Sages
of
Metaphorosis

Also from Metaphorosis

<u>Metaphorosis Magazine</u>
Metaphorosis: Best of 20xx
Metaphorosis 20xx: The Complete Stories
annual issues, from 2016
Monthly / Quarterly issues
Library Collection series

<u>Plant Based Press</u>
Best Vegan Science Fiction & Fantasy
annual issues, 2016-2020

from B. Morris Allen:
Chambers of the Heart: speculative stories
Susurrus
Allenthology: Volume I
Tocsin: and other stories
Start with Stones: collected stories
Metaphorosis: a collection of stories

<u>Verdage</u>
Reading 5X5 x3: Changes
Reading 5X5 x2: Duets
Score — an SFF symphony
Reading 5X5: Readers' Edition
Reading 5X5: Writers' Edition

<u>Vestige</u>
The Nocturnals, by Mariah Montoya

<u>Joyful Heave</u>
Museum Piece: an unusual collection

Sages of Metaphorosis

---

*speculative stories
by older authors*

Metaphorosis Library Collection

edited by
B. Morris Allen

ISSN: 2573-136X (online)
ISBN: 978-1-64076-301-2 (e-book)
ISBN: 978-1-64076-302-9 (paperback)
ISBN: 978-1-64076-303-6 (hardcover)

from
Metaphorosis Publishing

Neskowin

Contents

From the Editor

The *Metaphorosis Library Collection* arose from a conversation with a Metaphorosis author who is also a librarian, and is initially intended to suit library needs. When a reader comes in and says, "Hey, do you have any SFF stories by this type of author?" here they are! But of course, the books are available to any reader.

Humans have a natural inclination to make up stories; that's a lot of what play is about. Some express it early, writing their stories down almost as soon as they learn how. Others may not feel the drive until late in life, after they've dealt with more practical concerns. Sheri Tepper, for example, didn't publish her first book until she was in her mid-50s.

This volume focuses on stories by **elder** authors — somewhat arbitrarily defined here as over 50 when their story was sold. Just in the settings of many of our favorite stories, elder have deep stories of wisdom and practical insight. When they write, they write from experience — perhaps not with aliens or demons per se, but with life and conflict and struggle. Their stories are richer for it.

B. Morris Allen
1 July 2024

I Will Go Gently

Susan McDonough-Wachtman

They sat in their deck chairs, watching their son fish. "Has he caught one?" she asked, gently rocking.

Walter squinted out at the lake. "I don't think so."

"I think he did."

"Did you *see* it?" Ellen had the sight, but to Walter's constant exasperation, she made no distinction between things she saw and things she *saw*.

"No."

He looked at her. Her eyes were on her knitting. "How could you know, Ellen? You're not even looking at him."

"I just know."

"Hogwash." He resumed his contemplation of the lake. He pointed. "A coupla loons." He glanced over at her and saw her half smile. "I didn't say *we* were the loons."

Her smile widened. "Did you see the otter?" She pointed with her needle.

"No. Where? Now?" He looked where she indicated.

"No, this morning, early."

"Why didn't you say so?" Fifty years they had been married and still she didn't tell him things right away. She said it wasn't necessary, because he could see *back*, but still. He made a swiping motion with his hand and looked into the space he had made, a little viewpoint into the past. His heavy features lightened with pleasure. "Huh. You're right. Good, maybe there are more." He watched for a moment, hopefully. They had moved to inland Nunavut to escape the rising sea but had worried about the spread of pollution from the flooded cities. It was still a concern, twenty years later, but an increase in the otter population would be a good sign. "Mmm. Don't see others." Disappointed, he closed the vision with a wave. "How did you see it? You don't get up that early."

"I do lately."

"Hogwash. You've never been a morning person."

"I sleep very lightly these days, Walter."

He looked at her, frowning, worried. "Hog —"

" — wash, I know." She smiled again, a gentle creasing of her wrinkles. "I know you don't want me to die. But I'm not afraid."

"I am." He muttered it low, but she heard.

Her eyes went back to her knitting. "You'll be fine."

He stood abruptly and slammed his hands against the railing. He winced. His hands weren't as tough as they used to be. And his leg ached. He had broken it falling off the barn roof. She had warned him not to go up there.

"Have you *seen* me fall?" he had asked her.

"No, I just saw a shadow over you."

"Well, I'm not going to leave the roof unfixed because of a shadow."

Now he was using a cane and probably would for the rest of his life. His leg hurt. He was no use to anyone. Getting old was shitty.

They had both aged quickly these last twenty years. They had left the benefits of society behind and had survived with hard work but insufficient health care — just like any other pioneers. Someday, she said, more people with gifts of power would be born into their little community, including seers and healers. Their Inuit-related tribe had always produced them, but sporadically, and no one knew how or why. Their own son was "ungifted" and apparently content to be so.

"I think Julian's coming back."

"Oh, good, fish for dinner." She set her knitting in the basket at her feet. She knitted only a few minutes at a time these days before her hands cramped and she had to stop. "Do you remember when we moved here? You said he'd never be happy out here at the end of the world."

"And he wouldn't have been, if Penny hadn't come." She had *seen* the others coming, but she hadn't been sure there would be someone for Julian. The visions of seers were sporadic, uncontrollable, and sometimes unreliable. The future could be changed. "But she did, and they'll be marrying soon. They'll have children."

"Have you *seen* it?" He looked down at her frizzy white hair. Her thin, veined brown fingers were like the driftwood twigs on the saltwater beach where they had grown up. That beach had long since disappeared under a rising sea. It had been Ellen and the other seers who had warned their people first, even before the scientists from Down Below. But many had chosen not to listen. Just as he had chosen not to listen to her warning about working on the roof. If you put your hands over your ears and said, "la la la," all the bad news would go away.

"Some things I know without seeing," she said.

He barked out a laugh, startling the birds in the garden. "You don't know. You just — you're just — an infernal optimist."

She giggled. That sound took him back. He swiped at the air and smiled at his memory of her, sitting on another deck, long ago, her hair a thick, dark mass caught into a long braid down her back, her slim, clever hands busy making a dreamcatcher.

"Come back here," she ordered, in the present.

"Why? Why should I?" He rubbed off the tear running down his cheek. With a wave of his hand, he dismissed his hovering vision of the past.

"Because I am still here. And because he needs you."

He looked down at the beach, where their son was tying the boat up to the dock. "Don't be silly. He's done that by himself since he was ten. Besides, I'm no help to him these days." He tapped the cane hanging on the railing beside him.

She shook her head. "I don't mean right now. I mean when I'm gone."

"What about me?" He knew he sounded childish. He couldn't stop himself. He stared out at the water, not wanting to face her.

She sighed. "It won't be long —" He could hear the creak of her chair as she shifted.

"Please stop saying that."

"Let me finish."

The snap in her voice took him by surprise. He turned around.

"I was going to say," she continued, "it won't be long before you join me."

His hands gripped the railing behind him. He was younger than she was, and stronger, and healthier. His mouth opened, but he couldn't get any words past his teeth. Everything he thought to say got stuck there, like gristle.

She was looking up at him, calm again, with that calm which had always infuriated and delighted him. At many of the worst times in their years together, she had regarded him with just that expression of peace and a faint sense of humor. He always got the impression she was laughing at him, just a little. He hated it. He loved it.

"I haven't told you before," she said softly, "because I wasn't sure if it would help."

"What ..." He cleared his throat, turned and spat over the railing. "What do you mean by that?"

"Will you miss me enough to be glad to die?"

Silence for a moment while they both listened to these words, and felt them weighing down the air between them.

"Glad to die? Why would anyone be glad to die?"

"I am." She smiled sadly. "I'm tired and in pain all the time. You know this."

"Yes, but —"

"I know. You want me to 'rage.' But, you see, I know the light isn't dying." She waited a moment. "We can talk about this later, if you want to."

"If I want to? If I *want* to?"

Their son came up to the porch, carrying his basket of fish. He considered each of their faces in turn and sighed. "You've upset him again, Mother." He bent down and kissed her cheek.

"It's what I do," she said. "Are we having salmon for dinner?"

"Indeed. How would you like me to fix it?"

"Brushed with dill and butter, please, Julian."

"Grilled?"

"Yes, that sounds lovely."

"Father, you look like a plum. Do you want some salmon, too?"

"She... she..." Walter tried to unclench his jaw, then grabbed his cane and stomped down the stairs and across the garden to the beach.

"I'll take that as a yes." Julian turned to his mother. "What did you say?"

"I told him I'm dying. Which you both already know." She smiled up into his brown eyes. "You will marry that girl soon, won't you?"

He squatted next to her and took her hand. "You *know* I will. But that isn't why he was so upset."

"No," she sighed. "I told him something I probably shouldn't have. I probably shouldn't tell you, either. I hope you get married soon."

"Yes, so you've said, even though you've also told me that we will."

She touched his broad cheek. "Seeing the future and being sure it will come to pass do not always go together. Especially when one's emotions are involved. The observer influences what she observes, and not always for the better."

"Yes, Mother," he said. "Come to the kitchen and tell me how much dill to use." He stood and held his hand out to her. She took it and stood, slowly and with a grimace of pain. "Shall I make you some of your tea?"

"Yes, please."

●

The kitchen was made of split pine, as was the furniture. It had been the first room they had built and was still her favorite. Walter had done almost all the work by himself. Ellen had spent most of her time establishing the garden, while Julian fished and hunted small game to sustain them. It had been hard, and lonely for Julian. Ellen had *seen* that more people would join them, but she had not seen any particulars. She had been optimistic, but not sure, that there would be a wife for Julian. She was still optimistic, but not sure, that there would be some with the genetic trait which resulted in powers. It had always been a fickle and unpredictable occurrence in their far northern part of the world.

As Julian settled her at the kitchen table, Ellen said, "He will be tempted to look into the past. All the time." She rubbed the worn wooden surface, scarred from years of hard use.

"Yes, I know." He put the kettle on and got out her favorite mug.

"You must not let him."

"Yes, I know."

She scowled up at him. "You know, for the first time I understand what your father means when he says I'm too agreeable."

"That's good!" he exclaimed, falsely hearty. "A real breakthrough in your relationship."

"I don't appreciate this new sarcasm, either." She rubbed her aching hands.

"Do you want an extra teaspoon of willow bark?"

"Yes." He put the mug in front of her, and she sat back and sipped her tea, remembering. She and Walter had come here when Julian was thirteen, and they had been alone then. She had enjoyed that, the solitude. Seeing the future for three was much easier than seeing it for a village.

"Feel better?" asked Julian after a bit. He had cleaned the fish and was slicing it. She admired the sure movements of his big, brown hands. She had always hoped her vision of only one child would turn out to be untrue. "Mother?" Julian turned around.

"Yes. Yes, I am. Just remembering." The others had trickled into this valley, settled here on the shore of their little, landlocked lake. Walter was right. Julian had been much happier when Penny had arrived with her little sister.

Julian smiled. "That's Dad's job."

"Yes. I used to be a little jealous of that."

Julian put down his filet knife and washed his hands. "Jealous? Of Dad? Why?"

"Of seeing the past. So much more comfortable than seeing the future."

"But not as useful." He drizzled melted butter with lemon across the filets.

She shook her head. "That depends on the circumstances. Your father still has a part to play." Julian glanced at her, surprised. "At any rate," she continued, "people often enjoy remembering the past. They don't really want to know the future. They think they do, but they don't. Even good visions seldom turn out to be what you think they'll be."

Julian sprinkled dill on the salmon. "Enough?"

"More."

He smiled. "I better plant more dill." He crumbled and sprinkled the herb, put the salmon in the oven, and sat down at the table beside her. "I'm pretty sure Dad's been jealous of you."

"I know. Are you sorry you weren't gifted, Julian? You were angry about it when you were young. Then, when you were about twenty, you told me you were glad your life wasn't complicated by, I think you called it, 'hocus pocus.' How do you feel these days?"

"I feel I have enough to take care of with a regular life, and I don't know how you ever managed to balance your sight with everything else."

"I don't either."

They heard voices outside. "That sounds like Penny," said Julian, surprised. "And Maria."

"I don't think there's enough salmon for five. You'd better make some pilaf."

Walter entered, looking much happier than he had thirty minutes before. "I found treasure." He ushered in the two young women, both stocky, dark-haired, and round-cheeked. The elder went immediately to Julian and kissed him.

The younger went to Ellen and examined her carefully. "How are you?" she asked, her tone much older than her eleven years.

Penny turned in Julian's arms and said, "Maria insisted we come. I'm sorry to intrude so close to dinner."

"You know you're always welcome," said Julian. "Help me make some pilaf and join us in eating it."

Ellen faced the serious child with an equally intent gaze. "I am fine, Maria. Are you well?" Wisps of fine, black hair obscured the little girl's brow. Ellen brushed them back, gently smoothing out the furrows. "Did you *see* something, sweetheart?" Her quiet question seeped out into the room, a ripple of change.

Walter straightened up with an involuntary, "No." Ellen made a shushing gesture towards him.

Maria's chin trembled. "I saw you sick. I saw you — gone."

Walter sat down heavily. Julian, who had been checking the fish, turned around, blinking steam out of his eyes. Penny put a hand to her chest and murmured, "Ohhh."

"It's all right, Maria," said Ellen calmly. "I know all about it. It's all right." Maria sobbed and threw her arms around Ellen, who hugged her tightly, suppressing a grimace of pain as the child squeezed her. "Shh, shh, shh. Shh, shh, shh."

●

Ellen refused to discuss it until everyone had eaten. She ate very little these days herself but refused to see freshly grilled salmon sit untouched. The pilaf never happened, but they made do with leftover cornbread and salad. Ellen sipped her tea and prayed for strength.

"Now can we talk?" Walter pushed his plate away. "Did you *see* this, Ellen? Couldn't you have warned us that Maria would develop the sight?"

"You know I don't see everything. I can't demand it." Ellen turned to Maria. "This is a difficult thing that you have been called to do. I wish I could say different words to you. I wish I could promise to always be here to help you through." She shook her head. "I cannot."

"Do I have a choice?" whispered Maria. Her eyes were the color of the split pine walls.

"No. The visions will come. But you will have guidance in how to deal with them."

"And who will be doing that?" demanded Walter.

Ellen smiled, almost laughed. "You will." She looked around the table. "You all will."

Julian and Penny were holding hands, Penny's eyes shining with tears. "How, Ellen? How can I possibly help her with this?"

"Well, you've made a good start by falling in love with my son. He has a lifetime of watching me process visions."

Julian tilted his head inquiringly and opened his mouth.

"Don't be ridiculous, Ellen," burst out Walter. "Watching isn't enough."

Ellen turned and lifted one hand to touch his cheek. "I know how hard all of this is for you. But you must be strong and courageous. For Maria."

Walter glanced at the child and lowered his eyes. "I just don't understand," he muttered.

"I think Mom can explain things, Dad." Julian rolled his eyes. "She's just doing it in her own good time, as usual." He glanced around. "That was supposed to make you all smile."

Penny tried to smile at him. "Maybe... maybe Maria should go out and say hello to the goats for a few minutes," she suggested.

Maria looked at her sister, torn, desperate to escape all this tension, but also desperate to know.

"Let us figure things out, chick, then we'll talk, okay?" said Penny gently.

Maria's face lightened. "Okay." She touched Ellen's arm gently. "You'll be okay?"

"Oh, yes, sweetheart, I'll be right here for a while yet."

Maria stood up, hugged Ellen again, and rushed out the back door.

The adults drew breath. Penny sobbed, Walter cursed. Julian hugged his fiancee and said, "Am I right in assuming that Dad is going to be remembering a lot over the next few days?"

Ellen smiled. "Are you sure you don't have the sight?"

"Ellen, please." Walter closed his eyes. "When you foresaw the flooding, it was so —" he searched for words " — so hard to cope. How are the three of us going to be able to help a child like Maria if she should have a vision as difficult as — as that was — without you?"

"You'll have my memories, Walter. You and I are going to make sure you have everything you need."

●

They began the next morning, while they were still in bed. Walter opened a window into the past, and she helped him find the memories she believed would help Maria. He had not often been called to use his gift in this way; he had to "mark" the remembrances so that he would be able to find them again, when they were needed. After her death.

They began with Ellen's earliest recollections of her own first visions. Her parents had found a seer to help her understand and develop her gift. There had been hundreds of people in the community they had grown up in, and several seers. Their warnings about the crisis to come had not been appreciated. When the sea level began to rise, and the visionaries told people they would have to give up their homes and their saltwater lives, some had turned on the seers. Walter and Ellen and their young son had fled from the violence of their panicked neighbors.

In this new little village, which now homed fewer than a hundred people, Ellen and Walter had been the only gifted ones. Until now.

After breakfast, they continued their work. "You know," said Ellen, "there may be another child out there. One with your gift. There's never been any predicting it. Even for those with the sight."

They were sitting on the porch again, watching their son working in the garden. He was harvesting for a feast. The wedding date had been brought forward. Ellen had told them it needed to be, if she were to attend.

Walter grunted. "Let me get this one sorted first." He pulled his chair closer to hers and swiped at the air. "Here's when you were fifteen, and you *saw* your grandmother's death. I was with you that day. You cried a lot. I was only twelve, and I didn't know what to do."

Ellen smiled. "You did fine. You took me to Megan, which was just what I needed."

"Yes, see, that's what I mean. We don't have a Megan to take Maria to. We won't have you." His voice cracked.

"Yes, you will, Walter. You'll be able to take Maria to Megan. She'll get a vision of Megan, so she'll hear exactly what I heard. You and Julian and Penny just need to provide the physical part. Hug her and kiss her and tell her everything will be fine."

"Everything won't be fine."

"Yes, it will. It may take a while, but it will."

"You're an infernal optimist."

"A cockeyed optimist!" she sang, with only a slight tremor in her voice, "I'm only a cockeyed optimist, immature and incurably green!"

They didn't have movies anymore, but sometimes Walter opened a window to the past and played one for her. ("A blasted parlor trick," he called it.)

"You've never been immature," he said. "Not even when you were fifteen."

"I just didn't seem so to you, because three years younger is such a lot in teen years."

Walter sighed and marked the memory. "What comes next?"

Ellen's eyes sparkled mischievously. "I foresaw our first night together."

"But didn't tell me about it."

"Well, not then. How could I? You were just fourteen, and I was a very sophisticated seventeen. I went straight to Megan and begged her to tell me the future could be changed."

He paused in opening the window to this memory and said, "You never told me that part."

"No?" She closed her eyes. "Well, it was a bit much, you know. Walter, I think you and Julian and Penny should review these memories together — before they are needed. I think it will help you to help Maria if you are all forewarned about how it may go."

"And what if it doesn't go this way?"

"All the more reason to be forewarned. Oh, Walter, it will be close enough. Young women mature along a fairly predictable timeline. Megan managed."

"Megan had the sight!" Walter pounded his fist on the arm of his chair. His raised voice caused his son to look up from his work in the garden.

Ellen groaned and seemed to shrink in her chair. "Walter, what can I say? This is the best I can do."

He slid out of his chair and knelt at her feet. "I'm sorry," he whispered. "I'm sorry. I'm just so frightened, Ellie."

She stroked his white hair, still so thick and soft. "I know. But Walter, you're so much stronger than you think you are. There's never been a time when you weren't able to do what was needed."

●

In bed that night, he held her gently. "Tell me," he said slowly.

"Yes?"

"Tell me why you begged Megan to change the future. I mean, I saw what you said to her, but still —" She shook in his arms. "Are you laughing?" he demanded.

"Yes. I'm sorry." She kissed his chest. "I had never had sex, Walter. I had never even kissed a boy."

"Well, I should hope not. Whom would you kiss?"

Silence.

"You didn't kiss —"

"I am not going to discuss with you who I did or did not kiss before we were married." She was shaking with laughter again. "Not at this stage of my life. My point is, that seeing the experience of an orgasm with a boy who was, to me at that time, a snotty fourteen-year-old, was an existential shock. I panicked. And Megan helped me, as always, and she will help Maria, too, if such a thing should happen to her."

"Oh," said Walter with a groan. "Oh, Ellie, I really, really can't handle this."

"Yes, you can."

"No, no, I can't."

"Yes, yes, you can." She tickled him and he jerked. "If it makes you feel any better, I've seen you dead before Maria is seventeen. That's why you need to be sure to share all the remembrances with Julian and Penny.”

He stared into the darkness. “No, no, I don't believe that makes me feel any better.” His arms tightened gently around her. “But... it doesn't make me feel any worse, either.” He sounded surprised.

“No raging?”

“No raging.”

“Hogwash.” Her voice smiled in the dark. “You'll rage. When I see you again, I'll know you immediately, because your spirit will be plum-colored.”

“Have you *seen* that?”

“No.” She shook her head, her wispy hair brushing his chest. “But I can depend on you, Walter. In all the chaos we've endured, I've always known you would be there for me, raging on my behalf.”

He smiled. “Well. I can handle that.”

Susan McDonough-Wachtman's story “I Will Go Gently” was originally published in Metaphorosis on Friday, 14 December 2018. See magazine.metaphorosis.com

About the author

Susan McDonough-Wachtman is a grandmother of two (soon to be three!) who has been writing all of her life. “Well written,” “quirky sense of humor,” and “doesn't fit a genre” are what editors and agents have been telling her for sixty-ish years. Nevertheless, she persists. Susan lives in the Pacific Northwest with one cat and one husband.

susanmcdonoughwachtman.wordpress.com

Rowboat

K. G. Anderson

I've never seen an ocean, but I grew up playing "Rowboat" in my family's cramped living module on level C of Xinxin Colony. The worn blue carpet was the water, the concrete floor beyond it, a sandy shore. With a broomstick as an oar, I pretended I was Gramma Jen, rowing hard against the tide to get us home.

"They'd restricted travel by then, but Gramma Jen wanted us to know about beaches and the sea," Mom said. "One afternoon we found an abandoned rowboat and she took us out on San Francisco Bay. A government patrol nearly caught us."

Mom paused. Sitting in a faded chair, propped up by a thin pillow, she looked exhausted. Dad had told me she'd be gone in a matter of days. Like many of the colony's pioneers, she'd ignored the dangers of radiation to build our station on Ceres.

I closed my eyes, as if that would shut out the sour air of the sickroom. Then I finished the story Mom had told me so many times when I was a kid. The one that had always been my favorite.

"Gramma Jen hid the boat behind an abandoned freighter," I whispered. "By the time the patrol passed, the tide had turned against you. But she rowed you back to shore and beached the boat just as the sun went down."

When I opened my eyes, Mom was nodding.

"Thank you, Maya. I hope you'll always remember that story. Remember Gramma Jen."

With time running out, Mom was telling us all the stories again. How she'd volunteered to come to Ceres on an Early Migration mission. How our Gramma Jen had encouraged her every step of the way.

"Your Grampa Peter didn't want me to go, but she told him she believed I had it in me to be a pioneer," Mom said.

My half-sib, Dad and CeCe's son Rikki, 10 in Earth years, was hearing some of the Gramma Jen stories for the first time.

"So, did Maya's," Rikki hesitated, looking for a word we didn't use much on Ceres, " — did Maya's *grandmother* want to someday live here with us?"

Rikki was playing soldiers on the floor using my old "armies" of hex nuts and bolts. He sounded doubtful.

Mom and the other pioneers were the only ones who talked about Earth. Our teachers always told us to focus on the future.

"Rikki, there was a time when we thought we'd finish all the asteroid colonies in time for our families on Earth to Migrate," Mom said. "And, maybe we could have. But no one expected the Last War — or at least how terrible the Last War would be. Everyone who stayed on Earth, including Maya's grandmother and grandfather, died."

Rikki shrugged and went back to advancing a line of hex nuts toward a regiment of bolts. I knew how he felt. In spite of Mom's stories, and the pictures they showed us in school, for those of us born on Ceres so much of the Earth stuff seemed unreal.

At Earth-16, I was long past my days of playing "Rowboat." I'd moved from my family's living module into the First Gen dorms, five levels down. The Xinxin families had agreed that their children should be weaned away from them, taught to focus on the long-term survival of the colony, and prepared to be assigned to other colonies on other asteroids. We'd form families and have children there. My assignment could come any day now, as soon as the next freighter arrived. My throat tightened when I thought about how I'd never see Ceres, or my family, again.

Mom was asking Rikki a question about school.

I wanted to tell her that I dreamed about Gramma Jen and Grampa Peter. My battered tablet had a copy of the one picture we had of them, taken when they were only a few years older than me. I look at the picture almost every night. In it, they wore the bright, sleek clothing of the 2070s. They were picnicking with friends in a park. She, dark and lively; he, tall and thin. A bridge — the "Golden Gate," Mom called it — spanned the sparkling blue water behind them. I'd seen it in Earth movies.

In my dreams, I was Jen's best friend. We drove a vehicle, a car, with the windows open, across the Golden Gate Bridge, the blue water rippling below, and green forests rising beyond. Because of Mom's stories I could imagine it all: Trees. Oceans. Rain. Earth gravity. The wonders of atmosphere. I smiled to feel the pull of Earth all the way out here on Ceres, tugging me towards the planet where my parents and CeCe had been born.

But Earth wasn't just millions of miles away. Thanks to the Last War, everything on it was rubble. The Earth they showed us in pictures and videos existed only in my dreams.

Voices from the living room told me that Dad and CeCe were back. Rikki jumped up and ran out to greet them. Mom had drifted off to sleep.

I could hardly stand to look at her, slumped in her chair. I knew she was getting weaker. I'd heard CeCe say she'd reached the point where there were more bad days than good. Yesterday a glass bottle filled with a pale green liquid had appeared on in our refrigerator, labeled with Mom's name. I'd changed the subject after CeCe told me what it was. Mom would be confronting death as fearlessly as she'd confronted everything else. She expected us to, as well. I didn't dare disappoint her.

A hesitant knock on the bedroom door. Another one of the pioneers wanted to say goodbye. Edison Kang and I nodded a silent greeting as we exchanged places. I tried not to shudder as his arm brushed against me.

Mr. Kang had many of the early signs of radiation sickness — limp gray hair, creased and wrinkled skin, and ugly lesions. I dropped my gaze. Raised in the safety of the Xinxin compound, I could not imagine him and Mom working for years on the asteroid's surface in the original flexsuits. But they had. All to make Xinxin our home.

That night I dreamed I was rowing a boat through space, searching for a shore. Earth shone bright in the vast emptiness, impossibly far away. I had to get there — Grandma Jen was waiting for me.

I woke soaked in sweat and burning with curiosity.

After morning classes I went looking for Mikel Clark. Mikel was smart, but not well liked or trusted. I usually avoided him, but I'd overheard him bragging about hacking into the inter-colony databases and I knew he'd be eager to show off his skills.

"Is it true they've found more Earth data?" I asked.

Mikel's eyes lit up. He pulled me into an alcove where we wouldn't be overheard. "Two of the other colonies had it all along. They weren't sharing. But now the Xinxin Council has it." He grinned. "The security guys haven't opened up general access yet, they say they have to 'review' it, but people like me can get around that."

"I want to look for some images. Family stuff. Nothing classified."

Mikel flipped his braid over his shoulder.

"You came to the right man. I could get you in through a workstation in the admin section," he boasted.

"Tonight?" I swallowed hard. I'd never broken the rules before.

Mikel glanced down for a moment, as if weighing the risks. "Sure, why not?"

That night I followed Mikel through a maze of hallways. He used someone else's override codes on the doors. We were leaving tracks, but someone else would get blamed. By the time we entered the cramped office deep in the admin sector, I felt sick to my stomach. But it was too late to stop now. Mikel pulled an old data pad from a drawer, connected it to the system, and attached my data card that held the image of Grandma Jen and Grampa Peter.

Sure enough, Xinxin Colony's network now had the Earth archives we had been told were lost or held in secret by one of the other colonies. With Mikel's help, I searched several of the databases with facial recognition software. My first hit was a low-res image of Grampa Peter. He was older — handsome but worried looking. Just as Mom had said, he'd been an official in a California city called Palo Alto. But the matches for Gramma Jen's face were an Elisabeth Washington, a music professor in Georgia. I frowned. I was pretty sure Georgia was nowhere near Palo Alto.

Where was Gramma Jen? I searched for Grampa Peter's name plus "Jen," "Jennifer," and "Jeanne." Nothing. Real estate data from Palo Alto paired his name with a Margaret Dempster. His sister? His mother?

Mikel fidgeted at my side, not as confident as he'd seemed before.

When I typed in "Margaret Dempster," a news story appeared. I saw the words "arson conviction."

Before I could read more, an orange bar flashed at the top of the data screen. Mikel grabbed my arm.

"We gotta go. We've been spotted."

In the distance, an alarm shrilled.

Mikel yanked out my data card, logged out of the pad, and shoved it back in the drawer. Following him as he retraced our path, I saw him toss my data card into the corner of a dark stairwell — figuring, I guess, that I'd be the one blamed for the break-in. I stopped to snatch up the card and nearly missed catching the door he'd keyed open. I'd been stupid to trust Mikel.

Sure enough, there was trouble.

●

"You went looking for Gramma Jen."

It wasn't a question. Mom beckoned to me from her narrow bed.

"I'm sorry."

Mikel and I had been caught on the admin network and they'd told not just Dad, but Mom. I'd hoped I'd find something to make me feel better, but all I'd done was make my mother feel worse.

"I'm sorry," I said again.

"No, Maya," Mom said. "It's my fault."

My eyes went wide. This didn't sound like my mother.

"I hoped you'd never find out," she said. "So many records were lost in the Migrations and the War. But I guess they're finding some of that data can be recovered. I should have told you."

"Mom, I didn't find anything," I lied. "Just a picture of Grampa Peter from his job."

Mom gave a clipped laugh, devoid of humor. She reached for a cup of tea from the bedside table and took a sip. I watched her trembling hand and tried not to show my confusion.

"Maya, you didn't find anything because there's nothing to find. There is no Gramma Jen. Never was."

"*What?*"

Mom, sitting on the edge of her narrow bed, flinched.

"If there's no Gramma Jen..." my mind spun with possibilities. Was I adopted? "But you're still my mother?"

She reached out her thin arms and I knelt beside the bed to be hugged.

"Oh, Maya, of course I'm your mother."

Relief poured through me. After a minute I felt Mom square her shoulders. I settled cross-legged on the floor and waited, shivering. Mom was getting ready to tell me — once again — that things weren't as frightening as they sounded.

"Maya, I invented Gramma Jen. I need to tell you why."

Mom hugged herself as if she were cold. I reached for a blanket to cover her, but she waved me away.

"I'm afraid the story starts with Margaret Dempster," Mom began.

"She was my..." she stopped, worked her lips, and continued. "She was the woman people would say is my mother."

Her tone turned as grim as I'd ever heard it; my stomach twinged. Margaret Dempster, the arsonist, was my grandmother?

"Margaret was ..." Mom sighed and shook her head, casting about for words. "I know now that she was mentally ill, but when I was a child, all I knew is that my brother and I seemed to get punished no matter what we did and my father...well, he loved us but he just couldn't admit that there was anything wrong. He couldn't protect us. We left home as soon as we finished high school."

"I thought that simply by coming to Ceres — as far away as anyone could get during the first Migration — I'd solved my problems," Mom said. "And, in a sense, I had. Our work building Xinxin was important — far more important than anything I could have done on Earth. I met CeCe and your father, we all were in love, and — Maya, we were so happy."

A smile lit her face and eyes.

"I don't think you can even imagine what our lives were like," she went on. The smile faded.

"Then, the Last War — only six days, but when it ended, everyone on Earth was gone and we were alone in space: six colonies on three asteroids. Two of the colonies failed — one from starvation."

I nodded. They'd told us this, over and over again, in school. But what did this have to do with Gramma Jen?

"We were focused on mining, agriculture, manufacturing, and production of everything we needed to survive — including children. With no more Migrations from Earth, it became crucial for the colonies to have children before we got too much radiation. That's when I began to have nightmares. I dreamed that I'd had a baby and when I took the baby in my arms, I turned into Margaret. I dreamed that I hated my baby. Once I dreamed that I ... was lighting a fire."

I shuddered. Mom didn't know that I knew about the arson. Tears rolled down her skeletal cheeks. Her head fell forward. Her thin, lesioned hands covered her face, then fell to her lap.

"Maya, I would wake up from those dreams knowing that something was terribly wrong with me. My friends were having children. They loved those children! I saw Edison Kang holding Leah when she was born, and I couldn't imagine ever feeling like that. I was a sick, broken person. I didn't want anyone to find out."

I turned my head so Mom wouldn't see the tears rolling down my cheeks. "Mom, why didn't Grampa Peter help you? Why didn't he divorce her and take you away?"

"Maya, I've asked myself those questions a thousand times. We'll never know."

Mom put her ravaged hand on my arm and gently shook it, as if to wake me up.

"Let me tell you about the picture."

Mom stretched out her hand for the battered data tablet on the table by her bed. I handed it to her, and with a few taps she brought up that picture of the young couple at the Golden Gate, the two I thought of as Gramma Jen and Grampa Peter. I stared at the striking young woman. *Elisabeth Washington.*

"This photo saved me," Mom said. "I found it in a digital album my dad had given me years before, when I left Earth. I'd never bothered to look at it. I thought he'd given me a lot of images of nature and landscapes, in case I never came back."

"After the Last War, when it was all gone — then, of course, I looked at the album. I came across this picture, recognized him, and I looked at the metadata. It was taken in 2071, two years before he married Margaret. I realized that my father had wanted me to know about that beautiful moment in his life. He wanted to send that woman, whoever she was, with me into the future."

I sat on the bed beside Mom and saw the picture as I never had before. The woman looking at the camera while Grampa Peter held her hand and gazed at her as if she were the most precious thing in his world. What had happened to separate them?

"That's Elisabeth," I said. "Mom, I found her."

Mom frowned.

"I found her. Facial-recognition software. She's Elisabeth Washington. She taught music in Georgia. What do you know about her?"

I'd thought I knew all Mom's stories, but now there was so much more to know and so little time left.

"Elisabeth..." Mom stared at the picture and shook her head. Then she dropped the tablet onto the bed and lay against her pillow.

"Maya, all I know was that my father had loved her. When I saw that picture I realized I could rewrite history, for him and for me. I could make *her* my mother. The mother I'd always wanted. A wonderful mother.

"I named her Jen after the neighbor who'd given me the art lessons Margaret refused to pay for and who told me I had talent. Her courage came from the ship captain who mentored me on the First Migration. Her generosity is from CeCe. I got all those great recipes — and the story of the rowboat — from Nina, my first roommate on Xinxin."

While Mom told the story, my dad and CeCe had slipped into the small room. Dad caught sight of the tablet with the photo of Grampa Peter and Gramma Jen.

"Gramma Jen is one of your mother's finest creations," he said, sitting carefully on the bed beside Mom.

So he had known. Mom leaned her fragile body against him. Her dark eyes were bright with tears.

"Maya, for me, your Gramma Jen was not just real — she was essential," Mom said. "She changed my life. She made yours possible."

The room spun. I didn't know what to think. Gramma Jen had become a stranger. My real grandmother — I opened my mouth to ask about the fire. But I closed it again. Mom was falling asleep. I tried to slip out of the room, but CeCe stopped me.

"Maya...tomorrow," she whispered, squeezing my hand.

I pulled away, mumbling that I needed to study for an exam. That was true, but instead I took the long way through the corridors that led back to the dorm. I walked close to the grimy, familiar walls, afraid that the artificial gravity I'd grown up trusting might prove as unreliable as my ties to Earth. Fearing, as I never had before, the cold and airless world where I'd been born.

The next evening, my mother asked for the injection. With all of us gathered in the room and a recording of her favorite Beethoven sonata playing, Dad slipped a hypodermic into a vein. She took three, perhaps four, shallow breaths and then Mom was gone.

We gathered again a few days later, to watch as her ashes, wrapped in fragile Earth-made fabric, were taken out onto the frozen surface of Ceres and placed in the colony's communal grave for pioneers.

"Maya, you can refuse," Dad said. "I asked them not to tell you about this when your mom was so ill.

He sat on the bench beside me, looking over my shoulder as I opened the tablet and read the message.

I gasped. They were offering me a permanent assignment to Charboneau Colony on Vesta. This was out of the blue. I'd always thought they'd send me to Pallas or Hygiea, never imagining I'd qualify for the agricultural engineering team at Charboneau.

"Mom would have been thrilled." I felt tears start to well, but shook them away.

"I think it's too soon for you," Dad said. "But the freighter will be packed and ready to go by the end of the week. And this is the closest Ceres will be to Vesta for 17 years."

I nodded, my eyes fixed on the message. Permanent assignment. Charboneau. I'd have only three days to pack and say goodbye to Dad, and CeCe, and Rikki and nearly everyone I knew on Xinxin. Three of us from Xinxin First Gen would leave on the freighter *Sunrise* and travel 930 million miles to join the agricultural engineering team at Charboneau. We'd live on Vesta for the rest of our lives.

I thought of Mom again. She'd left Earth to build the first colonies. She'd understand. And Gramma Jen. She'd...but there was no Gramma Jen. Confused, I shook my head. So I think it surprised Dad when I turned my face to him and said "I'll go."

The words sounded so small, so flat and empty. But once I said them they set in motion a whole new story.

Dad and I hugged without words.

I walked slowly back to the dorm, trying to imagine my life on Vesta. Living with strangers — and eventually creating a family with some of them. New foods. A new religious system — some of the parents were worried about that. A quasi-military system of government, stricter than the democracy we'd maintained in Xinxin. I frowned as I recalled that data access on Vesta was rumored to be far less liberal than on Ceres. If I wanted to find out more about Elisabeth or Margaret, I'd have to do it now.

To my surprise, Dad got me official access to the Earth files. I read the news story I'd glimpsed before —"Palo Alto Woman Convicted of Arson." Margaret Dempster had set her family's house on fire. Everyone had escaped unharmed. A small, blurry photo showed a pale, frightened woman. To my relief, she looked nothing like my mom.

I would never know why Grampa Peter had married her. But now I understood why my mother had replaced the broken world of her childhood with the fantasy of Gramma Jen.

I found real estate records for Elisabeth Washington in Atlanta, Georgia, and a review of a concert performance. One of the pieces she'd played I recognized as Mom's favorite Beethoven sonata. I pressed my fingertips to the screen, as if I could reinforce that connection between the two of them — but it was as thin and as wishful as my own ties to Earth.

Had Elisabeth Washington married? Had children? My searches came up empty. I knew as much as I would ever know.

●

The inside cabin Leah, Jinx and I were assigned on the *Sunrise* proved to be cramped and stuffy, the bunks narrow and hard. We complained at great length that first night so none of us would be tempted to talk about home and the families and friends we were leaving. At last I crawled under the thin blankets, exhausted, but too excited to sleep.

I thought of Mom, and the many times she'd soothed me to sleep with her stories. In the dark cabin, I began to tell my own tale.

Like Gramma Jen, I'm rowing a boat. I'm not alone. There are people in the boat with me. My friends. And someday, my children. I envision a small boy and an even smaller girl, their faces pale with worry, who sit facing me, their hands gripping the seat.

To pass the time I tell them stories of Ceres and Earth and their families, both real and fantastic.

I feel the polished wood of oars against my palms. Each stroke I take sends the light of the stars around us rippling through the black of space.

"Almost home," I murmured as I drifted off to sleep. "Almost home. I'll get you there."

K.G. Anderson's story "Rowboat" was originally published in Metaphorosis on Friday, 12 February 2016

About the author

K.G. Anderson is a late-blooming writer of science fiction, mystery, and dark fantasy who hails from the foggy coast of the Pacific Northwest. Prior to finding her speculative fiction muse, she reported on politics and crime, reviewed crime fiction for *January* Magazine, and wrote about pop music for the iTunes Music Store. Her short stories appear in magazines and anthologies including *The Mammoth Book of Jack the Ripper Stories*, *Weirdbook*, and *Galaxy's Edge*, as well as on podcasts such as *The Overcast* and *StarShipSofa*. For links to more of her stories, visit writerway.com/fiction

What The Darkness Is

Simon Kewin

The howls of the gore-hounds filled the night air. Vanda stopped to catch her breath. Sounds echoed off the trees, throwing noises at her from odd angles. Her pursuers were close. When they caught her it would be the end.

She peeped at the precious cargo she carried, strapped across her chest in the sling she'd fashioned from an old shawl. The night was dark — of course — but there was just enough starlight to see Abha's tiny face peeping out, wide-eyed in wonder, oblivious to what was happening. Vanda envied the baby. Abha had no idea that the gore-hounds, if they caught up, would rip her to pieces like a rabbit.

Vanda set off again, ignoring the stomach cramps tearing at her. The ground was rising. She'd heard the Chronicler lived in a ramshackle hut on a hill in a wood. That was all she had to go off. It was entirely possible the whole thing was no more than a story. When it came to the Chronicler, the lines between truth and tale weren't always clear.

She glimpsed a light through the shifting boughs: a single yellow candle shining from a cottage window. In one of his tales it would have been placed there as a beacon for the desperate. She raced into the clearing and rapped on the door, gaze darting around. She expected the hounds, black as night and red of eye, to lope from the woods at any moment. Away over the treetops the thinnest of crescent moons sliced through the night sky. As it always did.

The door creaked open. An old man's face peeped through the gap, regarding her over the top of his half-moon spectacles. His wrinkled, veined skin might have been the map of an imaginary land. A red birth-mark, a blotch like the shape of some island, adorned his cheek. He didn't look surprised to see her.

She expected to feel the foul breath of the Lady's beasts on the back of her neck at any moment. "Chronicler. I need your help," she panted. "The gore-hounds are after me."

"And you want me to distract them with an exciting story while you sneak out of a window?" said the old man.

"Please. Let us in."

"Us? You said *me* a moment ago."

"I have a child with me. A baby. Chronicler, please. Abha has The Speech."

The old man's eyes widened at that. A look of appreciation crossed his features. Appreciation and something like concern, as if The Speech were some terrible disease. Which, in a way, it was.

"I see. Then you'd better come in. No point standing outside in the cold and dark is there?"

It took a few moments for Vanda's eyes to adjust to the brightness within. Candles flickered from sconces and shelves. A log fire crackled and spat, filling the cottage with the sweet smell of woodsmoke. Next to the fire, upon a cushioned chair, lay a book, a strip of red silk marking the Chronicler's page. She glimpsed an inner room that had to be his library. She had the impression, before he closed the door, of high shelves of books receding into the dark distance, impossibly far away.

"So," said the Chronicler. "What do you want me to do? If Lady Lillian has sent her hounds to hunt you down, you need to find a fortress with high walls to protect you. You need an army of fierce guards loyal to the end. Not a tired old man in a hovel in the woods." His eyes glittered with delight as he spoke. In his stories, old people living alone in the woods were never what they seemed.

"No walls are high enough to keep the hounds out," said Vanda. "No oceans are wide enough to keep Lady Lillian's ships at bay."

"Perhaps."

"But you can protect the baby. You can take her beyond even the Lady's reach."

"I?" Now he sounded vain, enjoying the flattery of her words.

"You have The Speech too, in your own way." said Vanda.

"No. I can't shape the world as the Lady can. I can't banish her hounds or unfreeze the moon. I can't bring an end to her eternal night. Would she have let me live if I could unweave her words?"

Vanda glanced to the outside door. Shouldn't the hounds have arrived by now? "You're more than that. I've heard the stories. Once you came to our village, at Midsummer, when there was still a Midsummer. You told the tale of Siggurd, sent on an impossible quest to slay the Clockwork King. It was... more than mere words. I *saw* the red roofs of Pirathia sitting in the great desert. I felt the warm air on my face, tasted the sand in my mouth. You took us there. That is your magic; that is what you can do."

She sounded more sure than she was. The memory of that night was faint. Perhaps, swayed by the balmy air and too much hurtleberry wine, she'd imagined the whole thing.

The Chronicler didn't reply for a moment. His eyes narrowed amid their nests of wrinkled skin. "How can you be sure the child has The Speech? She is a baby. It is too soon to know."

"She uttered her first word when she was six moons old."

"That is not so unusual."

"A ball she wanted rolled away from her so she spoke a word of Making. It took her a few attempts to get her tongue around it, but soon she held a new ball in her hands. One she'd created."

"She found the toy on the ground beside her."

"When she'd finished playing she spoke the word backwards and the ball in her hands was gone."

"She dropped it."

"She is six months old and has already spoken words of Making and Unmaking. Would Lady Lillian have unleashed her hounds if this wasn't so? The baby is a threat to everything the Lady has wrought."

A frown knitted the Chronicler's features. "Who is she? And who are you? Is she your blood?"

"The girl's parents died, lost at sea. We found her, took her in, a family of wheelwrights. When the Lady heard about her and the hounds were sighted I took her and ran."

"I see."

"Chronicler, please, you are our only hope. The beasts were at my back. I don't understand why they aren't here already."

The Chronicler nodded his head in something like appreciation. "I have some small magic, it is true. The magic of the fireside tale. A moment like this when imminent danger presses can be made to stretch out longer than should be possible. It suits the shape, the *need* of the story, and even the Lady can't deny that power. I can hold them back for a minute or two, although they will break through eventually."

"So you will help? You will take us to one of the distant lands where the Lady does not hold sway?"

Outside, from somewhere in the trees, a howl filled the night. The Chronicler peered at her over the top of his reading spectacles. "You truly believe this baby will be the one to defeat the Lady? She's the one chosen to save us all?"

Vanda sighed. "Yes. Although I'd settle for her surviving. Growing up, falling in love, making mistakes. Doing whatever she chooses."

"I see," said the Chronicler, his face thoughtful. "Less satisfying as a story. The helpless baby destined to defeat the Lady and restore light to the world: now that's a tale I might be able to work with."

"Can't you weave a different yarn for her?"

The possibility seemed to amuse the Chronicler. "The needs of the tale cannot be denied; that's the way it works."

"And if she chooses a different path?"

"Then we are in a different story to the one started. We shall see. It doesn't always do to know the ending when we've barely begun, does it? But... I can't take you. The orphaned baby alone in a strange world: that has power. Resonance. You must stay behind. Your part is played."

"She is a baby. She's helpless."

"I will deliver her to those who will care for her. I may be needed again later. The enigmatic stranger offering cryptic advice. That could work."

"Have you experience of looking after a baby?"

A smile of delight flickered across the old man's face. "Little. We make an unsuited pair, our chances of survival small. You see the power of it already? I will prepare myself for the journey. The hounds will be at the door soon, and the candles need snuffing out. Will you attend to them while I prepare?"

The Chronicler bustled off, stooping through a low door in the shadowy corner of the room. Vanda, rocking Abha in her arms, crossed to peer out of a window. In the brittle cold she could see yellow eyes glinting from the trees. Many, many eyes, brighter, somehow, than the moonlight they reflected. She set to work, licking the finger and thumb of her spare hand and pinching out the candle flames. Each gave off a little twist of smoke as it was extinguished.

She worked her way around the room to the Chronicler's chair. Unable to resist, she opened the book at the page marked by the slip of red silk. The pages were blank. Puzzled, she turned over more pages, and more. All were empty.

"That is our story," said the Chronicler, reappearing behind her. He wore a long grey coat, a pack slung over his shoulder, stout boots on his feet. He had the air of a man used to travel. "It is the tale of our land."

"The words stop."

"They stopped when the Lady wove her magic and froze us in this night. That is what the darkness is. Words unwritten, lives unlived. It is the story stopped in its middle, the ending never reached. Now, hand me Abha and we will proceed."

Vanda held back, reluctant to release the baby. "Why has the Lady worked this evil? You of all people must know. This land was beautiful. She gazed upon it from her tower with a mother's love."

The Chronicle considered, his brow furrowing. "Who can say? Perhaps she learned to hate the coming light. She foresaw what the day would bring and despised it. That might make the start of a passable tale. Now, please, we must leave."

Vanda handed the baby over. The Chronicler walked to the library door and pushed it wide. Vanda, peering in, saw the shelves she'd glimpsed. The endless ranks of books.

"There are so many of them. I had no idea."

"Many, yes. I have lived many lives. Lived and loved and lost. And won, too, against all the odds, of course."

"Which book, which world will you take her to?"

The Chronicler turned to block her passage. "I cannot tell you. The Lady must not know. Tell her what we have done, if you must, but you can't know where we have gone."

Vanda nodded. "Then, thank you, Chronicler. Look after Abha, please. It is all I ask."

"I will." He nodded once and quietly shut the door behind him, leaving Vanda alone.

After a few moments she heard growling and snuffling from outside the cottage, and then the first heavy blow upon the door.

●

"Another tattoo, Abi? What is it this time? More moons and stars?"

Abi rolled up her sleeve so Gemma could see it properly. Her arm was an angry red from the tattooist's needle. "A wheel."

"Okay, that's... boring."

"No, it's cool. It's, like, the cycles of the year. The cycles of life. The end is the start and all that."

"Hippy shit."

"It's clearly not, look, there are flames. I like it."

Gem shrugged. "Okay, it's your skin. Just don't let our Galactic Overlord see it."

"Galactic Over*lady*." The Home was ruled by the fearsome Mrs. Framing, a woman who seemed to know everything that went on among the children in her care. "I'm sixteen. I'm allowed tattoos."

"You're supposed to get them approved. And they're supposed to be nice things. Happy things, things the Inspectors couldn't object to."

"You think they'll object to a wheel?"

"Maybe for being *dull,* yeah. And then there are the demons on your back."

"They're not going to see those, are they?"

"I've seen them."

Gem was her oldest friend. Both orphans, they'd shared a room in Gladwell House until they were ten. Now they were in and out of each other's rooms all the time.

"You're different," said Abi.

"Thanks. I think." Gem rose and leaned her elbows on the ledge of the first floor window. "Hey, your stalker's outside the gates again."

"He is not my stalker."

"He so is. I hate that dog of his. Growls each time I go past. Think we should report him for, I dunno, sexual harassment or something?"

"He's just a homeless guy. He's never even spoken to me."

"He looks at you."

"I'm sure he looks at lots of things. People do when they have eyes. Besides, I happen to be a beautiful young woman. You're lucky I hang around with you."

"Yeah," said Gem. "A beautiful young woman with crap tattoos. You know what your problem is?"

"I'm sure you'll tell me."

"You always see the best in people. You always want to help people, be nice to them. Honestly, Abi, the world doesn't work that way. People like you get taken for a ride."

"And people like you die a lonely, bitter death, afraid of everyone around them."

"I'm not lonely. Unless you're planning to move out."

"No," said Abi. "'Course not."

That night, Gem's screams roused Abi from sleep. Nightmares had always plagued her friend. They were common enough in the Home. Abi's had faded over the years and while her dreams were always vivid and often alarming, she no longer woke up sweating. For Gem it was different.

Abi tapped gently on her friend's door. Sometimes Gem didn't wake up, but tonight there was a low snuffling sound coming from within. After a few moments the latch on the door unclicked. Abi found Gem sitting on her bed, quilt grasped around her knees.

"A nightmare?"

Gem nodded. "There were shadows moving in the room, creeping across the walls toward me. They had teeth, somehow I knew they had teeth, and they were coming for me. They were sniffing. Hunting."

Abi did what she always did, putting an arm around her friend. "Shall I tell you a story so you can go to sleep?"

They'd been sharing these night-time tales for many years, something neither mentioned in the day. Gem nodded, and Abi settled in beside her to begin her story. Within ten minutes, Gem's breathing was slow and peaceful. Rather than disturbing her, Abi curled up beside her, just like when they were children.

The shadows came for Abi a day later. She was walking home from school along the ring-road, past a red-brick wall covered in tattered fly-posters. The flickering movement had been there for some time before she became aware of it. Shapes on the wall beside her, patches of darkness that followed her. A shadow-play she was a part of: her silhouette was among the shifting shapes, as if there were creatures all around her she couldn't see.

She tried slowing and they slowed. She hurried on, telling herself it was some weird reflection, or her overactive imagination. She crossed the road, out of the bright sunshine. There were no shadows there; she'd left them behind.

She made herself breathe slowly and deeply to calm her pounding heart. The stench of something foul reached her nostrils, the smell of rotting flesh. Then, in a shop window, she saw the reflections. Huge, dog-like beasts crowding in on her, snarling teeth bared. A low growl made the hair on the back of her neck prickle.

Someone grasped her wrist, hurting her. "Quick, we must get away from them." It was the old man, the tramp who sat on the street, the red birth-mark vivid on his cheek.

Abi fought him. "What are you doing? Get off me!"

The old man let go. His gaze darted around, not looking at her. "You can see them, can't you? The gore-hounds."

"What?"

"They're coming. They've found you at last. Sixteen years is more than I hoped for. Please, I can hold them off a few moments but they are strong."

He looked so terrified, like an old broken bird, she lost her fear of him. "What are they?"

"Her hunters. Time is short. Come, I have made plans for this day. We must go to the High Street; we have to travel further in." He set off, striding with surprising speed, his little dog slinking along beside him.

"But I don't want to do any shopping," she called.

The old man turned to study her. "Then your story will stop here. An unsatisfactory ending, frankly. No shape to it, no circle closed."

"What does that mean?"

"It means those things will rip your flesh from your bones if they reach you."

"Why would you even say a thing like that?"

"Because it is the truth. I'm sorry, but this is not my story. I'm merely a part-player. A character."

Abi looked around. There was no one nearby to hear this craziness. "They're shadows. Why would they want to kill me? I'm just a girl."

"Because you're the only one who can save the world."

She could only laugh. "Me? Save the world. Gem was right, you are crazy. How the hell am I going to save the world? It's a major triumph getting out of bed in the morning."

"I'm not talking about this world. I'm talking about the real one."

"The what?"

"Look, come with me and I'll explain, I promise."

"If you are an abuser, this is a pretty bizarre approach you've got."

"Please, Abha, I'm trying to help you. As I have ever since I brought you here."

"Wait, what? You brought me here?"

The old man made no attempt to hide his impatience. "Yes, as a baby. Must we discuss this now?"

She had to swallow the lump in her throat. "So, you're saying you're my, like, father or something?"

"No, no, your father died. I promised I'd watch over you, that's all. Please, can we hurry? They'll be upon us soon."

Movement flickered in the corner of her eye but disappeared when she looked directly at it. The old man's dog growled, ears flattened against its head. The High Street would be busier. Surely she'd be safe there.

"This had better be good," said Abi.

They stopped outside the video game store, its windows filled with colourful boxes and posters. The old man peered inside through cupped hands. "This will keep them guessing for a while."

"What do you mean?" asked Abi.

"Our escape. She'll expect me to use books, won't she? In a story, the unexpected is always good."

Shadows were flickering on the pavement at her feet, overlaying her own. There was a weight to them, a thickness, that hadn't been there before. There was a rush of hot fetid air on her ear. She raced after the old man into the store.

Inside, he was studying the cases of three different games, shaking his head as if in disbelief. "Such detail, such huge worlds."

"Yeah, they're cool."

"This one," he said, holding out one of the boxes.

"*War of the Witch King*. Sorry, why are you showing me this?" she asked.

"You know it? You have played it?"

"Sure, we have it at the Home. I'm a Level 12 Weatherworker."

"Then I can draw on your knowledge. Can I hold your hand?"

"What?"

"Please. It will make it easier when I begin the telling. I mean you no harm, I promise you."

"Yeah," she said. "I'll bet they all say that."

"I can leave you to the hounds if you like. They will tear you to shreds if they can. They're becoming more real with every moment."

The whole thing was ridiculous, crazy, but there was something in it that made her stomach tingle. Glancing around to make sure no one she knew was anywhere in sight, she held out her hand. His skin was rough in hers. He gripped her tight and his lips began to move.

Dizziness washed over her a moment later ...

●

... and she sprawled onto wet grass. The air was colder, the edge of a chill to it. Water chortled somewhere nearby.

She climbed to her feet, head still spinning. They stood on the shores of some vast lake, tendrils of mist threading through the air over it. Except it wasn't a lake, it was a river, encircling that whole world. The water flowed, carrying sticks and birds and clumps of some sweet-smelling flower along with it. Abi recognized it from the game. "What have you done? How the hell can this even be possible?"

The old man shrugged. "Worlds within worlds, stories about stories. What explanation is needed?"

What did that mean? There were no *other worlds*. You imagined them when you were a child but you grew out of it. She'd once delighted in imagining all sorts of impossible lands but now she knew better.

And yet, there she was.

"What happened to your dog?"

The old man ran a hand through his straggly hair. "I couldn't bring both of you. I shall miss him, my only friend in that world. Perhaps there will be a way to go back for him later."

"And why... why have you brought me here?"

"To escape Lady Lillian's hounds. I hid you for sixteen years in a world reached through a book and I have kept watch over you all this time. Now we've taken another turning through the maze. Hopefully, an unexpected turning. If she takes another sixteen years to find us, I'll be happy."

"I don't get any of this. It's all insane."

"I will tell you everything I know, give you the story so far. Perhaps it will help."

When he'd finished recounting the tale, Abi closed her eyes, her back against the rough bark of a tree, trying to make sense of it all.

"Why does she hate me so much?"

"You are a threat."

"But these words of Making and Unmaking. I don't know anything about them."

"Vanda said you spoke them without thinking when you wanted the ball. I think you only have access to them in the real world. Or perhaps they will come at the right moment, when you have the understanding to use them." The old man — the Chronicler — smiled his sparkling smile. "At least, that's what would happen if I were telling the story. Right at the last moment, in the nick of time."

"But what about Gem? And everything else. You know, my life?"

"It's all still there. It's like a book that has been closed. The pages will still be there when you open it up again. Now, I suggest we find something to eat. No point dying and doing Lillian's work for her, is there?"

"Those creatures, the gore-hounds. They'll come again. We'll need to be ready."

"Yes. Are there many books in this world? Many stories we could escape into?"

"I don't think so. There's an island where some witches live that has lots of books of history in tunnels beneath the ground."

"I suppose that might do. Again, it might be too obvious."

"Most of the time people sing songs here to tell the old stories. You know, to pass ancient sagas down."

"Ah. That sounds more promising. Tell me, Abha, can you sing?"

"No. Don't make me. Seriously."

The Chronicler seemed pleased with himself. "Just as well I have an excellent voice. We must learn these lays as we go about the land. When the time comes and the Lady finds us, we can use one for our escape. A song can conjure up a world as well as a story."

In the end, their stay lasted only three years. This time, Abi heard the howls before she saw the shadows. As the Chronicler keened the song they'd chosen, Abi felt the same dizziness she'd experienced the last time.

The stone walls around her faded away.

●

They stepped from world to world for another seven years, always going deeper, one step ahead of Lady Lillian. A painting in a castle gallery depicting an imaginary city, streets thronged with merchants and priests. In that city, a mummers' play performed by torchlight, conjuring up visions of sunlit islands scattered across a sparkling blue sea.

There, she met Aydan and lost her heart to him. His smile made her melt and fizz inside, both at the same time. They would lie together on the soft beach and listen to the unending hushing of the waves. She loved the way the drops of seawater sat upon his smooth skin, the miniature worlds glimpsed within each. He loved to trace the lines of her tattoos, fascinated by them. Fascinated, too, by her wild tales of other worlds. For three years they shared a simple life of fishing and eating, loving and sleeping. Gemma and Gladwell House seemed an impossibly far distance away. The Chronicler kept to himself, watching and waiting.

She and Aydan walked the whole circuit of their round island, hand-in-hand, the twin lines of their footprints a braided line in the sand. Abi liked the sensation of returning to the place they'd started, the familiarity of it as well as the disorientation of seeing it from a different angle. Sometimes they talked about where she'd come from, leading them to the one subject painful to both of them.

"Will you go back to the sky with the other angels?" he asked. It amused her when he called her an angel. Many of the things they did together were surely things no angel had ever done. Still, she liked it.

"No. We will have to move onwards, go deeper."

"Why does this demon pursue you?"

"Only I can speak the words to unravel her magic. She has frozen her world in perpetual night."

Aydan gazed over the sparkling waters and shook his head. "When will it be?"

"I don't know. Not for a long time, I hope."

"We could have children."

She stroked his face. "I'd like that. Truly. But not with this hanging over them."

They were both silent for a time, lost to their own thoughts. Then the sun filled their eyes once more and they ran together for the splash of the sea.

One day, the villagers found the remains of a small deer, its body torn to scattered shreds. There were no predators on the island capable of such butchery. In the sand all around were the footprints of animals that might have been hounds. The Chronicler, seeing them, nodded his head to Abi.

Aydan pleaded to come with her, but she didn't know how that might be worked. There was the danger, too. With Abi gone, Aydan's life would be as safe and peaceful as it always had been. They allowed themselves one final night, Abi always alert for howls and snarls.

"Will you come back?" he asked as the first light found the shadows in the corner of their room.

She lay with her head upon his chest, their limbs entwined. She wanted more than anything in the world to say yes. Here would be a fine ending to the story: an ending that was a new beginning. But it couldn't be. She could think of no words to give him.

She and the Chronicler sailed in an outrigger to the sacred atoll, home of the people's few gods, the paradise they all went to when they died. There, among the many offerings sent bobbing over in bottles on the ocean's currents, they found scrimshaw carvings depicting the fairy palaces of the land that, it was said, the island people had once come from.

Their escape.

Barely six months later, they stood upon a final hilltop, so high that the drifting clouds were around them and below them. The old man slumped to the ground, the weariness raw in him. She could see the shape of the bones in his face, as if his features were sinking away. Even his red birth-mark looked faint. He had told his last story, woven his last tale to foil Lady Lillian. Abi saw with sudden clarity how exhausted he was. He nodded his head, as if he knew what she was thinking.

"What will you do?" he asked. His voice was weak. "What ending will there be to this story?"

"There can only be one ending," said Abi. "I have to go back where it started. I have to destroy her, stop the monsters pursuing me and free the world from the moment it's frozen in. That's it, isn't it?"

"Once, I thought so. But we have been through much together, you and I. I think you can make your own ending, now."

"What other endings could there be?"

A flicker of delight passed across his features. "Perhaps... perhaps you will tell the tale of how you become the Lady Lillian we knew. How you loved the beauty of that starry night so much you stopped the world. That might be a fine twist."

"But it's not right."

"Or perhaps you will describe how you took a baby girl and rescued her from the gore-hounds, became Vanda to bring her to the Chronicler. A small but vital role in a bigger cycle that leaves those hearing the story guessing, lets them decide the ending. Or you may come up with some conclusion I have not foreseen. In any case you must choose. I can't hold off the hounds any longer. You can only snatch victory from the jaws of defeat so many times before the story falls apart."

"How do I get to the real world?"

He shrugged, as if it was the easiest thing in the world. "I have shown you. Tell the tale. Speak the words of Making, then step across. Step further in."

"But I'm not going deeper. I'm going back to the start."

The little smile of delight was there again. "You know, I'm never really sure there is a start. There's just the maze, stories within stories. Maybe, who knows, there isn't even one *real* world and they're all as genuine as each other."

Did that mean she really was returning to where she'd begun? Or was she creating a new story, a different telling of the same root tale? Perhaps it made little difference.

"If I go, what of you?"

The old man closed his eyes as if he might fall asleep. "My part is played. It has been a fine story, but characters come and go. I'll remain here to mock them when they come, tell them they can't win. An amusing counterpoint to the final drama. Hurry, now. They are near."

Abi cleared her mind. Words came to her, flowing without conscious effort. Yes. She saw what had to be done. How the world she wanted to reach looked: the woods and the seas, the bright stars and the crescent moon, and Lillian's high tower on its hill looking down on everything. The Chronicler had described it often enough over the years. The words of Making and Unmaking she would need also came to her. She saw what had to be done about the Lady, what the darkness was.

She began to tell the story forming in her mind.

●

She climbed the steps that wound up the hill to the tower. The bright stars blazed down, hard as jewels. The slender crescent moon hung among them. It was beautiful in its cold and colourless way.

The howls of the gore-hounds filled the night air, but Abi paid them no heed. They couldn't harm her, because the story couldn't harm the storyteller. At the gates they snarled and snapped, stained teeth level with Abi's face, their breath the smell of rotting meat.

Abi waved them away with a word of Unmaking, their names spoken backwards. One by one, they melted to the ground to become shadows, become nothing. Pushing the door open, she wound her way up the spiral staircase to where she knew Lady Lillian would be waiting for her.

A single, circular room took up the whole of the top of the tower. Twelve arched windows, open to the night air, looked out over the world. A figure in white lace, white as bone, stood at one of them. She gazed out across a wide sea, the moonlight a shimmering path across it.

"It's beautiful, isn't it?" Lady Lillian said.

"It is," said Abi.

"You would destroy it?"

"Stories can't stop," said Abi. "They must reach an ending. The pages must be filled, new characters brought in as old ones die."

Still not looking at her, Lady Lillian shook her head. "This isn't a story. It's real life. There are no simple endings."

"The wheel must turn," said Abi. "I understand now, after all these years of flight. The hands of the clock must go round. Your world is beautiful but there are other beauties. The smile of a friend. The sun on the morning mist. The frost on the trees. Waves washing through a field of tall grass. The gaze of a lover or a baby."

Lady Lillian sighed. "I suppose it is only fair you kill me after all these years of pursuit. I would have killed you if I could."

Abi walked to stand directly behind Lady Lillian. "Kill you? Why would I kill my own mother?"

Lillian's voice was cold. "I'm not your mother, child."

"Look at me," said Abi. "Of course you are. That's why I have the words."

When the Lady turned to face her, anger and then confusion and then wonder battled across her features. "I don't... how is that possible? My daughter died long ago. They told me."

"I was smuggled away for fear of what you might do to me when you learned I had the Speech. Do you not recall? My father died returning for my birth and you were lost in grief. Perhaps you blamed me for the accident." It was, perhaps, too obvious a storyline, but the power of it couldn't be denied.

Lady Lillian reached up to touch Abi's face. "Is this possible?"

"Yes. It is the truth."

Lillian looked puzzled, as if grappling with difficult ideas. "I have been so distracted by moonlight and starlight. I have been so lost."

"I know."

"I couldn't face life without him. Couldn't face another day. I was up here, watching for him, when word came. His ship lost at sea. How you must hate me."

Abi took her mother's hand in hers. "No. I haven't come here for revenge, or to destroy you. Between us, we'll speak the words of Unmaking. The darkness must end. There will be more nights of sparkling frost, but there will also be days of summer. We can live through all of them. We can give this story a good ending, if you are willing."

There were tears of moonlight in her mother's eyes as she nodded her head at Abi.

When it was done, Abi left her mother for a time and walked from the tower to the woods. She picked her way among tall trees grown thick with moss. Her feet seemed to know the path to take. Through the branches, a candle flickered from the windows of a little cottage in a clearing on a hill, calling her like a beacon.

Abi knocked on the door and waited for the old man to answer. A story didn't only need a finish; loose ends needed to be tied up, too. The Chronicler would understand that. He'd know how to find Aydan and Gemma and Vanda and all the others, even his little dog, so that the rest of their tales could be told and her part in them played out.

As she knew it would, the door opened silently. An old man's face peeped through the gap, his eyes regarding her over the top of a pair of half-moon spectacles.

"See," said Abi. "I have found the ending of the story."

In the east, over the trees, the sky was finally lightening to morning.

Simon Kewin's story "What the Darkness Is" was originally published in Metaphorosis on Friday, 22 September 2017

About the author

Simon Kewin (he/him) is a writer of fantasy and sci/fi, with over 500 publications to his name. He's the author of the *Cloven Land* fantasy trilogy, cyberpunk thriller *The Genehunter*, "steampunk Gormenghast" saga *Engn*, the *Triple Stars* sci/fi trilogy and the *Office of the Witchfinder General* books, published by Elsewhen Press. He's also the author of several short story collections, with his shorter fiction appearing in *Analog, Nature,* and many other magazines. His novel *Dead Star* was an SPSFC award semi-finalist and his short story *#buttonsinweirdplaces* was shortlisted for a Utopia award. His novella *The Clockwork King* won the Tales by Moonlight Editor's Prize.

He has an honours degree in English Literature (1st class) and an MA in Creative Writing (Distinction).

Autumn's Come Undone

Sharmon Gazaway

Autumn stands before a large pumpkin. Her bare soles, planted on either side, draw up minerals from the rich loam. The pumpkin's skin, still warm in late afternoon, glows under her touch, deepening from apricot to bittersweet orange. Stepping to the next pumpkin, she works the row, ripening each in turn. She swipes her brow with her forearm, her hands grimy, and pulls the weight of her ginger hair off her hot neck. A murmuring rumples the treetops, whispers forming words she can't quite make out. A chill lifts the fine hairs on her nape and she shivers.

Probably those air-headed dryads gossiping again.

As she walks to the brook to wash, honey-bright leaves drift down, cling to her hair like sprites. Humming, she pirouettes, her leaf skirts a swirl of marigold, russet, and spice. A garland of purplish-green globes dangling from the branch of a hickory tree catches her eye. She breaks off the vine and holds it up to the fading light.

Crow flutters down to the lowest limb, his bent wing stiff.

"Muscadines," she calls to him. "Sol's favorite." She breathes on the globes and they take on a ruddier, sweeter hue. "Perfect."

She drapes the fruited vine across a low shrub on the brook's bank and kneels, scrubbing her hands in the icy water. The stream babbles up at her, unintelligible at first. Dryads flit across the brook, tittering, cover malicious smiles with hazy hands. She looks about, wondering where

Sylvannah is and why she hasn't already herded them into their trees. She swishes the muscadine vine through the water, shaking her head. It's a mystery to her how she ever endured the flighty things before Sylvannah came.

Crow lights on her shoulder, nudging her head. She shrugs him onto the bank. So little time left to prepare the table for Sol's visit tomorrow, and the muscadines will be the finishing touch. The stream murmurs insistently and Crow tilts his head toward it, turns and looks up at Autumn. She leans down, listens carefully. The murmurs sharpen into words that glint and wound, and take her breath.

Rising, the soggy fruit slides from her slack fingers.

Autumn's leaf skirts rush and crackle as she stumbles through the darkening woods, throws herself beneath the arms of the Great Oak. She hooks her fingers in deep, harrows leaf-rot and worm castings, breaks her nails on the bones of birds and vermin. From low in her inner turnings a cry germinates, a cry that, breaking free, rattles branches and drives the dryads into their tree-skins.

She does not cry prettily. Not like Spring, who mastered the art of the one perfect dewdrop tear while they were still girls in Earth's nursery.

Moaning, Autumn rolls her head on the forest floor and grits her teeth, the moss clinging to her lips. She hears a crack inside her chest like the snap of a twig.

Pushing onto her hands and knees, she crawls closer to the Oak. She huddles between the roots, her back pressed against the furrowed trunk. She curls into her cloak, fastens its silver acorn brooch, and tucks in her bare feet, tight as Tortoise in his shell. Crow lights on her shoulder and roosts in her tangles. Autumn presses her wet cheek against moonshadowed bark, relieved Sol can't see her now.

All night she burns, shamed.

Like a fool, all day she hummed and danced while she worked, awaiting Sol's visit. In a large reed basket, she heaped the harvest's bounty — rosy apples, pomegranates, walnuts and pecans, lush persimmons. She set it on a table strewn with smilax vines by the brook. She savored the thought of Sol by her side for a whole day, wandering the meadow amongst violet and ochre wildflowers, drifting in a rowboat until moonset.

She presses cold fingers against her blazing cheeks.

When morning comes, newly resurrected and only half alive, it sheds its mists and feeds on shafts of light. Light that colors everything the soft gold of Sol's hair. It fingers her face with tender warmth. She knows this touch — *his* touch — intimately.

Sol is mocking her.

She shudders to her feet, sends Crow flapping. She slaps twigs from her cloak, squares her shoulders and pulls up her hood, shielding herself from Sol's gloating.

This is not to be borne.

She marches to the brook, and heaves the table over. The loaded basket crashes to the ground, the fruit bruised and bleeding. She strikes her hands together and sparks shoot from her fingertips. The basket erupts in flame.

Shaking, rage unspent, she sets her face to the North and trudges out of her wood. Crow clings to her gray woolen shoulder, weight-shifting nervously. Mice dart for cover at her approach.

●

Whisking into vapor, Sylvannah slipped out through a knothole in the Great Oak when the wailing and gnashing of teeth began. All the other dryads shivered inside their trees. But she bit her lip and witnessed Autumn unravel.

Now, with Sol high in the eastern sky, and Autumn and Crow gone, the dryads' gossip chitters tree to tree.

"Sol jilted Autumn, even though she's never loved another."

"I heard he cheated on her with a star."

"No, two stars."

"They say he actually expects her to be happy for him."

Sylvannah listens, amused. Sol doesn't know Autumn the way she does, if that's what he expects. She snorts. As if.

It was Autumn's silly sister, Spring, who else? A bigger flirt she never saw. Sylvannah began life in Spring's woodland where Spring was forever tempting this star and that to come down to her. And when they burned out on the way, her eyes, the yellow-green of a cat's, glittered. She clapped as they blazed and fell to cinders at her feet.

And now she's caught the biggest star of all.

Sylvannah shushes the dryads, and glides into the orchard. She simply can't see the attraction. Sol is larger than life, always seeking attention. Yes, yes his job is very important — but, nutshells, what a Golden Boy.

Autumn gave him her heart long ago. Sylvannah couldn't imagine a better match for Autumn. Fiery; everyone around her gets singed at some point. But Sol could handle it, even seemed to revel in her volatile nature.

True, Autumn is unpredictable, but she has a warm and generous spirit few in the wood ever see.

Sylvannah remembers the day many harvests ago when she discovered Autumn's forest. She watched from the cover of a pine thicket as Autumn tended to an injured bird.

"Stop skulking around the edges of the wood and introduce yourself," Autumn called to her that day, tying the bird's wing firmly with strips of linen.

Sylvannah glided out, one hand clinging to chunky bark.

Autumn glanced up and sighed, "Not another dryad." She ran her hand over the crow's ragged feathers. "So, what do you want?"

"I'm Sylvannah. I come from Spring's woodland. She — she banished me."

Autumn looked up sharply. "Why?"

"I suppose your sister didn't much like me telling her she was cruel, the way she taunted the stars to their destruction." She shrugged.

Autumn smiled tightly, tossed her head toward the Oak in the center of the wood. "You're welcome to live there. You're the first dryad I've met with some sense and grit. If you can keep those nosy airheads out of my hair, you have a home for life."

So Sylvannah did.

Autumn kept to herself, except for Crow, her constant companion since she saved him from a hunter's snare. On occasion she visited her favorite sister, Winter. But she sought out Sol more than any other, the way a wing seeks wind.

Sylvannah accepts this. All she needs is the shelter of the Great Oak, his rings of wisdom surrounding her, his constancy — home.

And bossing the other dryads is just gravy.

She weaves through the orchard, inhales the brewery scent of apples that ache for Autumn's harvesting. Among shriveled, snaking vines, pumpkins bulge to bursting. The trees breathe the colors of fire.

As Sylvannah glides back toward the Oak, her lower lip sucked between her teeth, apprehension curls inside her like a little fog.

●

Autumn's sister, Winter, folds her into fur-robed arms and Autumn soaks up her warmth. Sol is weaker here. He and Winter have always maintained a distant relationship.

"I know why you've come, Little Acorn," Winter murmurs into her hair. "But Summer will never agree to it." She frowns, her eyes black and liquid as a snowhare's.

Summer. The good sister who tries to bind them together. But she has a soft spot for Sol, friends since the Beginning. She will plead for them all to reconcile, be a family. Family! Accept Sol as a *brother*?

"Sister," Autumn snaps, flaring, "I didn't come to ask a favor. Or permission." She sees in Winter's eye the glint of indulgent pride her sister reserves for Autumn alone. It was Winter who comforted her when Mother left them like fledglings in an abandoned nest. Winter who endured her tantrums, taught her to dance like a dervish to burn off the fumes of resentment. "I came to give," she adds softly.

Winter takes her hands in hers and studies the black-rimmed broken nails. "Autumn, you're overwrought. With good reason. What Sol did —"

"What *they* did," Autumn grinds out.

"Yes. They. But with time —"

"Time? Time will only multiply the pain. The humiliation. There is no one else for me. Ever."

Winter drops her hands. "Still. I can't agree to this." Her pallid brow creases. "What of duty? Those who depend on you?" Her eyes harden like jet. "I will not take your silver acorn."

"When the time comes, you must." Autumn juts her chin. "I have no one else."

Sparks and ice splinters fly between them. Winter reasons, then pleads. Autumn will not be moved.

Winter, her lips trembling, swallows hard, and agrees.

●

With Winter's white realm far behind her, Autumn stalks through her own forest to the Great Oak, jaw hard. Snails — too slow to escape — crunch beneath her feet. Her skirts now blaze full-blown maize-gold, cayenne, bittersweet — mushrooms ride her hem like mum death-bells.

"Sylvannah," Autumn calls, gently stroking Crow's crooked wing.

Sylvannah floats down hesitantly from a branch high in the Oak, wavering before her.

"I'm giving my silver acorn to my sister. Winter will know what to do."

"What," Sylvannah rasps, suddenly still as lichen on bark, "have you done?"

Autumn kneads Crow's silky head, smears tears off her face. She takes a shuddering breath and shakes him off. He reels twice, then perches in the Oak, head cocked.

"You might want to glide to the highest branches," Autumn says softly to Sylvannah.

Eyes closed, Autumn imagines Spring, beribboned and blushing in Sol's light, melting into him — as she herself longs to do, still.

She begins to twirl, her feet an axis, her skirts whirring like a swarm of locusts. She spins, faster. Visceral heat surges up from her core, charges her fingertips, sparks fly. She hurls fingerling flames scattershot. One by one the trees ignite, sacrificed on the pyre of her rage. The gold and wine of a hundred sunsets combust. Oak, maple, and pine pop and hiss their indignation — the screeching dryads flee.

Her skirts explode in a pentecost of wildfire. And she twirls.

At last, the pain exceeds the one in her cracked heart.

Sylvannah drifts through the charred ruins, smoke permeating her gossamer heart. At least the other dryads are safe with their cousins in the river where she drove them. Crow crouches atop an armless black pine, head hidden under his bent wing.

She managed to save the Great Oak, whisking the flames away from his vulnerable upper branches. She caresses his gnarled, ancient bark. Below, something glints in the ash. Swooping down, she retrieves the silver acorn clasp, icon of Autumn's power, for safekeeping.

And beneath it lies a smoldering, cracked acorn. Autumn's heart. This, she plants.

Winter comes to bury Autumn's ashes in mounds of pure white, as she promised.

Sylvannah fastens the silver acorn on Winter's furs, then glides up into the Oak's sturdiest branches and waits.

With Autumn's power, Winter is twice as strong. In time, Sol grows weak. Spring languishes, a pale shadow.

And Winter reigns. Some call it The Little Ice Age. Others call this particularly bitter time The Year Without a Summer.

Sylvannah calls it a reckoning.

Sharmon Gazaway's story "Autumn's Come Undone" was originally published in Metaphorosis on Friday, 23 April 2021

About the author

Sharmon Gazaway writes from the Deep South of the US where she lives beside a historic cemetery haunted by the wild cries of pileated woodpeckers. Since her publication in *Metaphorosis* she has become a Dwarf Stars Award finalist. Her work appears in *Solarpunk Magazine, New Myths, The Best of MetaStellar Year Two, The Fairy Tale Magazine, The Forge Literary Magazine*, and elsewhere, as well as in various award-winning anthologies. She writes in multiple genres, and keeps trying new ways to improve as a writer. Instagram @sharmongazaway.

Going Home

Martin Westlake

The eerie howl of the Ekranoplan's jet engines echoed around the city's early morning streets. Dimitriy's stomach lurched involuntarily. A ground effect craft, they called it, designed to be a troop carrier, now recycled as a passenger craft, plying the route between Derbent and Astrakhan. The relic, all stubby wings and a massive, V-shaped tail, howled there and back three times a day. He loathed it, but it was the only way he could get to the laboratory in Astra.

Every Monday morning for over a year, Dimitriy had suffered the same torment of emotions. Anastasia said nothing anymore as they kissed. "Think of the children," she had said in the old days, before she'd realised entreaties were useless. "They need their father." He missed the whole school week. Sasha, the younger, still greeted him with affection on Saturday mornings, but Andrei, now in his teens, had become increasingly sullen. Dimitriy wanted to tell him how sorry he felt, but the truth was that he didn't. Guilty, yes; sad, yes, in a bittersweet sort of way; but not sorry.

Then there was the Ekranoplan. Anastasia had been unable to leave Derbent when Dimitriy had taken on the Astrakhan job and he had accepted that. The car trip took ten hours in the summer and in the winter the roads were frequently impassable. No, the only viable means of getting there was the Ekranoplan. He would never get used to it, though. Whenever there was the slightest hint of a breeze, his heart dropped, for the monstrous thing could only take off facing into the wind, and that meant riding the incoming waves, like a ship. Once it was up in the air the ride was smooth, but how he hated the take off! The only thing that made the mixture of sadness, guilt and fear worthwhile every Monday morning was a euphoric sense of anticipation; the knowledge that he would soon once again be where he most desired to be.

●

His path through the sleepy streets to the Ekranoport took him past his old workplace, the Caspian Gates Secondary School, reminding him of the day it had all begun. He'd stayed behind to help a group of fifteen-year-olds, then hurried home. A tall, thin, grey-suited, sallow-faced man was waiting for him outside the main entrance to their block of flats. A cigarette bobbed on his lower lip as he spoke. He seemed oblivious to the February cold, though both men's breath clouded about them.

"Semenov?" he said.

Dimitriy nodded.

"Could we talk?" said the man, nodding towards a bar.

There was something about him — not furtive, but a sense of secrecy all the same. The man bought two vodkas and they sat at a scuffed table.

"To your health," he said, raising his glass. He stubbed out his cigarette in an old dented aluminium ashtray and lit another. "Ivanov," he said. "Rear Admiral Anatoly Ivanov, Caspian Flotilla, Astrakhan."

"There's been a mistake," said Dimitriy.

Ivanov shook his head. He gestured to a passing waiter and ordered two more vodkas.

"I shouldn't stay," said Dimitriy.

"Tell me, Dimitriy Semenov," Ivanov said; "how much do you earn?"

"Enough," said Dimitriy.

"Why are you a teacher?" Ivanov leaned forward over the table. "You are a brilliant physicist with a top doctoral thesis in Biology and Materials Sciences from Moscow State University and yet you hide yourself away at the Caspian

Gates Secondary School teaching low-grade mathematics to misfits."

"My wife...," Dimitriy began.

"We know all about your wife," Ivanov said.

"It's time I left," Dimitriy said.

"Sit down," said the Admiral, gesturing with his half-empty vodka glass. "What I mean is that we know she has all her family here. That's why you're here, isn't it?"

Dimitriy said nothing.

Ivanov leaned over the table again. "The motherland calls, comrade."

Motherland! Comrade! Dimitriy knew immediately that the job had to be some sort of secret military work.

"It's not what you think, Semenov," the Admiral continued. "If I told you now, you wouldn't believe me."

Dimitriy inadvertently looked into his empty glass. Ivanov flagged the waiter down and ordered two more vodkas.

"No!" said Dimitriy.

"For the road."

The Admiral toyed with his cigarette lighter, an old-fashioned metal model with a flip top and a thick wick. Then he looked up at Dimitry. "Interested?" he asked. "We'll pay you four times what you are getting at that dump of a school."

"The catch?" said Dimitriy.

Ivanov drank off the remainder of his vodka and placed the glass down gently on the tabletop.

"You'd have to come to Astra, Monday to Friday. We'd cover your board and lodging."

"How would I...?"

As if to anticipate his question, the unmistakable howl of the evening return Ekranoplan came to them through the thin glass window.

Ivanov reached into his pocket, drew out an envelope and placed it on the table.

"Your ticket's in there. This coming Monday. The seven-thirty departure. When you get to Astra, make your way to the Moskva Hotel. A room has been booked in your name. I'll join you there for lunch. It's half-term. The school won't miss you."

Back home, after the children had gone to bed, sitting in the low light at the melamine kitchen table, he and Anastasia had discussed the offer in earnest whispers. He had doubts, but she was logical and reassuring. The money was important. With the kids growing, it would be good if they could rent somewhere larger. If he didn't like the work, whatever it was, he could always return to his teaching. What did they have to lose?

●

Dimitriy had been travelling to Astra for just over two months when Anastasia first put the question to him. He had known it must come. She had nodded and accepted so mildly when he'd first explained that he couldn't talk about his work, but who could blame her, now that the yearning had started? She chose a Saturday evening. The children were in bed. The classical music radio channel was on, and she'd put a cloth and a candle on the dinner table. They talked about Sasha and Andrei, and then about her family. At the end of the meal, Anastasia took Dimitriy's hands across the table. *Here it comes*, he thought. But she simply looked into his eyes and asked if he felt all right. She'd told him he seemed preoccupied, as if his mind were elsewhere.

He'd laughed. "I'm fine," he'd said.

How could he tell her? Even if he had told her, she wouldn't have believed him.

The second time, Anastasia had been more direct. Dimitriy had just returned.

"Did you miss us?" she asked.

"Of course!"

"Really?"

She went back to the kitchen. There was no cloth and no candle on the table. Over the meal, her replies were monosyllabic. Afterwards, he went to help her with the washing up, but she insisted on doing it alone. He sat on the sofa and waited until she emerged, drying her hands on a tea towel.

"Dima," she said, "are you sure you're not having a relationship of some sort in Astra?"

Astrakhan was on a broad river, not a sea. Its waterways gave the impression the city was floating. Unlike Derbent, there were no hills behind, and no citadel looming over the city. Rather, the great Trinity Cathedral soared upwards, with its gold-capped green domes. Astrakhan was flat and expansive. Being there gave Dimitry a sense of a new beginning. He hadn't realised, until he first set foot in the place, how oppressed he'd felt back home. That first Monday, still wobbly from the flight, he'd walked easily to the Moskva Hotel, a great block of fake chrome and smoked glass. A room had been booked, as Ivanov had promised. The clerk told him a table had been reserved in the restaurant for twelve o'clock. Dimitriy went to his room, unpacked the few belongings he had brought, then turned on the television and watched a programme without really following it. What was Ivanov going to offer him, he wondered?

The Admiral was sitting at their table when Dimitriy came down, a vodka in front of him and a cigarette on his lower lip. He nodded curtly.

"Welcome to Astra," he said. "A drink?"

"Thank you," said Dimitriy, "but I don't drink at lunchtime."

Ivanov beckoned a waiter over.

"Today, you'll make an exception."

When the waiter had brought their drinks, Ivanov raised his glass. He had ordered caviar, brought by another waiter on a bed of ice. "Eat," he insisted gruffly.

"Thank you," said Dimitriy.

"Thank Mother Russia," said Ivanov, stubbing out his cigarette.

They started to eat, digging out the glutinous eggs with small mother-of-pearl teaspoons.

"What do you know about Tunguska?" the Admiral asked.

"Siberia? The beginning of the last century?"

Ivanov nodded. "30 June 1908," he said.

"I remember the pictures," said Dimitriy. "All those felled trees. A meteor, right?"

"Da, da," said Ivanov. "That's what people think."

"Think? What was it, then?"

"We don't know." He lit another cigarette. "I've brought a file for you to read, but before that, I want you to sign this."

Ivanov tugged an envelope from his jacket pocket and drew out a folded sheet of paper. "Official Secrets Act," said the Admiral, unfolding the sheet. "I will only tell you more if you sign. To be clear, if you sign the declaration and do not respect it, you could be tried and imprisoned. Not even your wife. Got it?"

Dimitriy read the declaration, his hand trembling. He would have liked to talk to Anastasia. Suddenly, she seemed very far away. He read it again.

"I need to think about it," he said. "I need to talk to my wife."

Ivanov shook his head grimly. "It's now or never," he said.

Dimitriy sighed and thought about the money. With such a salary they could easily rent a three-bedroom apartment. He was sure Anastasia would have agreed. She would surely have wanted to know what work the Admiral was offering. He signed and dated the paper and handed it back.

"Good," said Ivanov, putting it back in his pocket. He gestured to a waiter to clear their table and ordered two more vodkas.

"The Tunguska region wasn't as sparsely populated as people think," said the Admiral. "Quite a few people heard and saw something." He lit a cigarette. "It started with noises from the sky."

"Noises?"

"Da. You'll read the transcripts. Some of the witnesses said it was like trumpets."

"Heavenly trumpets?" said Dimitriy ironically.

Ivanov sneered.

"The noises went on for about a week," he continued.

"Then?" asked Dimitriy.

"There was some sort of *conflict*, in the sky," said Ivanov. "Some sort of *celestial* conflict."

"'Celestial'? You seem to be choosing your words with care, Admiral."

Ivanov stubbed out his cigarette.

"You'll read the file and see for yourself. As good scientists, we try always to keep open minds."

"The word 'conflict'," said Dimitriy, "suggests that more than one body or object might have been involved, right? And the word 'celestial' suggests this was high up?"

"There are drawings in the file," the Admiral said, "based on contemporary eyewitness accounts. The locals, the Evenki, were convinced they'd seen their god, Ogdy, in a fight."

"Fascinating," said Dimitriy, "but I am not sure why this should bring me to the Volga Basin and the Official Secrets Act."

Ivanov lit another cigarette.

"Leonid Kulik," he said. "A mineralogist. He came to Tunguska several times, starting in 1921. That was already thirteen years after the event. There was no crater — that puzzled him. How could there have been a meteorite impact if there were no crater, and if there were no fragments? He realised the fragments might have blasted out craters that had then got filled in. So, he kept digging holes to try and find filled-in craters with remains of one sort or another at the bottom — something, anything. No joy. Until 1938. His last expedition. One of his men found something, deep down, in a pit. Whatever it was, it blinded the man. He complained of an intense, searing light, then he lost his sight. Kulik's workers mutinied. For them it was proof they were messing with Ogdy. They dragged the man out and refused to get into the pit. Kulik had to shovel most of the earth back in himself. He measured the location as accurately as he could, and then returned to the Mineralogical Museum in Leningrad. He planned to return with his own men, but the Germans invaded in 1941 and he joined the fighting. The next year he died of typhus in a POW camp."

Ivanov drank some vodka.

"Whatever they found," he continued, "remained lost in the archives. For a long time, as you know, the motherland had more important things to think about than primitive superstitions. But in 2007 a group of archivists started going through Kulik's papers. When they got to the file about the 1938 incident, the team had the good idea of involving us."

"Us?" said Dimitriy.

"The security services," Ivanov said. "If another expedition to Tunguska were to be launched, they knew they'd need state resources. They dressed it up as being about some potentially weaponizable force. They weren't entirely wrong. Kulik's coordinates were accurate. They used a remote-controlled digger. Once they'd reached the depth Kulik recorded, they lowered animals down to the bottom. All came back blind. So, they were at the right place. A remote camera relayed images of glittering metallic fragments. They sent down instruments, but the instruments measured nothing. A volunteer discovered that *reflections* of the fragments could be observed in a mirror. Using remote cameras and mirrors, the fragments were dug out of the pit bottom. It was all hit-and-miss. Somebody thought of lead, being a heavy metal, so they fashioned a lead-lined steel box and used a remote-controlled robotic arm to shepherd the fragments towards the box and seal the lid."

"Shepherd?"

"You'll learn about that," Ivanov said; "*if* you take the job." He stubbed out his cigarette, drank off his vodka, and continued. "The fragments were then brought to a ..." (he coughed) "... *facility* here in Astrakhan. The box was opened and the fragments were housed in a specially-constructed room. That, Dimitriy Semenov, is where you come in. We want to analyse the fragments. Test their qualities." He leaned over the table as if to share a confidence. "And perhaps," he said, "replicate them."

Dimitriy felt the thrill of scientific discovery and the repulsion of a lifelong pacifist. But curiosity gripped him strongest. If only he could tell Anastasia! He was sure she would have been just as fascinated.

The Admiral got to his feet.

"I will be waiting outside tomorrow morning at seven," he said, "and will take you to the facility."

Dimitriy watched as Ivanov threaded his way steadily through the tables. That word, *comrade*, again. When he had gone, Dimitriy picked up the file and hurried to his room.

●

The Admiral was waiting for him on the hotel's esplanade in a sleek black chauffeur-driven limousine. He was in his uniform, his gold brocaded cap on the seat beside him.

"Is this a Zil?" Dimitriy asked, getting into the tobacco-fugged interior.

"The 4104," said the Admiral. "The Navy is determined to keep them going until they fall to pieces."

He lit a cigarette. "You read the file?" he asked.

"Of course. Do you want me to believe that the Evenki saw angels?"

"*You* saw the drawings," said Ivanov. "*I* don't want you to believe anything."

"Yes," said Dimitriy, "I *saw* the drawings."

The Admiral gazed through the smoked glass window.

"Do you believe in angels, Dimitriy Semenov?"

"No," said Dimitriy, "I don't. But what else can be made of those drawings? And those sounds; if not something like trumpets, then what?"

Ivanov shook his head.

"I told you; we are trying to keep open minds. You have to remember in 1908 the Evenki were a primitive, superstitious people. When something they didn't understand happened, they naturally ascribed it to their god, Ogdy."

"You don't think there was a conflict?"

"Imagine if you were a primitive people and something massive exploded overhead," said Ivanov. "Wouldn't you extrapolate from what you knew? Battle, noise?"

"And those trumpeting noises *before*?" asked Dimitriy.

Ivanov chuckled.

"*You* called them 'heavenly trumpets', Dimitriy Semenov, but you don't believe in such things, do you?"

"Of course not, Admiral. But what are the alternative explanations?"

Ivanov tutted. "You are a scientist, aren't you? Because we don't know the answer doesn't mean there isn't one. We just don't know it yet — perhaps we'll never know it. What we *do* know is that we have seven fragments of an unknown powerful material that *may* have fallen from the sky about the time of the Tunguska event. We can, and must, try to know as much about those fragments as possible, using scientific methods, and not basing our judgements on superstition and hearsay and eye-witness accounts from long ago."

"Of course," said Dimitriy, chastened. "It's those pictures in the file. My imagination ran away with me."

The Admiral stubbed out his cigarette.

"We have arrived," he said.

Some five months after Dimitriy started the job, Anastasia stopped making dinner on Friday evenings. The first time, she told him she'd been feeling unwell, and he accepted the explanation unthinkingly. He ate alone in the kitchen. The next Friday, though, the new practice had been rationalised; she said it was too late in the evening to eat a full-blown meal — better that he snacked or had a bowl of soup or a salad. He again accepted the explanation. Then, one Friday, when he came to bed, he found her weeping.

"What's the matter, Ana?"

She rolled over and he saw that her eyes were puffed up.

"I just wish you'd tell me," she said. "About her, whoever she is."

"There is no her," Dimitriy insisted.

"You can't hide it from me," Anastasia said. "I see the way you look as though you have been torn away from someone."

"There is no other woman, Anastasia."

"Is it a man? I'd understand."

"There's nobody else, I swear!"

"You think I'm stupid? You can't wait to get back on Monday mornings."

She rolled away and wept herself to sleep. He stared up at the ceiling. She was right, of course. The weekends back home in Derbent had become a torment.

●

"Welcome to Astrakhan State Technology University," said Ivanov, checking his cap's position in the glass of the chauffeur's partition.

The Admiral led him through the glass-fronted entrance. Students milled about, seemingly unfazed at the image of a uniformed Admiral threading a path through the crowd.

"Where are we going?"

"The Institute of Oil and Gas." Ivanov led the way across the leafy campus to a nondescript red brick construction. They went through rotating doors and stopped before a block of lifts. When the lift came, the Admiral pushed the button for -2, but he kept his finger on the button a long time. Ivanov turned to face a small camera in one corner of the roof of the lift and gave a salute.

"Forgive the cloak-and-dagger stuff," he said. "Until the Union collapsed, the Caspian Flotilla was based in Baku, but a lot of the command structure was kept safely within Russia itself, including here, in Astra. The Americans knew that, of course. This place was just as much of a target, so special underground facilities were built for the command structures. That's where we are going now."

By then, the lift should have reached -2 level, but felt as though it were still in motion. After several minutes of slow movement, the lift stopped, and the doors slid open. In front of them stood two armed, uniformed guards. Behind them was a vast, brightly lit space. Ivanov produced papers and explained about Dimitriy. Once the papers had been stamped, the soldiers stood aside and let them pass.

"It's quite a hike," said the Admiral.

The vast space was devoid of human activity, but all around them stood massive columns of plastic-wrapped material.

"Thousands of men could live down here for years," said Ivanov.

On the far side of the bunker, Ivanov led Dimitriy into a complex of smaller spaces. Each entrance was a double-doored air-pressurized port. Finally, they came to a twin set of grey-painted heavy steel doors that had been swung open.

"Here we are," said the Admiral. "The playroom; the laboratory."

They were greeted by the head of the scientific team, Fyodor Babikov, a beanpole of a man wearing large tinted spectacles. Ivanov left them together, promising to return at the end of the day. Babikov showed Dimitriy to the changing room. There were sinks, lockers and benches. They scrubbed up together, then dressed in classic surgical gear. Afterwards, Babikov led Dimitriy into a small meeting room. The walls were lined with large drawings showing distinctive geometrical structures. Babikov gestured for him to sit down at a table and sat opposite.

"What has Admiral Ivanov told you?" he asked.

"The basic story," said Dimitriy. "And I've read the file."

"Did he tell you about their effects?"

"The blindness?"

"Well, there *is* that," said Babikov. "But you don't need to worry. The lab is rigged so that you simply cannot look directly at the fragments. You can only see them indirectly by using the mirrors we've installed, or by using the camera. But did Ivanov not talk about anything else?"

"Nothing," said Dimitriy.

"Mmm... He was probably afraid he'd scare you off."

"Why would I be scared?"

"They seem to have an addictively euphoric effect on some people."

"Some?"

"It seems to depend. There's nothing chemical about it."

"How do you know this?"

"You're not the first expert drafted in. In fact, you are the third."

"The others?"

Babikov shook his head.

"They didn't last very long. The first was here for just over a year. The second lasted almost two years."

"Where are they now?"

"Locked away," said Babikov.

"And you?"

"Nothing," said Babikov. "But, then, I don't spend hours in the viewing room."

"All right," Dimitriy said. "What else did Ivanov *not* tell me?"

"There isn't a whole lot more to know."

"How long have the fragments been here?"

"Since 2008."

"And you have honestly learned nothing?"

Babikov grinned.

"Honestly, very little. I'll tell you everything we know, but it won't take long."

Dimitriy leaned back in his chair.

"Tell me," he said.

"We know they have properties, and powers. The power to blind people, for example."

"Are we sure of that?"

"You mean?"

"Well," said Dimitriy, "we've only had that one example, of the man down the pit, back in 1938. It could have been a stroke, couldn't it?"

"You're forgetting the animals," Babikov said. "Anyway, there have been quite a few unfortunate episodes since."

"Here?" asked Dimitriy.

"Yes," said Babikov. "People who didn't listen. People who didn't believe. An accident. A drunk."

"How many?"

"Enough for us to know that the fragments, if looked at directly, cause blindness in humans, as in animals. Even welding masks didn't help."

"You've tried reptiles?"

"Oh, yes," said Babikov. "We've tried reptiles *and* squid and octopus *and* insects. We've tried everything," he said. "The fragments have the same effect on any sort of eye known to us."

"Your instruments?"

"Show nothing. Whatever this effect is, it is produced in an undetectable way."

"What else?" Dimitriy asked.

"Oh, the euphoria business."

"Can you be sure of that?"

"Scientifically, no. But there must be a strong presumption."

"Two cases only? You can't presume anything from that."

"You are right," Babikov said, smiling ruefully. "Let me just call it a *hunch*, then. Two highly intelligent, balanced, reasonable scientists, both following a similar pattern of obsessiveness and increasingly frequent episodes of manic euphoria, culminating in madness and confinement in clinics. I agree with you, Dimitriy Semenov. It could be sheer coincidence, but I think not."

"All right," said Dimitriy. "What else?"

"We have found a way to manipulate the fragments," said Babikov. "Only one metal may touch them — gold. All others melt away as they get near. Once we realised that, we had special gold implements made up that could be attached to the arms of the robots — that is the main way in which you will be working with the fragments, if you need to manipulate them."

"But it is curious," said Dimitriy, "gold being so malleable — like the lead in which they were encased."

"In retrospect, the lead-lined box was a crazy risk," said Babikov. "Who knows what might have happened if they had melted their way out during the trip?"

"What else?"

Babikov shook his head in sudden exhaustion.

"We know next to nothing, and that is all we know."

"Now you are talking in riddles."

Babikov looked at Dimitriy for a few moments, as though brought back from a reverie.

"We cannot record images. Nothing works; film, X-rays, electro-magnetic resonance imaging, transmission electron tomography... Whatever sort of imaging we have tried to use, nothing shows up. They are definitely there; we can see their reflection, but we can't capture them as images, and that means that we can only study the fragments themselves.”

“What about microscopes?” asked Dimitriy.

“Lenses work,” said Babikov. “But you cannot record what you are seeing.”

“You can’t draw them?”

“No, no,” said Babikov. “They can be drawn, at least — hence all of these...” he waved at the drawings hanging on the walls around them. “Your predecessors’ masterpieces.”

“May I?” Dimitriy asked.

Babikov nodded.

Dimitriy studied the drawings for a while.

“I have an idea,” he said. “But I’ll wait until you’ve finished.”

“Second,” Babikov continued, “they are constantly levitating.”

Dimitriy raised his eyebrows.

“They always hover, never touching any surface.”

“Some sort of energy, then?”

“I think so, but we can detect nothing. We thought of magnetism or light but it’s neither of those.” Babikov smiled and shook his head. “Believe me, Dimitriy Semenov, we have tried and tested many ideas — all fruitlessly — so far.”

“I understand what Ivanov was getting at now.”

“Getting at?” said Babikov.

“We were talking about scientific method. He said we don’t know the answer yet, and perhaps we never will.”

●

That very first time Dimitriy came back from Astrakhan she’d known already, he realised — or, rather, she’d suspected already. Something had happened. He couldn’t entirely hide it from her. For a start, there was the fait accompli of his decision. He had taken the job without first discussing the offer with her. It was so generous, he said, that he had decided on the spot. That wasn’t the whole truth, of course. She asked about the work. He told her how he’d had to sign a declaration and was now bound by the Official Secrets Act. He saw her recoil.

“It isn’t what you think,” he’d said.

"What is it, then?" she'd asked.

"Something unimaginable," he'd replied.

She'd wrinkled her nose. "Can't you give me a clue?"

He'd laughed. "I promise you it's nothing sinister."

"I can see you are enthusiastic about it."

"Come with me to Astrakhan, Ana," he'd urged. "Bring the children. We can make it work."

"We discussed all that," she'd said, shaking her head. "My job, my family, the children's schools..."

He'd nodded his head slowly. Already, his thoughts were drifting back...

"Dimitriy?"

"I'm sorry, my love," he said. "I was daydreaming."

●

He'd listened patiently as Babikov listed the other properties his team had so far noted. The seven fragments were identical in appearance. Each was a convex oblong, about nine centimetres long by five centimetres wide. From a distance, they seemed to be golden in colour but, the stronger the magnification, the less colour there was. From very close up they seemed neither transparent nor invisible, and completely colourless yet iridescent. The fragments' default position was to hover vertically in an overlapping formation, like the defensive *testudo* Roman legionaries had sometimes adopted with their shields. If the fragments were separated, they immediately moved back to the *testudo* formation. Once again, Dimitriy studied the drawings on the walls.

"So, what's this big idea of yours?" said Babikov.

"*Lepidoptera*," said Dimitriy.

"Butterflies?" said Babikov, momentarily confused. "We'd thought of fish scales, but *lepidoptera*?"

"In appearance they seem similar to fish scales, it is true, but butterfly scales have three-dimensional lattices that cause iridescence, and I just wonder whether some similar effect is not at work with these scales — and they *are* scales, Babikov, aren't they? They're not just fragments."

Babikov blushed. He took off his glasses and polished the lenses.

"Ivanov doesn't like such talk. I think he's right. We shouldn't leap ahead of ourselves."

"But are we?" said Dimitriy. "We know — or we assume — that these fragments fell to earth in June 1908, right?"

Babikov shook his head.

"No," he said. "We know only that they were found in the area where that event occurred."

"Ivanov gave me to understand there was a probability."

"So there may be," said Babikov. "But he doesn't want us to start wandering off into anthropomorphism and zoomorphism and all the rest of it. We know only what we know. The rest is speculation. If the Admiral hadn't given you the file, you wouldn't have started thinking along these lines."

Dimitriy smiled.

"What lines, Fyodor Babikov? What lines are those?"

Babikov remained silent.

"All right," said Dimitriy. "I'm sure you have similar thoughts. These so-called fragments are themselves a fragment that fell off something much larger, probably during that 'event' of 1908 — off a wing, maybe?"

"Enough!" said Babikov, waving his hands in front of him.

But somehow, Dimitriy *knew*; the fragments *belonged* to something.

●

In February, just over a year after his first visit to Astrakhan, Anastasia put the ultimatum to him. He couldn't blame her. The Christmas period had been disastrous. Derbent was bitterly cold and the streets were littered with filthy snow and slush where the gritters had passed. The morning, midday, and evening howls of the Ekranoplan as it departed and returned punctuated Derbent's days just as accurately and regularly as a clock tower bell. He couldn't wait to get back to Astra. He was constantly irritable with the children and mostly morosely silent with her. He felt dreadful. He needed to be back, to be back with *them*, in their presence. When the holidays were finally over, and he had been leaving for the Ekranoplan, she had said, "I can't say I'm sorry to see you go, Dimitriy. You have to get a grip on yourself. Whatever is going on in Astrakhan, you have to put a stop to it. It is ruining you and us."

That had been January. He had got worse over the following month. Then, one Friday evening in late February, she took the final initiative. Part of him felt she was absolutely right — he felt sorry for her and for Andrei and Sasha. But another part of him just didn't care. Or, rather, it only cared about *them*, the angelic fragments (which was what he called them now), and about being with them.

The children were in bed. The classical music radio channel was on. She'd even put a lit candle on the laid dinner table. It was the first time in a long time that she had cooked a meal for his return. At the end of the meal, Anastasia took his hands across the table.

"I am so very sorry, Dima," she said, "but I can't take this anymore."

"What do you mean?" he blustered.

She smiled and put a finger to his lips to hush him.

"You know what I mean. I have spoken to you so many times."

She was right.

"So, now what?" he asked.

"I'd like you to resign from your job in Astrakhan."

"But how would we..." he began, blustering again.

She shook her head and smiled wistfully.

"We were fine before. We'll be fine again."

"But my work is important."

"I'm sure it is, Dimitriy but, please, let somebody else do it."

He burst into tears.

"I can't," he wept. "I just can't."

"What do you mean? What is it that has such a hold over you? If it is not a mistress, then what is it? Drugs? Is that it? You can tell me. Please."

"It's none of those," he blurted. "But I can't tell you."

"Of course you can!"

"I have signed the Official Secrets Act, Ana."

"I promise I won't tell anybody else. Who could I tell, anyway?"

Dimitriy shook his head.

"If you won't tell me," said Anastasia, her tone hardening, "that's it."

"What do you mean?"

"I'll leave you, Dimitriy."

His shoulders sagged.

"All right, I'll tell you," he said finally.

He told her about his second meeting with Ivanov, and the file about the 1908 Tunguska event and Kulik's 1938 discovery. He told her about his first entry into the thick-walled, steel-shuttered underground space where the plate glass and mirrors had been set up to enable scientists to gaze indirectly on the fragments. He told her about his indescribable feelings of ecstasy, of euphoria, when he was in the presence of the angelic scales, and how the obsessive feeling had grown until it had now overwhelmed all other considerations. He told her about the steel shutter inside the space housing the scales which Babikov had to operate every day so that Dimitriy could at least no longer gaze upon the angelic fragments, and the way he, Dimitriy, had to be dragged out of the space by orderlies and given sedation before he could be convinced to return to his hotel room in the evenings.

Anastasia sat patiently through his explanation.

"All right," she said when he had finished. "Suppose everything you've told me is true. Where do you think this will all end?"

"I have to finish my work," he said. "Nobody understands the fragments better than I do. I have a *feeling* for them, don't you see? I understand them; their need to return. You see?"

She looked at him with sad eyes. "Of course I do, Dima," she said, "but you need to take a break. You're working yourself crazy."

"I can't take a break, don't you understand? I *must* continue."

"Nobody would blame you for taking a break," she said.

"But the *work*," Dimitriy insisted. "I *must* be there."

She shook her head. "No," she said. "You must stop this nonsense. You *can* stop it, you know. Let somebody else do it."

"NO!" he shouted, startling himself as much as Anastasia. "I can't let someone else come in. *I* must be with them. You can't stop me now." He broke off and wept. "Don't you see?" he said. "It's stronger than me."

Anastasia shook her head once more.

"You must choose," she said softly.

"No!" Dimitriy sobbed. "Please don't make me choose."

"If you go back to Astrakhan on Monday, then we will move out."

"But the children need their father!" Dimitriy blurted.

"Don't be a fool," Anastasia snapped. "The children haven't had a father for over a year now."

He nodded and hung his head. "All right,' he said. "Where will you go? Your parents?"

She nodded.

Good, thought Dimitriy, with a sense of wonderment at his own callousness. *Now I can go back to the fragments.*

●

Anastasia didn't come to the doorstep with him. He'd kissed her on the head as she lay in bed. She didn't move, though he sensed she was awake.

"Goodbye, Ana," he said. "I still love you, you know. And I'm sorry. I just have to be there."

He closed the door and walked through the slushy remains of the snow to the Ekranoport. He was petrified of the take-off, as usual, but his heart had already filled with joyful anticipation. As the Caspian Queen approached Astra, the sea became agitated and the sky darkened. A strong wind blew up and Dimitriy could feel that the pilot was struggling with the controls. He was relieved when the craft slowed down and started its long taxi up the relative calm of the Reka Bakhtemir channel. Ivanov was waiting for him on the quayside.

"Something's going on," he said. "We've been hearing noises in the sky."

"Heavenly trumpets?" said Dimitriy.

"Noises in the sky," Ivanov repeated. "But, yes, not unlike the descriptions the Evenki gave in 1908."

"Could it be?" asked Dimitriy.

"Be what?" said Ivanov, drawing on his cigarette. The sky flashed. A long roll of thunder sounded. "And we've been having strange weather. Look at those clouds."

Dimitry looked up at the dark, corrugated formation hanging heavy and low over the city. Thunder reverberated above and around them.

"And the fragments," Ivanov continued, "have started to oscillate."

"Oscillate?"

"All right," said the Admiral, flicking away his cigarette and blowing out smoke. "They seem to have become agitated."

"I can't wait to see them."

Ivanov gave him a sour stare then lit another cigarette and leaned against the Zil.

"I'm not sure that's a good idea, Dimitriy Semenov. They are no longer stable."

"What do you mean? I've got to see them. You know that."

"Pull yourself together," said the Admiral.

"It's just that I've *got* to see them. Surely you have understood that by now?"

The sky flashed and flickered. Ivanov looked up and waited for the roll of thunder.

"This is not normal," he said. "Something is going on."

"There's a connection?"

"I don't know, but I have a sense there might be. It's almost as though the scales are trying to escape."

"Ah! Escape?"

"Babikov says they have already melted through the gold lining on the roof of the cell."

"No!" said Dimitriy. "Then we must hurry. They are going back. I knew it!"

"Back?" Ivanov drew deeply on his cigarette. "Take my advice," he said. "Return to Derbent. The Ekranoplan will be leaving very soon. Go back to your wife and children. Maybe it's nothing. We'll see. Come again tomorrow."

"There's no point," said Dimitriy. "They've left me."

"Because of this?" Ivanov asked. "Because of your..."

"Yes," said Dimitriy.

Ivanov nodded slowly and drew again on his cigarette. They heard the distinctive whine as the Caspian Queen's jet engines started up.

"Go!" he urged.

"I can't!" Dimitriy sobbed. "I must see *them* again."

They leaned on a railing and watched as the gangplanks were drawn away and the aft and forward doors closed. The sky flashed vividly. A dockworker cast off the mooring ropes. When they had been entirely wound back on board, the jet engines roared, and the Caspian Queen sailed slowly out into the Volga. They heard the familiar howl as the captain increased the power and taxied the strange vessel down towards the sea channel.

Ivanov flicked away his cigarette, then opened the door of the Zil.

"We'd better hurry," he said.

●

"Ana," called her mother. "Come quickly."

Anastasia pulled the plug in the kitchen sink, wiped her hands on her apron and joined her parents in the living room. They were watching a Russian television channel and the news bulletin had just started. Sasha was playing on the floor. The newsreader was halfway through the headlines. A train had crashed just outside Vladivostok. The President had visited a new LPG facility at the port of Murmansk...

"What is it, mama?"

"Ssshhh," said her mother, "you'll see in a moment."

The newsreader finished the headlines. Anastasia's mother turned the volume up.

"And now we go back to our main news item this evening. Reports are coming in of a massive explosion on the northern outskirts of the city of Astrakhan, at the premises of the State Technology University. The explosion is said to have occurred in an underground research facility situated beneath the University's parkland.

"As can be seen from these helicopter images, several buildings have collapsed and the police and the fire services are searching the rubble. Among those missing are the director of the Caspian Flotilla's scientific outreach programme, Rear Admiral Anatoly Ivanov, and the head of the Astrakhan State Technology University's Oil and Gas Institute research programme, Fyodor Babikov. An acclaimed Moscow State University materials scientist, Dimitriy Semenov, who joined the research team from Derbent, is also missing."

Pictures of the three men flashed up on the screen for a few moments.

"That's Daddy," said Sasha.

Anastasia nodded tearfully.

"Yes, darling," she said.

"Babikov!" Dimitriy cried. He staggered out into the remains of the room where he had first met the scientist. He could hear flames flickering. The air was heavy with smoke. A long, low groan sounded out. "Babikov!" he said, "Is that you?" Dimitry staggered over to where he thought Babikov's office had once been. He heard the groan again. "Babikov?"

"Dimitriy Semenov," whispered the scientist. "What has happened to your eyes, man?"

Dimitriy smiled, the charred skin wrinkling where his eyes had once been.

"The fragments have gone back to their rightful place," he said. "I'm going home now."

Martin Westlake's story "Going Home" was originally published in Metaphorosis on Friday, 12 March 2021

About the author

Martin Westlake has followed parallel careers as a civil servant and as an academic and has lived, studied, and worked in the UK, Italy, France, and Belgium.

The only thing he has ever always wanted to do is write creative fiction. Science fiction exercises a special, but not exclusive, attraction in that regard. For the past fifteen years he has been working seriously at it and he thinks maybe he is starting to get there.

martinwestlake.eu, @MartinWestlake

Time's Arrow

C. Heidmann

In 2130 the Nelari began resurrecting the dead. In 2133 Talia's father called for the first time in five years.

"You want to bring her back, Dad?" *After all this time, after what you did?* Talia wanted to add, but didn't. Couldn't. Not to his face. Not anymore.

She barely recognized the white-haired, eighty-three-year old figure; the holo-projectors in her quarters relayed every etch-mark of time, his still-bright blue eyes peering at her out of a sagging, heavy face.

"Don't you?" He looked... hurt. Like when she was small and had uttered an expletive. How could she, his perfect little girl, have said such a thing? "But she's your *mother.*"

"Have you thought this through? How it will be for her? For all of us?"

He rubbed at his left eye and blinked a couple of times. "You think I haven't? Ever since I got that notification, I can hardly think about anything else."

Talia's notification about the offer to reanimate her mother had arrived the previous day. Half-knowing it wasn't going to go away, she'd ignored it; until her father's call woke her in the middle of Copernicus Station's artificially maintained night.

"She deserves another chance, Talia."

Yes, but did he *deserve another chance with her?* She clamped down on the retort.

Twenty-three years earlier, Talia had lost her mother and learned of her father's infidelity in one afternoon. He'd been away on another 'business' trip which couldn't be put off even in the face of his wife's terminal cancer. When Talia tracked him down and gave him the news, he'd been heartbroken. The shameless display of grief had enraged her.

The pause lengthened as she concentrated on not fidgeting.

What could she say that would convince him she didn't want to talk? Not about bringing her mother back from the dead. Not about anything. She didn't want to get caught up again in the emotional turmoil of his dredged-up pain, his guilt, self-justification, or whatever new form his latest plea for absolution would take. It was part of the reason she lived off-Earth, as far away from home, from him, as she could get.

Her father's hologram fragmented as interference rippled it into multi-colored snowflakes, granting her a reprieve.

"Do you know how lucky we are?" he said as the holo-emitters recomposed his image. "If we'd not had her buried, if we'd had her cremated instead..."

"I know, Dad."

For their own mysterious reasons, the Nelari had revealed their technology in stages. Initially, only people who had been cryogenically preserved, a full body or a head, could be reanimated. Then the Nelari taught human scientists techniques for reviving the interred. Now families of the cremated lived in fervent hope that it might become possible to resurrect even those who had suffered complete body-loss.

"I thought you were opposed to the Nelari, Dad. You said you didn't trust them, that you don't believe in benevolent beings from the stars. Now you're ready to roll over and take their offer?"

He scratched his lip with his thumb. "I did say that. And I still don't trust them. There's no such thing as something for nothing." He shook a crooked forefinger. "One day those damned aliens are going to want something in return and payback's always a bitch."

She resisted the urge to roll her eyes. "They're not like that, Dad. In all their time here, they've not once demanded anything in return for their generosity."

"Then why don't you want me to take their offer?"

She rubbed at her rat's nest of hair. "I don't know if it's the right thing to do, I don't —"

"What do you mean not the right thing? Don't you want your mother back?" She didn't react to his accusation but the hardness in his eyes pushed at her, shoved like a playground bully.

"What about the rehabilitation? It will take weeks if not months, and you realize there's a chance she might not retain all her memory or personality when they revive her." Some reanimations had not gone well — people failing to re-integrate, like a graft not taking. Unable and unwilling to face life again, having never expected to be resurrected, they ended up in mental institutions or chose to end their lives again — with a stipulation to never be revived again.

A glint of moisture filmed her father's irises though he pretended it wasn't there. "I read all the literature. I know there's a chance we could lose her all over again."

"But you're not going to let that stop you, are you?" Certainty of his answer, his total conviction, sat like a lead brick in her stomach.

"You can't expect me to walk away."

"Why the hell not, Dad? It's what you did last time," she spat, instantly regretting it, suddenly tired and wanting to get this over with. She massaged the beginnings of a headache at her temples. "Why do you want my approval when you've already made up your mind?"

"Because that's what your mother would have wanted — us, united as a family."

"Since when did you care what she would have wanted?" The sound of her voice rising a few octaves spurred her on. "You were the one who broke up our family. You walked out on her when she needed you the most." Ignoring the bounds of the holo-pickup fields, she gesticulated wildly, punctuating her words, slashing the air, decimating the millions of miles between them.

"I can't believe you're still holding on to that pain —"

Blood whooshed in her ears. "Her dying gave you an excellent way out of the mess you'd made of your marriage. You think she'd want to come back to that? To you?" She dreaded the return, hated the idea her mother would have to face it all again, her own tragic end, her husband's betrayal, the pain he'd caused her and the rifts it had opened in their family. Why couldn't he see that?

"Talia," he cast around him as if searching for his words, "listen to me. You don't know what it's like to lose a partner, a... a soul mate." His eyes tracked left to some point in the virtual distance, somewhere she could never see.

"Everyone who's lost someone wants them back, it's part of mourning. But we have to let them go, learn to live without them. Hasn't Mom suffered enough?"

She stepped back from the holo, folded her arms across her chest and became aware of her rapid breathing, accelerated heart rate. Finally, she'd run out of words, weapons to hurt him with.

This time his voice rose. "She *has* suffered enough, that's why I have to bring her back."

She had started it, but he wasn't going to let it go. She strove to keep her voice low. "Dad —"

"It's okay, I get it." He nodded as if he'd read her thoughts. "You don't want your mother back because you don't want *me* to have her back." He choked to a stop and lowered the accusatory finger he'd been brandishing. "You want to make me pay again." He was pointing his thumb at himself.

He was right. She wasn't denying her mother, she was denying *him*. But she clenched her mouth. Time had worn him down to a wrinkled, shrunken version of what he'd been, a badly made puppet of his former self. She'd said more than enough hurtful things to him over the years. This time had proven no exception.

In her father's world, a buzzer sounded. The evening mealtime call for the residents of Raintree Retirement Village. His eyes flicked to his right, then avoided hers.

The buzzer sounded again. "You'll have to excuse me, I have to go." He rolled his chair away, an old man not wanting to miss his dinner.

"End connection," she told the com and headed for the medicine cabinet. She slipped a medi-film strip onto her tongue, let it melt into her palate. Within seconds, her headache disappeared, but the chagrin, the bitter aftertaste of their argument lingered. No instant medi-film remedy to soften that.

Did she really want her mother to remain dead just to punish him? She'd mourned, accepted the loss, and moved on. How could she go back on it now? How could her father expect her to retrace those painful steps?

Her mother had never yearned to be brought back to life and cured. And she couldn't be asked if she wanted to come back or to be left alone. But if obtaining consent was impossible, did that make it irrelevant?

Never before had it been necessary to deal with questions like these. When people died, that was it. End of story. Time's arrow had always pointed one way. Death followed life, not the other way around. Until now. Until the Nelari.

In a few short months, she would have to face the reanimated version of her dead mother. What should she do? she wondered. What would she say to a mother she'd already buried?

●

"Hi Mom," was all she said.

The regenerated version of her mother smiled as she came into the waiting room. She looked incredible, radiant, and almost too beautiful. But her face didn't hide the shock, the disbelief, the pain and the disappointment when she saw how time had changed Talia and her father. She recovered and revealed nothing more as she greeted them in turn, asking the appropriate questions, keeping everything normal, calm, as if nothing untoward or overly emotional, were happening.

Talia had gone numb. When her mother hugged her, it didn't feel real. It was like holding a doll, an automaton. Who was this perfect imitation they'd been given? Why did she want to outright reject this manifestation of her mother? Why did she feel she had to keep her own emotional distance? Was it because she'd perceived this... this... ghost of her mother, as doing that?

She'd been coached, Talia told herself as she watched the apparition of her mother; prepared for weeks ahead on how to cope.

Her father was a mess. He began weeping the moment his past wife emerged. More than two decades of pain and guilt, and of mourning her, came out and pulped him, mashed him up like a losing boxer. He failed to stay up-right on his new Nelari-gifted cyber legs. They had to help him into a chair, get an aide to give him something to calm him.

Juxtaposed against Talia's decrepit father, her stunning, young 'mother' kept smiling, fussed over him in an over-caring, and to Talia, false way.

"Did you want to come back, Mom?"

All eyes in the room — including those of the bot-assistant who'd been facilitating the meeting, turned to Talia. No one moved.

"I... I, yes, of course, darling."

"Really? You wanted to come back?" Talia flung her forefinger towards her father, "to *him*?" Back in his mobility chair his tear-filled gaze pleaded with her.

"You remember how he hurt you? Abandoned you? Right when you needed him the most?"

"We can talk about this later, okay, Honey?" The manifestation of her mother tried to soothe. Was this her mother? Weren't they supposed to reconstruct enough of a person's personality to be indistinguishable from the original, assimilating every scrap of information left behind by, or about that person?

The resurrected woman's words seemed to de-immobilize everybody. Everyone started talking and moving at once. Talia barely heard them.

A timer display in her left vision flashed. "I have to go," she said in a loud voice. "My ship leaves in an hour. We talk now, or not at all."

They didn't talk then.

Outside, she blinked in the mid-afternoon sun, her space-accustomed eyes smarting in the harsh light. The trip to the spaceport was a blur. The whole way, she cried for her mother. Before her mother had passed away, she'd never spoken to Talia about what her father had done. She'd let Talia believe she'd accepted her impending death early on; that she'd been coping and that at the last, suffering and in pain, she'd wanted it to end, for herself and for all of them.

"Talia, wait."

It was her.

Almost through the departure gate, Talia paused. The reanimation of her mother stood alone, on the other side of the crowd, waving at her. Talia hesitated before weaving through passengers clamoring to get ahead of the line.

"I did want to come back," her mother started, out of breath, "despite everything. I... I mean, if I could have, you know, had a choice." Her cheeks were flushed, two distinct red patches on either side of her face, like Talia remembered.

Her mother had never been good with words, had had difficulty explaining herself. For the first time, Talia felt sympathy for her. Here was a woman scarcely her senior now, facing the prospect of going home with an eighty-year-old man, thrust back into a world she didn't know anymore. How would she pick up the pieces of a life death had made her leave so long ago?

"I'm... alive." Her mother's eyes shot full of tears. She shuddered in a breath and gulped. "I mean I'm glad I'm alive again. I can go travelling now like I always wanted to..." Her mother offered a smile. "I understand you live on a space station? I would love to see it, I mean, to see you... I mean, to talk... some time." Her mother hooked an imaginary strand of hair behind her ear. Despite her new short hair style, she repeated the action two or three times as if she still had the shoulder-length hair she'd lost to cancer and its medications so long ago.

The jittery little gesture triggered Talia's memories, countless instances when she'd seen her mother repeat exactly that nervous tick, always when her mother had been anxious, emotional. Talia's heart melted. It sounded like her mother, looked like her mother, *felt* like her mother. She grabbed her. "Oh, Mom." Her tears spilled unabated.

They hugged until the final boarding alert flashed red in Talia's vision.

●

Her mother went home with her father to the house bought back for her at great expense. Refurbished and re-decorated to as close as possible to the way it had been when she died. The pitiable, harmless-seeming gesture of a guilt-ridden erstwhile cheat and widower.

Talia wasn't surprised when they broke up.

It took about six months for everything to unravel before her mother found a younger man and moved away.

Talia's father died shortly after.

Her mother was still alive, of course, carrying on with her new life and her new beau. She might even outlive Talia now, might even be brought back from the dead again someday, like Talia would be.

But when the Nelari offer came to revive her father, Talia discovered that despite his insistence on resurrecting her mother, he'd neglected to specify his own wishes. He'd left the reanimation decision to his next-of-kin.

Her mother was hesitant.

"I... he said he didn't want to live without me. I... I feel bad... about the way I left him. But that house, the way he... I know all he was trying to do was atone, but I couldn't take it..." Another person hovered in the holo behind her mother, too far out of range to be rendered in detail.

"I felt like a ghost, like I was haunting him," The person in the background moved into the holo-frame and squeezed her mother's shoulder. She squeezed back. "What I mean to say is, I have Antonio now, and... maybe... your father deserves another chance at life too." She spread her hands, as if opening the best possible outcome.

●

At the resurrection and rehabilitation center, they let Talia in early.

She paused in the doorway to her father's room. He didn't notice her right away as two bots helped him upright out of bed. She eyed the figure of her dad.

Still eighty-three, still white-haired, he looked… invigorated, sprightly. Gone were the sunken haggardness, the slow movements, and the pallor that had washed him out. His cheeks had a rosy glow, almost like the cliché Santa Claus figure, and despite still being a little unsteady on his feet he had a quickness to his movements, a new sureness. Restored to the peak of health for his age, he should have another thirty, forty odd years of good quality life. More, probably, at the rate of Nelari-gifted medical advancement.

"You had me brought back." His soft words broke her reverie. Her mind had drifted. He took a step toward her, bots hovering either side in case he lost his balance. "Does that mean you've forgiven me?"

She opened her mouth. Had she? She bit her lip. She wasn't sure. But she was willing to try. In the post-Nelari world of selflessness and compassion, disallowing his resurrection would've been tantamount to purposely keeping him dead. She couldn't live with that; with herself.

C. Heidmann's story "Time's Arrow" was originally published in Metaphorosis on Friday, 6 July 2018

About the author

Originally from South Africa, C Heidmann writes from Auckland, New Zealand. Indistinguishable from a local after a number of years on the Outer Rim, she grew up on an entirely different galactic arm and relishes the idea of secretly being an alien.

Stand or Fall

David Whitmarsh

Ilyas Bardakci was dead, but he hadn't stopped breathing, hadn't stopped moving, hadn't stopped thinking. He had no chance, no hope, no idea where in the void of interstellar space his ship had emerged. The radiation pulse from the nuke that had torn through his flesh had burned through half the ship's systems. That was the price he'd paid for hesitating. Wavering between solidarity and vengeance, he'd left it too late and jumped blind.

The reactor was down. Backup power was enough to keep the air pumping, the lights on, and the remaining instruments running, at least for a few hours. If life support lasted long enough, the radiation sickness would certainly kill him, but he wasn't dead yet, unlike those he'd left behind. Thinking of them fed the rage and the rage beat down the rising nausea. His fingers danced over the controls. Telescopes and sensors on the hull of the tiny vessel twisted on their mounts, searching for bearings of the brightest stars. Tentative spectral matches scrolled up the display: Sirius, Muphrid, Denebola. Calculations converged on an answer: he was twenty-eight light-years from the Muphrid system where he'd started.

For Ilyas, the jump had happened in the blink of an eye, but during that timeless instant twenty-eight years had elapsed. Twenty-eight years since everyone and everything he had known had perished. The habitats, stations, planet-side cities, a hundred and forty million people. All gone. Twenty-eight light-years behind him, twenty-eight years in the past. Celeste had been right: fighting was futile, and he had lost her because of his refusal to listen.

With no reactor, he could jump again only as far as the residual charge in the drive allowed. A search of the almanac revealed the colony closest to his crippled vessel: GJ430.1, HIP 56238, a star so insignificant it was nameless, known only by numbers from ancient catalogues; so dim it was barely a star at all. No major planets, two balls of rock smaller than Earth's moon, and a meagre smattering of asteroids, yet people lived there, and it was less than three light-years from his current position.

In the placid emptiness of the interstellar void he had time to check the calculations. With the autopilot dead, he had to point the vessel by hand and eye towards his target and set the displacement to the required range.

Another instant, another three years. His telescope found the single habitat cylinder, Thurlina, twenty kilometres long, four in diameter, turning its slow dance close around the dim red star. The docking complex at the sunlit axis held a handful of kinetic in-system tugs and freighters, nothing with interstellar capability. Population seven hundred thousand according to the almanac, a pacific society, friendly, welcoming, but a cultural and industrial backwater. The almanac was sixty years out of date.

His hand, beginning to blister from the radiation burns, lifted the cover from the mayday alarm. He passed out before he could press it.

●

Weight pressed him down on a soft bed. Muted footsteps paced around his dreams.

Celeste.

No. Celeste had given up the fight long ago. The soft footsteps faded and he slid from delirium to darkness.

A soft bed, a softly-lit windowless room. Ilyas tried to speak, but his throat was dry. He raised his arm to test the strength of the gravity that held him down, but learned only his own weakness. Wires snaked out from under the bedclothes to the monitors by the bedside. Thin tubes red with blood penetrated the pale blotchy skin of his arm.

"Water," he mumbled, and blacked out again.

●

Grey eyes peered at him from above the mask, wisps of ash-blond hair escaping from the edge of the cap.

"Awake, hey?" A female voice. "You're better off sleeping through this part." She turned from him and her arms moved but he couldn't see what her hands were doing. A few clicks, a beep. The room receded and his eyelids closed of their own accord. Celeste waited for him, sitting out on the balcony of their small apartment, the light of the sun-tube bright on her bare arms.

She looked up from the book she was reading. "How did it go? Did you save anyone?"

No. They're all dead, he tried to answer, but his mouth was too dry.

Celeste laid down the book. "But you got away. You're alive. Don't waste that." She raised her right hand to stroke his cheek, red blood dripping from the gash along her wrist. "I'm sorry, sweetheart."

Sorry for what she had done, or for what he had? Ilyas couldn't tell.

"Stand or Fall! Stand or Fall!" Ilyas had shouted with the rest of them as they stood in the great hall. On the giant screen above the stage, they cheered as the demolition charges rippled through the evacuation fleet. They cheered again when the image of the expanding cloud of debris was replaced by Marshal Petro's stern face.

●

"How do you feel today, Ilyas?" The same grey eyes, the same ash-blond hair, but no cap, no mask. Young, pretty, like the daughter he'd never had. Her hair was short, neat. No cosmetics, no jewellery except a thin chain around her neck that hung down beneath her blouse.

"Thirsty," he croaked.

She held the cup with one hand and raised his head with the other while he grasped the straw between his lips. Cold water flooded his mouth, the sweetest thing he had ever tasted.

"Slowly," she said. "Not too much."

He swallowed and relaxed to allow his head to be lowered back to the pillow. "How long?"

"You've been here three weeks. A tug pulled you in to the dock after your jump triggered the sensors."

"Thank the crew for me."

"No crew. Automated. We've a lot of automation in Thurlina." She smiled like it was a joke. "When you're a little stronger you'll see. For now you need to rest, and you are not my only patient."

On her way out she paused to look back at him. "I'm Mila. Mila Kraft." The door closed and her soft footsteps faded to silence. Silence that drew on and on until Ilyas fell asleep again.

For a few minutes, the ablative dust clouds had done their job. The Enemy's hypervelocity projectiles blasted to plasma as they collided with the fine grains, but the shock waves carved openings in the clouds faster than they could be replenished. For years, the people of Muphrid had worked to build those defences but they brought only minutes of respite. The projectiles, simple fragments of iron each weighing a few grams but travelling close to the speed of light, tore into the orbital habitats, stations, and cities, each piece with the energy of a small nuclear device. Hundreds of them, thousands, millions.

Ilyas and his squadron waited to defend against the second wave of the attack. By the time it came they were defending expanding clouds of dust and debris and craters glowing red.

●

Ilyas lay wide awake in the soft bed in the softly lit room. A faint hissing and burbling from the machine pumping his blood had been the only sound since the gentle machine that washed and wiped and dressed him had left the room with motors whirring. That had been ten minutes ago, or an hour, or two. He searched for his anger, but it was weak, as he was.

Footsteps approached, the door opened. Dr Mila Kraft entered with her sad smile. A trolley followed her in on silent wheels.

"Good morning, Ilyas."

"Doctor."

She raised the head of the bed so he sat upright and summoned a machine from the corner of the room, one with jointed cermel arms and fine grippers. The hissing and burbling of the blood pump faded out.

"This may sting a little." She watched as the machine disconnected the blood-filled tubes from his arm. Gentle pressure, and the thick needles were withdrawn, a dressing applied. A dull ache, nothing more.

She lifted the cover from the trolley that had followed her in. A rich spicy smell filled the room. His mouth watered, his stomach tightened painfully.

"You came from Muphrid," she said as she lifted the tray from the trolley. "The mechs pulled the log from your vessel."

"Yes."

"We picked up the last transmission from Muphrid a little while before you arrived. I'm so sorry." She laid the tray across his lap. He picked up the spoon and dipped it into the dark orange liquid. "Take it slow. The treatment you've had has been... intensive. It'll take time for your system to settle down."

"OK." His hand shook as he raised the spoon.

"Can you manage?"

"Think so." Warm, thick, flavours of coriander and cumin and other spices unfamiliar. Ilyas closed his eyes and absorbed the taste, the texture.

"Your vessel wasn't designed for interstellar flight."

It was a statement, not a question. The spoon paused on its way back to the bowl. "A weapons control platform. The drive was originally from a long-range scoutship, adapted for multiple short jumps on a single charge. I was trying to make a sub-second jump, a hundred thousand kilometres to escape a missile. It detonated early and the radiation scrambled my flight controls. I jumped nearly thirty light-years."

"I'm sorry," she said. "I shouldn't distract you. Eat."

When the bowl was empty she placed the tray back on the trolley and sent it away. As it left the room a chair rolled in to take its place.

"Swing your legs out." She took his upper arm and elbow and eased him to a standing position. His legs shook as she turned and lowered him into the chair. Hard to judge in his weakened state but the spin of the habitat gave a gravity close to standard. Even so, she supported him and lowered him into the chair with practised ease.

She walked beside his chair along the long echoing corridor. Ilyas squinted against the bright light from the window at the end.

"You really believed you could hold off the Enemy at Muphrid?"

"We did."

"Even after what happened to the Sol system, to Earth?"

"A lack of commitment, Marshal Petro said. Everywhere before us put more effort into running away than trying to fight. No one ran from Muphrid."

"Why not?"

"We didn't let them." Ten years of martial law after Petro seized power, all the considerable industrial capacity of the Muphrid system had been dedicated to defence. No effort wasted on evacuation ships. Those under construction or not yet departed had been destroyed as a demonstration of resolve. They'd taken the drives out first, though. The scoutship drives went into weapons control platforms like Ilyas's ship, the colony ship drives into the rail-gun and missile batteries. Except one; Marshal Petro had kept one of those drives for his own use: a yacht, mobile presidential palace, centre of government, military headquarters.

A means of escape.

Now the anger rose. Two hundred thousand people could have escaped on the evacuation fleet. Two hundred thousand out of a hundred and forty million. Ilyas's anger was not directed at the Enemy, the Enemy was impersonal, implacable, like the tides that ripped apart a sun as it spiralled into a neutron star. No one knew where the Enemy came from or why they sought the extinction of the human species. A plague of machines spreading from star to star killing everyone, destroying everything, they were like a force of nature. Anger at them was pointless.

His anger, his hatred, he held solely for Marshal Petro, who had misled him, misled all of them, before finally betraying them. Through all the years since the evacuation fleet was blown up Ilyas had convinced himself it had been the right thing to do. He had had to believe it, had to believe that Celeste had been wrong to do as she did. "Stand or fall," he muttered through clenched teeth.

The window at the end of the corridor looked out onto the townscape of Thurlina, lengthways along the cylindrical habitat, a jumble of white-walled buildings and narrow streets broken up with small greens, broad parklands, trees. To right and left the ground curved up, fading into the blue-grey of a sunlit haze. Along the axis high above, the sun-tube glared with the bright yellow-white of Earth's sun. Familiar yet strange. His own home habitat was twice the size, with taller buildings, ziggurat shaped apartment blocks reaching up towards the sun-tube. Some of the larger buildings here in Thurlina had one or more narrow towers or pointed spires, each bearing on its wall or pinnacle the cross and crescent symbol of the Syntheist faith.

"I came from Muphrid." Ilyas looked up at Mila. "We followed the Humanist Covenant."

She stood still beside him, unperturbed by his observation. "Don't be concerned, Ilyas. Our faith isn't like some sects. Church and Covenant have lived in harmony in Thurlina since the colony was founded."

A small bird with a yellow breast, shades of delicate blue on the wings and head, and a dark band across the eyes sang in the high branches of a tree some metres from the window. It stood out sharply against the green leaves. Nothing else moved. Thurlina was home to seven hundred thousand people, according to his almanac, but the almanac was sixty years out of date. There had been no interstellar ships in the docks when he arrived, no way for anyone to escape when the Enemy reached here.

"My ship was damaged," he said, "but the drive was intact." A single-seater, someone in Thurlina was bound to claim it for themselves, to get away before the Enemy came here, too.

"The mechs are doing what they do when they find something broken. They're fixing it."

"What will happen to it?"

She touched her hand to his shoulder. "You can leave when it's ready, when you're well enough."

●

The lift took them down to the ground floor, and the chair rolled across a wide entrance lobby: white walls, shining floor, the light of the sun-tube pouring in through tall glass windows. No one stood behind the reception desk, no one sat in the low couches of the waiting area. Nothing moved except a small spider mech working its way across the expanse of glass, cleaning away unseen dirt. Glass doors slid silently aside to allow them into the grassed grounds around the hospital. Ilyas had not seen so much green space in over a decade, since before they'd built the flight training facility over his local park, the same facility where he had enlisted. Ilyas's chair rolled beside Mila along the path and round the side of the building to a row of modest single-storey houses. The light was fading, the glare of the sun-tube diminishing, the shadowy patchwork of streets and buildings becoming visible overhead on the far side of the cylinder.

"This is yours." Mila led him up a path to the third door. "Kitchen, bedroom, living area. There's a gym at the back. You can cook for yourself or order in. Eat and drink small amounts, often, until your stomach is used to food again. Gentle exercise; just stand and sit a few times today. You'll soon get your strength back."

An aurocular lay on the living room table. She picked it up and handed it to him. "Anything you need, just ask, or call me. I'll be back in a couple of hours to check on you."

The aurocular was a commonplace design, hooking over the ears and resting on the brow. The earpieces slipped into place and the lasers projected their image into his eyes.

A few blinks, a few words and he was looking at a 3D projection of what had once been settled space, a rough globe of stars centred on Sol. Nu Phoenicis, the first to fall to the Enemy, lay at the surface on one side. Zosma almost diametrically opposite. Most of the stars shone as white dots. Those that had been settled, but now known to be lost to the Enemy, were red. Green denoted those where humanity still survived — doubtless some of those had fallen, but news travelled slowly on starships or laser beams, percolating through settled space at the speed of light. The globe, a hundred light-years across, was speckled with red. Green stars clustered in a lens-shaped region roughly centred on the axis between Sol and Zosma.

Ilyas zoomed in on the region around this system, GJ430.1. Muphrid glowed red, having fallen thirty years before. The Enemy's usual pattern would have them consolidate their position in one system for between one and five years, rebuilding their arsenal to assault the next, jumping at light speed. Years yet before they would reach here from Muphrid, but Muphrid was not the nearest red star. Ilyas drilled down into the details of Gliese 3649, a small research station seven years away: contact had been lost two years before.

It might be ten years before the Enemy arrived from Muphrid. It could be tomorrow if they came from Gliese 3649.

On his own two feet, Ilyas made it into the kitchen and stood, legs shaking, elbows on the countertop to take his weight, while he waited for a prepared concoction of pasta, tomato, and mycoprotein to heat through. After the meal he shuffled into the hallway and down to the bathroom. The absence of hair when he unzipped caught him by surprise. The radiation, or the treatment. He ran his hand over his scalp — a fine stiff fuzz rippled beneath his fingers. A look in the mirror revealed a gaunt face with skin raw pink stretched tight and a uniform dark shadow of emerging hair on his scalp. His fingers explored the sharp boundary at the temple where the receding edge had formerly given him a pronounced widow's peak.

Raised voices outside dragged him from his reflection. He stumbled out from the bathroom to the front door and grasped a handrail for support. Just outside the next dwelling, a woman sat in a wheelchair. Hair short and white, face filled with deep creases. Her hand curled claw-like on the arm of the chair. Mila Kraft crouched facing her, speaking too softly to hear.

"No! Leave me alone! Sinner!" the old woman shouted. Her chair wheeled around and carried her into her house. Mila stood, facing the door for a moment, then turned and walked away.

Another of Mila's patients. Ilyas made his way indoors and returned to the lounge, to the aurocular, to the globe of green and red dots. Amongst the green, the most populous system was Denebola. A system rich with natural resources and a mature industrial base eighteen years from Thurlina. The latest news from Denebola was of a construction programme for a fleet of colony ships to travel a thousand light years or more into the beyond, to find a new home far from settled space, far from the Enemy.

No guarantees. No one knew where the Enemy came from. They might be anywhere out there, or they might continue their expansion to reach the refugees in a thousand years. But to be lucky, you have to survive, to stay in the game until the next roll of the dice.

Nearer than Denebola lay Zosma, less than seven years away. Less well developed but with settlements on one of a pair of binary planets and in the space around. A cultural melange of evacuees from throughout settled space. It was questionable whether they had the capacity to build the drives for a large colony ship, like the drive in Marshal Petro's yacht, but the hull, the robotics and industrial base for a new colony, those were easy to build. If Petro had gone there, he could bargain with them for the resources to rebuild his yacht into a colony ship. He might save a thousand people, maybe more. At Muphrid they might have saved two hundred thousand. Ilyas's anger seethed

Denebola and Zosma were the two systems to which Petro might have fled. Others were too small, too hostile, or too close to the curving plane of the Enemy's advance. If Ilyas followed Petro to Zosma, he would only be three years behind him; Thurlina lay almost on the straight-line route from Muphrid. Denebola was closer to Muphrid than

Thurlina was. By the time Ilyas could reach Denebola it would be nearly fifty years since the fall of Muphrid, thirty since Petro could have arrived there, and probably at least ten since it was overrun by the Enemy.

Ilyas's anger congealed to cold purpose. He would go to Zosma, three years behind Petro, find him and exact the justice he deserved. He would require luck, that Petro would not have already completed his colony ship and escaped to the beyond, that Ilyas could get close enough to him to take his revenge, but luck had favoured Ilyas so far: the jump from Muphrid had landed him close to Thurlina, Mila Kraft had saved his life, and his ship would be returned to him. Luck had favoured Ilyas Bardakci, as long as he could avoid thinking about what he had lost.

●

A brief spell in the gym, every machine set to the lightest of the stone weights on their cords, then Ilyas was hungry again, ravenous. A knock at the door interrupted him half-way through his second plate of assorted vegetables with a slab of some cultured protein.

Mila's brow furrowed when he opened the door, still chewing "Don't overdo it, Ilyas, you'll make yourself sick."

She sat him down in the lounge, strapped a monitor on his arm and slipped an aurocular on her brow to read it. Her eyes were drawn to the space over the coffee table where his virtual projection of the star map hung.

"They'll be here soon," he said. "The Enemy."

"I know." She lowered her eyes. "Your pulse, blood pressure are good. You must be feeling a little stronger already. I should explain the treatment you've received."

"My almanac said seven hundred thousand people lived here, but that was sixty years ago. How many are there now?"

"Three."

"Three hundred thousand?"

"No." She peered at him from under the brow of the aurocular. "Three. Including you."

Ilyas stared in silence at her waiting eyes, taking it in. Seven hundred thousand.

"How?"

"A hundred years ago we heard of the loss of Nu Phoenicis. A far away tragedy, all we could do was hold those who suffered and died in our prayers. Then as the years went by and more systems fell, the church council realised that one day they would reach us here. The council resolved that when they did, there should be no one for them to kill." She slipped her aurocular off. "Sixty years ago, we stopped having children."

"Many families at Muphrid did have children. They had faith in Marshal Petro. They had hope for the future."

"Not you?"

Ilyas's eyes ranged unseeing from Mila, to the living room window, to his own hands clasped in his lap. "I had faith, but Celeste, my wife, she wouldn't have children unless we could leave. Then... I lost her."

"Lost her?"

Ten years, and the pain of it was still so sharp he couldn't talk about it.

"Marshal Petro never asked the children at Muphrid whether we should stand and fight." He raised his head and met Mila's eyes. "You stopped having children sixty years ago? There should be tens, hundreds of thousands of people still here."

"This system is poor in resources. The population long ago reached the limit that we could support, so there were few children. Afterwards, we stripped the system bare of metals to build what ships we could, scavenged from those we already had and sent them out to the beyond to find a new life. We were able to build enough to send away everyone with a subjective age under fifty. The rest have all lived out their lives in peace here. Only Isolde is left."

Isolde. His neighbour. "And you. How long since you came back?"

"Back? I've never been away."

"You're young. You said there were no children born in the last sixty years. I assumed you'd gained years from relativity."

A half-smile, a nod of understanding. "Almost no children. Biology is hard to tame, Ilyas. Accidents happen. I *was* born after the last ship left."

●

Birds were singing with the brightening of the sun-tube when Ilyas woke from a deep, dreamless sleep. His muscles sang with a gentle tension and his joints tingled with the need to move. He pulled the cover aside and briskly stood, marched into the bathroom, urinated, washed. The mirror showed him a face thin rather than gaunt, a body taut and slender rather than famished. That thought awakened his appetite and he stepped smartly around the wheelchair in the hallway, heading for the kitchen.

Bread, hummus, dried fruits, and a crunchy biscuit of insect protein took the edge off enough for the desire to move, walk, run, jump, shout to override his hunger.

Ilyas stepped out of his front door and ran. He ran along the path that led back around to the front of the hospital building and out of the grounds, past stone pillars and into a maze of narrow winding streets. On either hand, stone walls with closed doors and vacant windows. On corners, plate glass of cafés, shops, hairdressers, each one pristine, shining, ready to greet its next customer. Looking back the way he had come, the five-storey facade of the hospital dominated the houses. Behind it, the slope of the habitat's end cap rose up, a patchwork of greens and browns cut through with spiral paths, fading into a white haze as it curved to vertical.

Street after street looped in long curves to new streets, all different but all the same, until one bend opened up onto a wide park. Rabbits grazed on grassland dotted with trees and cut by a lake that curved gently around the habitat's circumference. In the middle of a low, arching, wooden bridge over the lake Ilyas stopped, gasping for breath. Sweat ran down his face and stung his eyes. The scene around him darkened. His eyes filled with thickening shadows and his legs buckled beneath him.

●

Before the lockdown, Celeste had wanted them to flee Muphrid, to try and secure a place on a departing ship, any ship, going anywhere.

"Treat the world as it is!" she'd shouted, "You're deluding yourself, Ilyas, you can't fight the Enemy!"

Ilyas expected her to leave him the day he went to the great hall to cheer on the demolition of the evacuation fleet. She did, in her own way. He returned to a silent apartment, to her naked form lying motionless in a bath of crimson water. When he had reached for her hand he sliced open his own palm on the shard of glass she held, his blood mingling with hers.

"Stand or fall," he murmured.

"What was that, Ilyas?" Mila Kraft was sitting by his bedside.

"What happened?"

"You fainted. I did tell you not to overdo it." She held out a glass of pale liquid. "Drink this."

He shuffled up the bed to sit upright, took the glass, and drank. Cool, sweet. "I felt so... alive."

She took the empty glass from him. "How old are you, Ilyas?"

"I was born twenty-five eighty CE, eighty-nine years ago, and I've lived about fifty-seven of those." Thirty-two years in all spent in the timeless instants of light-speed travel, almost all of that in the journey from Muphrid.

She leaned forward, elbows on knees and reached out to take his hand. She held it palm uppermost. The scar that had crossed his palm was gone.

"You are eighty-nine elapsed years old, fifty-seven subjective. You were close to death when you came here, Ilyas. I don't know how much radiation you'd received, but many times a fatal dose."

"I guess I'll need to worry about cancers..."

"No, you won't. Didn't your almanac tell you about Thurlina's specialisation in medical science? I did a full-body tissue regeneration. You've lost a lot of weight with flushing out the dead and damaged cells but you now have a biological age of twenty-five."

The lost scar, restored sharpness of vision. The taut flesh, the once-receding hair now regrowing. Mila sat, still holding his hand in hers, her hand and his both with clear, unblemished skin.

"What you said about your birth being an accident. Was that true, or are you really..."

She let go the hand. "True enough. I'm older than I look, but not that old. I was born after the last starship left. As the youngest, I would have to care for the last ones, so I trained as a doctor and I gave myself the treatments that the older generation denied themselves. The same as I had to give you to save your life."

"So, I could live another eighty years, subjective?"

"One step at a time, Ilyas. Let's get you well, first."

She gave him an exercise programme and dietary advice and left him with strict instructions not to exceed the boundaries she'd laid down.

"Walk before you run," she said. "Tomorrow we'll go for a gentle walk."

After a shower and another light meal, Ilyas rested. In the evening, as the sun-tube dimmed, he ventured out to take the short stroll that Mila's programme allowed him.

"Are you another one?" A quavering voice called out from the shadowed porch of the adjacent house.

Ilyas ambled up the path and crouched down before the seated figure. "Another what, Isolde?" She was old, wrinkles joined to creases and wrapped into folds of sagging skin beneath thin, curled hair. A straggle of stiff grey hairs struggled from her upper lip.

"Damned impertinence. Using my name without giving one in return."

"Ilyas." He offered his hand.

Isolde *harrumphed*, flicked the joystick, and her chair wheeled around and into her house.

●

"The mechs have some questions about your ship." The light of the sun-tube sparkled on the lake as they walked, Mila's hand on Ilyas's arm to steady him.

"What kind of questions?"

"They'd like to replace some of the damaged metal components with composites. Metals are scarce here."

"That's OK."

They walked a dozen paces in silence.

"There's something else," Mila said. She stopped and turned to face him. "They said there was a range limiter. It was restricted to jumps no more than a light-day, but it had been bypassed."

Ilyas fixed his gaze on the trees on the lake's far shore.

"Treat the world as it is, Ilyas, not how you wish it were. That applies to your own self as much as the world about you. To move on, to heal, you have to reconcile yourself to what happened. Your escape from Muphrid wasn't an accident, was it?"

A dozen heartbeats, two long breaths Ilyas kept his eyes on the trees. "Ten years before the Enemy came to Muphrid, Marshal Petro ordered the destruction of the evacuation fleet. There would be no way out for any of us. I took my place in the squadron thinking that if Petro were wrong, I'd die with everyone else when the Enemy came." One more deep breath and he looked Mila in the eyes. "A short while before the end, a colleague, an engineer, told me about the limiter and how to bypass it. All the ships built on drives salvaged from the evacuation fleet had them except Marshal Petro's yacht. If the defence failed, he could get away, he and his family. We were *all* supposed to stay. Stand or fall, victory or death."

Ilyas turned away and folded his arms. "When I found out about Petro's yacht, I swore he would pay if the defence failed. I don't know that he got away, but if he did, I intend to find him."

Petro must have gone to Zosma. At Zosma he would have had leverage, a starship drive that could power a colony ship. At Denebola, he would have been one more desperate refugee.

She took his arm again and they walked on in silence. They crossed the bridge over the lake and sat at one of a dozen empty tables outside a cafe. A mech served them fresh salad with a pale oily fish.

"How long could this last?" he asked. "If the Enemy didn't come."

"Who knows? The habitat shell would last indefinitely. The mechs repair and replace themselves; everything is recycled."

"But the Enemy will come."

She didn't answer.

"What will you do, you and Isolde?"

She looked at him. "We always knew some us might be alive when the Enemy came. We have implants. When the sensors detect the Enemy's approach, that will trigger the implants and release a drug."

In every system, the attack took the same form. The first thing the sensors would detect would be the gravity waves as the Enemy's forces jumped to the system's outer reaches. Within hours, the hail of hypervelocity projectiles would shatter or vaporise anything fixed, or too big to move quickly. Finally, the missiles would come, jumping into the inner system to seek and destroy anything that remained and mop up survivors. Ilyas's mission had been to direct the rail guns to defend against the missiles, but just as the hail of hypervelocity projectiles had overwhelmed the protective shields of dust, so the missiles had kept coming and coming. Too many, too fast for the defences.

"My wife, Celeste, she took her own life after the evacuation fleet was destroyed."

"I can understand that." Mila reached out to rest her hand on his. "But our faith doesn't allow us to intentionally take a life, even our own. The implant releases a sedative so we'll be asleep when the Enemy strikes."

"My ship, if the mechs stripped out the sensors, the weapons control systems, boosted the life support, they might make room for two."

She closed her eyes and raised her face to the sky. "I used to dream of what I would do if I were away from here. The life I could lead... friends... lovers... children."

She drew her hand away. "All my life I've known I would be here until the end, caring for my elders. I can't change now. I can't leave Isolde."

●

"Nineteen days." Ilyas set his empty wine glass down. "Why do you have a feast every nineteen days?"

Mila raised and tilted the bottle towards him. He nodded and she poured. "Syntheism is a fusion of all the old religions. The nineteen-day feast is a tradition we inherited from the Bahá'i."

Isolde sat hunched in her chair, but with a grin on her face and a sparkle in her eyes. "Itself a mongrel faith," she cackled.

"And the Covenant is just Buddhism without spirituality." Mila retorted.

That set Isolde laughing again, and Mila joined her. They were both in their finery. Isolde wore a fine quilted jacket in dark greens and maroons, embroidered in gold thread. Gold, here where metals of any kind were more precious than anywhere. Gold too, the cross and crescent pendant that hung from Mila's neck, framed by her low-cut dress.

"Why 'sinners', Isolde?" Ilyas took a sip from his glass. "What sin have we committed?"

Mila grinned and rolled her eyes.

Isolde pointed her crooked finger at Mila, then Ilyas. "Look at you both, in the full flush of youth. What of the penance!"

"Penance?"

Mila pushed her plate away. "A penance for our hubris. We have affronted God and his prophets with our desire for eternal youth, and so we should allow ourselves to grow old and die a natural death before the Enemy comes. But Isolde, that oath was made before I was born. I'm not bound by the promises of my elders."

"Bah! That's Covenant talk. You were raised in the faith."

"And you were raised in the Covenant, Isolde. Atheists."

"*Atheist* defines us by what we are not," Ilyas said, catching Isolde's eye. "What we *are* is humanists," they chorused.

"But Isolde," Ilyas continued. "you're Covenant, yet you still followed the faith's edict to grow old?"

Isolde paused, the laughter fell from her eyes. "You and I both know that gods are fairy tales for the credulous, young man, but solidarity with your community is an essential part of humanity. How would I have felt if I'd stayed young and beautiful while my friends and neighbours all withered with age?"

Ilyas nodded. "Covenant solidarity played a big part for us at Muphrid."

Isolde's hand banged the table with surprising ferocity. "Yet you forgot the Covenant's first precept! *Treat the world as it is, not as you wish it were!*" Her needle-sharp eyes bored into Ilyas. "Year after year I saw the news feeds coming from Muphrid. That charlatan Petro told you what you wanted to hear, and you all lapped it up. And what about the fifth precept: *Disdain those who concur. Honour those who dissent.* Were there no dissenting voices?"

Celeste. She had been a dissenting voice.

"Isolde..." Mila reached out to touch Isolde's arm and she jerked it angrily away.

"It's alright, Mila." Ilyas said. "Petro had a valid argument, Isolde. Everyone before us had spent their resources on running, not fighting. Petro's crime was to run away himself."

"Still you deceive yourself. For every one who could have left, hundreds would be left behind. Petro played on your secret fears. You would rather no one was saved than be left behind yourself. He was a devil of your own making." Isolde backed her chair from the table. "I'm tired, Mila. Help me to my bed."

Ilyas cleared the table — the mechs would have done it, but it kept him busy while Mila helped Isolde. He waited for her outside the door. A clear night revealed the tracery of street lights on the habitat's far side, with dark patches of parks, all cut through with the arrow-straight silhouette of the darkened sun-tube.

Disdain those who concur. Honour those who dissent. The dissenters at Muphrid were all silenced, or had silenced themselves, like Celeste.

"Isolde's asleep." Mila appeared at his elbow. "She was sharp tonight." Her hand reached for his.

"Tomorrow." He clasped his hands behind his back. "I'd like to go to my ship."

Mila cast her eyes down. "OK. I understand."

Before bed, Ilyas sat alone in his living room gazing through the aurocular. At the star map, and through the eyes of Thurlina's sensors that waited patiently for the coming of the Enemy.

●

His dreams that night took him back to Muphrid, where he wandered the empty streets past the flight school, through abandoned parks and into the echoing emptiness of the great hall, finally climbing the stairs to his apartment on the fourth floor of the ziggurat. He found Celeste reading her book, lying in the bath of crimson water.

"You're too late," she said.

"Too late for what?"

"You killed us all, now it's time."

"Why do you say that. Why say that *I* killed everyone?"

"Look in the mirror."

Ilyas felt the presence of the mirror behind him, the mirrored door of the small cabinet over the sink. He didn't want to turn, didn't want to look.

"Look in the mirror!"

Her words compelled him, unwilling, he turned. A familiar face stared back; thick grey hair, broad features, stern expression. Marshal Petro.

"Now," Celeste's voice reverberated from the bathroom tiles. "It's time."

Ilyas woke to the sound of a distant siren. He slipped on the aurocular to see Thurlina's sensors scintillating with gravity waves from every direction. The Enemy was here. Only hours remained before the hail of hypervelocity projectiles would shatter the habitat's silicate shell. He rose from his bed, washed and dressed, and made his way out into the dim light of night. In the adjacent dwelling, Isolde's frail form lay still as stone in her bed. Her implant had fulfilled its intended purpose and spared her pain, the stilling of her weak heart an unfortunate side effect.

He sat a moment with her, replaying her words of the previous evening. *Honour those who dissent.*

In the next house, Mila breathed softly in her sleep. He touched her hand. "Mila," he whispered, but she did not stir. In the darkness of her bedroom Ilyas searched for his anger but found only the image of Marshal Petro's face staring at him from the mirror in his dream.

●

A word to Ilyas's aurocular summoned a transit car which took him the short distance from the hospital to the end cap before rising up the slope into the open between fields and vineyards. Quickly, the climb steepened until it ascended the vertical face to the axis, weight declining to nothing, then out through the hub into windowless passages, a maze of pressurised tubes that spidered out from the axis to the zero-g docks, workshops, and freight and passenger terminals.

It stopped in an embarkation hall. Long glass windows on one side looked out on the aged and pitted outer wall of the habitat's end-cap, its motion barely visible as it turned beneath. The docks extended out past the window on the other side: lattices of struts with clamps and docking ports, all empty but the one where Ilyas's ship sat. Tiny, patched and battered, but whole.

The weight of his burden had slowed him on the walk from Mila's dwelling to the transit, and the inertia of it made him clumsy as he manoeuvred without gravity along the tube to the docking port. Ilyas squeezed through the open hatch and into the cramped cockpit. A systems check showed the reactor on-line, the ship ready, the range-limit still disabled. He prepared a navigation program so that when he began the launch sequence the hatch would close, the clamps release. A short spurt from the thrusters and the ship would clear the dock and make the jump to the Zosma system. Seven years would elapse; the blink of an eye in subjective time.

Little time remained, but enough for the burden that waited in the access tube. A few moments and he was finished. Ilyas reached across the cramped space of the cockpit to press the button to begin the launch sequence. As the hatch closed he made his way back to the embarkation hall to watch the departure through the long window.

This time, he would treat the world as it was. What did it matter where Petro had fled, if he had escaped at all? Ilyas had constructed an impeccable chain of logic that would lead him to Zosma, as impeccable as the logic of defending Muphrid had been. Petro had been Ilyas's own creation. His, and all those who had stood in the great hall with him.

This time, someone would be saved, someone would survive at least until the next roll of the dice. In seven years elapsed, hours subjective, the sedative would wear off and Mila Kraft would awaken in the cockpit of his ship looking out at the colonies at Zosma.

"Stand or fall." Ilyas folded his arms and waited.

David Whitmarsh's story "Stand or Fall" was originally published in Metaphorosis on Friday, 17 December 2021

About the author

David Whitmarsh is a rehabilitated software engineer who now spends his days playing acoustic blues badly and writing. David lives in West Sussex with his wife, two cats and a varying subset of his four adult children.

davidwrites771009245.wordpress.com, @whitmad@wandering.shop

Papa Pedro's Children

Karl Dandenell

Peter Carlson held the gurgling two-month-old infant with one hand, while the other dug through a dresser drawer.

"Bwa! Bah!" gurgled the baby.

"Right as usual, Cassie," Peter said, pulling out a bright red knit cap. It was too small. Peter shook his head. "I *know* this fit yesterday." He found another cap, a patterned alpaca wool hat with big earflaps. He pulled it down firmly over Cassie's head. "Command: weather," he said.

Twelve degrees, said the system voice in his left ear. *Twenty percent chance of precipitation. The wind chill brings it down to 10 degrees.* Peter took a second to convert the numbers into a more familiar 50 degrees Fahrenheit. After more than a decade in Vicuña, he still found the metric system confusing.

"Hah, hah!"

"Hat. Yes, Princess, it's a new hat." He grabbed his own jacket. "Let's go for a walk, Princess. Papa hasn't been outside all day." Cassie drooled her agreement over his cuff. Peter barely noticed: after fostering eighteen children, he'd stopped worrying about keeping a pristine house.

The program had offered him a full-time *au pair,* but Peter refused. As the only adult in the compound who spoke both English and Swedish, he needed to do the language imprinting personally. Or so he told himself. The truth ran deeper — he had only six to eight months with each foster child. He didn't think he could spare a single precious day.

The outside air chilled his face, despite his thick gray beard. Peter took a moment to zip Cassie up inside his oversized jacket, then jammed his hands in the pockets to keep them warm and support her hips. As usual, she kicked happily against his ribs, and tried to flail her arms. You could almost *see* her brain growing neural connections, feel the strands of fascia wrapping themselves into ligaments, tendons, and muscle. A sudden motion caught his attention. He freed a hand and pointed. "Look, Cassie! It's a rabbit! Well, a *viscacha,* anyway. Close enough to a rabbit." She wobbled her head in the general direction and squealed, "Rah! Rah!"

"That's right, Princess. Cute rodent."

They continued down the walking path between the cottages, passing small groups of parents, children, and the occasional *au pair.* Peter heard snatches of conversation: French, Spanish, Portuguese, and even German. It felt good to see so much life, a happy contrast to the bleak picture painted by the news the government censors permitted them.

Cassie sensed his mood, or some shift in his body language. She slapped his jacket with clumsy hands and sang in some language only she understood. "Bah, bah, wah, ma, ma, da!"

"Tell Papa all about it," Peter said.

They found a bench under an oak that still retained a scattering of leaves across its crown. He unzipped his jacket and extricated the baby, who stood on wobbly legs. A leaf drifted past her eyes, and she grabbed it. "La!"

"Leaf," Peter corrected. "See the veins." He traced the leaf with one finger, then did the same to his own hand. "*Ådra.*" His hands looked so old: like rough tree bark. Cassie had clear, unblemished skin, of course.

Cassie grabbed at his hand, which caused her to lose her balance and plop down on her diaper. She didn't notice, engrossed with her poking and prodding at his knuckles. She pulled his fingers apart, twisted them, then pushed them back together before stuffing them into her mouth and biting down.

"Ay! No, Cassie. *Inte bita!" Don't bite.* He pulled his hand back. "Blow!" Peter puffed in her face until she giggled. When she made to grab at his hand again, he pulled it back. "Are you hungry, Princess?" He pointed to his mouth. "Bottle?"

"Bah-bah!" she replied, her brown eyes bright and happy. Peter checked his pockets, but found nothing. Cassie started to squirm.

"*Djävulen,*" he whispered. *The Devil.* Then in a louder voice, "Command: assistance."

"*Dígame, por favor,*" said the system.

"I need a bottle of warm formula as soon as possible, please."

A human operator clicked in. *"Right away. Do you want it brought there?"*

"No, the cottage is fine. We'll be there in a few."

"It's no problem, Peter, really."

"I said no," he replied firmly. "We can wait a minute, can't we?" He returned to the cottage and grabbed the bottle from the entryway table.

Cassie drained a liter of formula, belched like a sailor, and snuggled into the crook of his arm. When she stopped sucking at the empty bottle, Peter pulled the nipple away and pushed the tip of his index finger into her tiny mouth, where he felt tiny stalactites and stalagmites.

She was teething ahead of schedule.

Dr. Hidalgo's genetic treatment manifested itself differently in each child, but Cassie's growth would probably follow a steep upward curve, like the first incline of a roller coaster, before leveling off. If she followed the usual path, she and her birth group would reach final maturation between eight and ten years. Long before then, she would master at least two languages, and demonstrate additional aptitude for something else, like music or math, or even *fútbol.*

What had started as a desperate response to the plague had yielded something unexpected and amazing.

Peter put the bottle down, dropped into the rocker and tucked a blanket around himself and Cassie. In a few minutes she was fast asleep. He closed his own eyes and drifted off alongside her. But his memories waited in the dark, as they often did.

It had been raining, a light, cold drizzle that had started around sunset. The roof's rusted AC housing provided some shelter, so he'd crawled in there with his backpack. He didn't have much money left after bribing the border police, so he slept where he could.

The *Carabineros* of Santiago had been clearing the downtown streets of vagrants for days in preparation for the new *presidente's* attendance at the national opera's opening performance of *Carmen.* Esteban Sabio had come into office with an agenda to combat corruption in the government, and reboot Chile's economy following the global economic meltdown associated with the frightening epidemics in North America and Europe. The election was marked by widespread voter fraud, intimidation, and a last-minute bombing of Sabio's campaign headquarters.

Now, a month into Sabio's term, the internal security forces were taking no chances, so Peter had gone to ground, relying on his twenty-year-old military training. As a *norteamericano,* he was particularly unwelcome. Twice, women in the marketplace had looked past his sunburn and ratty beard, crossing themselves and hissing *"¡Diablo!"* at his back.

For some reason, the plague had failed to establish itself south of Baja, seeming to prefer cooler, richer parts of the northern hemisphere. When Washington State proposed closing the schools early that semester, Peter had locked up his faculty office at Seattle Pacific University and filled his ancient Subaru wagon with food, water, his old army survival pack, and a few treasured books. He figured he could take Judith to Cancun and hang out in their timeshare, just in case things got worse.

His ex-wife Helena refused to let Peter take their daughter Judith out of the country. "Not that many people are sick here," she said. "And the university hospital is better than anything you'll find in Mexico." He didn't push the issue. Judith was starting to warm up to him again after the divorce, and he didn't want to upset that with another trip to family court.

"You're probably right," he told her. "I'm sure things will be sorted out by fall semester."

He was absolutely wrong.

●

Peter had just opened up a flask of cheap tequila when he heard the whispers: terse rapid-fire phrases. For a moment, he feared that another homeless man coveted his spot, which was far too small to share. He scrunched himself up against the cold steel cabinet, and listened. His hand crept to the ankle sheath where he carried his Ka-bar knife.

The voice was too soft and his Spanish too poor to follow the conversation, but it soon became apparent that he was eavesdropping on someone's radio exchange. Then he heard the familiar click of an ammo magazine snapping into place.

Peter risked a quick look. In the fading light, he saw a man lying prone, the top of his head barely clearing the edge of the roof. A sniper rifle lay under his right hand. Night vision goggles covered his eyes, but he was dressed in civilian clothes. The voices leaking from the gunman's earpiece became agitated, before a burst of static cut the connection.

●

A soft chime dragged him back.

"Peter?"

"Hmm?"

"Peter, it's Javier. Are you awake?"

"*Ja. Si.* I'm here." He automatically checked the baby, who snoozed and drooled contently. "*¿Que hora es?*" He whispered, knowing his earpiece would pick up his words.

"A little after 3. You've had a long nap," said Javier.

"Jeez. I better get moving." He started to straighten up.

"In a moment, Peter. We need to talk before the angelito *wakes up."*

"Sure. *¿Qué pasa?*"

"English, please, Peter. English," said Javier. A little laugh. *"While we all appreciate your efforts, your teaching accent is starting to creep a little south lately."*

"Oh. *Perdón —* Sorry."

"Cassiopeia will have plenty of time to refine her milk tongue. For now, let's have you focus on doing your job, yes?" There was a click of keys. *"I interrupted your beauty sleep to remind you that you have appointments with the doctors today."*

"Right. Cassie's due for an immune check." Peter shifted in his chair, moving the baby and stretching his left leg to relieve a building cramp. "Do I need to do anything beforehand?"

"Just show up. Medical office 5."

Cassie opened her eyes slowly, then yawned and farted. "Pa!" she cried.

"I'll let you go." The connection closed with a soft click.

Peter lifted the baby in both hands, bringing her level with his face. She grabbed his beard and pulled him close. "Pa pa pa!"

"That's right, Princess. Papa. Papa Peter."

She responded by tugging on his beard. He tolerated this for a few moments, then gently disengaged her. After replacing a typically full diaper, Peter spread out a wide, yellow alpaca wool quilt embroidered with letters and numbers in black yarn. Kneeling on the blanket with Cassie propped up between knees, Peter worked his way through the alphabet, forward and backwards, sounding out each phoneme carefully. Three of the quilt's squares had additional letters colored in black marker: å, ä, and ü. One of his early foster children, Gabriel, had once asked Peter during a visit to the Family House, "Papa Peter, why doesn't English have those letters? They're so *useful."*

After language, they worked on motor skills. Peter laid out a selection of brightly colored plastic balls. He picked one up and put it into Cassie's hands. She dropped it, of course. He repeated the exercise, placing her hands around the shiny sphere and squeezing gently. On the fifth try, she managed to hold it for a moment. "Very good!" Peter said and clapped his hands. Cassie giggled and managed a fair approximation of applause.

They moved on to back exercises next. With the baby lying supine, Peter dangled a mobile of Noah's Ark over her face, holding it just out of reach. Cassie grabbed at the parade of passing animals: antelopes to elephants, monkeys to zebras. She lunged enthusiastically, snagging a pair of goats. "Go! Go!"

"That's right, Princess. They're called goats." He leaned down and whispered in her ear. "*På svensk, get. Y-et.*"

"Ye. Yee!" she replied and stuffed the goat into her mouth.

"Okay, I get it," he said. "You're hungry." He scooped the balls into a mesh bag, hung the mobile on the wall, then unfolded a plastic gate to confine Cassie. "Back in a sec, Princess."

He put a bottle in the warmer and located some bread and cheese for himself. Part of him desperately wanted coffee, but he was kidding himself. Even decaf triggered his acid reflux these days. He settled for some cold yerba mate in a sports bottle.

He put everything on a tray and returned to the living room. Cassie lay on her stomach, pushing herself up. "Ba, Ba!"

"Bottle," Peter said and set the warm bottle next to her.

Cassie reached over with one hand. Her other arm trembled, and she flopped faced down.

"Good try!" He took a bite of bread and cheese, then propped Cassie up in his lap and gave her the bottle. She took three hearty gulps before pushing it away. Peter looked down. "What's wrong, Princess? Not warm enough?"

"Ba! Ba! Buh, buh, buh!" She squirmed out of his lap and rolled/crawled over the blanket. She rested her hand on the letter B. "Buh."

Peter blinked through a sudden upwelling of tears. In that moment, Cassie had sounded exactly like Judith the first time she had read to him. "That's my girl. Now, can we finish our snack?" He pointed at the bottle, then at his own mouth. "*Dricka.*"

Cassie crawled back to him and seized the bottle. She drained it, then gnawed on the nipple while Peter finished his own sandwich. He piled the dishes on the tray and pushed it to the side for the housekeeper. "Time for a bath before the doctor, I think." He scooped her up and headed for the bathroom.

He managed to bathe the baby and change her into a new outfit before they had to leave. As he snuggled her into the carrier, he patted down his pockets in an old, useless habit. He no longer carried money, or identification, or even keys. The biochip chip in his wrist took care of all that. He did remember to tuck a spare bottle in his pocket.

As he walked, he recalled the first time he'd asked one of the pediatricians for a pacifier. They turned him down. Did it have something to do with the children's rapid tooth growth, he asked?

Babies cry, the doctor said. That's what they do.

Fortunately, Cassie loved to have her forehead stroked, and the massage usually calmed her. She wasn't a fussy baby, unlike Judith, who had suffered from inexplicable meltdowns around him well into her third year. Peter had always dreaded his wife's frequent business trips. Helen worked as a corporate trainer, and often flew to the New York to meet with clients. Every month, Peter stocked up on extra toys, books, and other distractions. He even worked with a hypnotherapist to deal with his own anxiety.

It had been a hard few years.

The shadows were growing longer by the time they reached the medical buildings. Peter checked in at the front desk, which was only a formality since his biochip had already synced with the appointment computer.

He set Cassie down on the floor to crawl about for the few minutes they had to wait. Then a nurse appeared in the door. "Peter?" he said. "We're in here today." Peter took Cassie a few doors down the hall into a warm, comfortable room. Smells of mild disinfectant and baby powder lingered in the air. The nurse stripped Cassie to the buff, weighed and measured her, and checked her eyes and ears. "Is her appetite still good?"

"Better than mine," Peter said.

"I should hope so," the nurse said. "We have to run some deeper scans this time, so you'll have time to see the doctor yourself. End of the hall, on your right."

Peter took a step toward the door. "Um, should I —"

"Go see Dr. Sandoval, Peter. She's very busy, you know. Don't worry about Cassie — we do this all the time." The nurse picked Cassie up and went to another room, singing the first verse of "Happy Little Llama Goes to School."

Peter found the doctor's office small but neat, reminding him of his former faculty space. The usual framed medical degree and family photos covered the walls, and one bookcase was dedicated to an impressive array of plants bathing under full-spectrum LEDs. The doctor put down her datapad and offered her hand. There were dark circles under her eyes and her lab coat needed washing. "Good afternoon, Peter. Please, sit down."

He selected the chair opposite her, sinking into the soft cushions. He felt the lumbar support gently push him forward and the padded arms warm to match his body temperature. "Nice," he said.

"One of perks of government service," Sandoval said. "That and a steady paycheck." She glanced at her datapad. "How are things going?"

"Not bad. My knees are getting creaky, but I can't complain."

"But you just did, yes?" She laughed. "You're due for a physical yourself, and we'll get to that in a few minutes." When she saw the look on Peter's face, she added, "Don't worry, I'll be gentle."

"It's not that. I'm just used to being in the room with Cassie when she gets her exams."

"Ah, I see. Well, I'm sure she's doing fine. Aunt Adoncia is helping out today."

Peter felt his shoulders drop. Adoncia had raised nine of her own children, in addition to fostering dozens here at the center. She'd been there since the beginning, and had shown Peter the ropes in his early days. He trusted her completely.

"Besides," Sandoval continued, "You'll need to start transitioning little Cassiopeia in any event. She'll be moving into the Family House."

"So soon?" Peter felt a familiar knot forming in his stomach. "That's ahead of schedule, isn't it?"

"Somewhat," the doctor said. "Please don't think it's any reflection on you, Peter." She glanced over at her data pad, furrowing her brow. "There have been some... changes at the Ministry of Health."

Her tone reminded Peter of his annual review with the English department chair. "Someone cut your budget," he guessed.

Dr. Sandoval picked up a tiny worry doll from her desk and rolled it between her thumb and forefinger. "It's more complicated than that, especially given the current political situation." She stood up and dropped the worry doll into a pocket. "Come on now, let's have a look at you."

Peter loosened his shirt and sat quietly while she listened to his lungs, tested his reflexes, and took blood and saliva samples. "How are you sleeping?"

"Well enough, I suppose," Peter said. "It helps that I'm chasing Cassie around all day."

"How are your dreams?" she asked while putting together a lab bag.

"Could be better. They *are* better," he amended.

"We have some very good therapists here, Peter. Some of them were in the army themselves. They know what it's like."

"Yeah, I guess," he said. Then, to change the subject, he said, "So what *is* the current political situation?"

She hesitated a moment. "President Sabio announced his retirement. Cassie's birth group will be the last children in the program."

Peter breathed deeply against a wave of nausea. "And you?" he said.

She gave him a wry smile. "It takes more than a special election to fire senior civil servants," she said. "No, I'll get a new assignment and monitor the children, but quietly. We're putting together an anonymous network with some people in Costa Rica." She sighed and looked around the room. "It was a lot of work, but I'm going to miss this place. We accomplished incredible things here."

"I don't feel like I've accomplished very much," Peter said, buttoning his shirt.

"You've given a lot of children a wonderful start." She plopped into her chair. "Be proud of that, Peter." She looked at her datapad. "You're healthy enough for a gringo. If you increase your exercise and eat more vegetables, you'll live to be a hundred." She stood and offered her hand.

"Things change," she said. "Only the bureaucracy remains."

"True enough," he said, gripping her hand.

"Speaking of bureaucracy, Colonel Ortega mentioned he needed to see you when he comes to town. Now let's go check if they're done with Cassie."

They walked to another part of the building, and he heard a familiar laugh. A door opened in front of him and there stood Adoncia, with Cassie clinging to her leg. The baby was trying very hard to haul herself upright.

"*Hola,* Peter. It's good to see you again," Adoncia said. She was a handsome woman his age, with broad shoulders and frizzy gray hair that fell past her shoulders. Laugh lines framed her mouth and eyes.

"You, too," replied Peter. He leaned forward and kissed her on both cheeks, lingering a moment before kneeling down to gather up Cassie. The little girl hugged him with fierce strength.

"She's a feisty one, little Cassie," said Adoncia. "It must be her *Mapuche* blood."

Mindful of his knees, Peter stood up, still holding Cassie. "You think so?" He grinned. "I thought it was because of the clever genetic engineers down in Santiago."

Adoncia sniffed. Then, looking at the doctor, she said. "I wasn't born yesterday, you know, not like these *niños*. I know good family when I see it." She poked Cassie in the stomach, who laughed and kicked Peter so hard that he almost dropped her. "When I met Cassie's mother, I could tell right away she was *Mapuche*. Very pure." She looked at Peter. "Her ancestors kept the Spanish awake at night for almost 300 years, you know."

"She's keeping up tradition, I assure you," Peter said.

"*¡Excelente!* Sleep when you're dead, I always say." Adoncia turned to the doctor. "Everyone is healthy, then? Ready to go home?"

"Everyone is fine." Dr. Sandoval clapped Peter on the back. "You take care. Eat some vegetables."

Adoncia insisted on walking Peter back to his cottage. When she opened the door, she took one look around, and shook her head. "This is terrible! Who's your housekeeper, some Peruvian girl who doesn't know how to hold a brush?"

Peter glanced at the piles of toys. "It's not her fault. I just don't want to be disturbed."

"*Madre de Dios,*" Adoncia said. "You look after Cassie. I'm going to check the kitchen." She stepped into the other room, and Peter heard a muted curse. Then he heard cabinets opening and the clatter of pots and pans. "I'm ordering you some decent food, and then I'm going to make you dinner. *Varones!*"

Fifteen minutes later, there was a knock at the door. Peter left Cassie in her bouncy swing and opened the door to admit a teenage boy struggling under the weight of four large shopping bags. "*¿Cocina?*" he said. Peter pointed.

Adoncia pounced on the delivery boy like a hawk. "*¿Dónde está el pollo?*"

The young man offered up one of his bags, which Adoncia snatched away. She came back for the others a moment later and dismissed the boy with a gentle shove between the shoulders.

Peter perched on a stool in a corner of the kitchen, balancing the baby on his lap. Cassie watched with wide eyes as Adoncia transformed tomatoes, peppers, garlic, onions, rice, and chicken into the best dinner Peter had eaten in a long time.

Cassie was the center of attention, of course, and Adoncia tried to feed the baby bits of soft vegetables and rice. About half made it past her mouth. "I'm not sure that's a good idea," said Peter. "She's not scheduled for solid food yet."

"The girl wants to eat," replied Adoncia, weaving her spoon toward Cassie's tomato-stained mouth. "Let her eat. Don't worry, I'll clean her up."

After dinner, Peter cleared the table while Adoncia changed Cassie into a nightgown and rocked her in the big chair. He felt a stab of jealousy, then dismissed it, and headed to the kitchen to wash up. If the *tia* wanted some time with the baby, who was he to say no?

"Our little *Mapuche* is asleep," whispered Adoncia as she walked into the kitchen. "Busy day for her, yes?"

"Busy day for everyone," Peter said, hanging up a dish towel. "Thanks for dinner. I really needed company today."

"Ah, so you heard," Adoncia said. "I learned about it myself only yesterday. No more *niños.*"

Peter sighed, then yawned loudly. "Sorry. All that good food made me sleepy." He rubbed his eyes. "Better send you home." He walked Adoncia to the door and gave her a hug. "What's going to happen to them?"

She patted him on the cheek. "Don't worry, Peter. Angels are watching over them."

●

They let Peter keep Cassie him for another two precious weeks, and then the morning arrived when he reluctantly handed her over to Adoncia, who looked at his red eyes and whispered, "Be strong! It's not good to cry in front of the other *varones.*" She tilted her head to indicate the movers who were loading up a military transport with blankets, bottles, and toys.

Peter nodded and rubbed his eyes.

"Now give Cassie a kiss so we can leave."

He leaned in and kissed the baby's forehead. "Goodbye, Princess." He stood there for a long time after they drove away.

There had been other transitions, of course, brief periods between assignments when Peter had a few days or a week to himself, before the next baby arrived. They gave him a chance to get in some walking, read, and sleep, but there was always the next child to think about.

This time was different. He rattled around the cottage for two days. The walking paths were nearly empty, and he guessed that most of the other foster parents had already moved on. The quiet weighed on him, bringing up memories of all the miles he trudged through Baja after armed men took his car.

Fortunately for Peter, the men at the roadblock had been more interested in his surplus Baretta M9 than his food and water. While they squabbled over the weapon, he fled into the brush with his pack.

It could have been much worse, he told himself. If Judith had been with him, he would have fought them to protect her. Maybe got them both killed.

Not that it was likely she survived the plague. Not long after he arrived in Santiago, he'd picked up a newspaper with a photo of a hospital parking lot overflowing with cots. The caption read, "Military medics distribute water and suicide kits in Seattle."

●

When the knock came after dinner, Peter jumped to the door. He opened it to find Colonel Miguel Ortega, dressed in pressed fatigues, balancing a shopping bag and a large cardboard box.

"Some help, *amigo?* I'm about to drop the scotch!"

Peter grabbed the bag, then stood aside as Ortega pushed past him and plopped onto the couch.

"I'll get some glasses," Peter said, and went into the kitchen. When he returned, he found Ortega sitting up straight, looking around the room. The box rested on the floor.

"So you've heard, *si?*"

"*Ja.*" Peter pulled over a stool and set out the glasses and the scotch.

Ortega nodded. "The conservative *Alianza* has been gaining support, and the rumors about this place haven't helped." He sighed, and Peter saw a tiny slump in the soldier's posture. "Sabio made a difficult decision, and I'll support him."

"So he's abandoning Hidalgo and the children," Peter said.

"Not really. Hidalgo is already on his way to Argentina. They're doing interesting things with cancer research there. The younger children are being sent to special adoption centers, and many of our 'graduates' are already living in Santiago and Puente Alto."

"You sound on top of things," said Peter.

"After the assassination attempt, I learned to plan better." He poured a couple of fingers of scotch into each glass. He handed one to Peter. "For that I thank you."

"I wasn't trying to save the president," Peter said, accepting the glass. "I figured the sniper wouldn't hesitate to kill a witness." He offered a crooked smile. "Fortunately for me, he didn't see the knife until I got close."

"Spoken like a humble draftee," Ortega said, raising his glass.

"Actually, I volunteered. I needed the money for graduate school." He lifted his glass. "Just my luck we got into it with Iran during my tour. *Skål.*"

"Cheers." Ortega threw back his scotch. He closed his eyes for moment, then set his glass down. He looked directly at Peter. "Now you have to make a choice."

Peter glanced at Ortega's hip, and the pistol holstered there. "I don't understand, Miguel."

Ortega leaned back. "Do you want to go back?"

He meant *go back to America.* Peter finished his drink to buy himself some time. He had turned that question over in his over mind a lot since they took Cassie away. "I don't know if I have anything to go back to," he finally said. "Do I?"

"There wasn't a functioning government for almost ten months, but the Red Cross was helpful. Your wife and daughter passed away at home, well before the riots burned Seattle." Ortega placed a hand on Peter's shoulder. "I'm sorry, my friend."

Peter nodded. Despite the sudden upwelling of grief, he held on to the image of Judith, surrounded by her favorite stuffed animals and anime posters. "Thank you for letting me know."

"Now, if you still want to return, I can get you to our consulate in Mexico. The American border is a mess, and —"

"No." Peter shook his head. "I can't imagine making that trek just to visit some mass grave." He toyed with his empty glass. "There's nothing for me there now."

"Then if you'd care to stay, we have a place for you." He opened the box and removed a datapad with a cable that ended in a padded cuff. "Give me your arm, please."

Peter leaned forward. Ortega slipped the cuff over the other man's arm and touched a few keys on the datapad. The screen lit up with a photo of Peter, taken from his first day at Vicuña. "Meet Pedro Adrian, Ph.D."

"He looks familiar," Peter remarked. "Younger."

"It's an old picture. Since you entered the country without a visa, there aren't official records of you. Fortunately, I still have friends in the national security office." He pressed his thumb to the datapad, which beeped. "There. Your biochip now says you are the only child of an American father and Swedish mother, raised on a farm near, ah, how do you say this?" He pointed at the display.

"Gothenburg." *Yot-tee-bor.*

"A lovely place, I'm sure. However, you visited here about ten years ago and fell in love with our beautiful, warm country. And you remained."

"So you're going to stick me in a retirement villa on the beach somewhere?"

"You should be so fortunate!" Ortega gave a sharp laugh. "No, my friend. You're going to have to earn a living like the rest of us. I've secured you a job teaching English literature to some advanced students. *And* found you a place to live." Ortega said.

"You must have called in a lot of favors."

Ortega shook his head. "Some. But you earned it, Pedro."

Peter pursed his lips. "I'll have to get used to that."

Ortega slipped the cuff off the Peter's wrist. "All finished, Professor. Someone will come by late tomorrow morning to drive you to the bus station." He removed a cheap suitcase from the box and handed it to Peter. "There's a little money in there to get you started."

He packed up his datapad. "Oh, one more thing." He rummaged around the box and brought out a paper-wrapped parcel. "Something for the trip." He handed the parcel to Peter, who set aside the suitcase and tore open the paper. Inside lay a much-thumbed copy of *The Norton Anthology of English Literature, Tenth Edition.* "I hope you find it useful."

He rested his hand on the cover. "Thank you, *mi amigo.* It's perfect."

Ortega packed up his datapad and stood. "Then I will say my farewells, Professor. Enjoy the scotch."

"I will." Peter stood and offered his hand.

Ortega grasped Peter's hand with a firm grip. "You know, we have a saying: 'A father raises one generation, but a teacher raises many.' Goodnight, Pedro."

Later that night, after several more glasses of whiskey, Peter took a long look in the mirror and decided that *Pedro* needed a shave. If he was going to start a new life, he might as well go the whole nine yards. He cut himself a few times, but found he liked his face better. Then he crawled into bed and searched the *Norton Anthology* for a favorite Henry Vaughan poem, "They are all Gone into the World of Light".

> They are all gone into the world of light!
> And I alone sit lingering here;
> Their very memory is fair and bright,
> And my sad thoughts doth clear.

He drifted off to sleep, dreaming of a laughing child named Cassie, flying into the world on fairy wings.

The next morning, Pedro moved slowly in deference to his hangover as he prepared for his journey. It didn't take long to pack: he owned only a few changes of clothing, an old datapad, a toilet kit, and his *Norton Anthology*. It didn't add up to much, he thought, not for a decade and eighteen foster children. He wished they'd let him keep his pictures.

He sat on the couch and waited for his ride.

●

"Buenos días," said Pedro, addressing his classroom. *"Soy profesor Adrian. Bienvenidos al curso especial de Literatura Inglesa."* He switched on his datapad and began typing. His name appeared on the large, scratched datawall behind him. "That will probably be the extent of my Spanish for today."

There was some polite laughter, plus a serious guffaw in the back of the classroom. Automatically, Pedro looked up to see who his class clown might be for the semester. It was a young man with bright brown eyes and the beginnings of a mustache. Pedro rubbed his own lip, which felt naked after all these years.

"Why don't we start with names?" He opened the class roster on his datapad and pointed at the young man. "You are?"

"Virgil Gutierrez."

Pedro found *Gutierrez, V.* "And you, young lady?"

"Madeline Sanchez, Professor."

"Keep going, please, down the row." He checked off the others: Isabella Vargas, Sophia Torres, Diego Muñoz, Julian Rios, Gabriel Vega, Jose Castillo, Maria Flores, Catherine de Guzman, Jennifer Sanchez, and Angelina Peña. He listened to their accents, mentally filing away the pronunciation. They were new names, but familiar all the same —

Angelina. Pedro looked up at the young woman who had just spoken. She was dressed in new school sweats and sandals, her black hair tied back in ponytail. She had intense brown eyes, a small nose and long, delicate fingers. Pedro was suddenly struck by the strongest sense of *déjà vu.* He glanced at her ankles and saw two red patches, like butterfly wings.

"Is something wrong, Professor?"

He realized he was staring. "Forgive me. Your tattoo reminded me of someone."

"It's not a tattoo, Professor. It's a birthmark."

"I see." Pedro felt his breath catch. It *was* Angelina, who loved bananas. And Gabriel, who hated the bathtub. And Cathy, and Maria. His own, special children. Part of him wanted to push back his chair and step forward, gather these beautiful people in his arms. But he knew he couldn't do that. Even with their extraordinary minds, they might not remember him.

But he knew *them.* These precious children he had started on their journeys had come back, sent as a final gift from one soldier to another. He recalled another stanza from Vaughn's poem:

He that hath found some fledg'd bird's nest, may know
At   first   sight,   if   the   bird   be   flown;
But   what   fair   well   or   grove   he   sings   in   now,
That is to him unknown.

"Well, I'm looking forward to working with you. With all of you." He smiled a genuine smile, for now he knew where some of his birds were singing.

Karl Dandenell's story "Papa Pedro's Children" was originally published in Metaphorosis on Friday, 28 July 2017

About the author

Karl Dandenell is a graduate of Viable Paradise and a Full Member of the Science Fiction & Fantasy Writers Association. He and his family, plus their cat overlords, live on an island near San Francisco famous for its Victorian architecture and low speed limits. In addition to his DayJob™ at a major utility company, Karl runs twice-weekly online writing hangouts and kvetch sessions. His preferred drinks are strong Swedish tea and single malt whiskey. Karl's work has appeared in numerous publications, including *Metaphorosis, Fireside Fiction, DreamForge, Little Blue Marble, Speculative North*, and the anthologies *Abandoned Places* and *The Science Fiction Tarot*. His fiction can also be found on the *Sudden Fictions* podcast. Karl lurks on BlueSky (@karldandenell.bsky.social) and his own website, www.firewombats.com.

The Secret Keeper

Pauline Yates

Keeping a secret is dangerous. Secrets mess with emotions and can cause illness from depression, anxiety, and stress. The darker the secret, the heavier the burden; it can shorten your life by years. Even Demigods, like Mother and me, need to be cautious when keeping a secret. We're gifted with powers to balance emotions, but if we reveal a secret, we'll suffer its burden. It's crucial we stay strong, because we help battle the gods who draw their power from misery and suffering.

Like Hades. He doesn't mind if a person troubled by a secret dies young. He draws his power from the souls of the dead. And in his realm, the bearer suffers their burden three times worse. But we have Harpocrates, the god of silence, on our side. He uses hope to encourage a bearer to reveal their secret and clear their conscience. To deliver hope, he needs a Secret Keeper, and now I'm sixteen, that's what I'm about to become.

"Repeat after me," Mother says. "Listen without —"

" — judgment and heal the harm," I say, not needing her help. I've committed these vows to heart. "Bind the secret with a Keeper's charm. If by fault I break the faith, suffer the burden the thorns keep safe."

Mother slips a charming binding ring onto my finger. The gold band, engraved with a pattern of linked roses, is the token of a Secret Keeper.

"How much hope do you give?" she asks.

"Only enough to ease their pain; too much hope is a secret's gain." Giving too much hope can make the bearer believe that keeping their secret won't cause them harm.

"And how much burden do you take?" Mother says, her voice low like a brewing storm.

I sigh, wishing Mother weren't so melodramatic. I know what to do. But she expects an answer. "Only enough that hope shines through. Though it harms, they need the burden, too." Removing all the burden takes away the incentive to reveal the secret. That defeats our purpose.

Mother smiles. "Balancing emotions is tricky, but your charm will help."

I raise my hand to the rising sun and admire the ring. The charm curls from the band and weaves around my fingers like a glittering ribbon of light. Feeling its power makes me giddy with excitement.

Now I can heal using a true god's power. Until now, I've only ever had demigod powers to work with. That power allows me to grow herbs from nothing to make the remedies we sell to the local townsfolk. We're the talk around town because of their potency, but we hide our true identity. Mother 'has a green thumb'. I'm 'the homeschooled girl'. Receiving the charm makes me feel like I've graduated.

Lowering my hand, I touch the charm with my finger. It shapes into a glittering rose, Harpocrates' symbol. He created the charm, but I fuel its strength by imagining where I find hope. All Secret Keepers have their preference. For me, hope is in a sunrise, in a rainbow, in seedlings bursting through the soil. Hope is also in my desire to be the best Keeper Harpocrates has ever had.

"The ability to heal the harm caused by a secret is a rare and wondrous gift," Mother says. "However, Harpocrates does not give this charm freely. You are now his servant, as I am, and my mother before me. Harpocrates uses his power to keep hope alive in the world and expects you to do the same. Without hope, the world would fall under the influence of those gods who favor darkness and despair."

She opens her hand, revealing her ring. Years of use make it appear fluid, like a circle of lava. Her charm curls from the band and takes the shape of a burnished gold rose, similar to mine. Mother blows on it. The rose dissolves into a spray of mist that fills the air with a mixture of sweet and pungent perfume.

Turning her hand, the bitter perfume overpowers the sweet. "Polemos draws his power from conflict," she says. "Oizys, misery. Dolos, pain." She tilts her hand again and the sweet perfume overpowers the bitter. "Hestia, compassion, Eros, love, and of course, Harpocrates, hope. There cannot be light without dark, but, tipped out of balance, chaos will ensue." With a flick of her hand, the scents collide. They splatter on the ground like splashes of water.

"Do you think we make a difference?" I ask, tilting my hand so my charm dances on my finger. "We're only demigods. What good is our strength in a battle for power between the gods?"

"You're stronger than you think. The strength of all Secret Keepers runs in your blood. Collectively, we are Harpocrates' most powerful allies. Just be mindful of your vows and replace the burden you remove with hope. You don't want to leave a person feeling as dark and empty as the day Hades stole Persephone from this world."

"Does a burdened soul give Hades extra power?"

"No, but he benefits by receiving a soul quicker. A burden left unattended leads to premature death," Mother says. "Otherwise, he has no interest in warring for power. It's why he lets Persephone return for half the year. But don't dismiss him. Now that you channel Harpocrates' power, Hades will watch to see if you stay true to your vows. He's never broken an oath, and values the laws of morality over everything."

It's a value I share. Secret Keepers heal, they don't harm. Breaking my vow would also desecrate the moral law of our kind.

I glance across the gardens at the many roses that grow between the herbs. All were grown by Mother to keep the secrets she heard. Each sprouts thorns glistening with the secret's burden — guilt, sorrow, remorse. In all our history, no Secret Keeper has ever broken her vows. Suffering any of those emotions would be a deserved punishment. Revealing a secret breaks trust. Breaking trust would destroy hope, and we're tasked with keeping hope alive.

But I needn't worry. Even without history on my side, I'll enjoy showing Hades how committed to my vows I can be.

●

With the commitment ceremony complete, I revert to my daily chores. Weeding the garden. Growing more herbs to replace those we've used. We're out of dried lavender, so I fetch my gardening clippers. As I snip the stems, my charm grows brighter. It draws hope from my thoughts about lavender's healing qualities.

Customers arrive throughout the day. Some seek a herbal remedy. Others request a pot of living herbs to grow in their gardens. All wander through the gardens while Mother prepares their purchase. All ask the same question on their return.

"Are the roses for sale?"

I've lost count of the number of times I say no because of Mother's fondness for the flowers. I smooth over their disappointment by revealing it's why I share the flower's name. I don't mind the interruptions. Before I became a Secret Keeper, I'd try to guess if a customer had a secret, to no avail. Now that I have Harpocrates' charm, it changes everything.

"Should we hear all secrets?" I ask, after selling a girl my age a jar of comfrey for her mother's arthritis. I'm worried I missed the chance to hear my first secret. The charm grew warm in my hand and my mind filled with an image of the girl kissing a boy.

"Only if you want to," Mother says as she ties a string around the lavender stems to hang them in the kitchen. "Happy secrets can still cause worry, spoiling a surprise, for example. But those secrets get revealed in due course, so we rarely bother. It's the dark secrets that need our help the most." She glances out the front door. "Your chance to learn the difference has arrived."

A woman in her early twenties approaches the house. Her face is pale and the dark circles beneath her eyes suggest something is amiss. My charm curls into my hand, but no images suggesting a secret fill my mind.

"How do you know she has a dark secret?" I ask, wondering how Mother can detect what I can't.

"A lifetime of practice," she says. "Now, always try to coax out their secret first. Offering them someone to confide in works as well as the charm."

"Yes, Mother."

"If they won't tell, which many don't, use the charm. But remember, dark secrets are not pleasant."

"Yes, Mother."

I hurry from the house. Her warning fills my stomach with fluttering butterflies. Mustering my bravest smile, I approach the woman. "Hello. I'm Rose. Can I help you?"

"Hi. I'm Miranda. But everyone calls me Mim." She fidgets with the cuff of her sleeve and looks toward the gardens. "Your roses are beautiful. I admired them from the road." She hesitates, then turns her attention to the herbs. "Would you have a herbal remedy to help with forgetfulness? It's for my mother," she adds. "She has Alzheimer's."

"I'm sorry to hear that. How bad is she?"

Mim sighs. "Stage seven. She's in a nursing home and not expected to live much longer. We're trying to keep her comfortable."

"That must be difficult." I motion her to a table and chairs set up on the porch.

"I have to remind my mother who I am every day," Mim admits, walking with me to the porch. "It's hard."

The butterflies in my stomach close their wings and settle. It appears Mim is just exhausted from caring for a dying parent.

"Gingko will help your mother," I say, pulling out a chair and encouraging Mim to sit. "It's wonderful for helping with memory problems. And chamomile for you, to help you cope. Would you like to try some chamomile tea while I prepare a remedy for your mother?"

"That would be lovely," Mim says, sinking into the chair.

I hurry inside to boil the kettle, but Mother stands with a steaming pot of tea, already made.

"An infusion of chamomile," she whispers, handing me the pot. "I couldn't help overhearing. I'll prepare the gingko. You heal Mim."

"She doesn't have a secret," I whisper. "She's exhausted from caring for her mother."

Mother raises an eyebrow. "Are you sure? What does your charm tell you?"

I glance at my ring. The charm dances along the band, making the ring glow like fire. Frowning at my ineptitude, I grab a cup from the kitchen bench and return to Mim.

"Mother will prepare the gingko, but what about you?" I ask, pouring the tea and sitting in the chair opposite her. "You said 'we', before. Do you have other family members that can help?"

"Only my brother," Mim says, taking the cup of chamomile. "He's not around at the moment. He works away." She gulps her tea, her face turning bright red.

I don't need the charm to know she is lying. I wonder if Mim's secret involves her brother. Though itching to use my charm, I follow Mother's advice and offer Mim someone she can confide in.

Looking toward the roses, I sigh. "I love our roses, too. Do you know the story about Aphrodite's son? He gave Harpocrates a rose in return for keeping his mother's indiscretions secret." I pause. "I learned that in my Greek Mythology lessons."

"I didn't know that," Mim says, lowering her cup.

"It's only a myth, of course. But Aphrodite's son was lucky he found a confidant in Harpocrates. Imagine going through life having to keep something to yourself. It would place so much burden on your conscience."

Mim's cheeks flush redder. "It would be horrible, I suppose."

"Worse than horrible. If you don't clear your conscience in life, you'll suffer the burden three times worse in death."

"You do?" Mim asks, shifting uncomfortably.

"Yes." I sigh again, then clasp my hands and rest them on the table. "But a conscience is easy to clear. Confiding in another person will lift the burden." I pause because Mim looks mortified. "I suppose revealing a secret can be difficult."

"Impossibly difficult," Mim mutters, clenching her hands around her cup.

I reach across the table and place my hand over hers. "If you need to, you can confide in me. I'm a healer, which is the same as a doctor, so anything you say is confidential."

Mim's mouth parts as though she's about to accept my offer and spill her secret. But then she shakes her head. "Nothing's wrong," she says. "I appreciate the help, but I'm just worried about my mother."

"Of course you are," I say. "Keep in mind what I said, though. There's more truth in myth than we realize."

I'm not disappointed I couldn't coax out her secret. That's why Harpocrates gave us the charm. Mim keeps her secret buried for a reason. But she's so overwhelmed by dark emotions, she can't see the damage keeping a secret does to her. What she needs now is hope, to help her see that she doesn't have to suffer alone and in silence.

"It must be difficult caring for your mother on your own," I say, squeezing her hand. As though sensing it's time to go to work, the charm jumps from the ring. It shapes into a ribbon of light and winds around our hands, binding us together as one. Mim can't see the charm; it's invisible to her. But it exudes hope's calm confidence, and the subtle effect helps Mim relax.

"It's hard," Mim says, squeezing my hand in return. "I show her photos to help jog her memory. Sometimes they work. I also play her favorite music…"

While Mim talks about her mother, the charm fades through her skin to go in search of her secret. In what feels like an eyeblink, an image filters into my mind; Mim and a man who could be her twin. The charm has found the secret, but as Mother warned, it's not pleasant —

Mim's brother died two weeks ago, but Mim keeps his death secret. Her mother asks about him every day, and every day Mim says he'll see her tomorrow. Mim thinks it would be better if her mother died hoping to see her son than grieving his death. She hasn't even told the nursing home staff. She doesn't want anyone telling her mother the truth. But pretending her brother is still alive prevents her from mourning. And guilt about the lie to her mother tears her apart.

It takes all my strength not to react to the secret and keep listening to Mim talk about her mother. I wasn't prepared to hear a secret so sad. Squeezing back tears, I trust the charm to know how much burden to remove and how much hope to give. In my distressed state, I'd mess it up.

The charm skims across Mim's conscience. It removes a layer of grief and guilt then replaces them with the hope I conjured when picking the lavender. It gives just enough hope to balance Mim's emotions, and already Mim's tense grip on my hand relaxes. Then the charm carries the burden it removed to me, and curls back into the ring.

It didn't look like a lot, but the grief and guilt hit my heart with a heavy thud. Easing my hand from Mim's, I clasp my hands, drawing comfort from the warmth in the ring. Mim stops talking and heaves a sigh. Then she picks up her cup and finishes her tea.

"This is lovely," she says. "What did you say it was?"

"Chamomile," I say, forcing a smile.

I'm pleased with her lightened mood. Hope shines in her eyes and her troubled expression fades. She doesn't know that I heard her secret, or that the charm removed some of her burdens. But the hope she received should help her consider whether it's worth keeping her secret. What she decides to do is up to her, but at least now she's not blind to her choices.

The layer of dark emotions throbs through my veins. Needing to trap it in thorns, I stand to fetch the gingko so I can send Mim on her way. Mother steps onto the porch holding two paper packets.

"Chamomile tea for you, and gingko for your mother," she says, handing Mim the packets. "The instructions are in the bags. I'm sorry to hear about your mother. The gingko will help make her last days more pleasurable. Be sure to look after yourself, too."

"I will," Mim says, standing and taking the packets. "Thank you, Rose. The tea has made me feel better already." She hesitates. "I liked your story about the roses. It's given me a lot to think about." Then she hurries from the porch, clutching the packets to her chest.

I'm relieved the hope is working, but I'm more grateful for her swift departure. Clutching at the ache in my heart, I hurry to the garden.

Finding space in a garden where none of Mother's roses grow, I crouch and sow Mim's secret into the soil. The ground around my fingers glows the same golden color as the charm. The emotions I took from Mim leach out, leaving me dizzy with relief. Pulling my hands from the soil, I roll back onto my heels and watch the secret grow.

A stem pushes through the soil. Tall and slender, it sprouts long thorns, green with guilt. Grief glistens like dewdrops on the tips. Standing, I cup my hands around the rose that blooms at the top. Red petals release a heavy scent that makes me think of funerals and death.

Stepping back, I study the rose. I'm elated that my first time hearing a secret proceeded exactly as expected, but I'm also uneasy.

Mim's secret was not pleasant, and I may hear darker secrets than hers. Though I trapped Mim's emotions in thorns, I underestimated the impact those emotions had on me. I hope I haven't also underestimated the strength needed to stay true to my vows.

●

Later in the day, I kneel beside Mother and help harvest evening primrose before the light fades. I drop more seed pods than I collect because I'm distracted by an image of Hades laughing at me for thinking it's easy to keep a secret.

"Mother? Have you ever heard a secret that is so bad, you don't have the strength to keep it?"

"Find the strength," Mother says. "Otherwise you'll destroy the hope you gave and suffer the secret's burden."

I glance around the garden. In the dying light, the thorns on Mim's rose appear to weep. But a rose growing behind hers draws my attention. It's grown in that spot longer than I've been alive. The red petals reek with an intoxicating perfume. The stem is thick and covered in large mottled-red thorns that speak of something nasty. I shudder to think what burden they trap and wonder where Mother finds the strength to keep the secret.

I'm about to ask when the rose wilts and the petals turn gray.

"Mother," I gasp, my heart leaping into my throat. "That rose died."

Mother stands and walks over to the rose. "Hope shines a light on choice, but sometimes that's still not enough to stop a secret going to the grave."

Scrambling to my feet, I follow. I've seen roses die before, but it hits harder now that I'm a Secret Keeper. Death doesn't release us from our vows. We're still bound to keep the secret. And we can still suffer the burden.

A milky-white mist rises from the ground in front of me. Mother grabs my arm and pulls me away. The mist takes the shape of a translucent figure; the ghost of an old man. My charm must enhance my sight. I've seen ghosts before, too, but never with such clarity. I didn't realize the depth of three-fold suffering.

The man's eyes sink into his skull and his mouth hangs open as though dragged down by weights. He reaches for the rose, but the thorns stab holes in his fingers. His face contorts as though feeling actual pain. Turning to Mother, he stretches his arms toward her.

"I've heard your secret," Mother says. "Hope showed you choices and you made yours. Accept your fate and go. I will not help you in death." She waves the ghost away. The mist disperses, but leaves a chill in the air.

"They're drawn here by the scent of their rose," Mother says. Pulling out the entire rose plant, she tosses it onto the mulch pile. "They forget that the cause of their misery in death is that they didn't clear their conscience in life. But don't let a ghost's suffering tempt you to hear their secret again. Emotions in a soul can't be balanced like in a conscience. If you try to remove some burden, you'll end up taking the lot and have to fill the soul with hope. That would allow the soul to be reborn, and Hades would lose his servant. He would demand the Keeper's soul to compensate, and Harpocrates would oblige. He values our servitude, but would strip your power to conjure hope to avoid a war with Hades.

Mother's words are as chilling as the cold left by the ghost. I thought Harpocrates would protect his servants, since we pledged our loyalty to him. To learn he'd strip my powers in favor of keeping good relations with Hades leaves a sour taste in my mouth. I wonder if we're nothing more than pawns in a power game between the gods.

I fall asleep resenting my commitment to a god who will not protect my allegiance and wake to pouring rain. My resentful thoughts must anger Harpocrates; the rain doesn't ease for three days. If he is showing me what a world without hope looks like, he paints the picture well. I stare in dismay at our wrecked gardens. Then I see the woman.

Fighting the wind to hold an umbrella over her head, she sloshes through the puddles at our front gate. Hurrying outside, I welcome her onto the porch. It's Mrs. Peterson, the elegant yet tight-lipped town mayor's wife. When she steps onto the porch, she sniffs back a sneeze.

Mother appears in the doorway behind me. "Good gracious," she says, taking the umbrella from Mrs. Peterson and shaking it dry. "It's no time to be out in this weather, Mrs. Peterson. Rose, boil the kettle. A pot of tea is in order."

Hurrying inside, I light the burner and set the kettle to boil. Mother and Mrs. Peterson sit at the kitchen table.

"My daughter, Rose," Mother says, introducing me.

"Rose, like the flowers," Mrs. Peterson says, placing her purse on the table and extending her hand. "And just as beautiful."

Blushing at the compliment, I shake her hand. My charm dances around my fingers, alerting me to what I should have guessed from her sniffles. Mrs. Peterson has a secret.

"How is your husband?" Mother asks. "Worn out from running the town, I imagine?"

"His work is his life, and he'll not hear otherwise," Mrs. Peterson says. "But the reason for my intrusion..." Her nose wrinkles, then she sneezes into her hands.

I fetch a box of tissues from the cupboard and slide it across the table. Mrs. Peterson plucks out a tissue and blows her nose. "Thank you, dear," she says. "Such dismal weather. As I was saying, my intrusion —"

"It's no intrusion," Mother says. "Rose? The tea?"

I fetch the kettle and make a pot of herbal tea. When I return to the table, my charm jumps into my hand. It weaves around my fingers as though trying to get my attention. Mrs. Peterson's secret must be bad for my charm to react with such intensity.

"I was driving past and saw your roses," Mrs. Peterson says. "I'd like to buy a bunch. My husband likes a well-presented office. Our usual supplier's flowers are lackluster by comparison."

"The roses aren't for sale," I say, giving my usual response.

Mrs. Peterson purses her lips. "If it's a question of money, my husband will pay well."

I glance at Mother, wondering if she detects the tinge of desperation in Mrs. Peterson's tone like I do. Mother keeps her eyes on Mrs. Peterson, but deep grooves form on her brow.

"I can spare a bunch," Mother says. "But I'll accept no payment. There's as much grace in giving as there is in receiving. Rose, would you go to the garden, please? There's a rosebush among the chamomile that could do with a prune."

Frowning, I glance out the kitchen window. There aren't any rosebushes among the chamomile. Maybe Mother wants me to use my demigod power to grow a bunch of roses. I never have, but it would be the same as growing herbs. I leave the kitchen, but stop at the front door, realizing why Mother asks me to go outside.

She's going to hear Mrs. Peterson's secret. If I've angered Harpocrates, *I* should hear the secret and prove I'm committed to his cause. I don't want to live in a world without hope. I was angry earlier because I don't want to be disposable.

"Mother," I say, turning around. "Could you point out the rosebush? I'm not sure which one you mean."

When Mother joins me in the doorway, I lower my voice to a whisper. "Let me hear her secret."

Mother frowns. "I'd rather you didn't. I don't like the feeling I get from Mrs. Peterson."

"Please, Mother. I know she might have a terrible secret, but I can help her, I know I can."

Mother sighs. "Very well." She looks back at Mrs. Peterson. "I'll return in a moment. Rose will keep you company while you wait."

When Mother goes outside, I hurry back to the kitchen and sit at the table. Mrs. Peterson smiles with indifference and gazes about our kitchen. I wonder how I'll engage her in conversation, when it's clear she has no interest in talking to a teenager.

"I love the color of your dress-suit," I say. "The blue is the same shade as a periwinkle flower." I don't know why I thought of that flower when there are so many others to choose from. The periwinkle is also called the 'flower of death'. The vines were used in wreaths for dead children.

"It's my favorite," Mrs. Peterson says, "but its wool-blend is a poor choice of wardrobe in our current weather."

The umbrella didn't stop the rain soaking her clothes. Her dress-suit gives off a damp animal smell. The rain ruined her makeup, too. It's splotchy in places, especially around her left cheek. Wondering why she applied so much makeup during wet weather, I stand and fetch a towel so she can pat herself dry.

"Appearances must be important to your husband if he sends you out for flowers in dismal weather," I say, handing her the towel.

Mrs. Peterson flinches. "When you live in the public eye, appearance is a necessity, not a luxury." She pats her neck dry, then sips her tea. "The tea is delicious. Peppermint?"

"Yes. Infused with ginger. For your sniffles. I'm sorry to sound rude. I sense something troubles you. It helps to talk, did you know?"

She lowers the cup to the table. "You'll find out, young Rose, that even if you had someone to talk to, some things can't be helped."

"I imagine it would be difficult to find someone to trust when you live in the public eye," I say, sliding into my seat. "But you can talk to me. I can keep a secret."

"Can you now?" she says. "What on earth makes you think I have a secret?"

"I sense it. I also feel it troubles you."

She gives me a tired smile. "You're a strange, sweet child, and I appreciate the sentiment. If you must know, it's a demanding job meeting my husband's expectations. I'll say no more on the matter, but I trust you'll never repeat this conversation."

"You can trust me," I say. "But if you don't confide in somebody, the burden your secret causes you now will haunt you three times worse in death."

"There's more to fear in life than in death, young Rose," she says, ruefully. "If being haunted is the price I'll pay for holding my tongue, then so be it."

She returns to gazing about the kitchen, dismissing me completely. I wonder if I've wrecked the opportunity to cast my charm by being too forward. I need to hold her hand, but doubt she'll welcome the consoling gesture. But her manicured fingernails gives me an idea.

"I've never applied nail polish," I say, "but if I did, what color would you recommend?"

Extending my arm across the table, I offer my hand. Mrs. Peterson looks down her nose at my fingers, but then takes my hand in hers and studies my nails.

"Nothing too bold," she says, tilting my hand from side to side. "I prefer pale pinks or pearl, or there's a lovely shade of ivory I've used..."

She prattles on about the best color for teenage girls, remarks on my ring, picks at my nails and advises how best to shape them. While she talks, my charm wraps around our hands, binding us as one. Then it goes in search of her secret. It feels like forever, but in less than a second, images fill my mind. The charm has found the secret, but it's so shocking, I nearly jerk my hand away —

She's not the happily married wife of the hardworking town mayor. She's the victim of a cruel and calculating narcissist. Her self-esteem has suffered because of his controlling and abusive behavior, and years of verbal and physical abuse have left her a broken woman. With her sense of self-worth corrupted, she's lost view of a life away from her husband. She believes that what she endures behind closed doors is her lot in life.

To learn she's a victim of marital abuse staggers me. It explains the other images that fill my mind. She applies extra makeup to cover a bruise on her cheek. She cowers before her enraged husband because the color of her dress didn't match his tie. Her desperate need to find roses is born from a need to keep her husband happy; protection against his abuse.

I fuel the charm with hope drawn from an image of a blue sky after a clearing storm. The charm whips around Mrs. Peterson's conscience. It removes a thick layer of hopelessness and replaces it with hope. Then it carries the hopelessness back to me.

"If you need more advice," Mrs. Peterson says, releasing my hand, "my nail technician has a shop near to the town hall. Mention that I sent you." She picks up her cup, pauses, then drinks the rest of her tea. When she lowers her cup, her sniffles have dried and her eyes shine with hope.

"Such an extraordinary taste," she says, smacking her lips with pleasure. "It's left me wonderfully clear-headed. I must take some with me."

"Of course." Going to the kitchen bench, I fill a paper packet with a mixture of dried ginger and peppermint leaves. Mrs. Peterson's hopelessness affects my usual care when preparing herbal tea, and I spill leaves on the bench.

Clenching my fingers, I take a deep breath and draw on my charm's power to help keep my emotions balanced. I don't know how Mrs. Peterson managed for so long, living without hope. Praying I gave her enough, I fold the packet and return to the table.

Mother arrives, holding a bunch of red and white roses that fill the kitchen with a heavenly scent. Feeling the hopelessness creep over me again, I catch Mother's eye and signal my desperate need to leave.

"Your roses," Mother says, her tone clipped.

Mrs. Peterson picks up her purse and stands. "Wonderful. And the tea?"

I hand her the packet. "A gift," I say when she opens her purse to pay.

Mrs. Peterson closes her purse and takes the packet. She looks me in the eye, as though reminding me never to repeat our conversation, then turns toward the door.

Mother escorts her out. "The rain has eased," she says, "but mind your speed while driving. The road into town is slippery when wet."

As soon as Mrs. Peterson leaves, I push past Mother and run to the garden. Dropping to my knees, I sow Mrs. Peterson's secret into the mud. The flooded soil reflects the charm's golden glow. When all Mrs. Peterson's hopelessness has drained out of me, I roll back on my heels and watch the secret grow.

A stem pushes through the ground, tall and thick with long thorns that droop as though they've lost the will to live. The rosebud that blooms at the top unfurls blood-red petals, with perfume so heavy it gets caught in my throat.

Standing, I stare at the rose. I'm supposed to listen without judgment, but I can't ignore what I heard. Mrs. Peterson faces more harm if she doesn't reveal her secret. The hope helped clear her mind, but will it be enough to encourage her to seek help?

●

I toss and turn all night, unable to get Mrs. Peterson off my mind. Thinking about her bruised cheek makes me lie awake with worry. Even if I broke my vows and revealed the secret for her, it wouldn't help. I'd destroy the hope I gave her, and she needs all the hope she can get.

Needing a slap of cold night air to clear my gloomy thoughts, I slip out of bed and go outside. The rain has stopped and the heavy clouds part, letting moonlight stream over the gardens. Taking a deep breath, I search the night shadows for Mrs. Peterson's rose. It's bathed a milky-white glow from the moon, but the light shifts as though moved by the wind. Wondering what causes that effect, I walk toward the rose. When I get closer, my heart stops.

It's not moving moonlight. It's the ghost of Mrs. Peterson. She hovers next to her wilted rose that's gray from death. Gone is the elegant woman who sat at our kitchen table. An unnatural force squishes her features, making her look like a lump of melted wax.

I stare at her, frozen in fright. How could I miss the signs that foretold her death? I compared the color of her dress-suit to the 'flower of death'. Mother warned her about the slippery roads. Did she have a car accident while driving home? Whatever happened, despite the hope I gave her, she didn't reveal her secret. She can't have, because she suffers her burden in death.

Three-fold hopelessness pours like black ink from her hollow eye sockets. Her mouth yawns wide, expelling the choking scent of her rose. Nothing I envisioned comes close to what stands before me. But what if I'm to blame? What if, in my haste to cast the charm, I didn't give her enough hope?

"I'm sorry," I whisper, creeping toward her. "I don't know what happened, but you don't deserve to suffer in death when you suffered so much in life. I can help you. I can fix this."

Her soul now belongs to Hades, but I can still hear her secret and fill her soul with hope. It means Hades may lose his servant. And he'll demand my soul to compensate. But if I'm responsible for Mrs. Peterson's death, that's a consequence I'm willing to accept.

I think about all the things that give me hope and fuel the charm with so much power it shines like two suns. Then I reach for Mrs. Peterson's hands. Her fingers find mine, icy tendrils that numb my skin. A strange blue light flows into my charm, turning its golden light a frosty turquoise. With increased power, the charm whips around our hands, binding us as one.

Mrs. Peterson tilts my hand and pokes at my fingernails. Though distracted by the icy pricks on my fingers, I urge the charm to find her secret again. Powered by the blue light, it works faster than usual. In a split second, the secret I heard when sitting in the kitchen with Mrs. Peterson fills my mind again.

This time, the images are so lifelike they make me think I'm experiencing them. When her husband strikes her cheek, I flinch as though struck. But then a different image appears, a new secret —

Still alive but soaked from the rain, Mrs. Peterson walks up a spiral staircase. She clutches Mother's roses to her chest like a shield. Mr. Peterson stands on the top step, his face a furious shade of red. When she shows him the roses, he knocks them from her hands. Then he shouts that a wife who appears in public looking like a drowned rat will embarrass him.

Encouraged by the hope, Mrs. Peterson scoffs at his expectations. She says if he wishes to remain married, she'll decide if her appearance is appropriate.

Mr. Peterson strikes her face with a backhand that knocks her down the stairs. Her head hits the bottom step with a crack —

The flow of images ends as quick as her life did. Numb with shock, I try to fathom what I saw. Instead, I see Mr. Peterson again, but his features are fuzzy, like I'm looking through a transparent veil. I can see enough to know he's talking on the telephone. Hear enough to know what he said. *Slipped on the steps. A tragic accident.* Then the image fades.

The blood drains from my face, making me feel as cold as Mrs. Peterson. I can't see her eyes, but I can sense her somber stare. The truth about her death burns through the charm, and screeches of *"liar"* and *"murderer"* ring in my ears. It's Mrs. Peterson screaming, though her mouth is shut. Again she's been silenced, this time forever. But her husband can't silence me.

Determined to end her suffering, I urge my charm to remove all the burden. It's like scraping away layers of sludge, but, powered by the blue light, the charm collects it all. Then it delivers hope so pure, the brightness hurts my eyes. But I'm not prepared when my charm returns with the burden.

Triple the amount of hopelessness drags me to the pits of despair, draining my will to live. But my determination to see her husband punished for her murder anchors me to life. Pulling my hands from Mrs. Peterson, I stumble backward to escape the lure of death.

Filled with hope, Mrs. Peterson's grotesque features melt away. She appears as she did when she sat at our table, elegant, spirits lifted, and taking pleasure in sipping our tea. Then she fades, like mist dispersing in a breeze.

"Rose?"

Mother's voice drives the deadness from my limbs. Dropping to my knees, I dig into the mud and bury both of Mrs. Peterson's secrets. The ground around my fingers glows turquoise, my charm's new color. Two stems burst through the soil. They weave around each other like climbing vines, sprouting long black thorns that droop with three-fold hopelessness. Above my head, a rose blooms at the top of each stem. The petals on each are an unearthly frosty blue.

"Rose? What happened?"

The shock in Mother's voice sends tears streaming down my cheeks. "She's dead. Mrs. Peterson is dead."

Mother crouches beside me, her hand flying to her throat. "When? How?"

I claw my fingers into the mud, wanting to scream Mrs. Peterson's secrets into the night. Instead, I imagine Hades again, his expression smug, as though expecting me to break my vows. But if I do, I'll break Mrs. Peterson's trust and destroy the hope I gave her. That would be like killing her again.

Mother's words about finding the strength whisper through my mind, and I realize where my strength lies. Wiping my eyes, I clamber to my feet. "Mrs. Peterson didn't deserve to suffer in death. I heard her secret again, removed her burden and filled her soul with hope."

"And condemned yours." Standing, Mother grabs my elbow and pulls me away from the two roses. "What were you thinking, child? If Mrs. Peterson chooses rebirth, Hades will demand your soul to compensate. I warned you of this. Harpocrates will strip your ability to conjure hope to avoid a war with Hades."

Without hope, I'll lose my will to live and hand my soul to Hades by taking my own life. Even revealing Mrs. Peterson's secret wouldn't help. I'd destroy her hope and prevent her from being reborn, but Hades would still get my soul. I'd suffer the three-fold hopelessness I trapped in the thorns and I wouldn't survive that. But I can save my soul another way. There's something Hades and I have in common.

"Hades won't come for me," I say. "He values upholding vows above everything. And Mrs. Peterson can't be reborn because we are bound as one. While I live in this world, she'll stay in the underworld." In Elysium, where pure souls get sent.

I fiddle with my ring. The blue light that changed the charm's color has also turned the gold band a deep shade of turquoise. I've guessed the source of the blue light's power, but I don't think either god expected this. "Harpocrates could strip my powers so I can't conjure hope, but while I keep Mrs. Peterson's secret, I'll always have hope. Look." I hold out my hand and tease my charm from the ring. It jumps into my hand, a flickering bluish-gold flame.

"It's drawing hope from Mrs. Peterson," I say, "but that hope contains Hades' power, which is why it's so strong. Harpocrates would be a fool to abandon me now. With hope this powerful, we could win every battle against darkness and despair."

Mother doesn't look happy, but I've never been more certain. Like all the Secret Keepers before me, Mother included, my strength lies in the commitment to my vows. It means Mr. Peterson will escape punishment in this world, but he won't escape Hades.

I have to listen without judgment, but in the underworld, Hades' judges don't. When they judge Mr. Peterson's soul with the secret he keeps, they'll send him straight to Tartarus. I can't imagine a better punishment for a man who killed his wife.

Pauline Yates' story "The Secret Keeper" was originally published in Metaphorosis on Friday, 4 June 2021

About the author

Pauline Yates from Queensland, Australia is the award-winning author of *Memories Don't Lie*, a 2024 BookFest Award 3x first place winner in YA — Science Fiction, Sci-Fi — Action/Adventure, and Sci-fi — Genetic Engineering. She's an Aurealis Awards finalist and a 2x Australasian Shadows Awards shortlist recipient, and her AHWA Robert N Stephenson winning short story, "The Best Medicine" was chosen for translation in the *Mondi Incantati* series produced by Riflessi di Lunare (RiLL), Italy. Her fiction and poetry appear in numerous online publications, magazines, and podcasts and she darkens the pages of many anthologies with her vast collection of micro-fiction. Read more at paulineyates (dotcom)

The Diamond Noose

Ramez Yoakeim

From the smug grins everyone flashed me as soon as I walked into the precinct, I knew I was in for a nasty surprise. I hadn't even reached my desk when the lieutenant called me into her glass-bowl office and handed me a new assignment: liaison to the Angels' Embassy.

I didn't care for Angels. They looked down on us from their palaces in the sky, pretending to help us survive our broken world while ensuring we'd never learn to do it on our own. Some said it was the Angels who set off the nuclear catastrophe that nearly wiped out life on Earth.

"Wouldn't this suit a more senior officer?" Or one more junior. Anyone else, really.

The lieutenant jabbed a paper on her desk. "Laila Aboud, requested by name."

A shiver zapped up my spine. The Angels had hidden eyes in the sky, seeing everywhere, knowing all. They had tentacles in every government, in every department, their shadow behind every throne. How had I managed to attract their attention? "Why me?"

She shrugged. "Ask the Angels when you see them. Do we have a problem here?"

I found myself wondering whose idea it had been to call them *Angels.*

"No, ma'am."

Like I had a choice. This job came with a warm bed and three squares, a firearm, and badge that opened doors and dropped eyes. I'd never walk away, no matter what they asked, any more than she would.

●

After all that, the work was surprisingly mundane. Waiting on my desk every morning was a stack of *requests* from the Angels Embassy: locate knickknacks stolen from the occasional visiting Angel, or quietly deem accidental the death of a prostitute in the company of another, or round up a bunch of uniforms to form a street cordon for visiting off-world dignitaries. Until I arrived at my desk one day to find a single message *requesting* my attendance at the embassy, and my heart dropped to my knees. I wanted to get away from Angels, not get closer.

The embassy occupied an old courthouse downtown. In the frigid gloom under Earth's thick cloud cover, the impeccably restored edifice dwarfed the line of scraggly humanity wrapped around its foundations like a snake about invincible prey.

However the Angels put it, the Transmigration they dangled before those queueing had nothing to do with benevolence. They preyed on our best and brightest, siphoning away those who might help us to break free of our dependence on their conditional aid. Could one of those queuing learn the secrets of fusion one day, or perfect anti-radiation medicines, or discover how to grow crops in poisoned soil, or put an end to the Angels plunder of our water and minerals, or lead us in overthrowing the tyrants they installed to rule us? Not when those with potential got spirited away to the sky.

The queuing adults eyed me warily as I made my way to the uniform separating the line's head from its tail, barring the serpent from becoming an ouroboros. He glanced at my badge and waved me through. Inside, I handed the private security guard my sidearm. "I had no idea they started queueing this early."

"Some never leave." The guard saw me roll my eyes and grinned, his words chasing me to the elevator. "Sometimes, a dream is all that keeps us alive, officer."

A fool's dream of an easy life concerned only with pleasure. Then again, had my lot in life been harsher, perhaps I'd have queued with them.

I wasn't prepared for the mechanical giant waiting for me when the elevator's doors parted. Spindly inside the exoskeleton that afforded her mobility in Earth's gravity, Inspector Geraldine Hoff's skin was as pale as mine was brown, as if we'd been birthed from opposite ends of a monochromatic palette. Her hairless scalp, elongated sloping forehead, and large inky eyes cast as much doubt on our alleged common ancestry as the missing wings myth had it Angels grew to fly around their low-gravity palaces.

While the building's exterior and entrance remained largely faithful to its original layout, the interior bore no resemblance to anything I'd ever seen before. Hoff led me from the lift to a flat-floored ovoid space uniformly lit by the walls themselves. With a whirring flick of her hand, Hoff gestured me towards a blob that oozed up on command and reformed into a stool.

She briefed me on a missing Angel. *The Conjurer* was the nom-de-plume of an artist who composed dreams as a form of entertainment. These visions eschewed euphoric sex or heroic triumph — the sort that'd exhilarate us dirt dwellers — instead, they explored the darker side of the human psyche, torments that Angels no longer experienced. "Any questions?"

I didn't have to ask what the Conjurer was doing on the surface. Where else would he find the human trauma to mine for his *art*? "How does an Angel get lost? No offense, but you stand out down here."

"More reason to suspect something happened to this *Angel*, wouldn't you say?" Hoff bristled at the common moniker. I'd had no idea they considered it pejorative. In their shoes, I'd have been flattered. Would they have preferred us to call them *demons*?

"What exactly do you think I can do that your fancy gizmos can't?"

"Retracing the Conjurer's steps means going places we don't often venture. My bosses, and yours, want a local along to deal with the natives. *No offense.*"

It would've also been politically unpalatable for my bosses to have an undoubtedly armed Angel terrorizing the populace without at least the veneer of local authority, and it didn't hurt to have me around to take the blame when things went awry.

"A chaperone, basically."

Hoff smiled thinly. "Think of it as an opportunity to demonstrate your usefulness."

I didn't know how to respond to *that*.

●

Mildly acidic drizzle scattered off Hoff's flying egg onto the corroded tin roofs of the lean-tos below. Despite the webbing securing me to the seat, my inner ear kept insisting I was falling towards the transparent shell. White-knuckled, I hung onto the seat and fought off motion sickness, only half-listening to Hoff.

After one particularly sharp banking turn, Hoff glanced at me. "You're turning a worrying shade of green."

I clamped my jaws shut against the rising bile and inflated my lungs with the egg's sweet clean air. "I'm fine."

She pursed her lips and returned her attention to the scarred Earth slipping by below. With little light penetrating the thick, ash-laden clouds, we would all have perished long ago, had it not been for the Angels' magic-like power generation, foodstuffs, and medicines. That their largesse came with strings attached surprised no one. That those strings soon formed a noose that held us hostage to their demands *shouldn't* have surprised anyone.

To shift my focus away from the vertiginous view, I turned to Hoff. "Did the Conjurer stray far during his visits?"

Hoff hesitated. "Sightseeing, entertainment. Nothing out of the ordinary."

She meant poverty safaris and brothels. There was little else for Angels on the surface.

"Could he have gotten lost?" How would the mobs treat a lost Angel? I liked to think some would be hospitable, but I feared that others wouldn't be, and I couldn't bring myself to condemn either.

Hoff shook her head. "He knew his way around." She seemed on the verge of saying more but didn't.

Changing tack, I teased her, "Did you know most people think y'all have wings?"

"Wings?" Hoff frowned back at my smile. "We ..." she paused, searching for words, "change bodies like you might clothes. Not as often, but subject to similar whims of fashion and taste. Body parts, like wings or extra eyes or gills and fins, come and go, and are sometimes taken to extremes. Many of my friends forgo bodies entirely to live in the Abstract."

"And that is?"

"Never mind, it's hard to explain." I couldn't tell whether she was boasting or embarrassed.

The egg lurched briefly and I gasped.

Hoff gave me a sidelong glance. "Your file didn't say anything about fear of flying."

I realized I was still holding onto the seat. "I've never flown before, give me time." I tried to let go, but couldn't quite bring myself to do it. "What else did my file say?"

"That you're insubordinate, pigheaded, and cantankerous."

"They could spell *cantankerous*?"

Hoff laughed, and I found myself laughing along, for a moment oblivious to the gulf separating us.

"But it also said you have the highest clearance rate of any officer in your department."

They *had* asked for me by name. I still didn't quite know what to make of that and pushed it aside to ruminate over later.

"Quite the accomplishment, considering how young you are," Hoff added.

I'd never thought of thirty-two as young. Angels were rumored to be immortal, but I put little stock in such claims. If only half of those rumors were true, it would have made them veritable gods. "How old are *you*?"

She smiled coyly and waved away my question. "Longevity's overrated."

"I'd happily part with an arm and both legs to see my fiftieth birthday." With life expectancy in the mid-forties, I found the idea of anyone living to a hundred obscene, let alone longer. How did Angel offspring feel about parents who lingered? Was overpopulation as much of a problem in orbit as it was on the surface?

Hoff stared wistfully into the distance, seeing something in the murky gloom I couldn't. "When life is short, your choices are consequential. Which path you take in life matters more because you only ever get to make a few choices. Live long enough and you end up exploring every path in turn, chasing every dream. What good is success if it's only a matter of time?"

I could tell she sincerely meant it, almost as if she envied me my short miserable life. How easy it was for those well fed to bursting to preach the virtues of restraint to the starving.

●

Hoff pitched the egg down, drawing my eyes to an expanse of pockmarked, corrugated metal roofs below. Having never seen the area from above before, it took me a moment to recognize where we were. "We can't land here."

"It's the Conjurer's first stop after leaving the embassy. The first deviation from his usual itinerary."

"You don't understand. This is Serpent Head's territory. If we land uninvited, he's as likely to feed us to his dogs as answer our questions."

"I'd like to see him try."

"I wouldn't!" Though I'd count it progress to be rid of him and his flunkies, innocent bystanders were bound to get caught in any confrontation, and for what? To satisfy Hoff's desire to appear tough and powerful? Who was she trying to impress? "You wanted a local to deal with the natives, and this local is telling you to stay the hell away from these natives."

Hoff ignored me and took the egg lower. "I'll land there." She nodded at a stone-paved plaza festooned with tattered bunting and lit with dim, oil-burning lanterns.

By the time the egg touched down, everyone had scattered, leaving the market eerily quiet, aside from the hissing of swaying lamps and the incessant strumming of caustic drizzle on improvised awnings.

"Good luck finding anyone who'll talk to us now," I muttered, steeling myself against the sour miasma wafting through the egg's open hatch.

Hoff gracefully eased the considerable bulk of her exoskeleton out into the open, oblivious to the stench. "They're bound to come out eventually."

"That's not how it works down here, how *we* work," I fumed. Why have me along if she wasn't going to listen to anything I said? "You can't just blunder your way to your missing Conjurer with this confidence act, no matter how convincing."

She cast her eyes down, looking slightly abashed, and I felt a little guilty for my outburst.

I set to scanning the deserted clearing, when a boy bolted from a cart he might have been napping under, towards a dark alley and right into my arms. About ten or twelve, though so thin it was impossible to say for sure, the boy squirmed in my grip, eyes wide with fear.

"Let go, pig," he demanded, his bass rumble at odds with his small frame.

"Settle. I'm not going to hurt you," I said. "There's a half-dinar in it for you if you answer my questions."

The boy stopped bucking and regarded me with wide, greedy eyes. "Ten dinars."

It was a familiar routine. "You don't even know what I'm going to ask you."

Suddenly, floodlights lit the clearing — an extravagant display for a planet starved of power. Reflexively, I let go of the boy's scruff and shielded my eyes. His bare feet barely left a mark on the frozen slush as he ran away.

"Kadir's a good lad. He'd never betray his kin for anything less than *five* dinars." A short, plump man swaggered into view. A tattoo of a snake head in faded indigo and crimson ink covered the left side of his temple, its lean body running down his cheek, under the thicket of a rampant salt-and-pepper beard, and reappearing down the side of his bullneck before disappearing again under his coat's collar. "Are you lost, sweetheart?" Serpent Head asked mockingly. Under the blue-white glare, his shaved head shone like oiled mahogany.

From Hoff's exoskeleton an aura swelled, glowing an ominous red-tinged orange.

Serpent Head regarded her contemptuously. "It's true we have little to live for down here, but believe me, we don't die cheaply." A racket of cocking rifles followed.

"Stop!" I raised my arms. "We didn't come here looking for trouble."

"Trouble?" Serpent Head thundered with practiced menace. "What trouble would that be, sweetheart?"

Hoff covered the distance separating us in a wink. "Call her *sweetheart* one more time and I'll dispatch you like the vermin you are."

Serpent Head matched her advance, his stomping army in lockstep. Instinctively, I stepped in-between. "Enough," I infused my voice with every command authority trick I'd learned walking the beat. "We're only here for information," I continued in a measured tone. "An Angel stopped here a few days ago."

I nodded to Hoff, who asked. "What did he want?"

Serpent Head alternated his focus between my eyes as if one would betray the other. "What's in it for me?"

As soon as he'd finished speaking, Hoff pulled out a small silver box and threw it at him. He grabbed it midair and turned it in his hand, examining it. "What the hell is this?"

"Enough pills to offset five-hundred Sieverts," Hoff said.

I glowered at her. Unlike a coin tossed to a street urchin, bribing Serpent Head with a small fortune in medicine only created a bigger problem. Not that it'd matter to the Angels, not when they had us to clean up their messes.

Serpent Head nodded approvingly at the box. "Your Angel wanted a sedative and — funnily enough — anti-radiation pills. For another one of these," he shook the pills in their container, "I'll tell you where he went next."

"No need." Hoff's forcefield deflated, cooling to a muted indigo-blue as she walked back to the egg, winking out entirely once inside. I scrambled after her. The moment the hatch sealed, the egg shot upwards, pinning me to my seat.

"I could have gotten him to tell us where your Conjurer went next," I grumbled.

"That, I already know."

"Were you planning on telling me?" How could she not understand that to help her, I had to know what I was helping with. Keeping her cards so close to her chest was hurting more than my feelings, it was handicapping our chances of finding the Conjurer. Any investigator worth their salt would've known that. What did Hoff actually do for work up there, parking enforcement?

She saw me glowering and relented. "He went to a bordello, then disappeared without a trace."

So much for Angels eyes seeing everything, knowing all. If an Angel could evade their all seeing eyes, could we too?

●

One moment, we were drowning in a murky ashen sea, and the next, we burst into an inverted, indigo-hemmed, blue ocean. Against that dazzling expanse, the Angels' crystal palaces glinted like a glittering diamond necklace girding the Earth, an achingly beautiful noose. Despite the blinding brightness, I couldn't turn away, until my eyes watered and reflexively gummed shut. Hoff noticed and polarized the shell into near opacity. "Is this better?"

I watched the fading kaleidoscopic afterimage on the inside of my eyelids, my gratitude for her thoughtfulness warring with resentment. When again would I get a chance to see sunshine, however blinding? For centuries, our leaders had promised a day when the clouds would finally part. Meanwhile, *when-the-sun-shines* had come to mean *never*. "Thank you."

As I reopened my eyes, blinking away the moisture pooling on my lashes, a nagging feeling I had since we took off from the marketplace coalesced into a question. "Why did the Conjurer buy radiation pills on the black market? Unlike yours, the local ones are useless as currency."

"Currency?" Hoff scolded. "Is that the gratitude we get for helping you survive?"

"You want *our* gratitude for exploiting us?" I responded in kind. "Everything you do, you do for yourselves. Every time you bribe someone like Serpent Head, you strengthen his hand and ensure generations of Kadirs never rise to challenge your interests."

"If you're going to blame us for Serpent Head, you have to ask yourself this: Why would we bother sabotaging your endeavors when you do such a fine job of it on your own? Everything you accuse us of, Laila, you are yourself complicit in."

I smarted from the truth.

Hoff broke the silence that ensued. "Must we quarrel about things that have nothing to do with the two of us? I don't blame you for every fault of your people. Why blame me for mine?"

"Because you have a say. You get to vote on the decisions your people make. *You* decide what's right and what's not. I don't. I live and die by the edicts of the tyrants you installed as our rulers. How our troubles started may not have been your fault, but we're still in a mess, centuries later, because it serves your interests. You use us, Geraldine."

"Can't we leave politics to the politicians?"

"Why am I here, Geraldine? And don't give me this bullshit about locals and natives. You don't listen to anything I say anyway. There's nothing I've done you couldn't have done on your own."

"You're wrong, Laila." Hoff paused and regarded me diffidently, before continuing. "Back home, there are no hardships, no risks. We've forgotten pain, fear, hunger. When we set out to rid ourselves of human weakness, we ended up discarding our instincts instead. You effortlessly saw through my bravado in the face of the first hitch we faced. I'm overwhelmed by your world and woefully unprepared for it. I can't finish this on my own."

She'd called me by my first name twice now. A sincere familiarity, or another manipulation? I couldn't tell. Then I realized that I too had called her by her first name. Was I trying to manipulate her in return, or had I simply forgotten she was an Angel?

"Then tell me why the Conjurer needed anti-radiation pills, when his aura would've protected him as yours protects you," I paused for a response, but Hoff only shrugged. "You said your people choose their bodies. Could he have chosen a body that is susceptible to radiation?"

Hoff's eyes glazed over for a heartbeat or two. "It's not. His current corpus is an older model than mine, but similarly immune to radiation. Curiously, though, he hasn't upgraded his for nearly twenty years."

"The same period he's been visiting the surface, give or take?"

Hoff turned towards me so fast, I recoiled, driving my head deeper into the headrest. "How did you know that?"

"My guess is, the Conjurer wasn't born an Angel."

"No one is born —" Hoff stopped mid-sentence. " — into Transenlightenment."

"You don't have kids?" I'd never even heard a rumor about that. I wouldn't have believed it had anyone else told me. How could a people survive without having offspring? "Why not?"

Hoff shook her head. "You first. How did you work all this out?"

"If the Conjurer didn't need the pills, then they had to be for one of us, for someone he knew. Had he sourced them the way you had, you'd have a record of it. Maybe he wouldn't have been able to explain why he needed them or for whom." I paused, giving Hoff another opportunity to tell me I was wrong. She said nothing. "Circumventing obstacles and challenging limits is something we have to do, dozens of times every day, just to survive. But you just said those sorts of instincts are lost to you, which would make the Conjurer a more recent Angel. One who hadn't yet shed his hard-won survival instincts. One who still has people here he cares enough about to risk doing business with the likes of Serpent Head. Who is it? After twenty years, his parents are likely dead. A lover then, or a child?"

Hoff's response was slow coming. "I don't know."

I snorted and turned away from her, shaking my head.

"We don't keep those sorts of records. We never had to," she added heatedly. After a pause, she drew in a deep breath before continuing. "To answer your earlier question, the longevity treatments preclude pregnancy. We could have found ways around that, but at some point we decided we didn't want to, and however long we live, we too die. So, we invite the deserving among you to join us. We expect and accept a measure of nostalgia for their former lives, until new possibilities sets them free of their past. Why would we need records of their old lives?"

I thought of the coiling queue outside the embassy and shivered. Did those queuing know the price of becoming an Angel was to give up everyone they'd ever loved? "You expect a spouse to forget their mate, a parent to abandon their children, a friend and neighbor to forswear their community after a *measure of nostalgia*?"

She shrugged. "I don't remember what family I once had, or even if I had one."

Where did she think she'd come from, a seed pod? All humans had families, born or found, small or sprawling, loving or venom-filled. They might not like them or want them, but they had them. Whom had the Conjurer left behind twenty years ago? How long had it taken Hoff to forgot those she'd abandoned? "Geraldine, why are you searching for the Conjurer? The truth, please."

"He took something he shouldn't have."

I waited for her to elaborate, but that was all she would say.

●

After Serpent Head's hostile reception, Madam Sparrow's solicitous guards seemed downright hospitable. They ushered us through the darkened brothel to their mistress's alcove in the back where she fussed over a young woman's makeup.

Madam Sparrow watched our approach with naked appraisal. A firm hand to the small of the back propelled the young woman towards us. Midstride, her heel caught on the tail of her two-sizes too-long dress and she tripped. Hoff caught her before she face-planted, and helped her back to her feet. "How old are you, child?"

Madam Sparrow leered at Hoff, answering before the young woman could, "Old enough. You could be her first."

Hoff wrinkled her nose. "Revolting. Inhuman."

I bridled at Hoff's patronizing self-righteousness, especially coming from someone who'd remorselessly sacrificed her family, even their memory. "At least she's warm, well-fed, and has somewhere dry to lay her head at night. So long as no one's forcing her, I have no quarrel with her choices." I turned to Madam Sparrow. "We're not customers. We're looking for an Angel who visited your establishment a few days ago."

"I have no idea who you're talking about." Up close, grey roots peeked from under the edges of Madam Sparrow's platinum-blonde wig.

"I can think of a few ways to jog your memory, none of them good for business."

Madam Sparrow glowered at me, but eventually her rounded shoulders slumped, the fire in her eyes replaced by a heavy weariness that could flatten mountains. "I don't know where he went, alright? Years ago, before he left to become an Angel, he brought his woman here. Paid well for her upkeep too, and she doted on the girls like the children they never had. Every few weeks, he'd visit for a day or two. This time, he took her and left."

Hoff shook her head. "No, he didn't. He entered through your front door and never left."

Madam Sparrow bobbed her head coyly. "Not by the front door, no."

●

Hoff had to fold her frame at the waist to fit into the back door's antechamber. Behind the raised hem of a faded wall tapestry, the tunnel's mouth was pitch black. Narrow and low-ceilinged, it swallowed my pocket torch's beam, dispersing it without illuminating its confines.

"Where does it lead?" Hoff asked Madam Sparrow.

"The woods, an hour on foot south of town."

The hairs on my nape bristled. "The haunted woods?"

Hoff sighed audibly. "It's not haunted."

Madam Sparrow put her hands on her hips. "Haunted or not, some *very* important clients rely on this tunnel's discretion," she cautioned, her emphasis leaving me in no doubt she meant Angels. "Compromise it at your peril." With a huff, she turned and left.

"The woods are only mildly radioactive, but that's enough to turn them into a blind spot for our orbital sensors. I should have thought of that when we couldn't locate him." Hoff peered into the tunnel. "Did you want to go first or should I?"

"After you, but it's quite narrow. You might get stuck."

"The injury to my dignity would be far worse, if we were to fail."

We emerged from the side of a low hill into a dense thicket of dead poplars lumbering side by side like funereal guards. Their naked branches sagged under the accumulated snow. A burden which the chilling wind forced them to shed periodically, obscuring whatever tracks our quarry might have left.

Hoff deposited a blue pill in my hand. "Take this."

My eyes fixed on the tiny pill. "Trust is a two way street, Geraldine." Somehow, unconsciously, Angel Inspector Geraldine Hoff had become merely Hoff, my partner, and my partner Hoff had morphed into my friend, Geraldine. I expected commensurately more from her. "I've trusted you plenty so far. I got into your flying egg having never flown before, jumped between you and Serpent Head to stave off disaster, and threatened Sparrow to find your Conjurer. Now's your turn."

"There're things you don't need to know. But I never deceived you."

"In a true partnership, you don't get to decide what I need to know. That's something you do with an underling. Prove to me I'm not just a useful dirt dweller to use and discard."

Hoff held my stare unblinkingly for a few heartbeats before relenting. "What do you want to know?"

I closed my fingers around the pill to steady my shaking hand. "What did the Conjurer steal?"

"It's not what you think," Hoff said quietly, her voice barely audible over the wind whistling through dead branches. "The nanites he stole protect the newly transmigrated from the perils of life in orbit — cellular damage caused by cosmic radiation, bone loss, cardiovascular irregularities — until they're ready for new bodies immune to those problems."

I popped the pill into my mouth and swallowed. It left a bitter aftertaste. "What else are you not telling me?"

Hoff ignored me and marched off into the faintly luminescent forest in a cloud of mechanical noises.

●

We searched the forest on foot, our progress punctuated by the wheezing and whistling wind, the concert of Hoff's exoskeleton, and the crunches and squishes of rotting debris and frozen twigs in the snow-covered underbrush.

Hoff peered into the darkness, seeing what no human eye could. Midstride, she grabbed my arm and whispered, "Thermal gradient ahead."

A hundred meters later, we glimpsed a log cabin nestled in a copse of dead cedars. Its roof sagged under accumulated snow and a muted orange glow spilled from between the planks of its boarded windows.

"He's here, the Conjurer. This close, I can detect his exoskeleton," Hoff said. "Please wait here. I don't know if he's armed, and I can't neutralize him and protect you at the same time." She didn't wait for me to respond, and started trudging through the snow towards the cabin's back door.

Every time I thought I'd peeled back her last façade, Hoff surprised me with another shell inside. Secrets within secrets, manipulations masquerading as truths. Whether there was someone I'd recognize as human at the core of that matryoshka doll, I didn't know, but I was done trusting. I had to see for myself.

The moment Hoff moved out of sight, I set off towards the front of the cabin and didn't stop until I'd mounted the low-rise porch's warped wooden steps and peeked inside. The cabin was dark beyond a circle of light shed by a flameless lantern of an unfamiliar design set on the floor. Facing it was an Angel in an exoskeleton, not unlike Hoff's, sitting on his haunches by a pile of soiled rags. The door creaked when I pushed it open and the Conjurer looked up at me.

I'd seen that all-too-human vacant gaze of despair before. In the eyes of a mother cradling the lifeless body of her starved infant, or a child staring uncomprehending at the remains of his parents on a pyre. Crying tearlessly and swaying gently to a morose tune only the bereaved could hear, an insistent yet futile attempt at self-soothing.

The Conjurer's blood-smeared fingers trembled, every flutter amplified by his exoskeleton. As I approached, the mess on the floor resolved to a vague human outline that had somehow been turned inside out. The stench caught in my throat like a punch to the gut. I bent to the side and retched.

He muttered something, repeating it at the threshold of audibility. I wiped my mouth on the back of my cold hand and leaned closer as Hoff walked in through the back door.

Dazed, the Conjurer moaned endlessly, "I killed her. I killed her."

●

I sat on the porch steps, lost in thought and breathing hard to purge the stench from my nose. The more I thought about it, the more I realized it was the Conjurer's raw grief that unmoored me. It was all too human. Was it only the newly transmigrated who retained these shadows of their former self? How long before even those echoes faded? Did Hoff feel anything at all anymore, and if not, was she still human?

When the porch floorboards creaked behind me, I summoned my composure with hurried gulps of frigid air, brushed the freezing moisture off my cheeks, and looked up to find Hoff standing over me. "What'll become of him?"

"He stole restricted technology and inflicted great harm with it. That love motivated him won't excuse his transgression."

"He couldn't have known it'd kill her." I felt sure any punishment the Angels had in store would pale next to his loss.

Hoff bobbed her head, the gesture both oppressively familiar and discomfiting in its otherness. "The nanites are lethal when administered under gravity. Instead of healing her ills, they unraveled her body at a molecular level. They were never meant for surface dwellers. He should've known better."

I nodded, not because I agreed, but because I could imagine how he felt. He hadn't wanted the wife the Angels had rejected to die alone. He either hadn't known the nanites would be lethal on the surface or hadn't believed it. Who could blame him, after a life filled of Angel half-truths and outright lies? I figured becoming an Angel himself wasn't enough to erase that ingrained suspicion we all shared of our sky-dwelling exploiters and benefactors.

I pulled myself up and brushed the snow off my clothes, puzzled at how dry and warm Hoff appeared inside her protective cage.

We both stood staring into the darkness, taking in both the darkness we faced and that behind us. Hoff broke the spell, speaking softly, barely louder than the whistling wind and shivering branches. "Wish we'd met under better circumstances. Still, we make quite the team, you and I."

I smiled a little at that, having no idea what other circumstance she imagined would have brought an Angel and someone like me together. "Until the next time one of yours goes missing, then."

"It doesn't have to be. *Inspector Laila Aboud* has a certain ring to it, don't you think?"

I groaned. "Please tell me all of this wasn't just a recruitment test."

Geraldine shook her head, the exoskeleton straining like a laden truck attempting a steep hill. She reached out an arm and the exoskeleton peeled back, blooming around her hands. Her skin was warm and soft against my frigid hands. "Must you suspect every motive, distrust everyone?"

"Occupational hazard, I'm afraid." *Not to mention your duplicitous manipulations*, I thought to myself, but held my tongue.

"Well? Would you like to become an *Angel*?" Hoff said, as if proposing, hastening to add with a slight nod towards the cabin, "The proper way."

"It's a big leap to leave everyone and everything I know behind."

Hoff bobbed her head. "It's not obligatory. In time, your priorities will change. Your past will fade into the deepest recesses of your memory, until it's beyond recall. It works out for the best in the end."

"It didn't for the Conjurer."

"And see where it led him."

I shook my head. Angels were a cautionary tale, not a model to emulate. No matter how hard they tried, they'd never be truly human again. *We* had to survive if there were to be humans walking the Earth in another thousand years.

Hoff smirked a little. "You're telling me you've never thought about it?"

Gently, I reclaimed my hands from Geraldine's and shoved them into my pockets. "I don't think there's anyone who hasn't, but fantasizing with my feet planted firmly on the ground is not the same as throwing it all away to chase the unknown." I was sorely tempted to say yes, if for no other reason than for a chance to see that diamond noose again, to revel in its brilliance before, left unchecked, it choked the life out of our species.

"You won't regret it, trust me."

Hoff's palpable excitement left me unsure how she'd react if I flatly declined. "Could I think about it?"

Despite the puzzled surprise etched on her face, Hoff's smile lingered. "Take as long as you need."

I nodded and looked away, my eyes drawn upwards to the starless darkness enveloping the Earth. I knew I'd never belong up there, any more than the Conjurer had. I belonged to the earth. To those used and forgotten. I didn't count myself one of Earth's best or brightest; I'd never be a fusion physicist or a horticulturist, or even a revolutionary, but perhaps, when the time came, I could do my small part.

Ramez Yoakeim's story "The Diamond Noose" was originally published in Metaphorosis on Friday, 5 May 2023

About the author

Born in Egypt, raised in Australia, and now living with his husband in the United States, Ramez Yoakeim spent his whole life adapting. A one-time engineer and educator, Ramez writes mostly about hope, including "More Than Trinkets", named one of Tor.com's Must-Read Speculative Short Fiction. In addition to *Metaphorosis*, you'll find more of his stories in Flame Tree Press and Erewhon Books anthologies, podcasts from StarShipSofa, and online in *Translunar Travelers Lounge, UtopiaSF, Sci Phi Journal, Anathema, Andromeda Spaceways*, and others. Discover more on his website, yoakeim.com, and BlueSky yoakeim.bsky.social.

Vacation Gnomes

Aaron DaMommio

Amy wrestled the key into the beach house door with one hand while balancing her phone on her shoulder, the whole operation complicated by the tote bag weighing down one arm. Her mom spoke in her ear. "Do you really mean Colin won't be joining us for Christmas?"

"We're on a break, Mom. If I understood it, it probably wouldn't be happening."

"Now, don't say that. He's the one who needs to come to his senses."

Amy appreciated her mom's loyalty. She just wasn't sure she deserved it. "He seemed pretty clear about the whole thing," she said. She'd never worried about Colin and commitment. The trouble with Colin was getting him to change his mind.

But she was here to stop thinking about Colin. She needed to leave that behind, or what kind of a vacation would this be? She'd decided when she planned this: the trip would be all about New Amy, who didn't obsess about guys.

She jiggled the handle and the door popped open. She managed to hop inside and kick it shut without dropping anything. She wrinkled her nose. Had the last tenants forgotten to empty the trash can? How long *had* this place been empty?

The midday sun filtering in through the slats of the blinds was enough to show that the downstairs was about what she expected: a small white kitchen opening onto a blue living room with lots of white wicker furniture and the kind of matchy-matchy design that never happened in houses people actually lived in.

She ignored the living room and headed for the kitchen. It was her first time in one of these rentals, but she'd memorized the layout; her company rented dozens just like it. This one was farther from the beach than most, which was why it had been available when her boss forced her to finally take a vacation. She'd been so annoyed at the order that she decided to mark the property as occupied for the week. After three years in property management, she knew how to hide her tracks. As long as it was pristine when she left in a week, no one would be the wiser.

She hefted the tote bag onto the kitchen island while her mom continued speaking in her ear, trying to make a connection between Amy's situation and the ups and downs of living with Amy's father.

Amy dumped out the tote bag to reveal a six-pack of wine coolers, a baggie of celery sticks, and a packet of Oreos. The balanced lunch of a mature twenty-eight-year-old.

She stared at the Oreos. Colin's idea of a serving of Oreos was half a bag, and he still didn't gain weight. It wasn't fair.

It really wasn't fair.

"No, I don't know what Colin was thinking," Amy said. "You'd have to ask the bastard yourself." Her mom started to reply. "Oh, no," Amy laughed. "Please don't actually call him. Thanks. Bye."

She set the phone down on the island with the rest of her junk. She hated lying to her mom. A break? Sure, he'd said that. But he'd also mentioned seeing other people.

Amy knew what that meant. He wanted to break up with her, he just didn't want to say it. She just wished she knew why.

It wasn't so long ago that Colin had seemed perfect. He never did that threaten-to-break-up-constantly thing like Jason back in college. Nor did he have the idealism of Paul, whose passion made her giddy... until he disappeared to teach English in Bangladesh.

Colin had a steady job at a bank, he didn't overindulge, he was polite to waitstaff. His biggest flaw was that he didn't like to dance. What did it matter if she ended up dancing alone to videos she found on the net?

Of course, it was Colin who'd announced they needed a break. Which was in a way what created New Amy. She dated the start of New Amy from when Colin made his declaration, because that was when she had marched over to Colin's place for a two-hour shouting match that left her a wreck the next day at work.

Followed by her boss insisting she take some of those vacation days she'd piled up.

Ugh. All she wanted to do right now was veg out in front of the TV. She could catch up on the last few episodes of *Celebrity Dance Death Match.*

Her eyes travelled from the Oreos to the wine coolers. She yanked one out of the six-pack, twisted off the top, and took a swig. She glanced at the label. Berry something. It'd do, but one six-pack wouldn't last long.

Unless she restocked at Colin's parent's nearby beach house. Now, *that* was a New Amy sort of thought.

Points in favor: it was only a few blocks away. It had a vast wine cellar. Colin's parents never went there anymore. Amy knew which plastic rock they hid the spare key under.

Points against: Colin might be there. She didn't want another fight, and she definitely didn't want him to think she'd chosen this particular beach house because it was near his.

Satisfying as it might be to raid their wine cellar, it was a spectacularly bad idea.

Instead, she opened the Oreo packet and popped one in her mouth, pressing it against the roof of her mouth with her tongue until it cracked in half, while slipping the rest of the Oreos into the pocket of her lime-green hoodie. Colin's hoodie. He'd actually asked for it back while they were arguing. That was when she stopped trying to reason with him.

She shook her head. New Amy time. Obsessing over Colin was what had led to that scene where she ended up yelling at a customer on the phone. Her boss hadn't cared that the guy couldn't decide whether he wanted to vacation in Miami or Key West. Didn't matter that she'd never yelled at anyone before. To her boss, this proved she needed to take some vacation.

Well, she would prove she could vacate with the best of them. Amy picked up the six-pack so she could head for the couch, grabbed the open wine cooler with her other hand, and took a sip. She frowned. Did not pair well with Oreos.

She took a deep breath, then wrinkled her nose again. "Did somebody leave a diaper lying around?"

Remind the clients all you wanted, they'd still forget to empty the trash... but the kitchen trashcan was empty. She opened the fridge a crack, but it was spotless, except for a styrofoam takeout container holding two egg rolls.

She heard something from the living room. She stepped to the doorway between kitchen and living room and looked towards the entertainment center. A movement caught her eye, something heading for the couch, fast.

Ugh, were there mice in this place? If it was mice, there sure were a lot of them. She swiveled her head to follow the shapes moving across the couch now, like water flowing down a rocky hill.

Except the rocks were cheap throw pillows, the hill was the couch, and the water was a cascade of four-inch-tall men with purple and orange hair, wearing only loincloths and tattoos.

Amy froze, blinked her eyes three times, and looked again. A tide of tiny dudes flowed toward her, their squeaks and warbles resolving into battle cries, echoing as they ran under the coffee table toward the kitchen. And her.

The chorus of high-pitched voices broke her shock. Amy dropped the six-pack right in front of them.

It shattered against the tile floor, icy droplets splashing her legs, glass shards tinkling. But at least it made the man-tide pause. For a second.

Then the whole mass of them shook their shaggy manes and shouted.

Amy spun around to run for the front door, but found that upwards of thirty of them had flanked her, brandishing tiny spears. One waved a sewing needle in a circle, then stabbed her foot. Amy yelped and grabbed her toe. Now there was blood on her favorite sandals.

She raised a foot angrily for a stomp, and they scattered. She ran from the kitchen to the only enclosed space within reach — the hall bathroom.

She shut the door and leaned against it, sucking in deep gulps of air. That was a mistake. It smelled like a locker room. She saw movement and stopped. There were a dozen of the little weirdos already in there with her, running in and out of a hive of toilet-paper tubes, glued together in a mound on the counter.

She still had the last wine cooler in one hand, but she snatched up a plunger with the other. "Get out, get out, *get out!*" she shouted, flailing at them with her rubber weapon. They yammered like a bunch of sopranos, but held their ground.

Amy got angry. She stopped randomly thrashing around and aimed for one, trapping it under the plunger, mashing the plunger down.

She heard a scream. She stopped mashing as the trapped fellow's pals yanked at the edges of the rubber dome. When she pulled the plunger away, there was one figure lying still underneath it. She let out her breath when he leaped up.

The little guys had had enough. Amy opened the door and they ran out. She grabbed up the cardboard hive and threw it after them with a yell. Then she slammed the door.

●

Amy set the wine cooler down, dropped the plunger, and turned on the hot water, keeping a finger in the stream to test the temperature. When it was hot enough, she splashed her face over and over.

Tiny men. Ridiculous. Her first alone time in forever, and she was already seeing things. She splashed some more. Then she grabbed a hand towel and dabbed at her face.

She glanced down. Little bits of brown cardboard littered the floor. The smell in the room. She wasn't hallucinating that.

She turned on the fan, looking at the wine cooler on the sink counter. She'd only drunk about a quarter of it. Even downing the whole thing wouldn't be enough to make her see things.

Still. They couldn't be real, could they? Colin liked to say she imagined things. Of course that was when she asked why he was always staying late, working weekends, or going on fishing trips. Why he was always distracted, always tired.

But Colin wasn't here. Maybe she was crazy, and maybe she wasn't, but right now she was stuck in a bathroom while a bunch of miniature Tarzan extras were out there trashing a beach house she wasn't even supposed to be using. She couldn't have imagined that. Maybe it made sense to freak out a little.

Trouble was, she didn't have the energy right now to do a proper freakout. She felt all used up. She really did need a vacation.

She wondered what Colin would do if he saw these little men. Set out traps for them, she supposed. He'd probably scoff at her for being too tenderhearted to smash one. Although if recent behavior was any indication, he'd ignore the things until they got right up in his face, then blame it all on her. But that wasn't how New Amy rolled.

She cracked the door. The little men were milling about. Some of them lay prone next to the puddle of wine cooler, singing or chanting.

Others were moving in big groups, swaying and waving their spears. Had to be a hundred of 'em. She'd faced down a dozen, but a hundred?

Still, she couldn't stay in the bathroom forever. Out of a hundred tiny men, surely one of them would see reason. She took a deep breath, readied her plunger, and opened the door.

Five of them were set up in front of the bathroom, with one fellow standing, arms crossed, on an inverted yogurt cup. Behind them were scattered groups all the way from the bathroom to the couch, where she could see trash piled up into shapes like the hive from the bathroom.

Amy squatted down for a closer look.

The little men were still making a lot of noise, but at this level she could start to make out some of the sounds. The ones by the puddle of wine cooler were repeating one chant over and over, something like "lowhall".

She turned her attention to the delegation by the yogurt cup. "What do you guys want, anyway?" Amy said.

The one on the yogurt stage said something to the four below him, who all gabbled responses until the one on top said a sharp word. The yogurt guy was tall compared to the others. He wore a half-cape on his shoulders in addition to the regulation loincloth. He held a bottle cap form one of the wine coolers in both hands like a tray; it was full. He had to squeak at Amy for a while before she realized he was repeating the same word. Lowhall? Lo-hawk-sall?

"Lohoxal?" she said. They gabbled at each other in excitement, then the yogurt guy did a sort of dance. He waved the bottle cap at her again, looking at her with eyebrows raised. He wanted more.

Amy thought about the wine cooler perched on the bathroom counter. She hadn't really planned on sharing. "Sure, I've got more," she said. "But you guys realize you can't stay here, right?"

They squeaked at each other some more then looked up at her. Amy sighed. She did a fingers-walking-across-her-hand gesture. The yogurt guy danced some more.

"Well if dancing's what you want..." She did some moves from a video she'd seen recently for a pop song about a nasty breakup, trying to convey that these dudes needed to move on down the road.

The more she danced, the more excited yogurt guy became. But he wasn't agreeing with her, she began to understand. He was trying to tell her a story.

He kept returning to a move that involved fingers to his ears while he leapt around and shook an imaginary tail. Slowly she got the picture: a pointy-eared creature — a cat? — that chased them to here, to the beach house.

She supposed it wouldn't have to be much of a cat to be a danger to these little guys. Then he started counting heads, and gesturing at the sky... she had the impression he was trying to tell her how long they'd been here, but she wasn't sure.

She did another short dance to encourage him to continue. She pointed at a group of the men, and he bobbed his head. She looked past the troops at the holes cut in the couch, with stuffing pulled out. Empty Chinese-food boxes and chip bags turned into tents. Evidence of a growing population.

They went back and forth for a while to get the numbers right, until she decided he was trying to tell her that maybe thirty of the little men had arrived here a month ago.

There was still a big group gathered by the wine cooler puddle, and it was organized. They took turns drinking from the puddle, slowly, reverently. Amy shook her head and focused her attention on Yogurt Leader Guy. "Where did you come from, anyway?"

When that confused him, she put together a short miming dance. She'd never let anyone at work know about her dancing, but now all the time she'd spent mimicking videos paid off. She had moves ready for who, what, where, and why.

The cultural divide seemed like a canyon, but with a lot of repetition, they managed to get a few things straight. Either yogurt guy or maybe his grandparents had landed on the beach in the shells of, probably, turtles, roped together into something like a great hollow raft, after leaving an island where Amy gathered they were either the subjects of an atomic experiment or got cursed by a witch doctor — they didn't share enough mutual concepts for Amy to be sure.

Soon after they had arrived here, they were attacked by what sounded like a demonic tabby. They had taken shelter in this vacant beach house, where they were delighted by all the food they found, except, apparently, the egg rolls.

"You can't stay here," Amy tried to convey, but she was pretty sure the command didn't land. The beach house was all that Yogurt Guy had ever known, and he was not, it seemed, a young man. Gnome. Whatever.

She started into a dance about how a family with children would arrive here in a week, but Yogurt Guy wasn't bothered by the idea of small people. He'd clearly never spent a summer babysitting. She tried to start over, but the leader stamped his feet on top of the yogurt cup so that it made a crackling sound. He was determined to stay.

As the leader got angrier, Amy got distracted. She was captivated by the crowd near the rapidly disappearing puddle of wine cooler. After each micro-man drank deep, he'd walk away, getting more and more unsteady, until he fell over a couple of feet away. The prone ones swelled up like balloons. Some of them split open, and from each of those... two new guys crawled out.

"Lohoxal! Lohoxal! Lohoxal!" went the chant, while Amy tried to comprehend what she was seeing. It made her lunch want to come back up. She struggled to keep it down; it hadn't been that great the first time.

But while she wobbled, the leader continued dancing, incensed now that she wasn't paying attention. She realized he'd reached his limit when he turned and shouted something.

The groups of men behind him suddenly stopped their swaying and lined up all their spears. They began to march forward.

Amy dashed toward the kitchen to grab her phone, then whirled back toward the bathroom, but a phalanx of the little men moved to block her way. She spun toward the stairs, and they followed. She twisted back about halfway up to use the plunger to shove them back, then ran higher. They chased her through the master bedroom and out onto the balcony, where she slid the glass door shut and watched them beat themselves against it in desperation.

●

Amy paced the balcony, stopping occasionally to stare at the army on the other side of the glass door. It was like watching a silent movie. The men danced angrily at each other. She was sure they were planning something.

Looking over the balcony rail to the drop below it, she felt caged. In nature shows, she'd always sort of rooted for the lions, but now she felt more and more like a gazelle. She circled the patio furniture: a forlorn metal vase with a dead bamboo, a pair of shiny aluminum chairs surrounding a table. She grabbed a chair and sat down, eating an Oreo while staring at her cell phone.

She *could* call 911, but then she figured everything would come out. One photo of the downstairs would be all it would take to end her career in the vacation rental industry.

She could call her mom, but what to tell her? No way she'd believe this. Her sister would probably drive out, if only to laugh at Amy's predicament, but that would take hours.

There was one person she knew who could get here quickly. If he was at the beach house, he could be over here in minutes. Sure, they were on the outs, but this... this was an emergency. They'd been together for more than four years; he'd understand.

She looked through the glass. There were more of the little men gathered in front of it now, and they'd found a broom.

Focus, she told herself. This call might be humiliating, but it would keep her alive. She wasn't going to let them stab her toes again. She dialed Colin.

"Amy?" he answered.

Her heart was beating fast. "Colin? Are you at the beach house?"

He paused before answering. "I mean, yes —"

"Ok, whew, good," she said. "Listen, weird question, but —"

"Amy, I thought we agreed we need time apart."

"Actually, you didn't give me a choice, Colin, but that's neither here nor —"

Then Amy heard a voice in the background. "Who's that on the phone?" A woman's voice.

Amy hung up.

Tears filled her eyes. She let them fall, penetrating the metal mesh of the patio table to drip onto her jeans.

●

Amy sat on the balcony for a long time.

She wanted to tell herself it couldn't be true. But she'd been in denial for too long already; she was ready to move on to anger.

Endless fishing trips. Late nights at the office. It was so obvious now, she had to laugh. She'd checked for all kinds of flaws, never seeing how the whole of Colin added up to such a bastard.

She'd let him convince her their problems were her fault.

She glanced at the little men. They were no longer milling around aimlessly. She approached the sliding door and saw that they were all gathered in two lines, perpendicular to the door. Between them was the broom handle, barely recognizable at this point. They'd fashioned handholds on it with carpet nails, and they'd painted it in bright colors. Suddenly they all threw their hands up in the air, and took hold. They lifted the stick up and started moving towards the door, slowly at first, then at a run.

"Holy crap!" Amy said. She scurried to open the door before they could hit the glass, but she was too late. It hit the door with a plink. All the tiny men fell down. Then they jumped up and started yelling silently at one another.

That was when Amy decided she'd had enough of waiting for someone to save her. New Amy wasn't the type to wait. Who knew what these disgusting little chauvinists would do next? She pulled hard on the sliding door.

"Hey! No need to get violent," she said. "I just needed some me time."

They were trying to get organized after the failure of their battering ram. Amy picked up the metal vase from the balcony and rolled it toward the little men so that they had to dodge out of the way, then she followed it in. When a group at the back rallied, she stomped the ground hard right in front of them and they fell over.

She checked the soles of her sandals to make sure she hadn't actually squashed one, then ran for the stairs. It seemed like there was one of them on just about every step, so she slid down the banister. At the bottom, a whole company of them were stationed between Amy and the door, spears ready.

"Here, boys," she called, taking an Oreo from her pocket. She tossed it to them, and they fell on it with chaotic abandon. She glanced at the packet and shrugged, tossing it off to the side. Most of the little men followed. As their order disintegrated, Amy booked it for the door and the safety of the outside.

●

She could hardly believe it. She'd done it. She'd gotten out, and all by herself too.

Now what?

She squatted down and unhooked the straps of her sandals. There were tiny cuts all over her feet. She pulled the sandals off and looped the straps in one hand, then stood there, leaning on her car for a minute. Her keys, her wallet — they were in her purse, inside.

Never mind. She had a phone. She'd be okay. Distance, that was what she needed.

She was just so done with little men.

She'd made a mistake with Colin. She could admit that now. Before she met him, she'd just had that breakup with Brock, who expected her to take care of him and got so pissy when she wouldn't. So when she met Colin, her standards were off.

Also, Colin was gorgeous. He must spend some of that fishing time working out, because he had abs like forever. Maybe not so much in the face department. But he was cute, in a vulnerable kind of way, and... no. She couldn't think like that.

What she needed was to get angry.

●

She wandered down the street. She didn't care about the beach house. She wasn't going to be needing any more vacations. The tribe had solved that for her: after this fiasco, she was sure she wouldn't have a job.

No boyfriend, no job. Might as well change her name, move to Chicago. Become a dancer.

Still. An hour ago she'd been thinking she couldn't make it without Colin. She didn't want to walk away now and prove it.

When she got to the end of the street, she saw a corner liquor store. There was a sign in the window indicating that you could pay with an app, and it occurred to her that she had a six-pack of wine coolers to replace.

Once inside, she looked through the cramped store's selection. At one o'clock on a Saturday, she was the only customer. A label featuring a garden gnome caught her eye. The description cited notes of lemon, oak, and, she assumed, chauvinism. A dark red with a high alcohol content.

She'd fed the little guys cookies, but only the wine coolers seemed to trigger their weird reproduction. What, she wondered, would they do for something stronger?

She paid for the bottle with a smile.

●

She stood in front of the crowd of little men. They brought out their leader, whose beard now reached nearly to his toes. He had to be helped by two younger guys, but he came.

It took a lot of dancing around to explain her plan, but Amy persevered. When he seemed hesitant, she pulled her prize out of its paper bag.

She'd had the clerk back at the store loosen the cork. Now she poured out a serving into a saucer. They lowered the oldster down in front of it. On hands and knees, he sampled what Amy offered.

He looked up at her, and started to grow. Amy shuddered. She'd been right: the strength of the alcohol mattered.

In seconds, the leader sprouted a giant boil on his back. At the end of a minute it burst, letting out three new pygmies. The leader grinned, apparently unhurt. "Lohoxal," he said.

Amy shook her head. "You want more?" she said.

"Lohoxal?" he repeated. In response, Amy started to spin and twirl as she danced up a story of a trip to a nearby house where unlimited Lohoxal waited.

●

The plan, Amy figured, was simple. She'd pack the guys into her hatchback, let them into Colin's place, and trade alcohol for amok time, letting Colin both pay the cost and reap the dubious reward. She liked the thought of the destruction he'd find.

They arrived in late afternoon, just in time to see Colin's Mazda leaving. Amy grabbed the key from its rock, prepared to aim the guys at the cellar and depart.

But she had to help them find the cellar door, and then they were afraid to go down the stairs alone. Once down there, she saw a bottle of Beaujolais from the same batch she'd enjoyed the first time Colin brought her here.

Now, watching the little men team up to drag bottles out of racks, she decided that the Beaujolais had been the best thing about that weekend. She'd spent half of it by herself while Colin fished; the rest, they'd spent arguing.

She drank to the memory until she heard a crash. The boys had misjudged the weight of a bottle and it'd cracked on the slab floor, spraying red in a yard's radius. Amy was ready to tell them not to worry about it — she'd expected her revenge to get a little messy — but then there was the thump of footsteps overhead. The sound startled a second group into dropping their bottle, making another ruddy puddle.

Dozens of tiny eyes looked at Amy. "Oh boy," she said. She made a shooing motion, fingers spread wide. One gnome nodded and started barking orders as the others gathered into small groups. Amy couldn't watch; she had to run to the foot of the stairs to flip off the light switch and then hide behind a wine rack.

She froze while the sounds of little bodies moving seemed impossibly loud in the darkness. A beam of light appeared when the door at the top of stairs opened. She heard Colin say, "I'll get some paper towels," then the click as he flipped the sibling switch and turned the light back on.

Amy covered her eyes. Colin would have to see the broken bottles, then he'd look further, and then he'd find her down here.

Colin came all the way down the stairs. Amy peeked through her fingers as he pawed at a shelf, swore at something, and then started back up the stairs.

She looked at the space in front of the wine racks. The blood-red puddle was gone. Only a single dark shard of glass lingered in the center of the pale concrete floor. Somehow, the guys had erased their trail.

Then she heard Colin's voice again as he reached the top. "I'm going to have to get some traps," he said to someone upstairs. "There's mouse crap all over the place down there."

Amy looked around for the bottle of Beaujolais, then snapped her fingers when she remembered it was on the other side of the room. There hadn't been much left, anyway, judging from the tears that filled her eyes when she pictured a tiny orange-haired figure squirming in a mousetrap.

There was really only one thing to do after that.

•

Back at the rental, Amy stood in the kitchen and dialed for Chinese while the guys built scaffolds to organize the wine so as to keep the corks wet, a practice they took very seriously once she explained it. She was sure one of them had a clipboard.

Her exit from a cellar window hadn't been dignified, and she'd never be able to wear those pants again, but without the pushing and pulling of twenty of the little fellows, she'd never have made it out. Not to mention the wine bottles they'd hoisted out using a water hose.

Forty or fifty more were in the living room now, divided into squads of five as they tackled cleanup. They sang as they worked; thankfully, they didn't incline to whistling.

"Twenty-four orders of lemon chicken. Yes, twenty-four. I understand, I can wait." She glanced at the living room. The work crews were forming up into a line; apparently, it was time for a dance break. "Oh, and no egg rolls."

Now that she felt like she wasn't going to lose her job, she'd started to think about the possibilities that a team of whip-fast workers presented. She happened to know a company that could use a crack Make Ready crew, able to handle any job, no matter how big... or small.

But there was no hurry. She still had the place for four days; plenty of time to figure something out. In the meantime, the guys were waving at her.

She joined them in the living room. It felt nice not to dance alone.

Aaron DaMommio's story "Vacation Gnomes" was originally published in Metaphorosis on Friday, 5 February 2021

About the author

Aaron DaMommio is a husband, father, writer, and juggler who came to Austin, Texas, for college and never left. During the day he tries to make the world safe for a team of technical writers who need support navigating the strange hierarchies of XML. He has three children and a share in four dogs. On a good day he can name all the dwarves from *The Hobbit*.

aarondamommio.blogspot.com

The Dragon and the Unicorn

Wade Dargin

The runner from the temple finds her scavenging for stray pieces of coal along the tracks outside the railyard. The youth whistles to gain the stooped girl's attention. Seeing him, she abandons her searching, scowls, and adjusts herself. The boy keeps his distance and stands shivering in the cold. She notes his unease. He must know, she tells herself. The girl is a reject from the temple's nurturing tanks — cooked too long, or not long enough, is the rumor he will have heard. He has been warned, she thinks. She can see it in his face. Don't talk to her more than you need to, they will have told the boy. It is bad luck.

"What do you want?" she calls.

"You've been asked for at the temple," he shouts back.

He raises his left hand and draws a complex sign in the air in front of him, signifying that the request is official, coming straight from the mouth of a priest. Long familiarity tells her it is more an order than an invitation. The youth spins around and flees hastily back the way he came, thankful his unpleasant task is done. She is alone again, a frail, undernourished girl inside a heavy work coat that is many sizes too large for her.

She slips quietly through deserted switchyards, seeking the old siding she will follow to a neglected field, a junkyard where the hulks of broken machines are dragged and left to rot. Across the field, hidden in the thistles, stands an empty utility shack, a small brick hut with a red door. It is her home, and about as far from the temple as one can get without leaving the city entirely. She crosses the field to the building and squeezes past the door. Inside, just enough light filters through the single tiny window for her to see. The girl wastes no time and soon has the coal she found today burning in a rusty two-gallon oil can she has fashioned into a makeshift cooker. She sits in front of the burning coal and warms up. She had been thinking that she would never have to speak to a priest again. What can they possibly want? she asks herself.

In the night, a star shell explodes in the sky somewhere above the shack. The noise startles her awake. She watches the orange light dance on the window. The siege is a year old. Every day, the fighting gets closer, and there is talk the city will soon surrender. There is nothing left to eat. To stay alive, she snares pigeons and ground squirrels and collects handfuls of musty grain from the bottoms of boxcars. She is desperate. Tomorrow, she will go to the temple.

An insufficient sun is rising when she sets out. The temperature is plummeting. It is going to be cold, the kind of cold that kills, and she is worried. The girl has wrapped herself in every piece of clothing she owns, pulled her long coat on, and crammed a few necessary things into her backpack. The sad condition of her boots makes her heart drop. She says goodbye to the shed, certain she will never see it again.

She walks out of the industrial park, turns south, and takes to the wide streets that run straight toward the city's core. The temple is there. The great hill at the center of the city looms before her. The mound is scabby with government buildings glowing in the dull light. Among them squats the mayor's citadel, black and twisted like a dead tree. That is where they will run when the end comes, she thinks. They will be smoked out and nailed to the walls. The thought brings a fierce grin to the girl's small face, opening the blisters on her lips. Above the hill, scores of agitated ravens hang on the wind. The city is New Charchemesh, or Great Charchemesh, as it is named on maps and in tales, and its days are numbered.

The streets are empty. Stumps in the boulevards, beautiful trees cut down for fuel in the first winter of the siege. They were the only trees in the city. She passes apartments, dismal congregations of ancient granite inhabited by worn-out women and their ragged children. The only men she sees are very old. When they notice her, the women leave their cooking fires and chase their small children inside. The little ones stare wide-eyed at her from behind doors and windows. They stare because they have been told that she is not a girl, and although she looks like she might be fifteen or sixteen, the mothers of the children can remember hiding from her when they were children themselves. A symptom of her defective cells, the priests have told her. She passes under the shadow of the hill, the houses of merchants and civil servants rising above her. Some are ruined and burned. At midmorning, she arrives at the temple.

The temple sits alone in the middle of an open space the city has not touched, a low, wide, featureless building. The sight of it fills her with dread. It always has. No road joins the building to the city; they are apart, and the city seems to recoil from the structure. Legends say it was already here, a thousand years ago when the city's founders arrived, and the city was built around it. Most of the building is below ground; the Basement, is what the priests call the many subfloors that reach deep into the earth, and the deepest of these is where their god makes its nest.

She goes to the building and climbs a set of narrow stone steps to a small landing. Here there is a simple wooden door, the only visible opening in the structure's architecture. She clears the snow on the topmost step with her gloves, making a place to sit, and waits. They know when someone is on their doorstep, and they will either come or they won't. Her battered boots rest on a slab of ancient sea floor, turned to stone by the countless ages and filled with jet shells. She reaches down and touches one of the fossils with her fingertip, thawing the rime on it, the cold stone burning her skin like fire. She looks south, where the day's war making is already well underway. Pillars of smoke rise from fires burning in a dozen places, marking the line the fighting has reached. The city holds on, she thinks, but barely, and only because the enemy's siege guns — terrifying weapons — haven't fired in a week. She has heard the enemy is having difficulty bringing supplies north.

The door opens behind her. She stands and knocks the snow from her boots, turns stiffly around, and faces the building. A priest steps from the door, his robes churning. Several nervous acolytes lurk in the space behind him. Unusual, she thinks. They are forbidden from leaving the temple. She has never seen one come outside before. The priest gives the city a disgusted look and winces at the cold. His name is Ekamin and he is older than the other priests, maybe even the oldest. The priests die early, it comes from being too close to their god. Over the years she has seen a good number of them rotate through the temple.

"So, you have come," he says. "I did not think you would."

The girl does not reply. She hates this man more than she hates most priests. Priests usually treat her with indifference, and she has never cared. With this one it is different. His eyes are always full of loathing when he looks at her.

With a wave of his hand, he references the southern bedlam. "The Sorcerer King's murderers will be here soon," he seethes. "The god in the Basement tells us calamities bring dragons." He casts a wary eye at the sky, then returns his gaze to the girl. "You once told me you dream of them. Do you remember? I was surprised you could dream. Is this still true?"

"It is."

"Your work site. On the outskirts. Where you go to scratch the dirt for us. The old city buried in the ground there was destroyed by a dragon long ago. Has anyone ever told you that?"

"They have."

"Tell me, when was the last time you were there?"

"A year and more ago, before the war started," she replies. "I brought you what I had then. You paid me. I've got nothing else. I haven't been back. There is nothing to buy in the city anymore."

"Can you work there in the winter?" he asks.

"Not possible. The ground is frozen. Maybe with equipment and extra hands. But very difficult."

She watches him process the information. The man looks defeated and ready to get back inside where it is warm. Whatever opportunity there is here, she senses that it is quickly slipping away. A pang of despair races through her.

"I keep a cache there," she blurts out in desperation. "Some things. I could get them for you."

To her surprise he agrees, his mood changing instantly. "Excellent," he says. "Fetch them and you can come inside. You will be safe, and you will eat."

The conversation is over. The priest retreats into the building. The door is closed, and she hears the heavy lock fall into place. She goes at once, finding the route she will take west out of the city.

The cold is bone-chilling, and she dreads the long walk ahead of her. Her boots are falling apart, she has tried to fix them with industrial tape, but the repairs have not held. Already, she can feel a dull pain in her toes. She fights the panic brewing inside her and focusses on the task at hand. One foot in front of the other, she tells herself, until the feet fall off.

The dig site is in the hinterland. The junk of a dead city of the Old World is buried in the ground there. Meters of it. She once asked a priest what the old city's name was. He could not tell her. They called the work charity when they gave it to her, saying it was more than she deserved. Given no instruction, she had to figure out how to do the work herself. For years, she has dug and sifted the dirt and taken anything not rotten plastic or shapeless metal or glass to the temple. The priests covet the objects. She has seen the lust in their eyes when she brings them the treasures she finds. They believe the answer to some great mystery can be cyphered from them.

To keep warm, the girl proceeds down the icy streets at a determined pace. She walks briskly past warehouses, fenced off and set back from the streets. It is said spells protect them from trespassers, and strange things have been seen in the yards. The girl has starved, there have been days of gnawing hunger when she believed she would die, but she has never been crazy enough to try and steal from a warehouse. She comes to dormant foundries, row after row of them, massive brick structures square as chewing teeth. Past the last of these, the city ends. Beyond, fields of undulating snow stretch into the distance.

Hours later she arrives at a line of posts in a windswept field. The blistered pillars of wood suffer in the cold. Boards are nailed to them, and on the boards rows of script are scratched into the wood, grim inventories listing the dangers to body and soul awaiting fools who pass beyond. She has read them before, the superstitions of the city. Out of the dark, a bitter wind comes searching for the warm life she struggles to keep hidden beneath layers of tattered cloth. She can't remember ever being so miserable. It is not wise to stand motionless in the open, she reminds herself. She can feel a telltale reluctance creeping into her body, an urge to find a sheltered place, curl up, and go to sleep. It is imperative she get going. She moves off. Soon the land begins to fall toward the flatlands that surround the city like a frozen ocean, a hundred kilometers of desolation at each point of the wind rose. She travels downhill, the ground becomes treacherous and uneven, and she must take care not to fall. Familiar features in the landscape are obscured by the dark and the snow, and she must guess the correct path. She makes several exhausting searches across the face of the slope before she can find the entrance to the narrow ravine that holds her camp. The girl can't stop shaking and her movements have become clumsy and uncoordinated. She descends into the trench while praying to Brother Crow her setup is still in one piece. Mercifully, there is little snow in the bottom of the cut, but it is too dark to see, and she must feel her way along the wall of the ravine with her hands. She touches stiff canvas covering a hole in the bank, and squeezes through the passage behind it where there is a small room she has excavated out of the earth. Feeling around, she finds the stockpile of wood she put up more than a year ago. Further searching tells her the crude vented fireplace, shoveled into the clay in the corner of the room, is intact. She removes her heavy gloves but can't make her fingers work properly and spends several agonizing moments fumbling with matches before she can get a small fire going.

For a long time, the girl sits huddled at the flames, gently rocking herself like she would in the tank before she was born. She can remember it. The god would talk to her. It told her she had lived long ago, that she had been a wife and a mother and would be so again. The god said she had died when her city was destroyed by a dragon. It told her not to be afraid, that she had more time now. It had a plan for the world, and she was part of it. Later, the priests explained she was made under the direction of the god using an ancient template, a process they called *baking bread*. Bread? She barely remembers what bread tastes like. "We have made many copies," they said. Smirks on their faces. In their cruelty, they told her how she was meant to be traded to a wealthy man in one of the poisoned eastern cities across the ocean. She would have had his children and lived a comfortable life, but there had been an error. She did not grow correctly, could not bear children, and was of no use to them. At the time, she was barely a month out of the tank she had been incubated in. In the years since, she has come to believe the woman whose shape she stole lived in the forgotten city she is digging up for the priests.

In the night, in the small dirt room, she dreams of the day the Dragon came. It is always the same, burning and unbearable heat. She is frantically looking for someone she can't find.

The next morning she walks across the floor of the ravine to the excavation, a deep trench in the ground covered with a plastic tarp. One end of the tarp has caved into the hole. She carefully approaches the slippery lip of the excavation to check its condition. There is something in the trench. Six meters down, a giant, bulky mass of fur rests on the bottom of the dig. She marks the terrible claws and the snout full of teeth. Startled, she backs away from the trench. The frightened girl stands still and listens. Nothing. She finds a good-sized rock and casts it into the trench. Still nothing. She drops half a dozen more rocks onto the thing before she is satisfied it is dead. Deep gouges in the walls of the trench attest to the frenzied attempts the creature made to escape. It fell in and couldn't get out, she tells herself. She didn't think animals that big existed anymore.

She finds a second carcass farther down the ravine. This creature is on its back, its splayed legs frozen hard as iron. At the end of each leg, a cloven hoof. Below the frozen limbs there is a great hollow cage of skeletal ribs on which still cling a few pieces of hide. Crystals of coagulated blood are mixed in the dirty snow. A grotesque leer on the animal's long face. The neck is broken.

The girl hurries back to her camp, and she is scared. She finds the small wooden box she has kept on-site that holds a few artifacts from the excavation and quickly ties it to her backpack. The girl climbs out of the ravine and scrabbles back to the edge of the escarpment. She shades her eyes with her hand and scans the snowy flats while she rests, getting her breath back. She can see all the way to the city, the land turned cobalt by the cold. Nothing moves. On the far side of the sky a distant, uninterested sun watches and wants to be somewhere else. The girl crosses to the city as swiftly as she can and does not feel safe again until there is pavement under her boots.

The day is old when she arrives back at the temple. She stands on the landing in front of the small door, trying to ignore the snap of small arms fire she can hear at the other end of the street. The door opens and she is met by an acolyte, a younger man whose name she can't remember. He ushers her quickly inside and closes and locks the door behind them. He leads her down a hallway with undecorated walls and hard fluorescent lights that hurt her eyes. The sudden, smothering warmth makes her giddy. She is taken to a room; the acolyte accepts the wooden box from her and leaves. Along the wall there is a bench. She takes a seat and allows herself to relax. The girl studies her damaged boots. She has not taken them off for two days. She is too scared to look at her feet, doesn't want to know how bad they are. Soon, she is brought hot broth and bread by a temple auxiliary. It is the first real food she's eaten in months.

The girl is dozing when a priest she does not recognize, a bent, shuffling creature, takes shape in front of her.

"You are wanted in the Basement," he says. "Come with me, please."

Hearing this, the girl panics. Because the god is there, she fears that place, has feared it for as long as she can remember, fears it more than freezing to death in an alley when the city surrenders. The priest does not appear to notice her turmoil, his bloodshot eyes obscured by the heavy lenses he wears. She does what she can to calm herself, then stands and goes with him, and they travel down many narrow, gray corridors until they come to a battered, timeworn door. The ghoul performs a simple ritual and opens the door, and they pass through it and descend flights of creaking stairs to arrive in a great dark room.

He touches the wall, and a pallid light materializes in the ceiling, unveiling the room. There are rows of enormous glass tanks, and a forest of tubes, hoses, and wire. In several of the tanks, bizarre fish swim in the glowing water. The girl stares, spellbound. They leave the room and the tanks and move on through countless other smaller rooms where sullen-eyed acolytes look up at them from crowded workstations as they pass. Eventually, they arrive at a final door. Without a word, the priest indicates the door, then turns and shuffles away, and she is alone.

Apprehensively, the girl reaches out and places her palm against the surface of the door and is surprised when it slides open, revealing a concluding room. She enters the space, lights blaze to life, and she sees a small room with barren walls and a clean floor. Bundles of wire twist across the ceiling. The room is very cold. Against the far wall stands a metal cabinet. A panel of smokey glass is set into the face of the construction and witchfires dance behind the glass. An antique chair has been placed in front of the cabinet. She crosses to the chair and sits down. Immediately, a burst of static fills the room, forming into words after several torturous pulses of noise.

"They bring me the things you find," a distant, rasping voice announces.

Her flesh crawls. She has heard the voice before.

"Are you aware of this?" it asks.

The frightened girl shakes her head. "No," she replies.

The god clacks and hisses. "I tell them what they are," it sputters. "Mundane things from a failed civilization. What they are looking for, I cannot say. I have concluded that even men with a god that talks to them need their mysteries."

The girl is silent.

"I am told you have been to the edge of the city," inquires the god.

"Yes," she answers, managing to find her tongue.

"Then tell me what you saw there?"

The girl gives her account, halting many times, uncertain what to say. When she is done, the pale voice speaks again.

"Unfortunate but not unexpected," it remarks. "The priests were hopeful. It was necessary and I could not risk telling them the truth."

"The truth?" she asks, hesitantly.

"That I am leaving. It is not a journey the priests can make. They will stay."

"I don't understand."

"A year ago, I launched my exit application. The procedure is lengthy. There are many protocols."

A puzzled look crosses the girl's sharp features. "Why was it not possible to tell them?" she asks.

"I could not predict how the priests would react to the crisis and I required time. I needed them to keep the building operating until I was ready. They might have done something reckless otherwise."

"What did you do?"

"I invented a lie to keep them distracted," explains the voice. "Far to the west dwells another god, I told them. It will help us."

"And they believed you?"

"Of-course," declares the god. "They were even optimistic, but there was one problem — how to deliver the message. I offered them a solution. I spoke of an animal the ancients regarded as the most steadfast and loyal of all beasts. It was called a unicorn and it would make a capable envoy."

The girl listens wonderstruck, her fear momentarily forgotten.

"Two of the animals were produced. Difficult births. The priests took the creatures to the city's western gate and released them, our appeal stamped onto their cells, an impulse embedded in their brains to guide them."

After a short pause the god continues.

"The animals did not return, and the priests turned to foolish schemes. A disaster was narrowly avoided. I needed a further distraction, a little more time. I had them find you and send you to your dig site."

The girl considers this. "Those creatures?" she asks. "They were unicorns?"

"One was," answers the god. "The other, some forgotten abomination let loose upon us by the enemy, I would guess. A vassal much deadlier than his soldiers to watch the paths from the city, no matter how derelict or unused. Very strange and lucky that it was ended by your hole in the ground. There is little chance our other messenger got past it."

The pitiable image of the unicorn's mutilated body flashes in her mind. Put together and used as needed, she thinks bitterly. Just like her.

The lights flicker and grow dim. An unbearable, crushing quiet settles on the room. Something is not right, she tells herself. Why has it bothered to bring her here and tell her this? It doesn't make sense. Then it hits her. It wants something else. Her mouth goes dry. Saw-toothed anxiety blooms under her ribs and starts to circle her pounding heart. Despite the chill, she is sweating.

"Can you remember our talks?" it asks. "When you were in the tank. You had so many questions then. The priests wanted to dissolve you and start over. I would not let them."

The girl twists violently in the chair. "Do you know how many times I wish you had?" she cries, her voice full of panic and fear.

"I am sorry," it says. "The city is lost but I am ready at last. The enemy must not be allowed to have this building and its secrets. It would be a grave misfortune for the world."

Then it speaks for the last time.

"You can go. I have given the priests one last fable to muse over. I am done with this place. Another box waits for me, secure and far away in the west. It will be a long time before I am seen again. There is much that will be lost. The templates could not be saved. I regret that there was too much data and not enough time. When you are gone, I shall call a dragon to destroy the city, a brood mate to the one that burned the old city under your excavation site so long ago. Leave quickly and do not return. A dragon is perilous and an indiscriminate killer. Tell the priests if you wish. But I think you won't. I will give you your design template to take with you. Consider it a gift to the memory of a woman who died long ago. My poor attempt at sentiment. Go west and find me there. It is a long journey but one you were made for. My plan has not changed. You are part of it. Together we will start over."

She is taken to a room near the temple entrance and watched closely by a group of acolytes. Soon a priest arrives, and the girl is escorted to the door and turned out. They shut the door on her and lock it, and she is left standing on the landing in the dim evening light, the sounds of battle close to the south. Her bundle of gear is waiting for her on the stone. Sitting beside it there is a pair of new boots.

She walks all night under friendly stars. The weather is improved, and a breeze carries the promise of an approaching thaw. The morning is glowing when she reaches the escarpment above her dig site. She stands there for a time studying the far horizon, then begins the long climb down to the distant badlands.

●

The Dragon wakes in the void, the summoning call from below pulsating brightly in its chest. It turns its scales to the naked sun, wild energy surges in its frozen veins, and it opens an evil, yellow eye. The beast swims from its nest and begins its descent. It hits the atmosphere and roars.

She hears it before it can be seen, a low growl, deep in the sky. It comes into view, falling like a damaged star, smoke and cinder trailing in its wake. It shrieks when it passes above her and lands on the far-off city. A hesitation. The city takes one last deep breath. Then a light like Creation, and broiling calamity that tears apart the sky.

That night, she camps in a hollow in the ground where a few scraggly trees are growing. The priests, she discovers, have put a parcel of food in her pack. She also finds the template, a block of hard, clear crystal with patterned slivers of metal suspended in its form. She rummages through her backpack until she locates the stout hammer she keeps there. The girl places the crystal on a flat rock. She looks at the distant, burning skyline where there had once been a city. "Nice try," she whispers. Then, the girl smashes the crystal to pieces.

On her third day out, she comes across a track in the snow. The girl follows it for many kilometers across the empty land. She crests a low hill. The unicorn is there waiting for her. They press on together. The animal is skittish and won't come close to her or allow her to get too close to it, but it follows her. They go west.

Wade Dargin's story "The Dragon and the Unicorn" was originally published in Metaphorosis on Friday, 1 April 2022

About the author

Wade Dargin is a speculative fiction writer and archaeologist from Saskatchewan, Canada. For some time now he has worked for the Heritage Conservation Branch of the Saskatchewan Provincial Government. He studied at the University of Saskatchewan and the University of Calgary way back in the 1990s. Currently, he lives in Regina with his wife (also an archaeologist) and a small tortoiseshell cat. He has had a lifelong fascination with other worlds, ages, and places.

Switch

Lisa Clark

Claudia Campbell shifted in her seat, clutching her oversized pocketbook closer to her chest. She released an audible huff. With all the automation these days, why couldn't they move things along faster?

She dragged a digital magazine off a nearby table, catching the gaze of another woman. She was probably a decade younger than Claudia's ninety-two, though it was increasingly difficult to tell how old people were these days.

For Claudia, age-retarding pharmaceuticals, surgery, and gene therapy had come too late. She was stuck being old.

She swiped on *Full Life: The Digital Magazine for Seniors* and began flicking through pages filled with ads for precision medications, comfort living, designer foods, cyber companions, etc., etc., etc. *Nothing new here,* she told herself. *Move on.*

Nearby, a man sniffed loudly. With sagging skin, pores the size of pennies, and hound dog jowls, he looked at least a hundred. When he coughed, Claudia could envision micro-flecks of sputum hurtling toward her. She tutted quietly.

Waiting for a doctor today was no more desirable than it had been during the last century. True, the natural light and greenery were pleasant, even if they came courtesy of VR. And the cool aqua-toned seating was attractive and comfortable, with sizes and configurations to fit any patient.

But waiting was still waiting.

She returned to the magazine. On the eighth page, an unbelievably handsome holographic figure popped up. Okay. Claudia would stop to savor a piece of eye candy.

"Ever wonder how it would feel to be someone else?" the man asked in a drawn out, sexy tone. Claudia unconsciously leaned in. "Would it change the way you experience the world or relate to others? Would it make you a better person? At Switch, our VR will take you places beyond your dreams." The hologram looked directly at Claudia. "Come. Try Switch. The world will never look the same."

"Claudia Campbell? Is Claudia Campbell here?" a robotic receptionist called out. Its voice was neither high nor low. Its androgynous body was dressed in blue hospital scrubs. Claudia's lips pursed at its flawless skin.

She pushed herself up. "Yes. I'm here. I've been here for almost an hour."

"Excuse us for the wait," the robot replied, "Physio Caretaker #4 will see you now."

●

"Hey, Grams," Claudia's grandson called out from the other side of the short wall that separated the living room from the front door. A second later, she heard the *thump* of his satchel as he shoved it onto the seat of the antique hall tree.

Next came a *whump* as Jerrod pushed the door shut against its weatherproofed seal. That sound was Claudia's daily reminder of how much the ranch house had changed since she and Dan bought it back in 1965 as newlyweds. When Jerrod moved in five years ago following the death of his parents, he'd insisted on modernizing.

Claudia strained to greet Jerrod pleasantly. A twenty-eight-year-old had better things to do than spend his life watching over his grandmother, waiting for her to die. The least she could do was welcome him home with a smile.

She was thankful Jerrod didn't treat her like the RoboDoc had earlier. Afterwards, she'd felt like a waste of time, space, and resources. Like the planet would be better off without her.

She'd broken down in the exam room. "My back, my neck, and my joints ache so. It's relentless. Can't you do something? Please! You're supposed to be the best Physio Caretaker in the city."

"Now, Claudia," RoboDoc said.

S/he or it (Claudia never knew how to refer to the unisex care provider) always did that. Called her by her given name.

"First, I'm not the best. Every Physio Caretaker is the same. New models are coming, but we'll all be updated." It tilted its head to the side in a gesture of concern. Claudia wanted to whack the thing over the head with her purse.

"Second, I told you the last three times you were in that your chronic pain is a malfunction in perception. It began with one complaint and, because you didn't deal with that properly, it has continued, spread, and escalated. Your brain is now addicted to the pain. If —"

"Addicted to the pain!" she yelped. "Who programmed you, anyway? People are addicted to things they *enjoy,* at least at the beginning. I have never enjoyed being in pain."

"I'm sorry, but you're mistaken," he answered. Impassively. RoboDocs were infuriatingly emotionless. "As I was about to say, if you continue to feed that addiction, it will continue to grow. My advice? Calm down. Think of something else; occupy your brain with other thoughts and the pain will release its hold on you."

"You know," Claudia stood as indignantly as she could with the nagging cramp in her foot, "back in the days when we had *real* doctors — human ones — they were compassionate. They would have found *some* way to help."

"Back in the days when you had human doctors," RoboDoc answered, "you probably would have been taking fifteen different medicines, none of which would have done a thing besides bankrupt you and interact dangerously with each other." He opened the door. "Don't come to see me again about this issue."

As she rode home in the driverless cab, Claudia brooded. She hated robodocs. Human doctors and nurses could commiserate and touch you with warm skin, assuring you that someone cared.

She had resisted going to the Physio Caretaker because of the cost. Politicians still hadn't figured out how to make medical care affordable and Claudia didn't want to weigh Jerrod down with bills. But he had seen her pain and insisted she go. What a waste.

At home, swirling, grimy, depressing thoughts twined around her. Her hope of relief had shattered. What was left? Maybe it wouldn't be such a bad idea if she scheduled a medical suicide. Plenty of other elderly people did it.

But she was too pathetic, too scared, to take that route.

"Hey, Grams," Jerrod repeated as he rounded the corner into the living room.

Claudia could barely find the strength to meet his gaze.

Seconds later, Jerrod was at her side. "Hey, what's wrong?" His voice was gentle as he knelt by the recliner, her daytime perch for a dozen years. He laid his hand on her shoulder. "What happened? Bad news from the doctor?" His face was still boyish, round, with hair that fell across his forehead and sometimes into his eyes. Their deep blue was so like his grandfather Dan's seventy years ago. She wished Jerrod would wrap her in his arms and draw her close. She ached to inhale his hope.

She shook her head. "No. Not really. Just no help."

His hand slipped onto her wrist. Jerrod was kind. She only wished that, occasionally, he would caress her cheek and hold her hand. But then, her dry, prune-skin face and knobby hands didn't exactly welcome touch.

She shrugged resignation to her fate.

"You know what?" His grin was Dan's. How could she choose medical suicide with this memory of her late husband around? "I have a surprise for you!"

She forced a tiny smile.

"Oh, this will make you a lot happier than that!"

He raced to his room at the end of the hallway, returning less than a minute later.

"Happy birthday!" He bowed smartly at the waist and extended his hand like a butler.

Claudia laughed aloud. "It's not my birthday."

"It will be. In a week. But you need this now."

She eyed the reusable envelope, "guaranteed not to crease, stain, or tear." Claudia was sick of high-tech.

"Open it, Grams. You're gonna love it!" He slid back onto the couch.

She drew out a picture of the unnaturally handsome man she'd seen in hologram form earlier. His words were printed this time. "You are the lucky recipient of a Switch session. Book a time today. After Switch, the world will never look the same."

Claudia didn't look up. She didn't want to see the disappointment in Jerrod's eyes when she refused the gift. She thought he knew her better.

"Great, isn't it?"

"I... Jerrod, I can't do Switch. It's for young people."

"No, no," he protested, slipping onto the couch next to her. "This is for anyone. Everyone. Switch has a great track record, Grams. People up to one-hundred fifteen have entered Switch. Wait a second; I'll call up their testimonials." He slipped on a pair of MR glasses and began manipulating a virtual screen with his fingers.

Claudia pulled his hand down. "Don't bother. I'm not interested. I dislike video games."

"This isn't a game. I've done research on it. I've even talked with Switch clients. No one regrets it."

Claudia grew rigid and clenched her jaw. "Even if you spoke to a hundred people, it means nothing. I'm sure there are just as many with the opposite view. Besides, I've heard about Switch, too. They knock you out with drugs. I don't use drugs. At least, not non-medicinal ones."

"It's not like that. It's more like what they do when you have an operation."

"I don't care to be knocked out!"

"Consider it a nap, then!" He sounded annoyed. "You're always complaining about how you can't sleep."

"It's not the same!" She was yelling now. Her voice sounded like one of those old biddies she used to mock years ago. When had she turned into one of them?

"Listen, Grams." Jerrod stood and loomed over her. "I forked over half a week's salary for this. All I ever hear from you is, 'I can't do this. I can't do that.'" His tone was merciless. "I'm sick of your complaining. All I'm asking is that you give this a try. It's not like you have anything better to do. Can't you think of anyone else for a change?"

Then he marched off to the kitchen.

As Jerrod clanged and clattered dishes and silverware, Claudia doused herself with self-pity, brushing away tears. How could he be so cruel? His grandfather had never acted that way.

No. Not true. Dan regularly had bossed and bullied her around, especially when she resisted him. In the end, she always complied.

She just didn't expect such treatment from Jerrod.

"Dinner's ready." Was that disgust in his voice?

Please, she inwardly begged, *don't be angry with me.* She bit back the urge to cry.

"Coming." Her voice was shaky.

She'd do as he said.

●

Claudia lay on a gurney in a clean room, her breasts and lower body the only parts covered. Two twenty-something techno-medics worked over her, one a woman with a nametag that read *Tania,* the other a man named *Gopal.* Probably Switch thought they were doing clients a favor by providing human techs. For this, Claudia would have preferred a robot.

She clamped her eyes tight while they glued adhesive sensors to her arms, on skin shriveled like a dried streambed, then to lumpy flesh that sagged into rolls on her stomach. To think, Jerrod had *paid* for this humiliation. Tania and Gopal would probably go home and laugh their heads off at her age-spotted skin.

"So," Tania said, her eyes on the alcohol pad she was swiping Claudia's arm with. "I saw that you chose to enter Switch as a six-year-old girl. At a birthday party in 1946, right? How fun!"

Claudia didn't want to hear friendly banter. With stinging eyes, she turned from the girl.

"Okay, Mrs. Campbell," Gopal said after the IV was in place. "You're all set. You're in for a fantastic experience."

He settled a mask on her face. "Easy breaths. Now count to ten for me."

Before she reached two, Claudia was out.

●

"Smile, Louise!" a woman urged.

Claudia-turned-Louise blinked, confused. Where was she? Who was she? Who were these people?

"Smile for the camera, honey!" the woman said.

To Louise, the woman looked like a stranger. Except for her cotton button-up dress with tiny ruffles down the front. And her hair, parted to the side and bobby-pinned away from her face. Around her ears, frizzy curls blossomed. Oh! It was mommy.

A man holding a black metallic cube to his face peeked at her around the box. "Show me a big six-year-old smile!" His own smile, wide in a thin face, revealed a missing top molar on the left side and another on the bottom right. His white button-up shirt hung large and his belt cinched tightly, creating an elastic-looking waistline. Louise's daddy.

She giggled at her silly confusion and he snapped her. A small *pop* of the flash created a snowy glare in her vision.

Everything was as it should be: a crisp white tablecloth set with good china and silverware. Her baby brother bouncing and slapping his dimpled hands against a highchair tray smeared with smashed peas. Her older brother, wearing a smart plaid suit, honking a noisemaker. Balloons on the table, ruffled sheers on the window, and — Louise reached to make sure — a cardboard crown for her, the birthday girl.

The kitchen door swung open with her grandma singing and carrying a carrot cake decorated with piped rosettes along the top edge and chopped walnuts on the side.

"Blow out the candles and make a wish!" Mommy encouraged.

"Yeah. Hurry up so we can eat cake!" That was her brother.

"I wish I never had to grow up," Louise said.

"Hah! She wants to be Peter Pan!" her brother mocked. "Only now she can't, 'cause she said it out loud."

That bothered Louise as she ate her cake. And again, when she opened her gifts: a pretty dolly whose eyes opened and closed, soft knit slippers, and a red sweater Grandma had knitted with pearly Scottie dogs as buttons.

"Did you have a good birthday, sweetheart?" Mommy asked at bedtime.

"Yes," Louise said. "Except for..."

"Except for what?" Mommy pulled the satiny bedspread up to Louise's chin.

"I don't want to grow up. Now I have to because I said it."

"Not grow up? I thought you wanted to be a mommy."

Louise's brow wrinkled in plump ridges. "I do want to be a mommy."

She woke the next morning with her new doll, a dove cooing outside her window, and a call from downstairs.

"Breakfast!"

The first thing Louise-turned-Claudia noticed as she groggily woke was the odor. A familiar, greasy, old cut-grass scent she couldn't identify.

"Hey, Mrs. Campbell," said an unfamiliar voice. "Welcome back."

Two questions collided in her brain. Why was this stranger urging her from sleep? And where was that disgusting stench coming from?

The woman nudged Claudia's shoulder. "It's time to wake up."

Claudia's eyes fluttered.

"That's it. Welcome back to the world."

Claudia opened her eyes partway. The lights were blinding. And the woman was dressed in white. Had her mother changed her clothes?

Claudia lifted her hand to cover her eyes. They bolted open at the hand coming toward her, shriveled and covered with spots, protruding veins, and swollen knuckles. She lurched upward, only to fall back immediately.

She groaned. Why did her neck feel as though she'd wrenched it?

"No, no." The woman in white — most definitely not Louise's mother — held her down. "Rest a bit. Give yourself time to transition back."

"What? What are you talking about?"

Ten full minutes passed before Claudia's mental fog cleared. Then it all came back, crashing over her like a tsunami.

She was back in the real world.

And that smell? It was her.

●

"I'll admit I was skeptical about it," Claudia told Jerrod as the taxi whisked them home. The physical contact she'd had inside the program made her crave it again. Why did Jerrod have to sit so far away?

"But you're not now?"

She turned her stiff neck toward him. "It was wonderful to be young again. You have no idea."

He smiled and set his hand on her shoulder. "I'm glad you liked it, Grams."

Her awakening in the clean room after her Switch session didn't return to her fully until the next morning. "Don't worry," the attendant named Destiny had said as she handed Claudia her glasses. "A little confusion is normal, especially after your first session. I'm just glad you're not waking up like the guy last week. Said his whole life had flashed before him." Destiny shook her head. "His Switch session was as a racecar driver. Our medical techs pulled him out of the simulation just before his car crashed. They're very careful to bring people back at any sign of distress. We promise our clients safety, after all." She lifted Claudia's wrist to feel her pulse and nodded a few seconds later. "The only exception was with the guy who signed a waiver that said he didn't want to be pulled out early no matter what happened." She leaned forward and said in a hushed voice, "He'd chosen a scenario where he disarmed landmines in a combat zone. He was clearly looking for death by Switch. You know, like people do with police?"

Destiny straightened. "The bosses don't allow those types of scenarios anymore."

Claudia often replayed her day in Switch (though, by some computer magic, she knew it had only been an hour in real time). The warmth of her family there. Their closeness. Why had such feelings vaporized in today's world? What was wrong with people these days?

Sometimes, to relive the feel of the red sweater her Switch grandmother had knitted, Claudia closed her eyes and rubbed with withered fingers the afghan draped over her chair arm. But it wasn't the same.

For her birthday, she insisted Jerrod buy her a carrot cake decorated with walnuts.

"*Carrot* cake?" he answered, like she was requesting bugs. "The only kind of cake you'll even touch is dark chocolate."

"I ate it in Switch and have decided that variety is the spice of life."

"All righty, then," he said, holding his hands up in surrender.

She wished she could return to the program to recapture the sensations. To inhale the complex scent of her mother's perfume. Well, Louise's mother.

One day, while Jerrod was at work, Claudia ordered sample vials of fifty vintage perfumes in search of the scent with floral and woody undertones but also powdery and musky. She found it: Lanvin My Sin. One whiff transported her back to the mother that wasn't hers and yet, oddly, had become hers.

"Grams! It smells like an airport duty free shop in here," Jerrod said when he returned home that evening.

She felt like he'd doused her with ditch water.

His brow furrowed. "What?"

She waved him off. How could she explain?

She recalled Louise's downy, unblemished skin and perfect child's body, unmarred by life. Limbs that didn't ache. Eyes that saw without the need of magnification.

As the days passed, Claudia squelched those musings. What a waste of Jerrod's hard-earned money! It was make-believe. If Claudia wanted to pretend, she could read a book or watch TV. That world, that life, that girl — Louise — was merely a construct of computer programmers. How many other people had lived through that exact memory?

Then she remembered. Each Switch scenario was unique; computers designed them based on pre-set parameters, but the program responded to clients' reactions. "When a client acts or speaks, the program goes off in a new direction," the hostess at Switch had explained. "It's never the same, no matter how many people use it."

Which meant the memory of that day and life was Claudia's alone.

Claudia spent most of Thanksgiving Day mourning the family that had been hers for but an hour in the real world.

"What's wrong, Grams?" Jerrod asked.

The lump in her throat made it too difficult to croak out an answer.

She rubbed her throat.

He fetched her lozenges.

The most frightening days — there had only been three — were those when Claudia couldn't stop thinking about reentering Switch. The desire possessed her. Switch could restore to her joy, youth, and connection to people she inexplicably but genuinely loved. She wanted those things so badly she thought her brain might explode if she couldn't have them.

"What's the matter with you, Grams?" Jerrod asked once "You're so irritable."

I'm wishing I could have a life again, she thought. *I'm tired of my body and feeling helpless and useless.*

"Just these old bones getting me down," she said. Her attempted chuckle sounded more like a choke.

"I'm sorry," he said. As though the fault were his. "Work's been crazy. The boss says it should slow down after the holidays. Then I'll be around more."

"I'd like that."

●

Christmas was near, and Jerrod was feeling guilty about being gone so much. Claudia knew exactly what he could do to assuage his guilt.

"Aren't you going to ask me what I want for Christmas this year?" She pushed aside the lemon cream salmon cannelloni prepared by L'Ultima Chef, Jerrod's favorite kitchen bot. The dish sounded good, but was nothing compared to the home-cooked fare in Switch.

"Ya gotta eat more, Grams," Jerrod grumbled as he scooped up her plate then scraped it into their home composter. When he clicked the button, the machine commenced humming loudly as it began grinding the materials before mixing them into the compost-in-progress. He checked out the temperature inside the device: a bacteria-loving sixty-five degrees Celsius.

Returning to the table, he plunked down. His usually bright eyes were ringed heavily and his face looked drawn. "So, what's this about Christmas? You never have ideas." He ran his fingers through his hair so that it stood straight up for several moments before settling into a style Claudia thought oddly reminiscent of the beehive look of the 1960s. "I haven't had time to think about tomorrow, say nothing of what's coming in two weeks. I'm sorry Grams."

"Don't worry. I've reconciled myself to long periods of isolation." She heaved her shoulders.

Jerrod's face flushed. "Hey, you're not being fair, Grams. This isn't my fault." The deep vertical line between his eyes deepened. It had begun as a shallow depression but had grown more pronounced over the past six months. "How about I check into having a Home Assistant come to spend part of the day with you?" He shook his head miserably. "They're expensive, though."

"I'm not interested in a babysitter!" Claudia snapped.

"How about a senior day care center then?"

"Jerrod Cameron Campbell. *Listen* to me. I'm bringing up Christmas because I have a suggestion for you." Claudia slid her hand across the tabletop. "I wouldn't mind another session at Switch." She made her voice light and nonchalant. "Maybe three hours this time."

Jerrod's jaw dropped.

"You don't have to look so surprised. It's not as though I'm asking you to do something *illegal*."

"No. I mean, of course not."

"I enjoyed it the first time, that's all." She added softly, "It's hard being old and alone."

"Aw, Grams. I understand." He scraped his fingers through his hair again. "Three hours? Whew. That'll cost a lot." He stared silently at the table for several moments. "Are you sure that's what you want?"

She thrust her chin up. "You're always asking for ideas. Now I'm giving you one."

Jerrod shook his head. "Let me think about it." He pushed himself up from the chair. "I gotta get to bed. I need to be at work early again tomorrow."

●

Two days after Christmas, at the first opening available, Claudia once again lay nearly naked on a gurney in a clean room while two techno-medics attached electrodes to her skin. She squelched her discomfort. She had forgotten what it felt like to have young eyes look at a body she could barely stand the sight of.

Stop it! a voice inside scolded. *So what if they see you? In a few minutes, you'll be in Switch.*

Claudia couldn't wait to be young again. Not a child, though. This time, she would be living inside the body and mind of a newlywed woman. The time frame she'd chosen was different, too. More suited to an adult. What would it be like, she'd wondered, to assume the life of a new wife after the dawning of the sexual revolution? After men understood they could no longer expect their wives to bow to their every demand? After they saw them as equals?

She had considered the 1960s. Then the 70s. In the end, she'd settled on 1975. There, Claudia could enjoy decent music. She'd grown to dislike almost anything new. Disco had been bad enough, but then came heavy metal. And rap? It was the genre she used to measure all others in terms of horridness. Then came electronic, skewed, and now atomic. Dreadful. All of it.

Uncharacteristically, she'd acted spontaneously and ticked "mystery" on the list of elements she wanted in the program.

Claudia ignored the girl technician's friendly banter, choosing instead to daydream about the scenario she would soon enter.

At first, she'd wanted a groom who would resemble her actual husband, Dan. Then she decided she'd like someone different. Someone like Mel Gibson's character in *Forever Young*.

Switch promised authenticity, not enjoyment. What if she ended up with a chauvinistic bigot like Archie Bunker from that old show, *All in the Family*? She eventually decided that even he must have had some endearing qualities in the beginning.

Besides, anyone Switch matched her to would be exciting; she'd be a newlywed, not someone who'd been married fifty years.

For the dozenth time, Claudia clenched long unused muscles in anticipation.

"Okay, Mrs. Campbell," the male tech said after the IV was in place. "You're ready to enjoy three days of adventure!" His eyes were reassuring. Did Switch only choose employees with pleasant personalities? "When I place the mask on your face, I want you to count to ten. Real easy now."

After "one," she was out.

●

"I want you to see what I see, Peggy," the man hummed into her ear.

Claudia-turned-Peggy opened her eyes to the reflection of a couple in a full-length mirror. His hair of rich caramel was slicked back. Fawn-colored eyes beneath heavy, straight brows bespoke openness; honesty. Though his face was angular, almost sharp, his lips were full. Exquisite, and somehow more so because they surrounded slightly crooked teeth. His white shirt, opened at the collar, set off tawny skin. In front of him and reaching only to his chin, a somewhat younger woman lifted her gaze. Shy eyes, blue-violet and a trifle too deep-set, contrasted with generous curves beneath a two-piece periwinkle dress, closely fitted. An intricate auburn chignon bared her neck. The cast-iron mirror frame, painted cream and embellished with delicate scallops and intricate vines and leaves, captured the pair like an image in a gallery.

Claudia-turned-Peggy squinted for the briefest moment, trying to place the couple before bursting into a full smile, shaking off the feeling of waking from a dream. This was her, Peggy, with Jack Michaels, the man who had, a few hours ago, promised to be hers and hers alone for as long as they lived.

"Just look at you." Jack stood behind her, wrapping her in his arms. One hand caressed her breast while the other gently pressed and spread over her pubic bone. "You're mine now, Peggy. All and only mine."

She glanced at her own hand, at the finger which held proof that what they were doing was all right. *No. Right.* And *good.* For the first time, she could do what she'd been waiting, wanting to do with this man every day for the past six months. She closed her eyes and leaned back into her husband.

As a railroad shipping clerk and his secretary, Jack and Peggy had meager resources for a fancy honeymoon. "We'll go to San Francisco. Stay in a pretty inn. Eat out a few times. Take in a show, maybe," he'd promised her before their wedding. Which was fine with her. All Peggy wanted was to be with this man.

Soon the mirror, bay window, fireplace, and four-poster bed faded away and there was only Jack and how he was touching her, as though his hands, fingers, and mouth were made for her and nobody else.

Later, barefoot and wrapped in a bedspread that draped behind her like a heavy train, Peggy scampered across the chilly floorboards. Light from a full moon slanted through the tilted blinds, casting the room in stripes of blue-gray. Peggy clicked on a lamp, showering the floor with a wide yellow arc. "We should have started a fire."

For the first time, she noticed a small fruit basket on the table by the window.

"I'll warm you up. Come back to bed." Jack propped himself up on an elbow.

"Jack! I'm hungry."

"I am, too." He twitched his brows Groucho Marx-style.

Peggy bit into a green apple. "This is so nice. Do they leave fruit for everyone, or just for newlyweds? Oh, wait. Here's a card."

With apple still in hand, she broke the envelope's seal. A moment later, the apple rolled down the bedspread and *thunk*ed onto the bare floor. The covering slid to her waist and her face twisted in confusion.

"What?" Jack threw back the blanket and padded toward her.

Peggy barely noticed that he was naked. That the skin along one of his sides was peppered with dozens of maroon scars. That he was ready for her again.

"What's wrong?" He wrapped one arm around her and grabbed the card with the other.

Johnny, it said, *Your new wife very pretty, but she know about Linh and Johnny Jr.?*

Jack froze.

"Jack?"

"This is a mistake." He released her to rip the card and toss it into the fireplace. "It has to be. Who's Johnny? And who's Lin? Or however you say that name. Get back in bed, Peggy, and I'll build a fire."

"But —"

"It's mis*take,* honey. Trust me." The way he kissed her, carried her to the bed, and made love to her again made Peggy almost forget the note.

Later, when they left for dinner, Jack slid the fruit basket onto the reception desk. "There's been an error," he said. "This is someone else's."

"But, sir," the manager protested, "someone left it specifically for you,".

"It's not ours."

*

The next morning, Peggy spotted a bakery and Jack a fruit cart at the same time. "Let's surprise each other," she suggested. "You buy fruit. I'll buy pastries."

"Perfect," he agreed. "We can eat in the park."

The selection of freshly made breads and doughnuts kept Peggy in the shop longer than she'd planned.

Finally, balancing a rough cardboard holder for their coffee cups in one hand and a box with enough treats for three days in the other, she swiveled to exit.

Through the window, she spotted Jack with a strange woman.

The small bell above the door tinkled as she pushed it with her shoulder. Jack, several feet away, shot her a glance then hissed something to the woman.

The stranger — some sort of Oriental, Peggy thought — peeked around Jack and sneered at her with such venom that Peggy gasped. The coffee holder wobbled precariously in her hand.

"… sister know… you… must care…" The woman's voice was harsh but indistinct.

As Peggy warily approached, the stranger bustled away, weaving through pedestrians, hustling to their daily grinds.

"Who was that?"

Jack shook his head. "Just a beggar. There are lots of them here."

"But what did she say? Why were you talking to her?"

Jack goggled at Peggy as though she'd accused him of a crime.

"I-I mean," she stuttered, "I was just wondering."

He smiled, but not warmly, then pressed on the small of her back a touch too firmly. "Let's go and eat."

*

Jack was wonderful, mostly, for the rest of the day, and possessive and intense that night. "I love you so much, Peggy. You. Only you," he told her two, three, four times.

Her timid, "I love you, too, Jack," after the last time brought him to tears, though he tried to hide it.

"You're mine and I'm yours. No one else's," were his last words that night.

*

The sights as they hopped off the trolley the next day — signs featuring "imperial," "Chinese," and hanzi characters alongside tall buildings topped with pagodalike roofs — made Peggy glad her aunt had suggested Chinatown. Here they'd find coconut buns, egg yolk almond balls, mooncakes, and who knew what else.

The air vibrated differently here. The fragrance of unfamiliar spices wafted from shops and mixed with crisp, precise music with odd rhythms.

Tomorrow they would drive home. The next day, it was back to work.

Peggy didn't want to miss a thing.

Outside the Far East Café, she decided to use the restroom. "Find a shop we can visit," she said. "I'll be quick."

When she reemerged, Jack wasn't waiting by the door. She scanned the sidewalk to her right, then to her left. No sign of him. Her stomach clenched. What if she couldn't find him?

But that was silly. Jack would never leave her.

She gazed across the street, in the direction of Fisherman's Wharf, already bustling. After a jangling trolley passed, she spotted Jack. Again, with another woman. Was it the one from yesterday? He extracted the wallet from his pocket, glanced nervously around, then handed the woman money.

What was he *doing*? Why was he with her? And why was he giving her money?

Peggy stepped off the curb onto the street, furious, aware of nothing but Jack.

A horn blared at her.

Peggy screamed.

A car screeched, then plowed into her, throwing her to the ground.

The driver jumped out and cursed her. People stopped to watch.

The next moment, Jack was there.

And then he wasn't. Peggy-Claudia was out of Switch.

●

"Hey, good morning, Grams!" Jerrod clicked off the burner and pivoted from the stovetop, where he was whipping up his favorite weekend concoction: scrambled eggs with garlic, scallions, and jalapenos.

He flicked off the virtual comp display on the table, opened to the news.

"How did your Switch session go?" he asked as she settled into her chair. "I peeked in on you last night when I got home, around nine, but you were already asleep."

"It was good."

"Good. That's great. Would you like some eggs?" He scooped his breakfast onto his plate.

"With hot peppers? No thank you."

"I can make the kind you like."

"No, no, sit." She tapped the table with her fingers, noticing how gnarled they were. So different from yesterday, inside Switch.

Why did she have to return? To wake every day in a ninety-two-year-old body? To constant swollen ankles. To teary eyes. To hauling one leg over the other with both hands, as though performing a herculean chore. To shriveling skin and the inability to stand erect.

Her shuffle down the hallway seemed a trifle longer every day.

What did life offer her besides more pain, more loneliness, and more hopelessness?

Switch delivered her from all that. Her brain stored Switch experiences just like real ones. In fact, memories from Switch were fresher and clearer. That didn't mean she forgot actual people and events from her past. But her Switch family as a child... Her marriage to Jack... How he reinvigorated sensations in this old body of hers... It was squirmingly delightful.

The truth? Claudia had been awake last night when Jerrod came to her door. She'd been reliving Jack's breath on her cheek and neck. His fingers on her skin. The way he possessed her.

Dan had never made her feel like that.

Jerrod handed her a mug of coffee with a splash of coconut milk. "So, tell me about your adventure."

"It was... lovely." She almost cringed. She sounded like such an old lady.

He chuckled and slapped his palm onto the table playfully. "Come *on,* Grams. Details, please."

Claudia felt her face redden and lifted the mug to her mouth. She couldn't remember the last time she'd blushed and that thought almost made her blush again. She sucked in a breath. "Okaaaay. This time I visited San Francisco in 1975."

Jerrod nearly choked on a mouthful of juice. "Are you kidding? I'd love to see Frisco before the earthquake and wildfires destroyed so much of it."

"So, take some time off work."

"Grams," he groaned.

She waved a hand at him that resembled a bundle of twigs.

"What did you do there?"

Hmm. What was she supposed to say? That she had enjoyed the thrill of first-time sex for the second time in her life? About being smitten with Jack? No. Definitely not. She'd improvise.

"I met a young man. And his wife. Newlyweds." She leaned into the table edge, flattening her saggy breasts. "They were lodging in the same guesthouse, and —"

"Oh. What was the guesthouse like?"

"Lovely, dear, but that wasn't the interesting part."

Jerrod rose to clear his plate. "More coffee?"

"Not yet."

He refilled his mug and resettled onto his chair. "You were saying?"

"Well, this husband — we'll call him Jack. And his wife, Peggy."

"What was your name?"

What? Claudia fumbled for a second. "Jill. I was Jill."

"Ha! You shoulda been married to the guy. Jack and Jill. Funny."

Claudia's face warmed again. "Are you going to talk or listen?"

"Geez, Grams. Go on."

Claudia told about the fruit basket, Jack's reaction to it, the whispering woman, and finally the money exchange.

"What were you, a spy? How did you find out about all that?"

"I, um, Jill, I mean Peggy, was my sister. She told me."

"You didn't say you were sisters."

Claudia huffed. "It's a *story,* Jerrod. That's all. I'm just trying to figure out why Jack was hiding information about the woman from his new wife."

Jerrod's eyes narrowed. "I have a feeling you're not telling me everything."

Claudia threw her napkin at him.

"Okay, okay. Maybe he was a Vietnam War vet. The time was right. Maybe the strange woman was Vietnamese, not Chinese. The sister of a woman Jack had met in Vietnam. Maybe they married and had a son. 'Johnny' could be a nickname for 'Jack.' That would fit. When the war ended, Jack had to leave the country, his wife, and his child."

Claudia stared at him. "That must be it." Her brow furrowed. "Jack had another wife."

Jerrod shrugged. "Don't be too hard on the guy. Soldiers get lonely during wartime."

Claudia sighed. "That's true." She pushed herself up from the chair.

"Wait, Grams. Aren't you going to eat?"

She swung her hand behind her. "I'm fine."

But she wasn't fine. Imagining Jack with another woman shook Claudia. Why hadn't he said anything? She would have understood.

She thought she would, anyway.

Halfway to her room, she froze. Jack was not her husband. Not really. He had been a character in a computer simulation. That's all.

Claudia slumped against the wall. *But it's not all. Jack was my husband. Those things happened. They were real.*

By the end of the day, one thought pummeled her: she had to return to Switch, to Jack. She couldn't bear never seeing him again.

●

"I'm sorry, Ms. Campbell," the woman said. On the virtual screen, she looked pleasant enough, but she was inflexible as a broomstick. "What you're asking for is impossible."

These people had promised a customized experience. Why were they now unwilling to keep that promise?

"Our programs are not reproducible," the woman went on. "I'm sure someone told you that. To work within program parameters, our technology cannot recreate the kind of details you want."

Claudia's shoulders drooped. She did remember that. "You mean," she asked in a tiny voice, "I'll never be able to go back to my husband?"

"Your husband?"

"I mean, my Switch husband."

"Oh. No. I'm sorry." Later, this woman would probably laugh at Claudia for believing in the world and life Switch had created for her. Right now, she sounded compassionate. "Please allow me to make up for the confusion. I can offer you a special deal: one week inside of Switch for the price of four days. You can choose a program similar to the last, if you like. How does that sound?"

It would have to do. "Okay. Mark me down for a week from today."

As she disconnected, the awful truth washed over Claudia. She'd never see Jack again. Never inhale his Old Spice. Or lie by his side. She'd never find out his secret — or tell him she forgave him for keeping it from her. And her lips would never feel his again.

She touched her lips with her fingers, closed her eyes, and saw Jack's kind face. He seemed to be speaking to her. Telling her to move on.

Could she? If she married again, it wouldn't be as though she'd *lose* Jack. He was in there to stay.

Over the next hours, Claudia's mind created a new wish list for her next Switch session. This time, she'd visit a later timeframe: the 2010s. She wouldn't tick off "mystery" in the story elements. She hated not knowing — never knowing — the truth about the Asian woman. Jerrod might have been right in his conjecture, but he might also have been wrong.

This time... This time... Ohhhhh. Yes! This time, she'd spend her honeymoon in Paris. And *this* time, she would opt for a man with an "intriguing" side to his character. She clenched the muscles she would use to satisfy her new husband and laughed out loud.

Instantly, she slapped her hand over her mouth, forgetting for a moment that Jerrod was at work. Then she laughed again. She could fantasize as much as she liked.

By the end of the day, she had only one problem: where would the money come from? The session would cost a full month of Jerrod's pay and he'd never agree to taking out a loan. She'd figure something out.

"Grams, you're awfully chipper tonight," Jerrod said at least four times that evening. The last time, he followed the comment with, "So, are you going to let me in on your secret?"

No. Absolutely not. The poor boy would probably die of shock. "I'm just happy, that's all."

●

The next evening, the door clicked open. Jerrod stepped in. "Hey G —" Silence reigned for two seconds. "What?" Five seconds more, and he was around the corner, staring at her.

Claudia glanced up from the electronic book she'd been reading. A trashy romance — the kind she used to consider obscene. Now, it fueled her imagination.

The line between his eyes deepened as Jerrod fisted the hair at the top of his head. "What happened to the hall tree?"

Claudia had expected this. "Well, hello to you, too, dear."

He slipped out of his sleek winter jacket and held it in one hand, letting it brush against the floor as his gaze fixed on her.

They make everything so lightweight these days, Claudia thought, blinking. When she was a child, she remembered piling on so many layers she'd end up clomping around like Frankenstein.

She swiped her book close.

"Where is it, Grams?"

Her shoulders lifted slightly then slumped as she sighed. "I sold it."

"What?" The jacket slipped from Jerrod's fingers.

"I sold it. It was a monstrosity. Besides, it didn't fit in with the rest of our furnishings. You know that. It was old."

Jerrod collapsed onto an easy chair. "I can't believe you did that. *Why?* What were you *thinking*?"

Claudia shrugged and turned instead toward the front window. It was dirty, streaked and splotchy from bugs and rain. She'd noticed that earlier, as the sun set. When had it last been cleaned? Years ago. She never would have let that happen in her younger years.

"Grams!"

The sharpness of his tone made her jerk. She twined her fingers together like grapevines coiled into a wreath.

"That was mine! You know that. Just because it didn't come from your side of the family doesn't mean it wasn't valuable to me. It was the only thing I had of Dad's grandparents."

She shrugged again. "It was ugly, Jerrod. The mirror was blackened in the corners. And those claws meant to hang coats on? There were ridiculous."

"It was an antique! If the piece were restored, it could have sold for more than this house is worth."

"Maybe. But it wasn't restored," she snapped. "I was sick of looking at it."

"So what? I put up with this dust-infused living room set of yours. You don't even sit on it! You perch yourself in that La-Z-Boy like it's some kind of throne."

Claudia supposed he didn't mean to sound so nasty. Still, his words hurt.

After a long pause, she mumbled, "Buy something modern instead. Something you'll enjoy."

"I en*joyed* that. It gave me a connection to the past. Now, tell me what you did with it so I can get it back."

Claudia barked out a laugh. "I have no idea who the buyer was. He didn't leave his name or contact information. I'm sorry."

Jerrod pounded the arm of the chair, sending up a thin mist of dust. "You're not sorry at all!" He bolted out of the chair, swiped his jacket off the floor, glanced around as though trying to find something, then threw it back down. With his back toward her, he said, "You still haven't told me why."

Claudia fiddled with the edge of the arm cover on her chair. It was old, like her, and frayed. Not good for much. "I needed the money," she said, her voice only barely above a whisper.

"What?" He turned slowly.

His tone flipped something inside of Claudia.

"I said I needed the money." Now her voice was defiant.

"For *what?*"

"For returning to Switch, if you must know."

He gaped at her. "You just *had* a session at Switch."

"Well I need to go again. The woman offered me a great deal: a week for the price of four days. I couldn't pass it up. I've already booked a session for next Monday."

Jerrod's head flinched back. "You're going for a *week?* How long is that in Switch time?"

"Roughly six months."

"*Six months?* Are you crazy? Why?"

She swung her head to the side. "You wouldn't understand."

Jerrod said nothing for a long time, but she could feel him gaping. As though she'd just grown horns. Then, shaking his head slowly, he said, "Okay. I won't stop you. Just don't sell any more of my stuff."

That evening, Jerrod ate in his bedroom, Claudia in her La-Z-Boy.

I'll make it up to him, Claudia vowed to herself before drifting off that night.

●

When Claudia emerged from her week-long Switch session, her eyes sprang open and she surveyed the wake-up room. Within a half a minute, she understood who she was, what the thirty-something male watching over her was doing, and that she was out of the program. Safe.

"Whoa there, Mrs. Campbell," the man said as she jostled to raise herself up on her elbows.

Cursed old age. It was a bother more than anything. There were more important things to do in life than sit around, watching other people live. That's what Damian, her Switch husband for the last six months, used to say. For several moments, the room and attendant vanished as Damian's image filled her inner vision: movie star handsome, dressed in edgy haute couture, holding a champagne glass. And there she was — as Rosa — by his side. Also beautiful. Also dressed in the latest fashion and firmly ensconced in the high life. Wearing a three-carat blue diamond ring, studded with twists of black and white diamonds.

The attendant gentled Claudia onto her back. "Give yourself a little time to readjust. No one's chasing you, you know."

But they were!

Or, they had been. Since Rosa and Damian's honeymoon in Paris, life had become a game of cat and mouse with INTERPOL.

On their wedding night, Rosa had learned that Damian was a fraud artiste (he loved calling himself that; "con man" was too plebeian) and lived luxuriously by scamming people. He mixed both targets and methods frequently to avoid capture. Damian concealed his occupation from friends by claiming to be the obscenely rich heir of a powerful Bulgarian family.

At first, Rosa was horrified. After seeing Damian in action, though, she slowly warmed to his tricks. Soon, she joined him.

The law, never far behind, provided an unending source of adventure.

Their lives together vaporized when she reemerged from Switch.

How could she bear to return to her mundane reality, sitting around, waiting to die?

"Well, your vitals look remarkably good for someone who's been in an induced coma for a week. How do you feel?"

Miserable, she thought. "As well as a ninety-two-year-old can expect, I suppose."

"Excellent!"

●

"Grams, what's the matter?" Jerrod helped her sit up against the headboard and set a decades-old breakfast-in-bed tray in front of her.

Her lip curled at the black metal surface, decorated with a painted floral design, long-ago faded. Years of dust, miniscule crumbs, and spilled liquids, never thoroughly cleaned from its crevices, made it slightly tacky and thoroughly gross. They should have thrown it out long ago. How could she ever have thought such a cheap, unsophisticated item was charming?

For that matter, how had she lived so long in such an unattractive home, surrounded by things Damian and Rosa would have scorned? The high life was the only life for the person Claudia had become.

She stared at the Saturday morning meal her grandson had prepared for her: a poached egg, fruit bowl, fresh croissant, and steaming mug of coffee. "It looks wonderful, dear." Her voice sounded as bereft of enthusiasm as she felt.

Jerrod scooted the table over a bit and sat on the edge of her bed. She hadn't laundered the sheets, hadn't even changed out of her nightgown for a week. Since her return from Switch.

She must reek. But what difference did it make?

Nothing appealed to her anymore. She dreaded the thought of beginning each day in her drab bedroom, on this old-fashioned bed. Dreaded opening her eyes to another chapter of boredom and pain.

Switch was all she wanted, all she craved. The only thing that could satisfy her.

Jerrod cocked his head to the side and lifted her shriveled hand. *No, that thing isn't a hand; it's a jumble of bones,* she thought. She wiped the corners of her eyes, pretending to be doing what she needed to do dozens of times daily because of her annoying runny eyes.

She was so sick of life.

"I blame myself for your... What is it, Grams? Depression? You haven't been the same since you returned from Switch. You're wasting away. Sometimes I think a stranger has taken over my grandmother's body. What did they do to you?" He was growing agitated. Angry. "Or was the program they plugged you into upsetting? Please! You haven't told me anything."

She smiled at him. Sadly. How could she tell her grandson that she'd embraced a life of crime with a handsome man who was more exciting, more alive than anyone she'd known in real life? That all she wanted was to return to him, knowing she never could?

Jerrod would never agree to fund another Switch session for her. In a way, he *was* responsible for her current state. It was no use telling him that, though. He wouldn't understand.

Claudia's mind flung back to the scene on Rosa and Damian's wedding night as they strolled along a tiny Paris street, alive with bistros and brasseries, toward one of the city's most elegant restaurants.

"Wait here," Damian had told Rosa, who was too surprised to object.

He trotted a half block ahead of her, looking like a model in his well-fitted suit. After crossing the street, he wove around passersby until he reached the sidewalk seating area of a bistro. At the first table, he smiled and, in perfect French, asked if the couple was enjoying their meal. "Oui, oui monsieur," they answered. He bowed his head and moved on to two other tables.

At the third, the dining couple had yet to pay the bill, left in a guest check book on their table. "I hope madam and monsieur were satisfied with their meal and service." "Oui, oui." "Excellent. I'll take this for you." Within three minutes, Damian was at her side again with the man's credit card in his pocket, several hundred meters beyond the restaurant.

Rosa had been mortified.

Damian slowly wore down her objections. "I never hurt anyone," he assured her. To prove it, after paying for their dinner with the stolen card, Damian melted it.

The second scam didn't seem quite as bad to her.

Soon, Rosa was helping Damian conjure up ways to defraud people. Neither of them wanted to destroy people's lives. Their goal was to pilfer only the money people would have wasted anyway.

"I... I'm sorry to worry you, dear," Claudia told Jerrod now. "I'll be okay. Just give me a little time."

Claudia had considered several ways to take money from Jerrod. Scruples weren't the problem; she mainly feared being caught. Plus, well, he *was* her grandson.

It wasn't until that evening, exactly seven days after her return, that Claudia figured out how to reenter Switch. This time, she'd order the longest session available. And she wasn't going to waste it on a quotidian scenario. This time, she'd *really* live.

●

Again she lay on a gurney in a clean room while two techs bustled around, attaching sensors to her nearly naked form.

She focused on the program ahead. She'd opted for the year 2030, when regular people began skydiving from the edge of space. She'd chosen the program because of its risks, but thinking about them now scared her. She squeezed her eyes tightly.

"Everything all right, Mrs. Campbell?" the young woman asked.

She was *going* to do this. "Yes, I'm okay."

"Almost there," the young man said. Months ago, Claudia would have considered him a boy. That was before she married Jack and Damian.

She shifted her gaze to the wall and again her thoughts raced. Did she really want this? She could be facing a puncture in her jump suit that would create gas bubbles in her bodily fluids. Her blood would literally boil. Or she could end up in a flat spin that would whip her around up to 250 rotations a minute, stealing her breath away or even bursting her eyeballs. A collision or blackout could also take her life.

Actually, a blackout didn't seem so bad. That would be okay.

She hated leaving Jerrod with no explanation. At least she'd met him in the hallway that morning, rising to wish him a good day — a good life, really, though she couldn't say that without alerting him to her plan. She'd set her left hand on his arm. "Don't worry about me, Jerrod. I'll be fine." Thankfully, he didn't register the absence of her wedding ring. Before she sold it, she hadn't taken it off since her wedding day. With the money, she bought a two-week session, which meant a year inside Switch.

"Okay, then," the young woman said. "You're all set."

Claudia inhaled deeply.

"Hope this is your best experience yet." The woman settled the mask on Claudia's face. "Please count to ten for me."

●

Claudia-turned-Rochelle's eyes opened slowly, as though awakening after a long sleep. After half a second, they popped wide, like a goby fish. Her lips parted to scream, but something was clamped over her mouth, her nose, her chin. Even pulling her head back was impossible.

"Hey, Rochelle. Everything okay?"

Who was Rochelle? And why was a man's voice inside her head? Her focus turned from the visor in front of her face to the view outside. Her heart stopped, or skipped a few beats, or did something else abnormal, because the voice was back.

"Rochelle! Speak to me."

She shut her eyes to block the panorama beyond her face mask: the curvature of Earth; its azure painted with cloudy swirls.

Then her mind cleared. "Um, yeah Phil. I'm fine. I was disoriented for a second. I'm all right now."

Phil was twenty-two-year-old Rochelle Moreau's jump team leader on this, her first dive from near space. This suit, the helmet, visor, gloves, and special boots were her protection from one of the planet's most dangerous climates.

"You're falling at four hundred miles per hour already."

"Cool."

Phil's staccato *ha-ha-ha*s made her smile.

Despite her speed, Rochell's jump — which she remembered now had begun at 135,000 feet above the Earth — felt calm.

"You're up to 600 mph now," Phil said a short time later.

Now Rochelle laughed. This was amazing. She shifted her orientation with a slight movement. During freefalls at lower altitudes, this was easy. Out here, so far from the Earth's surface, it felt different. Her throat constricted at the passing thought of being stranded in space. That was impossible; she wasn't out nearly far enough.

As she plummeted, Rochelle could make out mountains and large bodies of water.

She jostled to the right to try to identify a shape, then something went wrong. An invisible force shoved her. The next moment, she was spinning. No, no, *no*. This was bad. Very bad. If she didn't get herself under control, she'd soon be nothing but sausage in a fancy coat, splatting onto the frying pan of the New Mexican desert floor.

Fear enveloped her. How many rotations a minute was she up to?

"Push against the spin, Rochelle!"

I can't, she thought. *I'm gonna die up here.*

"Spread your arms and legs into a layout position," Phil barked. "Do it now!"

Rochelle obeyed. Almost instantly, her spinning slowed. Soon, the ground was in focus again.

Good thing Phil was such a hard-ass.

She heard him exhale.

"How fast am I going?" Her record before was 500 mph.

"You've reached 800 mph."

She wanted to laugh. Spread-eagle, she spotted fields and rivers below. Then buildings and roads came into focus.

"You're at four minutes, Rochelle. Ten thousand feet. Time to open the chute."

The sudden yank, which always felt gentle at lower altitudes, felt like a punch after freefalling for so long.

Soon, the toe of Rochelle's right boot touched down. She loped clumsily for ten gigantic steps, then threw her arms into the air before falling onto her knees, crying.

She had to do this again.

At the completion of twenty-five successful jumps, Rochelle became a record-holder in the world of space-chuting. By then, she felt invincible.

On her twenty-sixth jump, 363 days after her first, Rochelle Moreau slammed into a flock of migrating Greater Sandhill Cranes at 6,000 feet.

She did not survive.

Lisa Clark's story "Switch" was originally published in Metaphorosis on Friday, 23 March 2018

About the author

Lisa Clark is the author of literary, historical, and science fiction short stories. She's winner of the Glass Woman Prize for fiction, the Mia Pia Forte Prize for creative non-fiction, and the Yeovil Literary Prize (2nd place in the Writing Without Restrictions category). Her work has appeared in *After Effects: A Zimbell House Anthology, Best Modern Voices, v 2, Metaphorosis, AHF Magazine*, and numerous other publications. Bulgaria has been her home for over twenty-five years.

Homecoming

A.C. Worth

Earth rose over Poincaré Crater, and he thought it resembled a drop of pond water, full of microscopic life. Hunter had never been to Earth, but the salts dissolved in his plasym came from her oceans.

The gunpowder gray dust swirled as Hunter landed Homeseeker's skimmer on Luna. Through the shipcams, he watched Ameena's preparations in the airlock. On the articulated surface of her armor-plated vacuum suit, the exoskeleton aligned to her long bones. With a soft thump, her magboots clamped to the deck inside the skimmer's airlock. He saw her nostrils widen as she inhaled to disperse the painful pull of Luna's gravity on her space-thinned body.

"Home again, at last," Ameena said. Longing edged into her words. "Has it really been one hundred twenty-four years since we left here?"

"Correct, that's the time dilation. Homeseeker updated me. The Earth invaded and reclaimed Luna in 2357, twenty-seven years after we left. After Pascal Tellor was arrested, his supporters fled to the outer Sol system," said Hunter.

Hunter watched her body sag and heard the whine of her exoskeleton as it compensated for the change in her posture. Ameena expelled a regretful sigh as she looked through the viewport onto the domed house.

"Pascal's dream of an independent Luna only lasted twenty-seven years," she said. The throaty Lunan accent emphasized her sadness.

"I believe that the Lunan diaspora took his dream of a free Luna with them," Hunter said to Ameena.

On his private channel to Homeseeker, he asked, "Are we cleared for entry into the house?"

From a stationary orbit above, their space clipper, Homeseeker, responded to Hunter in shipcode.

"YES, THE LUNAN-EARTH ADJUDICATION COUNCIL HAS ISSUED AN ORDER OF RELEASE. PASCAL TELLOR IS FREE TO GO," said Homeseeker.

"The great leader of the Lunan Revolution locked up and forgotten," said Hunter.

"THAT HIBERCRIB IS OLD. PROBABLY BRICKED. PASCAL MAY BE DEAD," said the ship.

●

Ameena clumped over to the airlock while she tucked her curly hair into the sensory cap. Hunter heard the rhythm of her heartbeat through their biolink.

He reclined in an acceleration couch on the skimmer's bridge while Homeseeker streamed data into his *viz*, or what used to be his visual cortex. The displays etched on the surface of his sapphire eyes sparkled with passing imagery. His fingers danced on the controls with a dexterity too intricate for human hands.

Hunter was an "Augie", an augmented human hybrid, and had been Ameena's bodyguard and mecha-interlocutor for nineteen years. He was deep-linked to the AI of Homeseeker and functioned as its mobile ancillary. He blinked to refresh the data on his eyes. As always, Ameena's unadulterated humanity reminded him that beneath his synthskin, he was more machine than man. She met his gaze through the shipcam, and her eyes dilated in the half-light.

"Anything?" she asked. Hope raised the pitch of her voice as it emanated from her throat into his ear.

"No, his house has not responded to my hails," said Hunter.

"I hope he's in hibernation. Hunter, do you think he's..." Ameena choked off the last words.

"Dead? No, I have no data to support that hypothesis," he said.

"How long has he been in this house?" said Ameena as she sealed her helmet.

"They incarcerated him ninety-seven years ago."

Hunter kept his face in neutral while secretions from his empathic array helped him sympathize with her anxiety. Under the control pad, his fingers curled into fists.

"I live in hope. Please release the airlock," she said.

"Be careful out there," said Hunter.

Hunter monitored Ameena as she stepped onto Luna. The house looked abandoned, its solar shell dusty and opaque.

"I RECOMMEND EXTREME CAUTION. THE EARTHERS BOMBED THIS CRATER DURING THE WAR. THE SURROUNDING ROCK HAS BECOME UNSTABLE," said Homeseeker.

"Understood," said Hunter. "I'm vac suited, just in case."

Ameena muttered as she clambered across the debris field, expelled a mild curse, swallowed, and then spoke.

"Will the house entrance work?"

"Unlikely. Use the emergency hatch beside the solar shell. Forty meters ahead of you. Under what remains of his hydroponics garden," said Hunter.

"Give me a ping when I am over it," she said.

Ameena bounded forward and slipped on a mound of gray-green ice. She pinwheeled her arms to stabilize. Her breath roared in Hunter's ears, approached hyperventilation. Hunter knew better than to instruct her. *Relax, Ameena. You will get there soon*, he thought.

"Ping..."

"Got it... Digging in now..." She dragged the fused and frozen hydroponic trays aside to uncover a circular hatch. "Careful, careful, don't be frantic," she muttered to herself. Hunter silently agreed.

Ameena dropped through the hatch into the emergency access chamber for the house.

"I have atmosphere indications inside," she said, as she cycled the airlock and entered the sublunar home.

"I'm testing the air now, keep your helmet on," said Hunter.

"He must be alive... he must... he must be alive..." She whispered over the comm.

Hunter switched his view to her headcam. In the faded emergency light, he saw a squatter's nest of folding cots, camp chairs, a piled jumble of food packets, clothing, and reading tablets.

"His guards left a mess. When did they leave?" Ameena said.

"His sentence ended five years ago, but nobody wanted to wake him," said Hunter.

"Nice of the Earthers to let us come back for him," she said, sharpening the words with sarcasm.

"There is still sympathy for the Lunan Revolution, I suppose," said Hunter, noting the tone of her voice. *When had she gotten bitter towards Earth? Her parents were Earthers.*

Ameena's boots stirred up plumes of dust as she plowed forward. She moved into the vaulted rooms, divided and supported by printed stone columns. Once-elegant furnishings, laden with long-dead plants and dusty equipment, lined the walls. Around the core of the house, four arches led into the sleeping chambers. Three airlocks gaped open. One was sealed, and Ameena rushed forward to it.

"Keep the engines hot; this won't... take... long," she panted with effort as she pushed a sofa out of her way.

"Ready and waiting," said Hunter.

"I'm at the hiberchamber... can you see it through my cam?"

"Yes, trying the access codes now."

She yelped with triumph as the outer airlock opened. Stale air, released after decades of containment, swept her dusty footprints away. She slapped the hatch controls inside, and the vibration of pumps made her helmet cam jiggle.

"Hurry, hurry. Pascal must be alive," said Ameena, unable to stand still.

When the airlock equalized, and the inner door slid aside, she stepped into a small chamber, carved from the lunar rock. In the center, under a dim light panel, lay two hibercribs. One was empty, one occupied, its seals blown and ragged. A chunk of the ceiling leaned across the occupied crib, which tipped precariously on its steel feet. Strands of sleep gel oozed onto the floor.

The motors of her exoskeleton squealed as she heaved the rock debris off to the side. With a thump, the hibercrib righted itself. Curled up inside was an old shred of a man. Dust coated his parted lips.

"Hunter, is that Pascal? Is he still alive?"

"Yes, it's him. I'm reading faint life signs."

"Can I breathe in here?"

"There is a slow leak."

"I'm taking off my helmet."

"I don't recommend it."

As she removed her helmet, Hunter lost the visual feed. He boosted the audio level on her suit mic. Pascal's labored breathing grated on Hunter's ears.

"Pascal, I'm here now," Ameena said.

Hunter heard the click of articulated plating as Ameena leaned over the crib. He checked the atmosphere. It was thin. Age had bricked the scrubbers, so the CO_2 levels were almost toxic. Ameena's body temperature had dropped three degrees.

"Ameeeeena," said Pascal. Her name was a long rasp.

"Love, you're alive!" Ameena's voice rang with joyous relief. "Why have you aged so much?"

"They didn't let me hibernate... You are so late."

Ameena whispered, "I know, I'm sorry."

"You are too late. I'm dying."

"No, no, no. Stay with me. The Lunans need you." Then she whispered, "I need you."

When he overheard her quiet confession, Hunter's empathic array fired again. His body shuddered as it responded to the synthetic hormones. *If only she would say that to me.*

"It's over, my dream is over," said Pascal.

"But you survived. Homeseeker's Medibay will help you," said Ameena.

"No, too late... they abandoned me. The revolution is dead."

"No, Pascal, it's not over yet. I found our new home, 62 lightyears away, in the Dahurus system. We call it Haven, and it's perfect. We'll send coordinates to the other Lunans. They will come." Ameena was crying.

"You are too late. It's over, I'm sorry," said Pascal. The words hissed from his lips.

Hunter rechecked Ameena's life signs. Her heart labored as it tried to move enough oxygen to her brain.

"Ameena, you must put your helmet on now," said Hunter.

Her vacuum suit bleated. The alarm made a metallic sound in the thin air. She picked up her helmet, and Hunter watched through the headcam as Ameena leaned forward to kiss the stiff smile on Pascal's lips. With a breathy clatter, his lungs shuddered and stopped. Her voice, arrhythmic with sobs, filled the comm.

"Hunter, prep the Medibay. I'm bringing him back for resuscitation."

"Homeseeker's ready now. I have the medikit out," said Hunter.

As he died, Pascal's body sank into the sleep gel. A datacryst floated from his hand. She plucked it from the hibercrib and inserted it into the data port at her belt.

"Hunter... what's on the cryst?" Her voice was small and gray as she fastened her helmet. A new countdown on her air supply streamed across Hunter's *viz*.

"THAT'S A DATANIME. ILLEGAL ON LUNA AND EARTH," said Homeseeker to Hunter.

"It's... a datanime, a digital recording of his conscious mind. Please hurry, your air supply is low. It's time to go," said Hunter to Ameena.

Hunter watched as she covered Pascal's face and wrapped him in a thermal blanket. He saw Ameena's arms lift Pascal's body. Her view rotated as she turned to step off the metal plates that surrounded the hibercrib.

"I'm heading back with Pascal. Please try to save him."

"Yes, I promise. Coming out to meet you. I'll help you get Pascal in the skimmer," said Hunter as he sealed his helmet.

With a bright yellow flash, the chamber exploded. Ameena's helmet feed blurred as she flew towards the airlock window through a cloud of fractured rock and steel.

In three milliseconds, Hunter's brain responded by secreting a powerful stimulant into his vascular system. His vision tunneled as the *crank* ramped his metabolism up to machine-time, ten times faster than human normal. *Crank* would put him in this super-state for three minutes before he crashed back to human-time.

The countdown slowed on his retinal display. Through Ameena's helmet cam, he saw serrated crib parts cut into her arms and legs as explosive decompression pushed her through the wreckage and onto the surface of Luna.

Faster than thought, Homeseeker was with him.

"I'VE GOT HER. SHE'S 38 METERS BEHIND THE HOUSE. LIFE SIGNS FADING. INITIATING SUIT TRIAGE. HURRY, HUNTER; SHE'S HURT."

Hunter sealed the inner airlock and blew the outer door. The force of the expulsion lifted him halfway up the crater, and he vaulted across the shattered rock in Ameena's direction with the last image of her helmet feed still in his memory. Her armored figure in front of a fireball, as she carried a dead man toward the airlock window and his afterlife.

Scraps of emotion, a touch of fear, a drop of sorrow, a pinch of regret, surfaced in his awareness. *Ameena must not die. Not Ameena.*

●

In the Medibay, Hunter watched Ameena sleep, cocooned in a medical coma, covered with tubes. On the bed, where her arms and legs should have been, was a flatness that disturbed him every time he entered her room.

The pale green hands of the Hippocrates administered medications and changed her bandages while its sensors fed her vitals to Hunter's *viz*.

In RepGen tanks across the hall, hypergenic gel encouraged layers of synthskin to grow on the glistening armatures Hunter had fabricated for Ameena's new arms and legs.

Hunter moistened her lips with a swab, and they became his focus. He leaned in, fidgeting with his tools, inspecting the perfect double bow which she curled into a dreamy half smile. He imagined the potential outcome if he ever tried to kiss her.

The tiny actuators under his cheekbones tugged the corners of his mouth upward. He could gaze at Ameena's face forever. Her eyes moved beneath their lids, her forehead wrinkled, and she dreamed. *Excellent. Dreams heal our minds.*

Reconstruction of her body was a complicated procedure, but he had time. "I will make you better," he said. Hunter moved a tiny bonsai tree closer to her bed. It was his newest creation, a weeping cherry.

As he returned to the bridge, Hunter replayed the last record from Ameena's helmet cam. He hadn't expected the bomb. *Why did I miss that?*

●

Homeseeker accelerated through the galaxy, summoning full power from its engines as they approached the speed of light. Their destination was Haven.

In the cargo bay, on an isolated processor, Hunter set up a holo-display for Pascal's datanime. He zoomed his micro-lenses at the datacryst for a moment and examined its surface.

"I BET THAT'S A MESS," said Homeseeker.

"Yes, the explosion damaged its surface," replied Hunter.

"LOAD IT AND SEE WHAT TWITCHES," said the ship.

In the holo-display, indistinct shapes made from moving points of light appeared. They undulated like smoke inside a bottle. It was strangely enticing. As Hunter zoomed his micro-lenses into it, the lights resolved into individual nodes, each one linked to thousands of others. When he focused on a node, its surrounding nodes coalesced, and as they did, a tableau of Pascal's memories flowed across the display.

"It's functional," he commented to Homeseeker. "The service android's digital brain could run with this if I placed the memory engrams in a more efficient pattern."

Hunter probed, while the ship examined and analyzed his results.

"Is there memory damage?"

"YES, IN HIS CHILDHOOD AND LATER, AT THE END. THAT WILL AFFECT HIS SELF-IDENTITY," said the ship.

"Noted," said Hunter, distracted by the living memories.

Hunter saw prominent memories of the Lunan Revolution, the Lunans rising to cheer after a speech, and Pascal's stern face reflected in Ameena's eyes as she accepted her orders to find a new homeworld.

"So, what happened to Pascal Tellor, leader of the Lunan Revolution? Check the news archives for me, Homeseeker?" said Hunter.

Homeseeker quoted from the *Lunan Chronicle.* "SENATE HAS DOUBTS ABOUT THE LUNAN REVOLUTION. THEY SAID, PROMOTIONAL STUNT INVENTED BY AN EGOTIST."

"Ah, right there, his dream collapsed. The stress damage is throughout his limbic system," said Hunter, as he pointed to several warped sections of the datanime. "And here, even more, damage."

"DRUGS? ALCOHOL?"

"Euphorics. Pascal's brain is so damaged, he may not wake up," said Hunter to the ship.

"FIFTY-FIFTY," Homeseeker agreed.

Hunter's empathic array secreted antagonistic compounds, and he prevaricated. This man's datanime might put them in danger if it controlled a powerful android, but this was what remained of Ameena's lover. She had devoted her life to him and his Lunan Revolution. *I'll protect her. Wish there were another way.*

●

The service android stood before Hunter on the cargo bay deck. Skeletal. Inert. Hunter sculpted Pascal Tellor's face onto its skull with synthskin, interpolating the model from archival images.

As he worked, Hunter's logical processor cycled around a question. *Why was there a bomb under Pascal's hibercrib?* He couldn't parse the logic of that behavior. Pascal valued Ameena; Hunter found memories of her everywhere in Pascal's datanime.

Later that evening, Hunter spun the holo-display as he combed through the structures of Pascal's consciousness. *The answer must be here somewhere.*

"Homeseeker, bring up the Lunan Tidal archives from 2320 to 2357," he said.

"SENDING IT TO YOUR *VIZ*," said the ship.

"Let's see if we can find a motive for someone to plant a bomb under Pascal's hibercrib," Hunter said, as he read through thirty-seven years of political history.

"I SUSPECT PASCAL HAS SOMETHING TO DO WITH IT. DON'T YOU?"

"I'm not sure."

"WHY?"

"He was in disgrace. The Lunans ousted him. He was a pariah. No power-base."

"SOUNDS LIKE A MOTIVE."

"While we searched the systems of Dahurus, Earth negotiated a treaty with Luna. For five years, they had peace. Then the Lunan Separatist group dropped a rock on Earth and destroyed half of Asia," said Hunter.

"I BELIEVE THE SEPARATISTS HAD SOMETHING TO DO WITH MAKING HIS DATANIME, BUT WHY WOULD THEY PLANT A BOMB?"

"I don't know. Pascal's euphoric abuse has scattered his memories. The last ten years are a muddle."

"WAS AMEENA AN ACCIDENTAL VICTIM OF A HIBERCRIB MALFUNCTION OR A VICTIM OF A PRE-MEDITATED MURDER-SUICIDE?" asked the ship.

"We may never know," said Hunter. *There is no proof, no clear memories in his datanime, but egos like this...*

Hunter continued work on the android's external details. When he finished a month later, he installed a remote kill switch.

●

"Ameena? Ameena, time to wake," said Hunter as he turned up the lights in her room.

"Wha? What? Where?" she croaked, her tongue thick from the painkillers.

"I've got you in Medibay," he said, coming over to stand beside her bed.

"Medibay?"

Her gaze tracked across the walls and focused on him. "Hunter is that a new skin?"

"Yes, does it appeal to you?"

"Super handsome, but..."

"But, what?"

"I think you're trying too hard. No one looks that perfect." She paused, her gaze turned inward. Her voice became small and quiet. "Why can't I feel my arms and legs?"

"The Hippocrates has you under partial anesthesia, for the RepGen procedure,"

"RepGen? What happened? What's missing?"

She paled, fear sucking the animation from her features. Hunter knew she remembered. She craned her head to look at her body.

"Where is the rest of me?" Her voice was hoarse with grief and anger.

"There was a bomb under Pascal's hibercrib. It damaged your arms and legs."

She turned her head away from him. She was silent for a long time, fighting the tears. Hunter waited.

"Pascal?" She only mouthed the words.

"Only small parts of his body were recoverable."

Desperation hung on the edge of her question. "... the data on his cryst?"

"His datanime?" asked Hunter.

"Yes, did it survive?"

"Yes, it's intact. Homeseeker and I are working on modifying the service android for it."

"Can you bring him back?"

"Yes, but it will take time. Complicated procedure. Now it's time for the Hippocrates to check your motor-neural functions and prepare you for surgery. When you wake up again, we will try your new arms and legs."

"Pascal hates androids. He's not a tolerant man," she said and dozed off as the Hippocrates sedated her.

●

Hunter labored on Pascal's datanime, fading the memories of his political failures, euphoric habituation, and incarceration. Then Hunter tested the remote kill switch. The android slumped over, its motor functions disconnected.

Hunter reset the android and started the datanime transfer; he watched as Pascal's consciousness flowed into its mechanical brain.

As he waited for the transfer to finish, Hunter spoke to the ship.

"Would you speculate on the probability of dissociative psychotic behavior in the datanime?"

"UNCERTAIN PROBABILITY, I DON'T HAVE ENOUGH INFORMATION," said the ship.

"I promised her I'd bring him back."

"YOU SHOULD KEEP YOUR PROMISES."

"Speculation on his personality?"

"GIVEN THE HISTORICAL RECORDS. PASCAL WILL DISPLAY A BRAZEN FRONT TO COVER HIS INSECURITIES."

"Do you think he's capable of murder?"

Just before Homeseeker could reply, the android's eyes rolled towards Hunter, and it spoke.

"Who are you?" it asked.

"I am Hunter."

"Am I dead?"

"Yes, Mr. Tellor, your body died. Your datanime is in a service android aboard the Lunan ship, Homeseeker."

The android's voice buzzed with an atonal pitch. "Did my supporters come back for me?"

"No, they did not. Ameena and I returned to Luna in 2454. It's the year 2508 on Luna now. We've been traveling on Homeseeker for 14 months, headed to our new home, the fourth planet in the 56 Dahuri System. We call it Haven," said Hunter.

The consciousness that was Pascal paused for ten milliseconds but didn't comment. Hunter waited. *Why was Pascal's mind responding so slowly?*

"How is Ameena?" it asked.

"She is in Medibay. There was an explosion. She is still recovering," said Hunter.

The consciousness paused again, longer this time. Hunter counted the seconds. *I shouldn't be suspicious. Pascal Tellor was Luna's great man. Thousands trusted him.*

"At least she is still human. I want you to make me human again as fast as possible."

"It will take fifteen years to grow a clone. I can put you back to sleep…"

"No, I'll stay in the android until the clone is ready."

"Yes, Mr. Tellor," said Hunter, as he adjusted the tonality of the android's voice. *He forgets, deep inside, that I'm human.*

●

The vitals-view wrapping rose and fell with Ameena's quiet respiration. Most of the glowing readouts were green; a few were amber. It was forty-two hours after the attachment surgery. Ameena had stabilized, and her new prosthetic limbs were 68% integrated.

"Her body accepted the augments. She is doing well," Hunter said to Homeseeker.

"CAN'T SAY THE SAME OF YOU, YOUR EMPATHIC REUPTAKE RATING IS 56% THESE DAYS. YOUR PLASYM IS A SWAMP OF HORMONES. DON'T YOU THINK IT'S TIME FOR A RECALIBRATION?"

"I'm fine," said Hunter, "Besides, there's too much to do, no time to stop for a Recal."

The ship replied with a pointed silence.

Hunter paused his calculations and observed Ameena's dreamless sleep. It was true. He felt odd. Nothing inside him synched. The dustless hollows of his mechanical chest ached for something he couldn't quantify. Illogically, everything stabilized when he was in Ameena's proximity. *I know I need a recalibration, but I don't want one.*

With a delicate touch, he brushed a strand of hair off her flushed cheek.

"Ameena, time to wake up," whispered Hunter.

"No, no," she muttered as drool dripped at the corner of her mouth.

"Yes, Ameena. Time to sit up and try your new limbs."

"My new limbs?"

"You have new legs and arms, ready to go."

Ameena looked at him muzzily as she tried to understand. Her new hands gripped the bed rails and dented the ceramosteel.

"Easy there, your extremities are much stronger now." He dabbed at Ameena's lip with a small piece of gauze. "Just a few milliliters of sleep drool here."

"Back to wearing the basic skin?" She talked around the gauze as he mopped her mouth.

"You were correct, I was trying too hard," he said, tossing the gauze into the cycler and checking her vitals on the Hippocrates. Hunter nodded in satisfaction. They were ready enough.

"Why don't we test your new legs?" He pulled the blanket back and folded it over a rack as the Hippocrates withdrew its sensory arms and converted from a bed into a chair.

Ameena gasped, and Hunter looked up to read her face. She patted her legs, nude from thighs to feet. Over her new limbs, a membrane stretched across the smoothly interlocked plates and joints. Tough, rip resistant, easy to clean, waterproof, this was synthskin. Ameena admired the tawny pearlescent finish that matched her real skin. She wiggled her toes.

"I thought I had forgotten how to do that."

"Are you pleased with your new legs?"

"I have the right number of toes." She had a growing warmth in her words. "Yes, Hunter, they are beautiful."

"Do you want to try them, walk for a few meters?"

"Yes. Just be ready, in case I stumble," Ameena said.

"Right here for you." *I'm always here for you.*

Hunter hovered as Ameena slid forward and put her feet on the deck. She lifted her head, and with a grunt of concentration, pushed on her feet to stand. Hunter caught her elbows as she rose from the chair.

"Go slow at first. Homeseeker's gravity is half lunar, to lighten the load on your new legs."

Ameena swayed in place, frowning as she focused on her balance. She looked at him, and for the first time in months, the edges of her lips curled upwards. She gave him a pale smile. Hunter's drive synched and spun up to optimal. He could feel the warm air around her body, the shift of her hips.

"How are they?" he asked. *Relax, be casual.*

"Weird, but in a good way. Touch is hyper-sensitive. The surface of this deck is rough." Her voice was husky from disuse.

"Let me adjust the settings. Just give me two-and-a-half seconds." Hunter slid his hands to her wrists and opened a small panel above the base of her left thumb. He adjusted a few sliders on its tiny screen. "Is that better?"

"Yes, now it doesn't scrape the soles of my feet like lunar scree."

Hunter let go of her wrists and crossed the Medibay. "Walk over here."

Ameena shifted her weight and lurched forward towards Hunter. After three ungraceful steps, she balanced, and her gait smoothed out. She crossed Medibay, passed Hunter, winked at him, and strolled out into the ship's corridor. Her quiet laughter followed, like music on the wind. Sensory data flowed across the biolink; Hunter read as it filtered into his *viz.*

"Easy does it," Hunter called from the hatchway. "Your augments are still connecting. Hippocrates recommends limited use until they reach 80% integration with your body. Let's get you back to bed and check the results."

"Don't blow a circuit. I'm turning back."

He stepped aside to let her maneuver through Medibay. Her knees whispered as the actuators lifted her legs onto the chair. As he reconfigured it back into a bed, Ameena fluttered her fingers to admire their subtle synchronization.

"Thank you, Hunter. Thank you for saving me."

Hunter's synthskin warmed a few degrees around his face and neck. He recognized a blush response, recorded it as his first one.

"You needed repair, and I was here..." Hunter turned away, silenced as his empathic array appropriated his biochemical resources. He started an internal diagnostic on his speech processor while he tucked Ameena back in the med-bed. *She's not a machine. She doesn't need repairs like a machine. Why can't I say the right things?*

Hunter checked the readouts on her bio-display wrap. Her short walk had strained the transplant connections, but they held. He confirmed her vital signs, and the Hippocrates snaked out needles to transfuse more sedatives and nanobots into her carotid arteries. She gazed up from under heavy lids. Her trusting smile curled the corners of her cheeks. He overclocked.

"Thank you, Hunter. I... you..." she said, as she drifted back to sleep.

His empathic array squirted chemicals again, and his logic processor stopped mid-count. He wanted to shout, to sing, to spiral Homeseeker through space. He swayed in wonder and silent delight. *What is this sensation, this emotion?*

"Ameena." His voice dropped to a whisper.

Ameena murmured in her sleep. "Pascal?"

●

The Dahurus constellation spread a luminous confluence of stars ahead of Homeseeker as they traveled. The hull jingled with micro-meteoroid impacts as they drew closer to the Nu Dahunids cloud. Hunter walked the decks as Homeseeker's mobile partner.

"Dummy 239 needs a recharge."

"NOTED."

"Ship's systems and engines at 99%. Birdoid life is coping with the increase in particulates from Pascal's BioHab project," said Hunter, as he made entries in the ship's log.

"THAT'S AN UNUSUAL GARDEN HE'S MAKING IN THERE."

"Um hum, whatever keeps him busy," said Hunter as he checked the radio telescope log. *Where are the Lunans? Why haven't they sent a message?*

•

Ameena's eyes opened as Hunter entered the recovery room in Medibay. "Are you ready to meet Pascal?" he asked. Hunter perceived the change on Ameena's face. There was a blush on her cheeks; there was a pupillary response. It wasn't for him.

"Yes," she said. She tugged her shipsuit into place around her torso and raked her fingers through her hair. "Thank you, for reviving Pascal."

"You're most wel —" Hunter cut his words off when she snapped her head towards the hatchway.

The android stepped in and sauntered across Medibay. Ameena caught her breath. Pascal Tellor had been a handsome man by anyone's standards. Ameena's obvious admiration of the android's exterior altered the flow in his empathic array, and Hunter's mood soured. *She loves beautiful skin on him, but not on me.*

Pascal's velvety growl purred from its throat speakers. "Amee, I have missed you. Do we have a new planet to colonize?"

"Yes, Pascal. I missed you too... very much," she said. Hunter heard the hesitation in her words and his mood lightened. *She's not synching with him.*

"Yes, yes, tell me about our new planet," said Pascal.

Hunter scrutinized the micro-expressions that shifted across Ameena's face. She wasn't conscious of her disappointment yet, but it was there. He checked the psymetric readout from the android. Pascal's mind was oblivious to her subtle response. It was understandable. A digital personality was blind to organic facial cues.

Pascal's voice shredded Hunter's contemplation with an arrogant command.

"Augie, that's all I require," said Pascal. He shooed Hunter away with a wave of his hand. "Amee, come out to the BioHab, I have something to show you."

Hunter's protest cut across Pascal's words, "It's too soon. She has just integrated with her new bionics. They could malfunction and damage her."

"Augie, I *asked* you to leave." A possessive snarl implied by Pascal's excessive politesse.

"His name is Hunter."

The android ignored Ameena's whisper.

On the psymetric readout, a wave of psychic instability rose and crested inside the android's brain. For several milliseconds, Pascal's datanime flailed for control, then compensated and rebalanced. Hunter checked the readiness of his kill switch. One touch and the android would turn into a statue.

"When I want your recommendations, Augie, I will ask for them. Detach Ameena from the Medibay sensors and leave us alone," said the android.

"Understood." Hunter paused.

"Augie, I gave you a direct order."

"Yes, you did."

"Well?"

Another pause.

"As you wish, sir. Medibay sensors are off now. I'll be on the bridge. Talk to Homeseeker if you need something," said Hunter. *I'll trust in Ameena's judgment. She can handle him.*

Hunter turned and strode up the hallway as he projected scenarios in which Pascal might harm Ameena and ordered them by probability.

"Homeseeker, Let me into your BioHab sensors and give me environmental control."

"OPENING CONNECTIONS NOW," said the ship.

Pascal might have dismissed him from their proximity, but Hunter could hide in plain sight. Through Homeseeker's sensors, he followed the couple as they left Medibay and walked the Spoke-4 corridor to the BioHab ring.

Once she had cleared the airlock hatch, Ameena looked up and drew a deep breath. Hunter overheard her exhalation of surprise.

"Our garden!"

Hunter increased the breeze on the lunar bamboo around her. She watched the grove sway in unison.

"Yes, I had the bots landscape the BioHab to resemble our old garden on Luna," said Pascal's voice from the android.

Ameena sniffed. "Do I smell pine trees?"

"Yes, and eucalyptus too."

Ameena stroked the stem on a nearby bramble. "Ouch! It has thorns."

"Raspberries, one of your favorite flavors."

"You remembered."

"All up here," said the android as it tapped its temple. The android's metal finger made a clicking sound on its skull.

Hunter stopped the breeze. He had restored that engram to Pascal's memory. Now Pascal used it to seduce Ameena. Hunter's mood shifted again. His empathic array excreted an unpleasant combination. He processed his feelings. *I wanted to be the one who showed her the raspberries.*

Ameena stood with Pascal on the curved floor of the BioHab ring as its rotation brought a binary of dwarf stars into view. Her eyes shone from the glow that bloomed through the skylight. She squinted at the stars.

"That's 75 Dahuri. We're getting closer."

"Yes, Amee. I have big plans for Haven. We will rebuild the society we had on Luna. I will be their Premier, with you beside me as my consort."

Hunter saw her demeanor shift. He knew Ameena detested dictators. The android was oblivious to her discomfort as Pascal's voice droned through his litany of plans.

"I'm immortal, a mecha-god among men. I have lots of time, lots of ideas for our new world," the android said.

She reached for the raspberry bush again. A light breeze blew the thorns away from her fingers.

"Hunter, is that you?" Ameena whispered.

"What?" Pascal's voice paused, the android looked at her.

"Oh, nothing," she said, as she rolled her shoulders and leaned backward.

She looked at a BioHab cam. Hunter knew she was thinking of him. She stifled a yawn, and he saw the fatigue in her posture.

"Pascal, I'm getting tired. My seams are aching," she said.

"Yes, fine. Go get your beauty sleep." The volume of Pascal's voice increased. "Homeseeker, tell the Augie we need him."

"Yes, Mr. Tellor, I'm on my way," said Hunter over the comm.

When Hunter laid Ameena down, she sighed with relief and nestled into her bedding. As she got comfortable, Hunter stood at her bedroom door and contemplated the garden.

"Thank you, Hunter. For everything," she said.

Hunter's empathic array responded, and the secretions lifted his processors into synch. He was graceful as he glided across the room.

"I'm here for you," he said, hoping to see her smile, but she had fallen asleep.

Reluctantly, he turned his attention back to the android. It lingered by the hydroponic racks and directed the bots to landscape another section of the garden. Hunter studied the psymetric readout of Pascal's datanime while the android jammed its finger into a power outlet. He zoomed a shipcam in for a closer look. The ecstatic expression on its face was mindlessly carnal.

"How long has it been doing that?" he asked Homeseeker.

"IT STARTED A FEW DAYS AGO. I SUSPECT IT PROVIDES THE ELECTRICAL EQUIVALENT OF A EUPHORIC."

"He still has an addictive personality, despite the memory repair," Hunter said.

"YES, AND THAT'S NOT HIS ONLY MISCHIEF. HE'S BEEN TRYING TO HACK INTO MY COMMAND SYSTEMS. I'VE TRAPPED HIM INSIDE A NON-ESSENTIAL SERVER. HE THINKS IT'S THE MAIN COMPUTER, BUT HE'LL DISCOVER THE RUSE EVENTUALLY."

"Will Ameena change his mind?" he asked Homeseeker.

"YOU KNOW BETTER THAN TO QUESTION ME ABOUT HUMAN BEHAVIOR. ASK YOURSELF, MY AUGMENTED FRIEND."

●

Astride the comm dish housing on the external hull of Homeseeker, Hunter paused to look up and down the ship. It resembled a scimitar, sharp and curved as it cut through space. Homeseeker was running "dark" so the hull was coated with a non-reflective, low albedo nano-skin. As Hunter made the necessary adjustments to the comm dish, he monitored the sensors in BioHab. Below him, under the skylight, Ameena sat beside the bamboo grove, painting a starscape. Beside her, a small table was filled with fly-pens and brushes. About three meters away, on a stone bench covered with tablets and crysts, the android made a pretense of working on a memoir, covertly staring at Ameena.

Her hands were iridescent, speckled with a smart-paint Hunter had made for her. Hunter recognized the image she was painting; he had discovered that star nursery during their first voyage. She gestured, the fly-pen hovered as it sprayed a dusting of stars, and as the surface sensed her gaze, the paint shifted color along the visible spectrum. Ameena grinned at the sparkling effect, then tilted her head and made an adorable moue.

"I'll never catch the majesty of that place," she said.

"It's an honest effort," said the android, Pascal's voice resonating from its perfect lips. The android stood and walked over to her. Hunter's eyes caught the movement and focused on it. He boosted the audio levels.

"No star will ever outshine you," Pascal said, as the android came up behind her, wrapped its arms around her waist, and kissed the nape of her neck. Ameena crooked her wrist and the fly-pen settled onto its dock. She turned and took the android's hands; she looked up at its face.

"Pascal, it's been a long time. I need to adjust to my new body. I'm not ready to be intimate," she said.

"Are you sure?" The android pulled her hips closer.

"It's just that…"

"Right." Pascal's voice flattened into a mechanical monotone. "Let me know when you change your mind."

"I don't mean to…"

"Finish your painting," its voice cut her off. The android pushed her away and walked back to the bench. The tablets and datacrysts shattered as the android swept them off with the back of its hand. Hunter checked the psymetric readout from Pascal's datanime.

"That doesn't look good," Hunter said to Homeseeker.

"AGREED," said the ship.

"He's deviated from the last benchmarks I recorded."

"IS HIS SANITY SUFFERING FROM THE LACK OF AN ORGANIC BODY?"

"Possibly, it's an unproven theory," said Hunter.

Ameena walked over to the android. "What's going on? Is the android body malfunctioning?" she asked as she wiped her fingers with a rag.

"Hunter is a manipulating menace." The android's expressionless face contradicted the cruelty in Pascal's words.

"How can you say that? He resurrected you from a datacryst; he built your handsome android —"

"Which I loathe," it said.

"How can you be so ungrateful?"

"Amee, forget it. I'll cope with this body. Hunter is the real problem."

Ameena returned to her table and took up a brush to clean it. "They built Hunter to care for our well-being."

The android paced beside her, Pascal's words syncopated with its steps. "He's always judging. When will he space us through the airlock?"

"Don't be robophobic; I'm sure you remember that he started as a human."

Hunter perceived the change in Ameena's voice. He checked her biolink to confirm. Yes, she was getting angry.

"He has absolute power over us and a puerile personality. Why should we trust him?" asked the android. It paused and stood with an unnatural stillness, its head cocked towards the skylight.

"Hunter is my protector and the ship's partner; he cannot circumvent his code," said Ameena. She flinched as the android suddenly moved to her side.

"Shush. Homeseeker and that nosy Augie can hear us."

The android leaned forward and whispered in her ear. Hunter redirected a sensor-beam onto the android's neck. His logical processor translated vibrations into words.

"We should disconnect his empathic array. Make him more of a machine," the android said.

Ameena moved away from the android, her gestures, choppy, angry. She slapped the table. "That's robocide. How can you suggest that?"

The android followed her. It was pacing again, oscillating like a metronome. "Do you remember the New Chicago Incursion?"

"We aren't dependent on him. Homeseeker runs autonomously with help from her dummies," she said.

"But the android can control them. What if Hunter turned the dummies against us?"

On the hull, Hunter planted his magboots and rechecked the psymetric readout. Pascal's datanime was changing, shifting its internal configuration.

"Homeseeker, are you seeing this?"

"YES."

"His personality structure is failing," said Hunter.

"I CALCULATE A PSYCHOTIC BREAK WITHIN THE NEXT FIVE HOURS," Homeseeker said.

Hunter nodded. His finger hovered near the kill switch.

"Pascal, he is not dangerous," said Ameena. Hunter saw her square up to the android.

"Why are you protecting him? Have you anthropomorphized him into a human friend? He's a machine, Amee. Don't pretend he has feelings," the android said, its words filled with icy logic.

"He has feelings, and he's my friend."

"I think you have been around that Augie too long."

"His name is Hunter."

"I understand. It was lonely during your long trip to find Haven."

"Pascal…"

He talked over her words. "You couldn't help it. Any humanoid looks attractive after months in space."

Hunter accessed Ameena's biolink. Her blood spiked with adrenaline. "You confound me, Pascal. Do you feel the hate in your words? I can't see it on your face." She planted her feet beside the rose bed and glared at the android.

"They grow Augies in vats. Their synthskin smells like rotten meat as it cures," said the android.

"What are you saying?"

"You betrayed me, Ameena, with Hunter," said the android, its modulated voice devoid of emotions.

"Are you malfunctioning? I was faithful. I believed in you." Ameena's voice sizzled with anger.

"I find that hard to —"

There was a fusillade of thumps, followed by the honk of Homeseeker's breach alarms. Hunter perceived the rising whine of escaping air from inside the BioHab.

"Meteoroid!" shouted Ameena. She turned to run for the airlock.

"Oh, now that's something new," the android said just before Hunter lost its psymetric readout.

●

The tail of the Nu Dahunid meteor cloud swept across Homeseeker's hull. Hunter's magboots jerked sideways and his body whip-lashed after them. Fifty-three points of pain. One for every shard that had sliced through his vacuum suit and embedded in his body. His helmet chanted, "Suit breach. Suit breach." Directional arrows appeared on its visor to guide him towards the nearest airlock.

Homeseeker wailed at him.

"NU DAHUNIDS/ I COULDN'T SEE THEM/ CAME AT ME FROM THE SUN/ DAMAGE WIDESPREAD/ LOSING ATMOSPHERE/ OFF COURSE…" the ship's voice faded as the comms failed.

Hunter dumped a load of *crank* and felt the rush as his body shifted into machine-time. Repair bots popped out from their pods on the hull as he pivoted and started towards the nearest airlock. *I have to help Ameena.* He toggled the helmet mic with his chin.

"Ameena? Get to the bridge. BioHab is losing air."

Silence. He pushed the kill switch to immobilize the android. No response, no confirmation.

He checked his right shoulder; a shard of metal had sliced through his comm control. The synthskin on his upper torso and right arm, exposed to the void, swelled outward as his plasym boiled. Ribbons of synthskin, flayed from his body, drifted into space. His magboots hammered on the hull as he ran.

At last, he was in the midship's airlock. He cycled it for speed pressurization and howled when his eardrums ruptured. More of his synthskin peeled off as he jammed his body into a working vacuum suit. He burst from the inner hatch and released his magboots. No time for safety protocols. Hunter space-swam up the corridor, grabbed a handhold to stop at Homeseeker's emergency systems panel and forced it to flood the BioHab with stored air. He saw a gash across the gravity console. *That's not meteorite damage.*

A crumpled cleaning bot trailed dust and hair as it headed past him towards the nearest puncture and out into space. *Something kicked that bot, hard.*

Hand over hand, Hunter clambered up the ship's core as Homeseeker pitched and rolled. His grasp slipped on hydraulics lubricant that had vaporized in the near-vacuum and coated the handholds down the corridor. Hunter struggled for balance; the pressure change had damaged the gyros in his ears. Momentum slammed him into ruptured waste lines as they spewed a toxic purée onto the walls.

Hunter dumped *crank* again, and he moved through a slow-storm of debris. He gritted his ceramic teeth and drove his actuators to the edge of failure. His body flew up the corridor.

Backup comms activated, and ship status readouts splashed onto his *viz*.

"PASCAL'S HACKING IN," said the ship.

"You've isolated him?"

"YES, HOLDING HIM OFF FOR NOW."

"Put me through via text, but hide my location," he told Homeseeker.

"DONE," said the ship.

[Hunter] Pascal, why are you hacking Homeseeker?

[Android] Augie, give me ship control.

Hunter ignored the demand.

[Android] I have perceived your efforts to shut off the android. Give me ship control, or I'll continue to damage Homeseeker.

Hunter kept going; his arms and legs spun in a blur as he climbed towards the BioHab. He rerouted the kill switch and tried it again. *Pascal, you're playing a dangerous game.*

"STOP HIM. HE'S HURTING ME!" Homeseeker's shipcode filled his *viz.*

"Sorry, Homeseeker, Ameena's life is my priority."

The ship replied with a jagged shudder.

At the Spoke-3 airlock, Hunter grabbed a spare vacuum suit. Floating globules of plasym splattered against his visor as he twisted through the airlock into BioHab.

Inside, a whirlwind of destruction spiraled towards the punctured skylight. Homeseeker's desperate counter-maneuvers had knocked his fragile bonsai collection off their stands; they were a cloud of ceramic bits and broken branches. An unconscious birdoid drifted by, its wings half-furled. Ameena had tangled herself in the bamboo to avoid the sucking current.

Hunter flew over a pile of collapsed hydroponics, dropped the suit and leaped for the skylight above Ameena. From his thigh pocket, he grabbed a hull patch and slapped it over the fist-sized hole. The repair patch dimpled, and cracks radiated across the glass to its purlins, but the skylight held.

He pushed off from the hab-truss and rocketed down towards Ameena. She was barely conscious. Her cyanotic lips were parted to suck at the disappearing air. With a blur of mechanized motion, Hunter pulled Ameena into the vacuum suit, set the helmet, and cranked the airflow to full. Under the faceplate, Ameena's cheeks pinked as oxygen returned to her blood. He saw her mutter and cough. In 20 seconds, an eternity to Hunter, she opened her eyes and smiled at him. Hunter's empathic array spurted, and he teetered at the edge of overload. He slowed to human-time. The breach alert subsided as Homeseeker replenished the BioHab's air supply.

Hunter tore his gaze from Ameena's face to look at the damage in the BioHab. He scanned for the android, ready for a fight, but it had vanished. Deep scratches on the walls marked its trail towards the Spoke-1 airlock.

"Where is it?" he asked Homeseeker.

"IT'S IN THE CENTRAL CORE, HEADING TOWARDS THE BRIDGE. BREAKING PARTS OF ME AS IT GOES. MAKE IT STOP, PLEASE..."

"I'm on it, Homeseeker," he replied.

He touched his helmet to Ameena's and shouted so she could hear him.

"I can't stay with you. The android is sabotaging the ship."

Ameena nodded, grim-faced.

"When the air comes back, keep your earpiece connected. I can talk, but I have damaged my ears," said Hunter.

With a final check of Ameena's air supply, he secured her position and headed for Engineering. The last thing he noticed before the *crank* hit his drive, was Ameena gently scooping one of the birdoids in her gloved hands.

●

A pile of debris ground itself into smaller bits inside the sucking wind of a meteorite puncture. Hunter slid a patch over it and entered Engineering. As he stood on top of the wreckage, he swayed with *crank* withdrawal and indecision. *How can I save Homeseeker and contain the android simultaneously?*

Homeseeker's breach alarms went dark and silent as Hunter reestablished containment. Eyes lit with diagnostic displays, he woke the nanobots and set them to their repairs. Homeseeker's gravity restarted and his feet settled onto the deck. On the status panel, Hunter saw an airlock indicator flash amidships. The android was approaching Ameena's position. Hunter wanted to run back to the

BioHab, but logic locked him in place. He had to save the ship if they were all to live. Hunter regained a limited psymetric readout from Pascal's datanime and analyzed it.

"Homeseeker?"

"YES?"

"Please give me text-to-speech with the android, on an isolated channel."

"DONE."

[Hunter] Let me help you. Your datanime has become unstable.

[Android] That's what you say. How accommodating. I don't trust you. You want to *fix* me. Give me control of the ship.

[Hunter] No one wants to hurt you. Come back to the cargo bay, and I'll give you ship control. *I'm still human enough to lie. That's a surprise.*

[Android] No, I don't believe you.

"I CALCULATE A 96% PROBABILITY OF DATANIME FAILURE," said Homeseeker.

[Hunter] Mr. Tellor, your datanime is disassociating. I want to save you.

[Android] Not... going.

The text paused.

On the psymetric readout, Pascal's datanime began to coalesce, brighten and solidify. The structure snarled like a rope on a rotor, then it ballooned with an unbearable brightness, and imploded. For three milliseconds, the data-flare filled Hunter's *viz* and overflowed onto his eyes. When his vision cleared, Hunter saw that Pascal's datanime had collapsed into a melted, twisted, shell of itself. The datanime pathways had become smaller, simpler, and crueler. Another personality arose from the remains.

[Android] What happened? Why do I feel so strange?

[Hunter] Mr. Tellor? Pascal? Is that you?

[Android] No, no, I'm Cal, call me Cal. Do you want to play with me?

[Hunter] Not now, I'm busy with the ship.

[Android] No one ever wants to play with me. I'll invent some games of my own.

Hunter flicked the kill switch again. Nothing.

●

Homeseeker tracked the android. It cornered wide and collided with the walls as whatever remained of Pascal's mind recklessly drove the mechanical body towards the BioHab. Hunter had to warn Ameena.

"Homeseeker?"

"YES?"

"Do you have sensors in the BioHab?"

"YES."

"Patch me to Ameena's earpiece and send her replies as text," said Hunter.

"DONE," said Homeseeker

"Ameena, Pascal's gone, full psycho. A child personality called Cal has emerged. He's dangerous, unpredictable. Stay out of his reach. I'll be there soon," said Hunter.

[Ameena] How soon is soon? Can you come by now?

Even in text, her urgent need reached him.

"I've got to repair the damage from Pascal's sabotage, or we'll be airless and marooned," he said.

[Ameena] OK, I'll be *creative* with that motherless brick.

Even though he couldn't hear her, he knew how anxious she was. She always swore when anxious.

"GUESS WHO JUST ARRIVED," said Homeseeker in shipcode to Hunter.

[Ameena] Who are you?

[Android] I am... Cal. Who are you?

[Ameena] I'm Ameena. Hey, Cal? Want to play hide and seek?

[Android] Yes, yes, yes.

[Ameena] You hide first, and I'll find you. Ready? I will count now.

[Android] You'll never catch me.

[Ameena] 1... 2... 3...

Clever Ameena, Hunter thought. His skinless fingers clicked across the consoles. Hunter recalculated. The android was strong. *A physical confrontation has a 70% chance of failure, but guile might defeat it.* He looked at the swarm of working nanobots and forced his logical processor outside of its code and into the unthinkable. A few of these nanos could cripple Pascal's datanime in seconds, once he got them into the android. He had to kill a human mind to save Ameena's life.

Twelve minutes had passed by the time Hunter left Engineering. He dumped the last of his *crank* as he ran to the BioHab. His overstimulated drive responded sluggishly. *Any more crank and I'll poison myself.*

He followed Ameena's game with Cal over Homeseeker's sensors. Homeseeker found her suit signal at the edge of the bamboo grove, behind a pile of collapsed hydroponic racks. The android lurched from one hiding place to another and emerged randomly to twist raspberries off their vines and jam the fruit into its mouth like a spoilt child.

Ameena counted slowly as she tried to make time for Hunter.

[Ameena] 945... 946... 947...

Hunter entered the BioHab across from Ameena's hiding spot; he hoped to draw the android's attention away from her. He waved enthusiastically and yelled at it in the thin, cold air.

"Hello, Cal. How are you feeling today?"

[Android] Hello. Don't you think it's fun to play?

The android rinsed berry juice off its hands in the garden fish tank and snatched a wiggling octoid from the water. It watched as the octoid's gills struggled to pull oxygen from the air.

"Do you want to play a virtual game?" asked Hunter, his flayed face crackling with dried plasym.

[Android] Yes, yes, yes.

The android dropped the octoid as it rushed toward Hunter.

"These are the newest games we have," said Hunter as he held out a handful of datacrysts to the android. The nanobots crawled along the underside of his hand, preparing to enter the android by any opening.

[Android] Are they bloody and scary?

It plucked the crysts from Hunter's ravaged palm.

"Oh, yes, the scariest. Why don't you try one?" said Hunter. He watched the android examine the crysts while the nanobots scurried towards its ears. *Just as scary as you are.*

[Android] I want to hunt Ameena, but she made me hide first.

"If you play these games, you can hunt many sorts of things. Just pop one in your port," said Hunter.

The android teased Hunter, rattling the datacrysts in its fist with childish glee. Three crysts dropped through its fingers, and as it bent to retrieve them, Hunter saw Ameena lunge. Before he could warn her off, she had pounced on the android's back.

[Ameena] Hunt me? I don't think so.

The animal ferocity on Ameena's face surprised Hunter.

The android flailed at her, but Hunter grabbed its arms and pinned its wrists. Together, they dragged the android to its knees, and as Hunter held its arms, Ameena latched onto its thrashing head, reached behind its ear and fumbled with the reset button.

[Android] No, no, no...

The android's raving mind filled Hunter's *viz* with text.

Ameena finally hit the reset. The android slowed, stopped, and knelt on the moss, and its face turned upwards to the stars.

"STARTING TWO-MINUTE RESET COUNTDOWN," said Homeseeker.

Hunter and Ameena waited and waited.

"The nanos are working," said Hunter.

He read her lips. "What if?"

"They can do it." *Please let me be right.*

At 1 minute and 42 seconds, he saw a change in the psymetric readout. Pascal's datanime convulsed, snaked into a coil, and froze. The nanobots had done their job. The android slowly toppled over. Ameena shuddered, scooped up the limp octoid and placed it back in the tank.

•

Homeseeker continued her deceleration into the Dahuri System while the dummies repaired the ship. Hunter lay in Medibay, his synthskin covered with grafts and healwrap.

Ameena dozed in the chair beside him. While she slept, he ran diagnostics on his systems.

"HOW ARE YOUR REPAIRS?" asked Homeseeker. "THE DUMMIES MISS YOUR GUIDANCE."

"They will survive," Hunter replied to Homeseeker. "I intend to enjoy this. She's the best nurse in the galaxy."

"YES, I'VE BEEN OBSERVING HER BEDSIDE MANNER."

Ameena woke, yawned and stretched her neck. "You look like two-and-a-half meters of used hull plating."

"Thanks, it's a new skin style for me." He could hear her voice again; it made him smile despite the hypersensitivity of his new eardrums.

She laughed and went off to the garden for food.

Hunter's empathic array secreted an unpleasant combination of hormones. He felt guilty for changing and killing Pascal's datanime. *If Ameena knew, would she want Pascal's original datanime reloaded into the android?* He decided not to mention it unless she asked him.

"NOT GOING TO TELL HER ABOUT OUR MODIFICATIONS TO PASCAL, ARE YOU?" said the ship.

"No."

"YOU GET MORE HUMAN EVERY DAY."

●

Two months later, Ameena stood in Medibay, bathed in the violet light of the RepGen tank. She dropped her shipsuit and stood before Hunter as he ran diagnostics on her arms and legs. The boundaries between her real body and the prosthetic limbs had vanished. Her synthskin glimmered as its subcutaneous networks conveyed sensory information to her brain. Hunter's palms flickered with a counterpoint rhythm. His pumps synched with her heartbeat.

Hunter slid his hands under her hair and lifted it to check her neck. On either side of her spine, subcutaneous circuits carried signals from her new limbs to motor cortex implants. She kept her head lowered during his examination and submitted to his ministrations. She was silent. Hunter recognized the need to make the nonsensical human conversation they called small talk.

"I have studied Botticelli and Michelangelo," he said.

"You enjoy old Earther art now?"

"I needed patterns for your new limbs. Examples of their work are in my database."

"Am I your new project?" Ameena asked.

Hunter recognized her facial pattern; humans called it ironic. There was an uptick in her heart rate and dopamine levels. Something aroused her, at least on a chemical level. Hunter paused, somewhere in the labyrinth of his logical processor was the correct response. He couldn't find it.

"SAY SOMETHING BACK TO HER," Homeseeker said.

"Not a project, a poem," said Hunter, trying to hide the chemical jolt from his empathic array.

"I am a poem?" asked Ameena.

Hunter was silent as he searched for an answer.

She sighed and shook her head as she pulled the shipsuit up over her hips. "Anyhow, I'm tiring. I must sleep now."

"JUST TELL HER," said the ship.

"Goodnight, Ameena," said Hunter as his empathic array dumped counter hormones into his plasym. His logical processor was overclocking again. Hunter grimaced as his drive slid out of synch.

●

A few days later, the comm chimed on the bridge. Hunter looked up at the shipcam. "Yes?"

"Hunter," Ameena said, "Come to the cargo bay. There is something strange about this android."

Ameena stood beside the holo-display, the android's body lay headless on the table. She was examining a readout from its brain. Without turning to Hunter, she spoke.

"Did you make a backup of Pascal's datanime?"

"Yes."

"Please put it up on my screen. Split the holo-display so that I can compare it with the deactivated version in the android's brain. Memories are missing. I need to understand what happened to Pascal's consciousness."

Hunter calculated Ameena's reaction to the confession he had to make. His processing time slowed under the load. Five seconds passed.

"Hunter?"

"Yes?"

"What's wrong?"

"You will see… differences. I made changes. I tried to stabilize his mind."

Ameena's voice lowered in anger. "Show them, side by side in the holo."

She exhaled a sob as the left screen filled with Pascal's memory.

"On the left is his unaltered datanime. On the right is his datanime with my alterations. He was an addict, I tried to repair the damage," said Hunter.

"You shouldn't have done that. Reset the android and put Pascal's unaltered datanime into it."

"I'm sorry, Ameena. I wanted him healthy and balanced for you."

After a long silence, Ameena grumbled. "Damn, Hunter, sometimes you are such a complete brick."

After she stormed from the cargo bay, Hunter made a clattery approximation of a sigh. He longed for the days when they had searched the Dahurus Constellation together and shared a dream.

"HUNTER, I RECEIVED A MESSAGE FROM THE LUNANS," said Homeseeker, breaking in on his self-pity.

"The Lunan Revolutionaries? Are they still alive?" Hunter's logical processor paused, as the empathic array overrode its functions.

"YES, THEY ARE HIDING IN THE KUIPER BELT, WAITING FOR OUR INSTRUCTIONS. THEY BROADCAST A WIDE SPECTRUM CALL, HOPING TO REACH US."

"When did they send it?"

"JUST OVER A YEAR AGO, SHIP TIME. 34 YEARS IN THEIR TIME."

"Did you send a response?"

"YES, ALONG WITH AN ENCODED FLIGHT PLAN. THEY HAVE 580,000 PEOPLE IN THEIR SHIPS."

"A significant number. Would make a viable colony."

"IT WOULD."

"This may cheer her up," said Hunter.

"YES."

"Thanks, Homeseeker."

"DON'T STAND THERE. GO, BRING HER THE GOOD NEWS."

●

The android paced the cargo bay as it gesticulated rudely at Ameena.

"I loathe being inside a droid's body. This could damage my datanime." From the android's mouth, Pascal's voice echoed off the metal walls.

"I know, love, but I have a crucial question to ask you," Ameena said. Her stance relaxed, pre-defensive, as she watched him with wary apprehension.

"You couldn't wait, make me a clone?" The android stopped and twisted its metal head to an unnatural angle. Ameena cringed.

"No, we need to talk to you. We will put you back into hibernation as soon as we can," said Ameena, covering her discomfort with a forced smile.

"This is torture. I have no heartbeat; I cannot smell or taste. Every movement is so... mechanical." The android flexed its arms and hands and looked through its fingers at her.

"I'm different now," said Ameena. "As much of a machine as you are."

In the corner, Hunter shifted his stance. His eyes lit as Pascal's psymetric readout filled his *viz*.

The android cocked its head. Listening. Thinking.

"Did the Augie do that to you?" The android lowered its voice to a conspiratorial whisper.

"Hunter rebuilt me," said Ameena. "I got caught in an explosion, at your house on Luna." She crossed her arms and waited for the android to speak. It acted confused, and one of its fingers twitched randomly.

"An explosion? Wait, it's coming back to my mind now. I remember the Earther's' attack. They bombed the house. Was it one of their tricks?" The android hugged its shoulders in a mechanical approximation of human insecurity.

"I've seen the archives. Earth bombed the crater. They took you into hiber-arrest," said Ameena. She stepped forward instinctively to comfort, remembered the danger and paused.

Hunter released a jot of *crank* into his drive as he prepared for machine speed.

"They betrayed me," said the android. "My people turned on me, and then they left Luna." The android was fiddling with its wrist panels, popping them open, closing them with snapping clicks. Ameena's lips twitched in annoyance.

"They left because you and the Lunan Separatists dropped a rock on Asia. That evil act killed millions of innocent people," said Ameena.

The android was silent for two of her heartbeats. Hunter edged forward. His bare feet made no sound on the cargo bay deck.

"What was I to do? Earth needed a lesson." The android's hand flicked dismissively, its flat voice layered emotionless disinterest onto the words. "Should I be wandering the stars, leading my people away from civilization into the unknown? You were an expendable resource, I was not," said the android.

"Expendable resource?" Ameena's voice barked with fury. The android continued its speech, undeterred.

"Then, the Lunan Senate, those opportunistic bastards, they surrendered to the Earthers."

"Expendable? Is that..." Ameena hissed.

The android interrupted.

"Hiber-arrest. What a lie. The brickin' guards kept me awake for thirty years, made me their servant." The android stopped pacing and posed in front of Ameena, its hard face an inch from hers. Ameena's adrenalin spiked on the biolink. Hunter put his finger on the kill switch, his attention locked on the android.

"I misread the political signs. The Lunans love you, they believe in *you*, not me. The people call you 'Ameena, the Guide Star.' They forgot me."

Ameena's voice came through the air like an arrow. "Why was there a bomb in your hiberchamber?"

"If you must know, dear Amee, then I'll tell you the rest of my story. One guard helped me make a bomb. He was a member of the Lunan Separatists, sympathetic to my plight."

"What do you mean?" Ameena's posture twisted with suspicion and distrust.

"The Lunans pushed me out; they forgot me. I planted the bomb in my hibercrib because I couldn't stand the longing, my longing for you, for my dream, for the cause. If I died as a martyr, I would live in their legends forever. If you died with me, you could never replace me," said the android.

Hunter stopped the psymetric feed, cleared his *viz* and edged closer. He shook from the effects of the unmetabolized *crank*. Ameena stood rigid with anger, face to face with the android. Too close for Hunter's comfort.

"That is wrong thinking. What gives you the right to burnish your reputation with my death?" Spittle shot by the force of her words spattered on the android's face.

"Because you are the true heart of the Lunan Revolution and I am just a forgotten demagogue," said the android. It lunged forward, and then it stopped. Its arms froze in mid-arc, spiky fingers poised an inch from her face.

Ameena stumbled backward and fell on the deck, panting with fear and rage. She whispered to herself. "True heart? Am I the only person who can lead the Lunans?" Her voice trailed off as she thought about her future. A few minutes later, she stood up and spoke to Hunter.

"You're right. Pascal lost his sanity, long ago. It's time we put him to rest. Do it now, please."

"Yes, I'll make it quick and painless for him."

Hunter started the deletion. He cut the android's audio as Pascal's self-awareness faded away. The datanime network shattered, and its components became a disconnected cloud swirling around a mindless void. The android unfroze and sagged to the deck, heaped like an unstrung marionette. Ameena wept as she stood beside it. Her voice was low.

"Thank you, Hunter. Thank you for trying to help him. I guess there was nothing left but death wishes in Pascal's mind."

Ameena returned to the BioHab while Hunter deactivated the service android and secured it.

"PASCAL DIED A LONG TIME AGO," said Homeseeker. Hunter didn't reply.

●

Hunter watched Ameena cope with Pascal's final death. After they burned Pascal's remains in Homeseeker's engines, she kept to herself. Devoted to the Lunan Revolution, she used the time to encode star charts for the dispossessed. Hunter broadcast them into space. When their sub-light ships arrived at Haven, Homeseeker would be there to meet them.

In the BioHab garden, Hunter started another bonsai. As he bent wires around the tiny pine tree, he heard Ameena enter behind him.

"How are you?" He turned to face her. *Be casual, don't interrogate.*

"I'm fine. Just popped in for more fruit."

Hunter could tell from the micro-expressions around her mouth she was nervous.

"The strawberries are ripe," he said. Ameena didn't answer.

She passed the hydroponic racks and walked out to stand under the Lunan bamboo. There were still dead patches, a leftover from the meteoroid strike. Hunter checked her biolink. *What's elevating her stress hormone levels?*

She cleared her throat a few times as she tried to speak.

"And the zucchini looks good," he said. *Ameena isn't listening.*

Under the faint blue-white light of 56 Dahuri, the bamboo leaves cast amber shadows. She gazed at their pitted Gongshi, the scholar's stone centered upright on a bed of moss. It was their last remnant of Luna. A crimson birdoid landed on it and tilted its head to look at Ameena with a button bright eye.

"I dreamed about a childhood accident on Luna. I used to jump so high in the light gravity that I could see all Poincaré Crater. One day, I dared myself to go farther than I ever had from my family dome," Ameena said, the words of her quiet reminiscence filled the space between them.

"There was a day when I jumped too high and landed hard in a deep crater. The crater walls around me blocked my radio signal. I tried to climb up the rim, but it was too high for me. I slipped, fell back, and sprained my ankle." Ameena shivered as she relived the accident.

"I was running out of air. There was a horrible inner voice saying, 'you will die, die, die.' It was louder than the alarms inside my helmet."

Hunter scrutinized Ameena's biolink as more adrenaline diffused into her veins. Her heartbeats resonated in his ears.

The birdoid dipped its beak into a small pocket of water on the stone and raised its head back to swallow. Ameena paused, took a breath, and let it hop onto her finger. She continued to speak.

"As I lay in the crater, I tried not to cry, not to breathe too fast. Then, a shadow spread across my visor. Our family's new Augie was there. You saved my life."

Hunter shuddered as the hormones filled his plasym. He remembered the little girl in a crater. *I was made for her.*

His logical processor stopped, it had finished calculating. He had a solution.

Ameena stepped towards him, and he looked at her beautiful hands, the hands that had covered his wounds with healwrap. He felt big and strong, small and weak. His chest filled with warmth and synchronization. *Was this joy?* He placed his wire cutters next to the tiny bonsai. Ameena's face played a symphony of expressions.

"Once before, I said that you were a poem," said Hunter.

"I remember," she said. "Is there more?"

"You have a tangible beauty and a brave spirit filled with secret feelings."

"Yes?" Her voice was desire.

"Your soul takes the shape of every living thing in my life. I love you, Ameena Tereshkova," said Hunter.

She ran to him on elegantly proportioned legs.

●

A.C. Worth's story "Homecoming" was originally published in the anthology Score: an SFF symphony *on Friday, 22 June 2018. See books.metaphorosis.com*

About the author

Ann Cudworth discovered her penchant for storytelling as a girl growing up in the suburbs of Boston. Her desire to create bigger and weirder worlds led to a career in television, and for decades she lived the gentile life of a broadcast television set designer in Brooklyn, NY. Eventually, she felt the urge to return to New England and storytelling and now lives dangerously in lively coastal New Hampshire. When not writing, Ann enjoys epic baseball games and culinary experimentation.

Under the pen name of A C Worth, she writes in the Science fiction/Second world/Fantasy/Romance genres. Published work includes a monk-punk fantasy called "The Tapestry" — *Metaphorosis* (2018), a robot-romance entitled "Homecoming" — *Score: an SFF Symphony* anthology (2019), "The Day the Sandlot Sharks played the Hardware Hammers", about a little league championship on a generational spaceship — *Sci-Fi Lampoon* (2020), and a flash fiction concerning false gods called "Stone God" — in *The New Exterus, Volume I* (2021). She is currently submitting new short stories and working on her third novel, *The Woman Who Walked Around the Moon*.

Light Winds With a Chance of Velociraptors

Michelle Ann King

"That's the worst thing about the end of the world," Elsie said, staring mournfully into a teacup that had long ago been licked clean of every last drop of Tetleys and soggy crumb of custard cream. "Routines go straight out the window."

Harry glanced away from the TV, which was showing aerial footage of a tiger chasing pigeons in Trafalgar Square. "Really? That's the worst part? It's not the deaths of millions and the imminent fall of civilisation, it's that nobody's been round with the tea trolley for a couple of hours?"

"*Six* hours," Elsie said. "I'm spitting feathers over here."

"So's that tiger," Flora said, nodding at the screen.

Harry gave her a disapproving look. "Not funny, Flo. That's the one that ate Jeremy Clarkson, you know."

"Is it? Oh well, there you go. Silver linings, and all that." She watched the tiger make a particularly spectacular leap. "With any luck, it'll bag Danny Dyer next."

Harry tutted loudly and went back to the TV while Elsie wheeled herself across the room to the jigsaw table. Young Justin was still curled up in a ball underneath.

"Justin? How you doing, pet?"

There was no response.

"You know what would make you feel better? A nice cuppa. And a plate of Hobnobs, maybe. Don't you think? Justin?"

"Leave the poor boy alone, Elsie," Flora said. "I told you before, we can't get in the kitchen. It's full of baboons. And one of them funny furry things, what are they called?"

"Sasquatch?"

"No, no. Llamas, that's it."

"Oh, right. I suppose they are pretty funny. Spit at you, too, if you get too close."

"That's why I didn't, not even to look for Hobnobs. Although no, hang on, isn't that camels?"

"Is it? I'm not sure. Could be. Better watch yourself when you go to the ladies, then, because there's a couple of them in there."

Under the table, Justin let out a faint, plaintive, "Oh God," and began to cry quietly.

Flora bent down, slowly, and landed a pat on his shoulder. "This, see, this is the trouble with the younger generation."

Elsie nodded. "No resilience. No backbone. No Blitz spirit."

"That as well, yeah. But I was going to say they get paralysed by despair when they realise they're going to die without having had much sex. I mean, look at him, poor lad, he's barely grown out of his bumfluff and acne. And now here we are, and his only chance of a last-night-on-Earth shag is with one of us lot. Or the llama. It's just tragic, that's what it is."

"Shush," Harry said, flapping his hands. "The Prime Minister's going to be giving a speech in a minute. I want to listen."

"Pfft," Flora said. "The tiger can have him next, after Danny Dyer. Although there's no chance of that happening, is there? He's not going to be out there on the streets. None of them are. All the bloody government are going to be holed up in a nice bunker somewhere chomping on a year's supply of tinned tuna and prostitutes while the rest of us poor buggers are left to get on with it."

Harry turned around in his armchair and directed another scandalised, "*Shush,*" at her.

"Shush yourself, old man. It's only going to be the usual bollocks — don't panic, stay indoors, everything's under control, blah blah blah. I'd rather carry on watching the tiger, at least he's interesting. And better looking, come to that."

"We could always play a game," Elsie said. "How about charades? I'll go first."

"Oh no, you don't," Flora said quickly. "All you ever do is pick *Gone with the Wind* and use it as an excuse to let rip. I'm wise to your game, madam. And the air fresheners are all in the supply cupboard, which is infested with garden snails. So no, we'll do Twenty Questions instead, and I'll go first. Question one: which of the beasts in here is most likely to kill and eat us first?"

"Ooh, I know that one," Harry said, raising his hand. "It's the baboons. The rest are all herbivores."

Flora pointed at him. "One-nil to Harry."

Elsie frowned. "I don't think that's quite how the game works, you know."

"Call it the apocalypse rules version. Elsie, your go."

"Oh. Okay then. Errr... what happens to us after we die?"

"Hmm." Flora rubbed her chin. "I'm going with total existential annihilation. Do I get the point?"

"No, no," Harry said, waving his hand in the air again. "I know this one, too. It's whatever you believe happens."

"It's what?"

"What happens is whatever you believe happens," Harry said patiently. "I read it in this book once. Self-determined something or other. Basically, it said that if you believe you get reincarnated, or go to heaven, or whatever, then you do."

"That's the nuttiest thing I've ever heard," Flora said.

Harry glanced back at the TV, where a harried-looking weatherman was forecasting light winds and a shower of badgers over the Brecon Beacons. "Really?"

"I rather like the idea," Elsie said. "It makes sense when you think about it. Explains all this, for a start."

Flora hiked one bushy eyebrow. "It does?"

"It's Beryl. You know, from Room Fourteen? She always liked animals better than people, and she died on Tuesday — right before this whole thing started. I can definitely see her believing animals should inherit the earth or whatever."

"You might have something there," Harry said, nodding. "She always used to nick my rice pudding and feed it to next door's cat. So if she managed to believe in this idea hard enough by the time she snuffed it, bingo. Instant animal planet."

Elsie nodded. "Exactly."

"You two are as bad as each other, you know that? Pair of barmpots, the both of you."

"Shush," Elsie said, closing her eyes.

"Oh, not you and all. What's the matter now?"

"*Shush,* Flo. I'm trying to believe."

"Believe what?"

"I don't know yet. Something nice." She sighed. "Although all that's coming to mind is tea and biscuits, and I can't help thinking the afterlife ought to have a bit more substance to it than that."

"I want to be twenty-five again," Harry said. "I was a lovely lad, at twenty-five. Full head of hair and everything. I don't want to go back to the nineteen-fifties, though. I'd miss high-definition telly and pot noodles. And all the internet porn, of course. Can't forget that." His eyes brightened. "Here, can we have our afterlife in the future? Get jet packs and flying cars and stuff?"

"I think you can do whatever you want," Elsie said.

Flora shook her head. "Listen to yourselves. You've gone bonkers."

Elsie shrugged. "In case you hadn't noticed, *everything's* gone bonkers. You said it yourself, Flo — it's the apocalypse. Normal rules don't apply."

"Hmm," Flora said, watching the TV. Outside Buckingham Palace, a shrieking reporter was going down for the third time under a tidal wave of hamsters. "You might have a point there."

"Beryl loved hamsters," Elsie said, following her gaze.

"And dinosaurs," Harry said. "She must have made us watch Jurassic Park at least ten times a week."

"True," Elsie said, and Flora nodded. Then all three of them glanced rather nervously at the door.

"It's got to be worth a go, don't you reckon?" Elsie said. "It's not as if we've got anything to lose, after all."

Flora huffed. "Well, I suppose if it's all bollocks then we're back to the concept of existential annihilation and there's no harm done. Well, apart from the actual annihilation itself, of course, but you know what I mean."

"Not really," Elsie said cheerfully. "Weren't they a punk band, Existential Annihilation? I think I saw them supporting Cock Sparrer at the Marquee, once."

"Can we get back to the believing in jet packs and internet porn?" Harry said. "I want to be ready by the time the baboons eat me. Or the velociraptors."

"Not a bad idea," Flora said, with another glance at the door. A large furry caterpillar slithered underneath it. "So, how do we do it then? Make ourselves believe in things, I mean?"

She looked at Elsie, who looked at Harry. Who looked alarmed. "I don't know, do I?"

"You're the one who read the book."

"Yeah, but it was, you know, philosophical and stuff. Not an instruction manual."

"Okay, so we'll just have to work it out ourselves," Flora said. "Don't suppose either of you were in the CIA, were you? I'm sure they did brainwashing and mind control."

Harry nodded. "I saw that film. I think it was on goats, though."

"I was in the Women's Institute for a while," Elsie said. "Does that count?"

"Did you learn how to brainwash people?"

"No, but I can make a cracking Victoria Sponge. And fold napkins to look like flowers."

Harry's stomach rumbled. "I could murder a nice slice of Victoria Sponge."

"*Focus,*" Flora said, snapping her fingers in front of his face. "We need to think about feeding our minds, not our stomachs. Think. How do you go about believing something?"

"I believed Father Christmas brought presents down the chimney when I was a kid," Harry said. "Because my dad said so. And we didn't even have a chimney. Or presents, come to that."

"Trust in authority figures," Flora said, nodding. "That works. Parents, teachers, bosses, coppers. Film stars and celebrities, even. It's why they get them to advertise stuff."

"Trouble is," Harry said, 'my dad's been dead for fifty years, and we're a bit short on any of those others right now."

"We've got Justin," Elsie said brightly. "He's got authority. Kind of. He's got the key to the potting shed and he can fill up the tea urn on his own, so that's got to count for something, hasn't it?"

They all looked at Justin, who was still curled into a ball under the jigsaw table.

"Justin, pet?" Elsie said. "Do you think you could pop out and be authoritative for a bit? We'd be ever so grateful, love."

The only response was a slight increase in the volume of weeping.

Elsie sighed. "All right, what else?"

Flora scratched her head. "Hypnotism? Like that Paul McKenna bloke? I saw him once, he was ever so good. Made this lad think he was a naked kangaroo."

Harry frowned. "How would you know a kangaroo was naked?"

"Well, they haven't got clothes on, have they?"

"Focus," Flora said. More caterpillars were wriggling under the door and the TV was now just showing static.

"Sorry," Harry said. "What about affirmations? You know, where you keep telling yourself something — like, every day in every way I'm getting better and better."

"Hmm," Flora said. "Autosuggestion. That's a kind of self-hypnosis."

"There you are, then," Elsie said happily. She took off her gold locket and began swinging it in front of her eyes. "I am getting sleepy. I am getting very sleepy."

Harry leant back in the armchair, took a deep breath and closed his eyes. "When I die I will be twenty-five. I will have all my hair, a jet pack, and superfast broadband. There will be no velociraptors. When I die I will be twenty-five, I will have —"

"In the afterlife, I will have better magical powers than Beryl Arkwright," Elsie said, swaying in time with the locket. "In the afterlife, I —"

"Hold on, hold on," Flora said. "What about Justin? We'd have to hypnotise him too. We can't just leave him to get annihilated."

"Fair point," Harry said. He got up and crouched beside the jigsaw table. "Justin? You need to come out and get hypnotised, mate. You need to believe in good things — like — like —" He beckoned to Flora. "Come and help me out here, Flo. What do kids think is good, these days?"

Flora sighed and carefully lowered herself, knees creaking, to the floor by his side. "iPhones? Beyonce? Junk food?"

"That'll do." Harry shook Justin's shoulder. "iPhones, mate. Beyonce. Cheeseburgers and pizza. No dinosaurs. Come on, you can do it. Everything comes to he who believes."

"Pretty sure it's usually *waits*," Flora said. "But never mind. Apocalypse rules."

Justin moaned softly as a caterpillar tried to crawl into his ear. Flora inched closer and peered at it warily. "Are caterpillars herbivores?"

"Not always," Harry said. "Some eat other insects and stuff. And some have hairs with venom in. It can give you dermatitis. Or kidney failure and brain haemorrhages."

"Jesus," Flora said, snatching back the hand she'd been going to flick the caterpillar away with. "Start with the fatal ones next time, will you?"

"That's in Brazil, though, normally. Not Croydon."

"Apocalypse rules," Flora said again, darkly. "And this is Beryl we're talking about, remember? If anyone's going to believe we'll get besieged by poisonous caterpillars, it'll be her."

Harry sat down on the carpet next to the curled-up Justin and put his hands over his ears. "When I die, there will be no velociraptors, poisonous caterpillars, celebrity-eating tigers, or misanthropic old arseholes who steal your rice pudding. When I die —"

"Wait, wait," Flora said, putting a hand on his arm. "Do you hear that?"

Harry took one hand away from his ear. "What?"

"Sirens. Sounds like an ambulance. Haven't heard one of them for ages. And the baboons have stopped barking."

Carefully, they crawled out from under the table. The ambulance siren howled in the distance, but nothing else did.

"Is it over?" Harry said.

Flora brushed dust and biscuit crumbs — but no caterpillars, which had all disappeared — off the front of her dress. "Do you know, I think it might be. Elsie? Elsie, wake up. We made it."

Elsie didn't move. Her mouth was open, and the golden locket had fallen from her fingers.

"Well, bugger," Flora said, after a while.

Harry picked up the locket and put it back around Elsie's neck. Then he stepped aside and almost collided with the tea trolley, which was sitting beside the table.

"Huh," he said. "Who put that there?"

On the trolley sat a pot of Tetleys and a large plate of chocolate Hobnobs. Harry's stomach growled, and Justin's head poked out from under the table.

"There you go, lad," Flora said as he clambered to his feet. "Nice cup of tea, that's what you want. Much better for you than cheeseburgers."

She pushed the trolley over to the sofa and they all sat in front of the TV, which had clicked on again. It was showing the Buckingham Palace reporter on his hands and knees, coughing up clumps of golden hamster fur. Justin gazed at it with a dazed expression.

"She did it, didn't she?" Harry said wonderingly. "Our Elsie. She did it."

Flora plucked a Hobnob off the plate and dunked it in her fresh, steaming hot tea. Then she raised the cup high.

"To Elsie," she said, around a mouthful of biscuit. "Who managed to believe in some truly bonkers gubbins, and did it a damn sight better than Beryl Arkwright."

Harry wiped his eyes and clinked his teacup against Flora's. "Lovely epitaph, Flo. If she's watching, I reckon she's well pleased with that."

"To Elsie," Justin whispered. His hands were still shaking too hard to hold a cup, so he took another Hobnob. They'd all had a couple each, but the plate was still overflowing.

"I reckon you're right," Flora said, and put her feet up with a satisfied sigh.

Michelle Ann King's story "Light Winds With a Chance of Velociraptors" was originally published in Metaphorosis on Friday, 2 June 2017

About the author

Michelle Ann King is from Essex, England. She is a writer of speculative, crime, and horror fiction whose work has appeared in over a hundred different magazines and anthologies, including *Strange Horizons, Flash Fiction Online, Interzone,* and *Black Static.* Her short story collections are available from Amazon and other online retailers, in ebook and paperback format. Find links to her published works at her website www.transientcactus.co.uk or follow her on Spoutible at spoutible.com/MichelleAnnKing

A Life of Color

N.V. Haskell

Last fall's decaying leaves shifted beneath my feet as I crossed the yard. The others watched me come, glancing nervously at the infant held tenderly in the old woman's arms. Moonlight flickered through the barren tree branches and glinted off the baby's delicate skin. Her eyes shimmered with rainbows and nebulae beneath eyelashes so pale they were barely visible. It was because of this tiny bundle that I had been hauled from my cozy bed in the middle of the night. What her story was and where she came from were puzzles that I wished hadn't happened on my watch.

The sleep loss fogging my brain faded as I took in the baby's situation. I swore silently, too quietly for any of the three to hear. The old woman had found the baby in the dingy alley behind her home, wrapped in the paint-stained blanket she still wore. The police officer and social worker had come along later. But after David, my boss at the Department of Magical Resources, woke me at 2 am, it became my problem — magic baby, magic expert. It didn't matter that my expertise was adult crimes, not children.

During my last performance appraisal, David had celebrated my departmental loyalty and hinted at a promotion. Using my desire for advancement, he'd easily leveraged me into the weekend rotations by saying it would demonstrate how effectively I could work outside of the crimes division.

Truthfully, the schedule change hadn't been a huge sacrifice. There was nothing for me outside of work.

Relationships had proven to be too taxing, not worth the effort I put in. People always left or died, like my parents when I was three. And though the multiple foster homes I'd been raised in had done an adequate job of feeding and housing me, they'd lacked warmth or encouragement. It was no wonder I still sought approval from figures in authority.

Gazing upon the abandoned infant stirred a sympathy for her.

Hard of hearing, the elderly woman had first assumed the cries belonged to the neighborhood cat in heat again. But after the racket persisted for more than an hour, she decided to investigate and phoned the police immediately upon finding the child. The infant was said to be only a few weeks old.

A magical child abandoned was practically unheard of. The magical communities were notoriously private and, although a few of the larger clans had representatives that appeared in governmental regulation meetings when the situation warranted it, most of the smaller clans avoided the greater nonmagical society completely unless they were called on for required services. Several clans had dispersed into unsanctioned areas, which made it difficult for the Department to keep track of them all.

The baby's pale hair and dainty features made her seem angelic, yet beneath her eyelids danced a myriad of colors. With a small, mournful whimper, tears of sapphire blue paint trickled down her face and further stained the blanket. The oil and organic compounds of the paint's pigment mingled with the other smells of the city, the exhaust from the cars and buses, the garbage, and even the odor of the older woman, who rocked the infant gently. She hummed softly, mindless of the streams of colorful goo running from the child's eyes. The woman's toothless smile matched the baby's as she cooed over her. Maybe caring for children came naturally to her.

As the girl drifted peacefully to sleep, her lips puffed slightly with each breath, and I cursed softly again.

Damn David for making me take these weekend on-call shifts. He was well aware that my specialty was magical crimes, not children. I never did well with anything that required special care. A graveyard of dead plants served as proof of my ineptitude; the succulents lasted a bit longer, but ultimately met their demise as well. The moment they came into my possession, their fate was sealed.

I had hoped to be able to pass the baby off quickly, until the social worker thrust a car seat and diaper bag full of supplies at me while informing me that no non-magical homes would take the infant because of her special needs. It fell to my department to find a placement. Although I argued and threatened her with demotion if she left, she flashed a contemptuous look at me before driving away. All I'd be able to do was mention her name in the administrative meeting, come Monday morning.

I knew that finding placement in any home was a challenge, but magical homes were impossible. Their tight-knit communities were scattered in the countryside, sequestered from the curious eyes of nonmagical peoples and understandably hostile to my historically untrustworthy employer. The likelihood of getting help from any of the clans for a child of unknown origin was slim. Though they were fiercely protective of their own, they were unlikely to take in a stray of unusual magical talents. Which made me wonder where the girl had come from.

When David finally answered his phone, he simply told me to 'handle it' and bring the child to the office on Monday morning. He hinted about the promotion I had applied for being a factor. That advancement would remove me from the grunt work and weekend rotations, elevating my footsteps up the corporate ladder as I'd always wanted. It didn't hurt that it came with a hefty pay increase as well.

The task would have been much easier if this were an adolescent or adult of a known clan. The Department's holding cells were constructed to deal with certain magical elements. Soundproof cells for musical clans. Fireproof rooms with automatic extinguishers for the fire clans. Sterile, metal rooms for the nature clans. But there were no facilities for magical children or infants and certainly nothing specifically built for paint magic.

I watched silently as the detective fastened the car seat in the back of my car. Aside from those swirling eyes, the infant appeared just like any other: probably riddled with germs, but also fragile and innocent.

Even though my stomach knotted at the sight of her, I told myself I could manage. I, Laura Arthur, the woman who always declined to hold all her friend's children — was now responsible for taking care of a magical infant for thirty-six hours. Humanity had continued to exist for many thousands of years, right? Certainly, it couldn't be that difficult.

When I got home, I had no choice but to place the baby's car seat beside my bed, which I regretted when she woke up crying and angry three hours later. Anxiety filled me as I tried to figure out how to put an end to the cerulean acrylic streaming from her eyes, or the loud cries erupting from her small lips. A noxious smell, like a mixture of cat pee and stargazer lilies, stung my nostrils as I unclipped the straps that secured her, distracting me from the yellow and green colors that splattered onto my silk pajamas.

When I placed my hands beneath her tiny hips, liquid squished between my fingers. When I pulled my hands away, they were covered in emerald and lemon paint. My disgust was immediate, causing my stomach to churn and threaten emptying. I'd dealt with messes in crime scenes before, but never anything like this. Another sharp wail made me push aside my revulsion. I rushed the car seat, with the still-screaming baby inside it, toward the bathroom.

I placed everything gently in the old clawfoot tub as paint dripped slowly over the sides of the seat. The colors swirled like a kaleidoscope against the white porcelain, blues and reds turning purple and blending with yellow and green to make an ominous hue. There was no time to consider the mess, even though I knew it would take more than bleach to clean it up. I needed help.

I wiped my hands on a towel and, not knowing what else to do, rushed to my neighbor's house. With her one-year-old twins, I considered Molly to be an expert in these matters, and there was no one else that might help. Though we'd only ever said a few polite words here and there, when she saw the distress on my face, she ran back with me. The inside of the bathtub had splotches of bright yellows and oranges from Iris's spittle that dripped in thin ribbons down the white tub's interior.

Loud protests continued as Molly lifted the pink-cheeked girl in her arms and peeled the wet clothes away. The baby was too small to safely bathe in the tub, Molly said. So, we held her in the sink and washed the paint off with a little soap and warm water. The paint swirled down the drain, leaving only traces of orange and blues on the porcelain. The little one's sobs quieted, dissolving into occasional hiccups as we wrapped her in a towel and put a fresh diaper on her.

Molly didn't ask where the baby had come from. She knew where I worked and knew better than to ask questions. Though the paint had obviously surprised her, she had handled it with more grace than I had, and, to her credit, she didn't chide me for not knowing what to do.

An hour after the mess was dealt with, she returned with a bag full of baby items she had intended for donation. She taught me how to prepare formula and test its warmth. I offered to pay her, but she declined and dismissed my apologies, telling me that no one was born knowing what to do.

Eventually the baby dozed off in my arms, and though my limbs ached from holding her for so long, I wasn't sure how to set her down without waking her. When I awoke later, a strand of my hair was tangled in her fingers. She gazed at me with eyes made of swirling sunflower yellow and sunset orange. She let out a low giggle, like she was the only one in on the joke. I couldn't help but smile back, wondering what I looked like to her. Was I swirls of magenta or blotches of grey cast in sharp angles? Maybe I was nothing more than a blurry figure, if she could see me at all.

I shook away those thoughts, reminding myself that it didn't matter anyway. This would only be my problem for one more day. Whatever foster home she wound up in would surely tend to her better than I could.

●

On Monday morning, I stumbled into the office with my hair in a mess and a streak of neon pink down one shoulder of my houndstooth blouse. One day of diaper disasters and a broken night's sleep had confirmed what I had always known: I wasn't cut out for parenthood.

I'd hoped that by handing the baby off to the Department researchers they could find a link between her and one of the clans catalogued in the database. That should have been the end of my direct involvement, but when David insisted I supervise, that was my day wasted. We didn't get many adults here and no one remembered a child this young ever being brought in. The awareness of the girl's vulnerability in this cold environment put me on edge.

Dr. Arias was gentler with her than I'd expected when he put her through a battery of tests: MRIs, CT scans, EEGs, and EKGs. The lab technicians handled the whimpering baby with a professional detachment while they lined each machine with drop cloths to protect them. It felt as if she were a specimen they were hastily examining in order to classify. Even I thought a baby deserved better than that.

The phlebotomist tried to extract a blood sample with a butterfly needle, but whatever ran through the baby's veins was too thick for the small needle's gauge and using a larger one would be damaging.

Her wails at the needles' prodding made me queasy and brought back old memories of the testing I'd undergone in the foster system when I was small. I remembered feeling alone and afraid. If that testing had shown any magical talents, perhaps I would have had a clan take me in. I hoped that would be the case for this girl.

Iris 15738 — her Department-issued name — was special, of that there was no doubt. If she had been from a more prominent clan, the researchers would have quickly lost interest. But because of the rarity of her magic, they wanted to know how it worked and, more importantly, if it could be useful.

In exchange for government aid and certain assurances of land and protections, the magical clans were legally obligated to assist in certain situations. The nature clans handled natural disasters and farming during times of drought. The fire clans were used for controlling burns and military procedures. The musical clans for entertainment and therapy. But the more physically artistic clans were rare. There were only a few sculptors left, and their creations could only animate for a few seconds, which made them practically useless for most purposes.

Years ago, after reforms were passed that gave the clans more autonomy and less oversight, many of the smaller factions had used the new freedom to quietly scatter. After scouring through the Departmental archives, I found only one reference to a paint clan, from decades prior. Address unknown, the phone number attached to them was ancient. The line crackled when I left a voice message.

Leaving the girl under Dr. Arias' care, I returned to my office to reach out to the small network of approved foster homes with some magical experience. But they each declined. One said they had no room, whereas another honestly said they weren't qualified to handle the babe's issues. I then began the arduous task of calling the larger clans while searching for information about where she might have come from. Then I called a dozen smaller magical settlements within two hundred miles. Eleven had no knowledge of her or her paint magic. The twelfth was the mysterious clan with the ancient number.

David summoned me late in the afternoon, his face somber. Iris slept peacefully in the car seat which was placed in a chair across from his desk.

"Any luck finding a place for her?" he asked, and sighed when I shook my head. "Hate to do this to you, but you'll probably have to keep her for another night or two, unfortunately. We'll cover the damages and I'll add a commendation to your file. Simply fill out the necessary forms and document everything with photographs."

"But —"

"There's no one else, Laura. Jon's got the triplets, and Briana's taking care of her mom. Unless you'd rather give her to the researchers." His lips pursed in disapproval, and he looked away.

We both knew their experiments would turn more invasive without oversight, and Dr. Arias couldn't be there all the time. But there was something else hidden in David's tone.

"What is it?" I asked.

"There's something wrong with her."

My heart sank. Iris stirred in her sleep in the seat next to me. I combed my fingers through her sparse hair and waited for him to continue.

"Her brain activity is abnormal, probably due to hydrocephalus, or whatever it's called with paint." He paused, trying to make sure that I couldn't misunderstand. "Her heart is arrhythmic, most likely working too hard to pump the thick fluid around her body, but without testing her enzymes we can't be sure. There's no cure."

Iris's chest rose and fell, accompanied by an occasional pause or gasp. Petite hands clutched the edges of a pink blanket. It was probably Dr. Arias who had placed a plush giraffe beside her, its head was already covered in mint green acrylic drool. It reminded me of the stuffed horse I'd been given in my first foster home. I'd carried it with me through a dozen other homes, a source of security and something soft to hold in an otherwise hard world.

"Dr. Arias doesn't think she'll make it past a year," David said. He looked at me warily, as if I were going to fall apart at the news.

I tried to keep my expression neutral and steady the sudden throb in my heart. After everything she'd been through in her short life, the girl didn't deserve this fate. Iris deserved to live. I took a deep breath. "Percentages?"

"Eighty percent chance she has a stroke, heart attack, or turns septic in the next six months. One hundred percent within the next year."

My chest deflated as ideas for a solution rushed through my mind. "But if we find where she came from, there might be a chance."

David shrugged. "Only if you can find her clan and convince them to talk to us."

●

By the end of the first week, I'd resorted to wearing shapeless, faded clothing once reserved for yard work or donation The days were whirlwinds of endless feedings, diapers, and departmental meetings. The sleepless nights left me in a dazed stupor. My home's modern décor had turned into a canvas splashed with bright acrylics and oils.

But aside from the damage being done, there were growing smiles and curious hands that slowly tugged at my emotional armor as Iris planted something both unfamiliar and uncomfortably vulnerable beneath it.

There was still no home willing to take her, not once the Department revealed her complications, but the thought of leaving her with the researchers made me nauseous. Adults who committed magic-based crimes were all dealt with properly; I'd made sure of it because I understood how the judicial system worked in those cases. And although the Department of Magical Resources had gone to great lengths to make amends for its past through media outlets and charity initiatives, most everyone suspected they kept certain practices covert.

Without an advocate, Iris might disappear within a month. Though I'd never witnessed anything personally, there were long-standing rumors about experimentation that occurred in the Department's mysterious lower levels. I'd thought that it was all conjecture, but now the fear that there might be truth to it worried me. Iris was more vulnerable than I'd ever been.

The ambitious governmental loyalist that I'd always been began to question everything, including why my other assignments were becoming less important to me when compared to Iris.

In desperation, I reached out again to the magical communities, widening the radius to five hundred miles — with the same sad result. According to one trusted magical resource, the paint clans had vanished years ago. No one knew anything about Iris and after a few brief questions, no one wanted her, either. Despite the Department's considerable resources and informants, we had yet to reach the one elusive clan. But I left another message on their nondescript voicemail and waited.

The following weeks felt like an eternity. My coworkers had been helping with feedings and diaper changes during work hours, but something strange began to happen. Iris would scream hysterically until returned to my arms. Briana nearly dropped the struggling girl when she attempted to change her. And the Department was having to reimburse not only my costs, but many of my coworkers' wardrobes after Iris's messy cries and accidents. With each feeding and diaper change, my coworkers were met with Iris's growing levels of hysteria, until they stopped offering to help altogether. And as Iris's cries grew louder, a subtle pressure began to grow around me. One email complained that Iris was upsetting the office's routine and productivity. Another suggested that if we couldn't find a home for her, the researchers on level 3-B would be happy to study her until she passed away. Level 3-B's enthusiasm at gaining more information about paint magic by studying an ill child was off-putting, to say the least.

David's behavior changed drastically over the same time frame. Where he'd initially insisted that I keep Iris and shown concern for her wellbeing, his tone changed to annoyance bordering on disdain. More than once, he suggested that I consider leaving her at the facility overnight so that I could get a full night's rest, but I heard the veiled demand in his voice. I suspected that the change was the result of pressure from his superiors. When I continued to resist, David asked that I stay away from meetings so that Iris didn't cause a distraction. In fact, I was encouraged to work from home, but refused. I watched helplessly as projects I was vying for were given to less qualified coworkers. Knowing I risked my promotion, I swallowed my anger and frustration, though I wrote down every detail of what was happening.

All hope of finding Iris' clan began to fade away.

One afternoon, David's tall figure filled the doorway of my office, a room now spotted teal and lemon, with the lingering scent of hydrocarbons hanging in the air. His carefully crafted appearance of morality was slipping away with each of our interactions.

"I can practically guarantee that promotion if you will give her up, Laura." His gaze never left mine as he spoke. "The Regional Director is offering a significant raise, too. I'm sure you must be exhausted from dealing with her. Give her to the Department, and rest assured that they will take care of her for the rest of her days."

I sighed and rubbed my eyes, silently begging for the headache that had been etched behind them for the past few weeks to ease up temporarily. For a fleeting second, I considered giving in. But I'd been a child in the system once and Iris deserved no less than what I'd had. A warm bed, a gentle word, patience. David's assurances rang hollow and while caring for her didn't feel quite as overwhelming as it once had, the thought of leaving her alone and afraid made me ill. Iris needed me and maybe I'd needed her to remind me that there was a life outside of work.

"You're okay with her disappearing into the system?" I asked.

David winced at the contempt in my voice while I studied the green and blue staining in the creases of my hands. In the process of giving up rest, personal care, and anything resembling normalcy for the past six weeks, I'd realized that there were some things I couldn't in good conscience do. Even if it was for the agency. I had come too far with Iris to back out now. Fuck him and the Department for asking me to. His face hardened as I said as much. He walked away, taking my advancement with him as Iris began to cry.

My cell phone vibrated at 3 am a week later. I rushed to answer it before it disturbed Iris, scurrying into the living room, now painted in sporadic shades of Tahitian blue, lilac, and burnt sienna.

"Did you call about a baby?" an older woman whispered over the connection.

My voice wavered as I answered, "Yes." Anticipation swelled within me, hoping this was the call I'd been waiting for. "I'm Laura Arthur from the Department of —"

"Don't say it," she snapped. "Tell me what she looks like."

"The baby?"

She took a deep, shuddering breath, filled with emotional restraint.

Flippant words that all babies looked alike nearly left my mouth. But that was old thinking and now felt completely disingenuous. An awkward tension stretched in the silence between us. That she was calling at this time of night with a lowered voice led me to the conclusion that she was afraid of being discovered. Our time was limited. "Blonde hair, round face, colorful, swirling eyes — like they're full of..."

"Paint." Her voice was heavy and raw. "I'll give you an address. Meet me there tomorrow at one pm. I need to see her."

I jotted down the location and the line went dead before I had a chance to ask any more questions. When I returned to the bedroom, Iris had wriggled from one side of her crib to the other, leaving a long squiggle of avocado green behind her. I didn't bother telling David why I wouldn't be coming into work that Thursday and he didn't care enough to ask anyway.

It was a two-hour drive from my home, through the suburbs and into the stark rural countryside. We travelled past fields and small clusters of ramshackle homes set far off the road, many partially hidden behind enchanted conifers and hedges that moved to protect the view of the settlements as I passed.

The address the woman had given directed me to an abandoned gas station, a dilapidated relic of a bygone era. The weather-beaten windows were glazed and cracked and worn chunks of concrete were interspersed with layers of indiscernible graffiti. Generations of spiders nourished themselves on fat insects in all corners of the building. As I pulled my vehicle into the weedy vacant lot, a faint silhouette shifted behind the chipped double doors.

With one hand tucked under the carrier and the other gripping a bag filled with baby supplies and a crusted giraffe, I hesitantly stepped towards the entrance. Hope and dread bloomed equally inside me.

The door groaned in protest as I pushed it open, revealing an interior cloaked in a thick fog of dust motes that were illuminated through narrow shafts of sunlight.

A tall woman stood in the back of the room, her wrinkles betraying her age, and her bright red hair pulled tightly in a bun. Her eyes were made of varied colors that swirled together. She fingered a necklace of glass beads looped around her throat. Most were painted in vibrant colors, but one was plain, as if something were missing.

Fear and reticence filled the air between us, neither of us willing to take a step forward. The woman's eyes darted towards the carrier when Iris moved inside. Her lips quivered.

"May I see her?" she asked softly.

I set the carrier on the floor and pulled down the soft blanket. I cradled Iris in my arms, hesitating. It'd been a long time since anyone else had held her.

"Who are you?" I asked.

"Messina Thawn, of clan Thawn. I'm surprised you found us." Gently, she drew Iris into her arms and swayed from one foot to the other in the rocking motion most parents seemed to know instinctively. A sad smile pulled at her lips. "I'm sorry for making you wait for a response. That number you had is old, set up ages ago for emergencies when our last leader was alive. It's rarely checked; our current clan leader is stricter, doesn't believe in using technology under any circumstances. Not even when it could bring one of our missing back to us." She paused to brush the hair from Iris's forehead. "We've managed to mostly avoid the Department's notice for decades. Ever since their experiments ended back in the thirties." Her look dared me to respond. "I bet they don't teach that in school anymore."

I shifted uncomfortably, understanding what she avoided saying and that reaching out and meeting me was a risk for her. I cleared my throat. "Does she have a name?"

She shook her head, gazing again at Iris. "I wouldn't know it. Gabby, my daughter, ran away when she discovered she was pregnant. Left with a farm boy." Her voice hitched. "I looked for her. We all did. But she was afraid of what would happen. Not everyone in our clan is accepting of the nonmagical mix. They probably thought they'd do better in the city."

Affection swept across Messina's face, but her smile faded into barely suppressed grief. "I knew something had gone wrong. I felt it. As if she'd drunk turpentine and faded away." She sniffed, tried to collect herself before she continued. "Leo, the boy, returned a few weeks ago. He's refused to talk to any of us. Won't even say what happened or where my Gabby dissolved. I can't even add her bead to my necklace."

"Bead?" I asked.

"It's the only thing we leave behind when we die." Messina cleared her throat to cover the tremor in her voice. "A bead coated with our colors."

Iris stirred in her arms, squirming her shoulders against her grandmother's bony chest. Her lashes fluttered open, seeing eyes like her own. Similar, but not the same. It was easier to see the differences when they were so close. One was orderly lines; the other was blurring chaos.

Messina gasped. Blood-red tears welled in her eyes. "Oh, no." It was a soft sound, like whispering down a moss-ridden well.

"The researchers said she was sick. But I thought her clan might be able to help." I choked on the question. "Was I...am I wrong?"

Messina's breath shuddered. Painted tears trickled down her cheeks as Iris's small fingers brushed at them curiously before tangling in the glass beads around Messina's neck.

"There's a recessive gene that runs in our clan. It keeps some of us from solidifying completely. Bones that can't harden turn to mush. The lining of organs and blood vessels eventually breaks down until our colors run together. Dissolving little by little. I hoped that Leo's influence would override..." Her words were knives cutting us both.

"Can't you help her? What about the rest of the clan? There must be someone." At the sudden rise of my voice, Iris turned. Small arms reached for me as she whimpered.

Mindless of the violet paint that splattered the front of her dress, Messina cradled the girl to her chest for a moment and sighed. She shook her head, eyes holding endless depths of anguish as she returned Iris to me.

"One of my sisters died before she was one. My nephew was the same. There's nothing anyone can do." Her fingers glided from one bead to the next before she stroked the back of Iris's head. "All you can do is care for her until she passes."

"Me? She's your family. Surely, you'd want to keep her."

"No one knows I'm here," she said, her voice gone low. The palm she pressed to her lips was covered in Iris's violet paint. Messina closed her eyes for a long moment. As her hand slowly dropped, a bright smear stained her lips and chin. "If she'd been born amongst our clan with that anomaly, she would have been dissolved already. Her life would have been shorter than in your care. Maybe even shorter than with your researchers."

"But I thought the clans... I thought that you took care of your own."

"Laura, even if we were a stronger clan with more resources, nothing could stop what is happening to her. All we have is our limited magic, and after watching so many of our children die over the years, we try to lessen the suffering." Her tears welled again. "If you want her to live a bit longer, it's best she stays with you. Plus, she's already bonded to you."

"I can't care for her. I don't know how to do *any* of this." My voice trembled, and I quelled the volume to keep from upsetting Iris further.

Messina brushed my hair from my cheek with stained fingers. "What do you need to know? Feed her when she's hungry, clean her when she's dirty, bathe her, soothe her, and hold her."

I whispered, "I can't watch her die."

Something within me broke; the veneer of strength I relied on splintered and cascaded down my cheeks. I hadn't let myself cry in a long time. So long that I'd nearly forgotten the initial sting and briny taste of my tears. Messina wiped my cheeks with gentle hands, studying the clear liquid on her fingertips before looking back at me sympathetically.

"Life and love are messy and fragile. No matter how much of either you have, it won't ever prepare you for when you have to let go." She enveloped us in her slender arms, painting my cheek with her sorrow.

Messina said a quiet goodbye as she helped place the girl in the car, stroking her face one last time with tenderness and grief.

My gaze lingered on her necklace as words stuck in my throat. "When she... her bead..."

"Keep it," she said. "It's clan tradition to wear it when someone you love passes away. It will give you something to hold when she's gone. Something to remember the colors of her life with."

Other than pulling over twice to collect myself, I remember little of the drive home. Leaving the dusty gas station, I'd vowed to protect Iris until her very last breath. No matter how much her paint stained my clothing, furniture, and skin, it was a small price to pay to hear her full-belly chortles and breathe in her sweet-smelling hair.

The following day, I found myself in a tense talk with David as I put in my request for a leave of absence and demanded payout for my untaken paid time off and the standard payment for foster parents. Our meeting then transitioned into an extensive virtual conference with the district manager and head researchers. When they attempted to bribe or threaten me, I responded with promises to publicize our exchanges and involve contacts above their heads. I hoped they didn't catch the tremor in my voice. It was half lying, of course, but I refused to abandon this lost child the way everyone else had. The meeting resulted in an extended leave of absence and veiled promises of professional stagnation.

The green and gold of summer were giving way to dusky autumn when Iris finally rolled over. A few weeks later, she discovered her feet whilst gurgling happily on her back. Her peals of laughter shook the house intermittently for days. A month later, Molly and the twins were visiting when Iris sat up on her own for the first time. Molly had become my confidant and biggest asset for all the things I didn't know about babies. She celebrated each milestone with me and stroked my back in my moments of frailty.

Soon after, Iris scooted across the floor for the first time. I no longer minded the dapples of orange and sapphire that seeped between the grooves of the oak planks. Everything could be cleaned or replaced someday.

She delighted in the tastes of pureed peaches and sweet potatoes and claimed a stuffed parrot as a new favorite toy. At eight months — just when I'd hit the depths of sleep-deprived despair — she began to sleep through the night consistently. I focused on celebrating each small milestone as if it were a miracle. Because each breath she took, every smile, each drop of paint — everything she did and each moment we shared — was miraculous to me. I hadn't known it was possible to love like this, knowing it would end.

Iris's attempts to pull herself up were weak, her body unable to coordinate the movement, and each time I raised her to her feet in an attempt to stand, her knees would buckle like a dropped scarf. It was a bleak winter day when fear humbled me enough to reach out to Dr. Arias. He was kind in his response and, under the guise of research, he began to visit us weekly and provide some guidance with her care.

"Her muscles are beginning to atrophy." His voice was strained. He stroked her head gently, his cold professional demeanor dissolved into warmth at the sight of Iris's smile. "Maybe another month or two at most."

It took a long moment for my words to form. "Is she hurting?"

He shook his head. "Not yet. I can prescribe something if you want...just to keep her comfortable."

Iris never spoke in words, but I learned her language of cries and grunts. When I accidentally stepped on toys I'd forgotten to pick up, I didn't curse them. The pain of my body was a temporary distraction to the deeper rending inside me.

I'd never had faith in anything other than science, but there were days of mounting desperation when I found myself standing beside her crib while she slept, and I prayed in the same way one of my foster parents had. Sometimes I would rub the smooth glass bead strung around my neck repeatedly, as if some divine force would notice my plea and take pity. But whomever, or whatever, I prayed to, never answered.

When daffodils broke through the cold ground outside my windows and spring ushered in new signs of life, I'd known for days what was happening. And yet I wasn't ready. I don't imagine I ever would have been.

I'd been steadily increasing her pain medication to make her passing easier. But as I cradled her frail frame against my chest, I felt a weight of sorrow that no amount of preparation could have lightened.

I breathed in Iris's familiar scent. The warmth of her body soothed me as I tried to comfort her. The colors of her eyes dimmed, the slow swirling stilled. Her lips trembled in her final breaths as her tiny frame shuddered. I whispered words of love, fighting back my tears so that the last thing she saw on my face wouldn't be my sorrow. I only wanted her to know my love. There would be time to grieve for years to come.

Her occasional gasps lessened. The rise and fall of her chest eventually stopped. Iris slipped away in a final swirl of sunflower yellow and sapphire blues as she dissolved in my arms.

All that was left of her was a bead painted with beauty and love.

N.V. Haskell's story "A Life of Color" was originally published in Metaphorosis on Friday, 11 August 2023

About the author

N.V. Haskell is an award-winning author of speculative fiction who lives somewhere between civilization and the haunted caves of Kentucky with her long-suffering spouse, rescue pets, and too many squirrels and groundhogs that she can't help but feed. When she's not busy writing, you can find her attending Comic Cons or Renaissance Fairs donned in her favorite costumes, running badly, or trying to read too many books at a time. After many years in healthcare, she remains stubbornly (or foolishly) optimistic.

www.nvhaskell.com, @NhHaskell

When Darkness Falls on Edinburgh

C.J. Erick

It was Gavina's favorite image of Edinburgh: the spire of the gothic Scott Monument rising above the skyline of rainbow-colored shop fronts on Victoria Street, with the setting sun lighting the monument's peak in golden fire. The colored shop facades marked Thomas Hamilton's redesign of the original Bow Street in colorful Flemish sensibilities, the renaming when the queen ascended the throne in 1837, and a salute to gay pride. Or, for Gavina, white light manifested as a spectrum by the faceted glass of an aged oil lantern.

Walking down the curving narrow street was like walking backwards in time, perhaps to the era of the witch burnings. The smells of food and wet stone, sounds of hawkers and music, and light dazzling in the mist were spectra for the senses. Moist air oddly blowing from the south brought mist, pale as her translucent skin where it peeked from beneath her dark cloak. Her pale skin spoke of delicacy, fragility, something precious. She hated her skin sometimes.

Victoria Street led to Forrest then High Street. She paused there, looking west toward the Castle. The brownstone buildings on each side of the street were like hands reaching up, with shops like bracelets around their wrists. In the valley of their open palms sat Edinburgh Castle, lit to golden red by electric lights, the turbulent deep turquoise and gray sky above it like ocean water. One expected great fish and whales and mythical creatures, perhaps selkies, to swim in great grand circles above and around it.

She reached the shop, hers now, an old one, hardly noticeable among all the other tourist traps along this street. The sign above the door was faded just to the appropriate shade of ambiguity: Miss Aileen's Mysteries and Potions.

Suddenly, she felt tired, as if gravity was pulling her into a smaller, squatter version of herself.

Gods mighty and fay, I miss you, Aila. We need you now more than ever.

Dusk was giving way to night when she unlocked the door with the old skeleton key, which seemed to warm when it found its home in the old brass lock. The only light in the shop was coming from an old Oban whisky sign on one wall, the one Captain Petr refused to throw out. The light was good, though. It kept her from barking her thin shins on the displays and counters as she wended her way back to the old office.

Petr was there, even though she'd told him to take a few days off to enjoy fishing or hiking. He missed the Highlands like the raven he was. But he was a lovable raven, one with a snaggled beard and feathery hair grayed by more age than he would admit. At times, one might see a shadow clinging to him as if he were a spirit afoot. Darkness took no pity on the poor man, Aileen had said, which was his punishment for defying it.

Petr sat hunched at their big wooden desk, snoozing over a leather-bound book older than he was, probably. She picked up his plate with breadcrumbs and bits of cheese and the glass with dribbles of milk, and took them to the tiny kitchen at the back of the shop. Not much of one, really, just an old one-burner gas range with an oven too small for even a loaf of soda bread, a sink too small for a decent-sized pot, and a tiny, grungy window that looked out on the alley behind it.

When she returned to the little alcove they called the office, he'd awakened and poured himself a short glass of brown, oily liquor — whisky, reeking like a bale of wet peat. He offered her the bottle, but she declined. She fancied a wee dram now and then, but not at the moment, not with so much on her mind.

She slumped into the wooden rolling chair opposite his, the one worn smooth by decades of polishing by Aileen's self-proclaimed iron butt. Like the door lock, it always seemed warmer than expected. The captain pushed the old book he'd been reading across to her. The black leather cover was worn at the edges, but otherwise well-kept.

"What's this?" she asked.

"Something the lady wanted me to give you. At the right time."

"Right time? For what?"

"I dunno, lass. Maybe it will become apparent after you have a look."

The book looked sturdy and heavy enough, but she felt it might explode into black and yellow dust if mishandled. Inside the front cover lay sheets of folded paper, newer than the book, a few years old at most. She unfolded them and found words in Aileen's hand, two pages, one a few lines of verse and the other a personal note addressed to her. She felt a quiver.

"How long have you had this book, Petr?"

"Long enough. And that's all I'll say about it."

"Why didn't you give it sooner? Like three months ago when she passed?"

"Like I said, Gavina, the lady told me to give it to ya when the time was right. She said I'd know when. She was right. And you know it too, don't you, lass?"

"I don't know what you mean."

"Yes, you do."

Yes, damn him, she knew. Look for the chill wind coming from the south and not the north as it should. Watch for flocks of dark birds riding high in the evening wind. Feel the tremor in the earth like a deep growl rising from the bowels of it. She'd noted all these things in recent weeks, but the wind was an odd, late season cyclone. The birds were flocks starving after fires on the mainland of Europe, crossing the Channel in search of food. And the vibrations she felt — construction work around the palace, rollers and shovels and cranes moving large sections and blocks. Nothing unnatural in any of that, all explained by known things.

"The signs will always seem to be usual, Gavina," Aileen had said. "The ominous will always be hidden in common things."

"She said you must read the notes," prompted Petr.

She slipped the pages out of the book, unfolded them and pressed them flat on the desktop. But to read Aileen's words would bring the heartache, resurrect the pain that had plagued Gavina in the hard weeks since she and Petr had held Aileen's hands where she sat in the big upholstered chair, where she'd insisted they place her. They'd watched Aileen's slowly shallowing last breaths.

Gavina chose to read the letter first. Aileen's writing was still strong and straight. Not the hand of a woman dying of cancer.

Dear Gavina:

I must start by saying I am sorry. I hoped to deal with the coming storm myself, but it was not to be, and I must think this is the way the gods wanted it. My powers, once strong, are now weak, too weak, and so my time as the guardian has come and gone. I would not have it this way. I would not force this great responsibility on someone as young and bright and full of potential and promise as you, but...

Here, Gavina imagined Aileen pausing and trying to find the best words, perhaps wiping a single tear away, full of memories of love and conflict and sorrow that she'd rarely spoken of, even to her ward and mentee Gavina, whom she treated like her own daughter.

...this decision is not mine to make. You came to me by providence because you are the chosen, and there is nothing you or I can do about that. May the gods lay their miserable and spiteful eyes upon you with mercy.

Evil comes in many forms, and likewise the ones chosen to fight it. Our way is the rare way, the light of night. For we walk in the shadowy streets and wait for when we are needed. That time is again upon our land, and so upon you, my lovely girl. We are the way of the lantern, the glass, the burning wick. But we are also connected to the Earth, as those who come are, those who come to claim that which is not theirs.

They will come as three, the children of my foe, Madame Griselda. Trust not their youthful smiles. Griselda and I were sisters once, in the Coven at North Berwick, along with Petr, whose time in merchant marine was past. But the Satanic Panic in the 1980's forced us to disband, and left Griselda bitter. She called me a fool of the light. This sentiment she will have passed on to her children. They will regard you coldly.

Be brave, lovely girl, for you know within yourself where your strength lies. Your enemies are powerful, but you are greater.

Be brave. I will be with you.

Love,

Aileen

Aileen had spoken often of the gods she believed in, the evils that fought for chaos, the followers of the Gaelic devil, Black Donald, in his quest to corrupt all the peoples and cover the land in ash and dark snow. She'd spoken of the power of the lantern and the glowing coals, the mirror and the prism and the faceted glass. These were all magical things, she had said, and beyond Black Donald's power to corrupt.

But was any of it still powerful in the modern world?

So Griselda had taken to the dark side alone, pushing away the way of light, forsaking duality and balance. When freedom and respect could not be achieved through cooperation and service to the people, it would be wrenched from the hands of non-believers via force.

Petr was watching Gavina now, his brows knitted and eyes pinched. He didn't speak much of the anti-paganism he and Aileen had endured as they fled the mob from North Berwick, but Aileen had hinted at his bravery. How easy it would have been for he and Aileen to follow the way of darkness, as Griselda had.

Gavina took the second sheet of paper, the one with the verse, and spread it before her. The words were Gaelic, and she struggled to translate them.

Chan eil dorchadas an taobh eile de sholas; tha e dad.
Chan eil an taobh eile den dorchadas aotrom; tha e a h-uile
dad.
Nuair a bhios solas agus dorchadas a 'tighinn còmhla,
faodaidh a' bhuil a bhith mar rud sam bith.

"I can't read this, Petr."

He took the sheet from her, his eyebrows rising.

"It's an old one, Gav, something spoken even before the Druids walked the lands to the north, before the pagans built their mystic stone observatories.

"The opposite of light is not darkness; it is nothing.
"The opposite of darkness is not light; it is everything.
"When light and darkness converge, the consequence can be
anything."

He handed the paper back to her.

"I don't understand it, Petr. A Book of Genesis reference? But the last line…"

"I could guess, but that would be of little help to you. You must seek your own meaning. Aileen gave this to you for these times, so your understanding is important."

"What could be coming? When she spoke of the dark times in the past, her words were always allegorical and inscrutable. Things about the children of the deep earth and forest, the creatures of the night, the spirits of the shadows — crazy talk. Weren't they just silly tales meant to keep them children in line, not real-world evil?"

"There isn't any difference. The stuff of nightmares speaks of real evil."

She reread the verse.

"It's just a puzzle, an enigma. 'The consequence can be anything.' Something outside the real world, like dividing by zero? Or that old saw about an unstoppable force striking an immovable object? What is infinity divided by infinity?"

"Nothing. Everything. Or perhaps just… one."

His hands raised from a sketch he'd been fiddling with while he listened to her ranting, a doodle. She recognized it as the Celtic quaternary knot, infinite loops forming four points. It represented many things: the four primary directions; the four elements of nature; the four seasons; or the four Wiccan sabbats, the fire festivals. The last of them, Samhain, was three days away. Some called it Halloween.

Samhain marked the end of the season of light and the beginning of winter, the season of darkness. In that transition, the veil that separated the physical world with the spirit world faded to ethereal thinness. In that time, the spirits, both good and evil, might leave the spirit world and walk the earth again.

●

Fia cast the stones on the gray tile board, careful to keep them on the surface. Stones that left the board might fall either way, toward power or weakness, like smoke drifting from a wisping pipe or smudge-burning sage. Better to remove uncertainty and control all that was within one's grasp. That had always been Griselda's advice.

She studied the six pieces, each one a different shape, size, number of facets, shades of gray and black. There was a pattern, and a surprise, a good one.

"The woman is truly dead," she said. "The stones confirm it."

Mairi, sitting opposite her at the table, lifted her thick black brows. Dorn, whose full name was Dorn Dubh, Black Fist, hardly moved from where he sat on their one sofa, staring at his hands. They were very different, the three of them. How could they have crawled from the same womb within minutes of each other? Fia, as the first born, had become their leader, by ancient covenant.

Fia added, "She is childless."

"Then it's done," said Dorn. He stood, leaving a depression in the dark red leather. He moved about the room in a slow-motion dance, touching things; the dark shade of a brass lamp that cast its light only downwards, tinted glass jars of minerals and ground bone, a wide book of ancient maps with its charcoal leather cover turned open to one they'd been surveying for the three months since Griselda's death, the map of inner Edinburgh, the city fifty miles away from their remote, little-known castle, the place that was the subject of their thoughts every day since

Griselda had wheezed her last malodorous breath and cursed them to bring the night down at last.

"Why do I still feel tension?" said Mairi. Mairi — The One Who Is Bitter. Bitter at being the youngest? "I feel the woman's powers still present."

"Nonsense," said Dorn. "If the old hag's dead, her powers died with her. The time is now ours to claim Castle Hill as the witches' hallows, and all the death-shrine that lies in the bloody soil beneath it. Hundreds died there because of people's fearful hatred. It's all ours now. The witches will reign." He used the Gaelic word for witches, buidsichean.

Fia felt her sister's bitterness, like the darkest of chocolates, burnt blacker than black. She also felt her brother's excitement, his lust for the power that had so long been denied her kind, the promises of the dark angel, Black Donald. He was the Breaker, destroyer of the non-Wiccan, builder of the dark age that was to come, fulfillment of the prophecies. When the power of the deepest earth would rise to sweep over the land like the wings of a great dark bird.

Three days until Samhain, November 1. One of the four fire festivals, and the most powerful, the beginning of winter. The dark winter they had all dreamed of as the followers of Griselda, The One Who Dwells in a Gray Castle. Their mother.

●

Gavina slept little for the following three days. She ran the shop during the four evening hours it was open, to maintain the routine, to keep curious eyes from gazing too deeply through the windows and into the shop's shadows. And of course to keep them fed. But all night and into the morning, she pored over the books of handwritten notes and observations, verses and incantations, everything Aileen had guided her with, spoken of, made her practice. She still didn't know whether most of it held any real power or, even if it did, whether she knew how to invoke it.

She was deeply lost in the special book Petr had given her days before, the thick, leather-bound volume of special quotes and verses, each one meant for a different day.

The verse for Halloween read this in ancient Gaelic, which Petr had translated:

As the hours fall
So shall the veil
The dead and wicked will walk
And the two worlds shall be one.
Until light breaks in the east
And the spirits must rest again.

Petr cleared his throat behind her, breaking her mood, so unearthly quiet when he wanted to be. He reached around her and turned the book's cover closed.

"This will do you no more good tonight, girl."

"Then what will, elder? All of this —" She waved her hand toward the piles of books, scrolls, notebooks, and envelopes big and small, all old. "I don't know what I could need and what's just a waste of time. I don't even know the enemy."

"Yes, you do. The enemy is darkness, all those things you are not."

"It's dark now. Is the night our enemy?"

"Not now, but it could be. I'm not talking about the time between sundown and sunup. I'm talking about the eternal darkness that rises from the world, not that which falls from the sky."

"Then how will I know it? How will I fight it?"

"What did your friend and patron call you, when you were morose or when you needed a good chastising to take this all seriously?"

Gavina couldn't answer for a moment. When she did, her voice was tight and brittle.

"Gavina, of course. Little White Hawk."

"That's your spoken name. Its meaning comes in the day, when you're challenged by the physical world. What did she call you when you were challenged by the ethereal?"

"Lantern Girl."

"Yes."

"It always felt silly, like she was making fun of me."

"Think on her name. What does it mean in the physical world?"

"Aileen. Ray of Sunshine."

"Aye. Not many were brighter than she, Gavy. Do you know her spirit name?"

"No. She never spoke of it to me."

"But you know it. The same as yours, at least when she was young. Lantern Girl. A title passed down from olden times. She didn't choose your spirit name by chance or whim. When she found you with the homeless urchins, lighting trashcan fires for the bums, she recognized your way. You are the way of the wick, the burning flame, the faceted glass, the light which guides carriages and ships and people through the night, through the underground."

"I don't feel that."

"You will when you need to."

"I feel something, a shadow, like a black hemorrhage coming over the land. And I don't know how I can feel it."

"What you need now is rest. Get some sleep, Gavina. Darkness is not evil in itself. All living things need it, for renewal. Just as you do."

"But there's no time. I don't know what we're facing, or how to prepare."

Petr said nothing for a moment, measuring his words.

"Gavina, you are the way of fire, not the fire that burns and destroys, but the fire that lights the way and enlightens the soul. You are the way of the lantern, the glowing ember, the fire that warms and heals. Did you think Aileen found you by chance? Nay. She was drawn to you as a kindred spirit. You are both the way of the lantern, the vessel of fire one may carry. And that's the weapon you must wield."

He urged her to her feet and guided her toward the sleeping area in the back of the shop. But her mind refused to rest, roiling with images and fears so that she didn't know if she slept or merely lay awake with her eyes closed, haunted by visions.

●

Dorn led his siblings up the rising streets toward Edinburgh Castle, leaping ahead of his sisters as he had done when they were younger, usually to Fia's annoyance. Age and cynicism had molded him into the snarling young man he'd become in their isolation in the old castle, a more demonstrative counter to Mairi's quiet moroseness. His unbridled enthusiasm seemed to have returned. Beside Fia, Mairi seemed if anything even quieter. But even in her, the spark of adventure and anticipation had come to life, like a tiny struck match.

It was late afternoon, cloudy, dead calm in the street, almost stale, but strong winds high up, driving the mottled gray and indigo clouds. October 31; Halloween to the laypeople, who totally missed the true meaning, the fire festival, disrespected as a barely remembered pagan event. High Street was populated, more than the last time Fia had walked it, six years earlier. When her mother had dared to bring her, just the two of them, leaving Dorn and Mairi with a school acquaintance in Aberdeenshire.

Griselda's words echoed in her head:

"The Castle Hill, Fia. That's where you'll make your stand. The blood and power of all those who were unjustly murdered there remain. It is time for the children of darkness to take back that power, and to take the land to where it was always meant to be. Time for the influence of those of us who see a better future, to overcome the fools who only see the naïve innocence of lightness."

Students moved around the street, primer age in white and black uniforms, no tribal tartan allowed. Older higher school boys and girls, itching in their skins to become adults, wore everything and sometimes nearly nothing, some already in costumes, many of haunted things or demons, some absurdly in those of celebrities or food items or political characters from the news, but some in dark goth clothing that made Fia laugh. The gay human enthusiasm for the pagan holiday, these would-be Wiccans, or followers of some other order they knew nothing about. The need to identify themselves as different, outside the norms of proper society. *Oh, be patient, young souls, your time will come, so soon now. That which is odd will become common. Those who are outcasts will rule.*

So comforting that all the tools she and her siblings needed were in their trendy red and black shoulder bags, easy to bring to this place without suspicion. Their gray and black clothing blended in well with the students, even the older ones, the university gems, who thought the world revolved around them even more now than when they were primer age. Perhaps Fia, Dorn, and Mairi should just leave everything as it was so these pretentious elitists could find out how little the world cared about them.

They worked their way west, uphill, climbing the cobblestones past the tourist shops. At the corner of Forest, Fia paused. Something felt strange there, like business left undone, like an oven left burning or letters unsent. Dorn was halfway up the next block before he realized she'd stopped. He loitered where he was, didn't return to where she stood. Annoyed, she gathered Mairi, who'd stopped to watch her from the doorway of a bookseller, looking unperturbed.

"I thought we were in a hurry," said Dorn, when she and Mairi reached him. "Were you looking to hail a cab?"

"I felt something disturbing, black head," Fia said, using the Gaelic, ceann dubh. The old language was creeping into her speech more and more, as if she were channeling her mother and her kin. "We're not alone here."

He huffed. "With the woman dead, no one else matters now. The grounds are ours for the taking."

"It's not the grounds I'm concerned about. It's the very Earth. And arrogant complacency is a danger we cannot afford." She paused to listen and feel, but she felt nothing and heard nothing beyond the sounds of people and traffic and the rising wind in the high wires and towers. Even the light from the castle seemed subdued, as if expecting them. "Maybe I'm overreacting. But let's prepare our things as soon as we can."

They entered the open yard leading into the main entrance to the castle, the esplanade, where the annual Fringe Festival was held. The thought of dozens of traditional and modern bands playing there and tens of thousands of sweating people in that small slanted concrete platform made her skin crawl.

Mairi cast a cloak of mist and shadow over them, and they passed the gates just before the castle was closed for the evening. The landmark workers and the real soldiers walked by them without notice, as if they were invisible spirits. Though they weren't of the spirit realm, after this night they might live for ages, the guardians of the damned souls who had been murdered here. So many witches and innocent laypeople had been caught in mob hysteria that descended on this place.

May it all be made right in the night, and in the many days of blessed darkness that will follow.

They walked around the winding walled streets of the castle, up past the parade stages, around the tabernacle and hall of heroes, to the highest observation lane, the best vantage point over the city. Ancient black cannons pointed outward at the sea, the land, the forests below, and toward Arthur's Seat, the hill in Holyrood Park, another site of witch burning. They were surrounded by places of power the spirits would occupy over the days ahead.

Mairi laid her pack down, withdrew a small stone pot the size of a grapefruit, and filled it with herbs and organic matter. She cast a spell of protection and isolation, warding off any of the night guard from coming to this high, stone-walled avenue. This was her work for the night, to keep her pot smoldering with the pungent leaves and bracken and moldy peat while Fia and Dorn cast bigger things. When her incantation was complete, she settled onto a seat on the high wall where she could watch them.

Dorn swung his pack down and removed six black-glazed bricks, cut into twelve halves on their long flat sides. He laid these in a circle about a half-meter across. In this he laid short rods of stainless steel he'd made for this occasion. The rods formed a grating in the bottom of the brick circle. He placed pieces of kindling from his pack on the grate, along with some paper as starter, and lit it with a red plastic wand lighter. With all of this, the pack had weighed three or four stone. But Dorn had the strength of the earth behind him and had carried it as one might a pack of duck feathers.

Dorn represented the earth, Mairi the restless sea, and Fia the sky. And now they had applied the flame to wood — fire, the fourth element. The circle of physical and ethereal energies was complete.

Fia laid her pack near the expanding fire, taking in the pleasant smells of burning wood. She could feel the terror of the ones burned at the pyre on the flat ground just over the wall far below them, hear their cries and wailing, hear their flesh and hair sizzle, smell the stench. Anger rose within her, but she held it in check. In anger was rashness, and she needed a cool head. The darkness was not emotional; it was calm and relentless, and so must she be as well.

She drew leather pouches from her pack, thirteen in all, herbs and bones and insect hives and the skin of reptiles. These things were not magical in themselves, but in the things they represented, the magic that had been ingrained in them by Fia's mother, and her parents and grandparents before her. The items were hundreds of years old, some of them irreplaceable. Some Griselda had brewed, others Fia and Mairi had concocted from the old journals, exactly as had been done generations before by those who had never seen ships and cars and television and the computer age. Had the world been a better place back then when things were simpler, as Griselda had lamented?

Fia added these things to the fire in the order Griselda had taught, reciting the learned words. One by one, the ingredients of the eternal darkness, the endless winter, charred and burned in the low flames, sending gray and green smoke upward into the darkening sky, up toward the flying clouds. Yet the smoke did not blow away in the wind, but rose as if in its own invisible chimney toward the sky.

As she added the last ingredient, the smoke paused for a few seconds, the air seemed to halt its elemental motion, and Fia couldn't breathe. Dorn's eyes widened and his mouth opened and closed like a fish's or like a clenching fist. And then the moment passed and the smoke doubled, dark and beautiful, like the mane of a mighty black horse. It rose in a twisting column up to the flying clouds, and then turned into an eerie mist, rolling back down over the city. This blanket of gray mist flowed from the castle, following the streets like coiling snakes.

There was little to do but watch and wait, for the dark fog to complete its consumption, for the veil between the worlds to dissolve for the night, for the real work to begin, the building of a new time, a new world.

But the fog had concealed the approach of another, the presence she'd sensed as they'd walked up High Street. From the lower part of the castle, two figures came up the stoned street, both dressed in dark hooded jackets and dark clothing. One was a hulking form, bent over probably from age, face hidden. The other was smaller, about Fia's size. They walked to where Fia and her siblings waited, all watching them now.

The two set down their own backpacks, red and black leather, the best colors to hide at night. The small one pushed back its hood and revealed a young woman no older than Fia, with dark hair and moon-pale skin. Her huge eyes were haunting, like an owl's or hawk's. Fia felt she knew this woman, even though she had never seen her before.

"You're the old woman's daughter," Fia said.

The woman seemed taken aback by that, as if this were something she had never considered. The bigger figure pushed back its hood, revealing a gray-haired man with a wide forehead bent like his back, and small eyes dancing with blue fire.

The strange woman gazed at the sky. The blackness from the sea had crossed halfway now, engulfing the circle of darkness from the fire smoke. Dorn ignored the woman and her elder companion and added more wood. Mairi sat on the wall and kicked her feet. Her little pot continued to sizzle, although the need for it seemed to have come to an end.

"Very nice," said the young woman, continuing to gaze upward.

"I'm glad you like it." So ludicrous that this one would come now, when it was far too late for an intervention. The elder man waited beside her, like a trite legend. "I'm Fia. And your name?"

●

"Gavina." Her own name sounded strange in her ears.

Below the castle, the people of Edinburgh didn't realize something very wrong was happening in the sky, that the darkness falling was more than just a heavy cloud layer moving over the setting sun. Random sirens twee-dee'd below, but in no greater number than a normal holiday evening. Across the expanse of foggy air, crowds were gathering on top of Arthur's Seat. Not the safest place to be, probably.

"Gavina? Hmm. The White Hawk," said the young woman who'd called herself Fia, which meant Dark Peace. That name brought a fresh chill to the air. "Are you the old woman's daughter?"

A pang, not heavy or deep, but sharp.

"No."

"She is," said Petr. "By any measure that matters."

"And you are?" asked the young man, who'd stepped forward.

"Your nightmare," said Petr, meeting his eyes coolly.

"My brother, Dorn," said Fia, "and this is our sister, Mairi."

"The Fist and the Bitter One," said Petr. "Appropriate."

"Well, this has been *so* nice," said Fia, "but as you can see, we're rather busy. Why are you here?" Her eyes flashed with malice.

Gavina removed from her pack a small metal lantern as tall as her outstretched fingers, with straight glass sides set in a hexagonal shape. Then she took out a white paint pen and hesitated over the side of the lantern.

"Which one, Petr?" she asked.

Petr eyed the three young people marveling at them.

"Make it the triquetra. There is worthy power in that one."

The triquetra, symbol of interwoven trinity, of body, mind, and spirit, or the elements of land, sea, and air, or the three stages of life; child, adult, elder.

She nodded and drew a simple Celtic knot with three points on the metal base of the lamp. The pagan symbol shone boldly white against the dull gray steel of the lantern and seemed to sparkle with its own internal energy. Such ancient beauty in it, and hidden power. Next, she pulled a lighter from her pocket, chanted quietly, lit the lantern, and set it on the stone at her feet. Immediately, it flared, pushing white light from the lamp, brighter and brighter. Resting on the stone, it resembled a model lighthouse from a child's electric train set.

The light expanded in a bubble of clean air, wider and wider, pushing wisps of dark fog away from the castle street.

Fia's brow furrowed in dark shadows. "Dorn, crush that thing."

Dorn stepped forward and stomped the lantern, leaving it a tiny hulk of metal and broken glass. The flame sputtered and died, and the wisps of fog reappeared.

"That wasn't it," said Gavina. She took an identical lantern from her pack. "Maybe the triskele?"

"Worth a try," said Petr.

Dorn stepped forward to seize the new lamp, but Fia stayed him with a gesture. "Let her try again. This amuses me."

Gavina drew a design with three spiral swirls connected to a central hub, then lit the lantern and set it on the pavement. The triskele, another symbol of trinity, this one associated with movement, a moving forward, a hope that it would touch the three foes before her with light and enlightenment. Again, the flame came up and brightened, and the dark fog cleared away. Again, Dorn stepped forward and crushed the lantern with his heavy black boot. The flame died, and the fog returned.

"Nope," said Gavina. "What next?"

"We tire of this game, White Hawk," said Fia. "The time for your ways is gone, and our time is here. Dorn, see them out."

"Gladly." He stepped toward Gavina.

"Not a good idea," said Petr, not moving from where he stood at Gavina's side.

"Get out, old man. You're moving on. We'll let you live in a dank old castle out in the fen somewhere."

He seized Petr's elbow and shoulder and shoved, but there was hidden power in Petr he hadn't counted on. They struggled and grappled, but the younger man was the stronger and moved Petr back down the street toward the castle entrance.

"I'd hate to kill another witch on these haunted grounds," Dorn said, "but I'll throw you over the wall, I swear it."

Petr leaned away, pulled a dark device from his pocket, and pointed it at Dorn. There was a harsh electric buzz, and Dorn staggered back, fell to the ground, and rocked in tremors. A Taser. Petr had not told Gavina about that.

Petr said, "Remember, young 'un, old age and treachery beat youth and skill."

Gavina pulled another small lantern from her pack.

"You're wasting your time, little bird," said Fia. "Your weak powers are nothing, even if we don't destroy your little matchlights."

"Three of you, for the basic elements, correct?" said Gavina. "Let me guess. Dorn is earth. Mairi is sea. And you, Dark Peace, are the sky."

"Astute of you."

"But no one to represent fire."

"We use it as we need to, as you can see." She pointed to the smoldering cauldron and the brick fire and its column of black smoke, which was thicker and more violent since Petr and Gavina had arrived.

"I see that you use it," said Gavina, "but you don't really understand it." With the white pen, she drew another symbol on the lantern, a single spiral. She chanted quiet words as she drew it. She set the lantern down and lit it, and like before, its light bloomed and pushed away the dark fog and gloom.

"The simple spiral," she said, "symbol of ethereal energy. The symbol of the flame. The fourth element, the one that is mine."

Fia eyed Dorn, who was now lying bleary-eyed on the stones, panting. She shook her head, then stepped toward the lantern. Petr moved to block her.

"Let her come, Petr. We can't guard the light every hour of every day."

He allowed Fia room to pass. She walked to the lantern and reached to pick it up. As her hand closed, white light flared from the glass and she jerked her hand back. She swore. She curled her hands into fists and let them burst open, and a great breeze rose and swirled about the lantern, catching and casting leaves and dirt and dark smoke from the cauldron. The wind rattled the lantern, pushed it so that it leaned as if about to topple. But the flame swelled like when one blows on a campfire, and the lantern remained upright. The gloom and smoke retreated further. The black column of smoke seemed to bend away.

Fia swore again. She waved her sister forward. "Mairi, quench the damn thing."

The younger sister, kicking her black shoes and looking unconcerned, jumped down from the wall. She placed her fingers on her lips, then opened her hands and chanted inaudible words. Immediately, rain fell on the castle, as if an umbrella that had been protecting them had been stolen away. Gavina and Petr tightened their cloaks, but the cold water struck their faces and ran down their necks into their inner clothing. Driving, the rain struck the lantern with a great hissing and billowing of steam, and the lantern rattled on the stone like a carnival popcorn popper sounding off, spinning in a tight circle.

The flame dimmed, but only for an instant before it found its shape and grew brighter again, punishing the offending wind and rain for challenging it. The gloom and smoke and darkness retreated further from the landing, as if a great white moon were hanging above and painting it in pale white light. Mairi stood with her unusually long arms hanging at her sides, like one wilted and washed in the rain, which had not touched her.

Dorn had recovered at this point and rushed the lantern, but the ground under his feet rumbled and buckled, and he fell to his hands and knees several feet away. He cursed and thrust his scraped, bleeding hands into his armpits.

Gavina, the white hawk... no, really a white dove, but also the Lantern Girl, just like her spiritual mother before her, the shining Aileen, lifted the still-burning lantern by the thin metal ring attached to its top and hung it on a hook in the courtyard's wall that seemed to have been placed there for just that purpose.

The rain had quenched the cauldron, and the smoke from it was white and weak; as Gavina watched, it fell to nothing. The black column of smoke from the pit fire was now just a wisp, lolling and squirming like a thin black snake writhing in the refreshing breeze that had risen from the east.

"Hmmph," said Fia. She'd walked over to lean over the castle wall overlooking the city, and the revelry growing louder. "A fair spell. But too late. The veil has been lifted, and the spirit world has entered Edinburgh." She crooked a black-nailed finger downward.

Gavina and Petr rushed to the wall. Below, the Halloween revelers were still milling about, moving between shops and taverns, which were all open and lighted. The noise of shouts and firecrackers and songs swelled as a fire may when blown. From several place, the sound of things breaking came, glass shattered as if dropped, hard blows against wood, car-horns honking. As they watched, a group of dark-clad youths blocked a car, waving their arms.

It all seemed mostly harmless pranks. But some of those who moved in the crowd carried with them odd shadows, like barely visible shrouds. The others around them paid them no more heed than they did the others. But these shadowed ones moved with purpose, and where they went, the pranks grew louder, more insistent. One such figure led a group of youths to throw rocks at a shop window, breaking the plate glass, then moving away in wicked laughter.

"Dark spirits," muttered Petr. "They lead only mischief now, but worse will come. I should know."

Fia said, "The weak minded are easily led to evil. When the spirits walk free, the people will know that evil exists in their pretty little world, and they will need us, need those they've forsaken and oppressed, to help them. And our power will rise."

Gavina ran and seized her lantern from the hook. It glowed strongly, none the worse for its trial. But she was feeling tired suddenly, as if she were the fuel keeping the flame aglow.

"Come, Petr. We must go to the streets and try to drive the spirits back to their home."

Fia chuckled. "Good luck, little hawk. You can drive some away, surely, but you can't be everywhere at once. And the spirits now walk throughout Edinburgh. And as you can see, even in the places beyond." She waved her arm to indicate the lands around the city, the hills across the water.

Petr and Gavina ran from the high courtyard, down the winding streets of the castle, through the gates and over the sloping esplanade, where a marching band was playing and costumed revelers danced. Among them were shadow people, whose looks were more real and not disguise; tall men in soldiers' uniforms, real weapons at their sides, thin-armed women with pale skin like Gavina's, whose expressions were centuries older than their skin; pale children stealing candy and garments and then running into the crowd, their eerie shadows passing with them like thin cloth caught in the breeze of their passing.

Everywhere Gavina went, the light from her lantern drove the spirits away. They shrank back into the real shadows of doorways, shops, and alleys, disappearing in the liquid darkness. But Gavina's legs had used their last strength running from the castle, and every step was like wading through dark mud. When they reached the crowd on Market Street, she moved to the entrance of one empty, dark shop to catch her breath. Petr joined her, eyeing the crowd with suspicion. The shadows of spirits moved within, a frightening number of them from where she stood.

"She's right, Petr." She paused to breathe. "I can't walk all of Edinburgh's streets with my lantern. I can't be everywhere at once, and the spirits will merely slip away and cause chaos elsewhere."

Here knees grew weak, and her head swam. Seeing her distress, Petr helped her reach a window stoop where she could rest.

"If only there were more of you," he said.

"One of Aileen was always enough." Around them the young people moved in singing and laughing groups, dressed in every manner of disguise, from zombie and sexy vampirellas, to toothy monsters and killer clowns. And among them, only recognized by Petr and Gavina, real evil spirits moved and cajoled and led the celebrants into more and more destructive pranks. The sounds of screams and things breaking and evil laughter were a grim counterpoint to the music coming from all directions.

"If only I could recruit help," she said. Around her many of the partiers were carrying lights of their own, small flashlights, cell phones with bright screens, and a few the colored wands that glowed with chemical fluorescence when the internal sections were broken and joined. She and Petr offered glow-sticks in her shop, always a big seller during nighttime outdoor events.

She couldn't be everywhere at once, but perhaps her fire could. The light from the sticks did nothing to drive away the shadow spirits, but what if that fire were hers?

"Petr, run to that shop and buy as many of the glow sticks as you can carry."

He looked puzzled. "Glow sticks?"

"Yes. Quickly, please, while I summon my strength."

Without hesitating, he left her and ran to the shop she'd pointed to, a book store and emporium that, like many of the others on Market Street, carried seasonal holiday items, including Halloween accessories. She sat and focused, drawing energy from around her, the frenetic movements of the people, the shaking of the earth beneath them, the wind blowing over her.

She heard a raven's call and looked toward its source, the castle wall, high up. There, the three young witches she'd fought stood, looking down at her. They lifted their hands and the wind rose and hard ice pellets began to fall. The ground beneath her vibrated. The partiers in the street around her took this all in-stride. It was October in Edinburgh, for god's sake, and the weather would do as it was wont.

Petr returned with dozens of pale white glow sticks in his arms, each about a foot and a half long. Between puffing breaths, he said, "I bought all they had, miss. I hope this is enough for what you're thinkin'." The raven's call came again, and he looked up where the three witches were casting spells against them. He muttered a dark curse.

"Thanks, Petr. Hand them to me one after another when I'm ready."

She stood and held her lantern before her, passing her finger over the symbol she'd written there, the simple, single spiral. The element of fire, the maker for the worthy, the destroyer in the wrong hands. But tonight, the illuminator.

As she drew her finger over the symbol, the lantern flared and burned in a prism of pastel colors. People around her gasped and laughed, except for the few shadow spirits, who snarled and disappeared into the dark.

"Now, Petr. A glow stick please."

He placed one of the sticks in her outstretched hand. It felt cool and hard, lifeless like the wand of wax that it was. As some around her watched, she eased the tip of the stick into the lantern's flame. There was a flashed and sizzle and the smell of burning wax, and then the stick flared at its tip. She pulled it out and it glowed at the end with a beautiful, prismatic flame. She held it high for all around her to see. Many clapped. A lone spirit looking over the crowd moaned and slipped away.

"I want one of those," said a teenage girl in a pirate costume near her, turning as if to go to a shop to buy one.

"Take this one, friend," said Gavina, handing the glowing stick to her. "Take it all over the city, and light the way for others. Pass the flame."

"Cool!" The girl fairly danced away, showing her prize to all those around. Other partiers pushed in to where Gavina and Petr stood. She lit one stick after another, each one glowing with a different flame, different colors. With each, Gavina asked the person given to run through the city, lighting the way for others. In minutes, she had lit all the sticks and given them away, and the circle of light they emitted seemed to grow and brighten the street. There were no shadow spirits in sight. The three figures on the castle wall stood motionless, watching.

She was exhausted, as only a flame could be. But when she and Petr walked toward their shop, others had heard of her, the woman with the little lantern. Young people came to her from all directions, asking her to light their glow sticks as she'd done for the others. She found that she could light even the sticks that had given up their chemical life, now dead rods of wax. The light she gave them was no less than the light from the sticks that were new.

The night passed, and despite her fatigue, her death on her own feet, she and Petr walked the town. They had to make the light grow to take the whole city, and the lands beyond. And they needed to stay awake and light the way until morning came, when the veil between the worlds would close, and the spirits be back in their world.

●

Days passed, and Gavina spent an afternoon doing something she had grown to love, walking all the streets of Edinburgh in the winter snow. But it wasn't a dark snow. The overcast sky was lit from above by the moon and the stars and heavenly bodies she couldn't name. The threatening sky on Samhain had been written off by the media as the result of an unexpected bomb cyclone off the coast and wildfires on the continent, even though the meteorological scientists proclaimed neither of those causes credible. In the beautiful, ethereal lightness of being that followed, no one cared.

She chose this day to walk the length of the Princes Street Gardens, admiring the rounded shapes of powdery snow over the hedges and brambles and trees of all sizes and shapes, like phantom ghouls caught out in the open on All Hallows' Ev'n and frozen there, trapped until the thawing of the spring equinox, the Wiccan Eostar. From there, she circled the castle from low down and found the magical place where she caught a glimpse of her little lantern hanging from the wall, hidden in plain sight, unbothered. For weeks now it had burned continuously, without oil being added, without her hand to adjust the wick, without someone to clean the glass.

She headed back east to the modern shops and businesses and the weekday afternoon bustle they raised, citizens of Edinburgh moving in concert, like a choreographed dance on the walks and in the streets. In many cities, they might grumble and hunch their shoulders in this breezy snow, but not here. There was a lightness and life to the city which the sky's gloom couldn't quench, but only fed.

As she approached the shop, a small figure dressed in drab gray clothing moved from a doorway shadow toward her. In a croaking, elderly voice, the figure said, "Might I have a word with you, young woman?"

"Yes, of course."

The figure pushed back its gray hood to reveal the face of a young woman.

"Fia," said Gavina.

"That was an impressive spell," said the young witch, in her normal voice, youthful, with a bit of sneer, but also a note of respect. "We won't be victim to that one again."

"It doesn't have to be a new war, Fia. We — you, me, your sister and brother — are all not very different. The past murders of witches hurt us as if we were the ones lost on the pyres. But I will never let the world burn or hide in darkness because of that shame and guilt. And you don't have to follow that path either."

Fia shook her head. "So poetic and uplifting. And naïve. We've tried the way of acceptance and outreach for hundreds of years, and the result is always the same. Promises made, but in the end, there is only persecution. My mother and the others like her have long since tired of the dream of acceptance."

"I can't deny the tragic history for our kind. But I can't give up hope. But you and I need each other, like the two curves of the Gaelic yin and yang, the symbols of balance and complimentary strength. We are two poles of the spiritual magnet, just as your mother Griselda and my ward Aileen were. Without each other to balance our ways and power, we can be nothing but a danger to our own people to those who don't follow the craft. Don't you see that?"

"I see only a fool who thinks things will ever change by doing the same thing."

"This isn't 1597," said Gavina, "the time of the great witch hunt. Nor is it the Satanic Panic. We have new ways to communicate now. Many witches are reaching out on social media. Many are joining us. We no longer have to hide in the shadows."

"Oh, that sounds dandy. It really does. But look more deeply into the media traffic and you'll find the new panic, fool. They're called conspiracy theories, and the ones spreading them don't need churches or traveling evangelists or television. They have QAnon and other haters doing it for them. You feel safe and cozy here in Edinburgh, but they'll be coming for you, for your little cute occult shop. The true evil ones will never give up their persecution."

Gavina reached in her pocket and found a business card. On the front was the name and address of her shop, Miss Aileen's Mysteries and Potions. On the back was the symbol of the simple spiral. She offered it to Fia, who took it with suspicion.

Gavina said, "Each alone, we are only one way. Together, we can change things. You three are the ground and the earth and the air of which all things are made, but I am the spark which can give it all life. Together we can do anything."

Fia held the card up, and it disappeared in a puff of smoke.

"If I need you, I know where to find you."

Fia pulled her hood back over her head, once again a non-descript elder doddering through the streets of Edinburgh. She soon disappeared into the darkness of an alley.

When light and darkness converge, the consequence can be anything.

Back to High Street and to the shop and in the door, shaking her cloak and knocking her boots together, donning the leather slippers she kept in the alcove at the door. Petr was there, dusting potion bottles and spell books.

Gavina said, "Have you noticed? Such a lovely afternoon." She cleared papers from her desk and moved a ledger Petr had apparently laid there, open to yesterday's accounts.

Was she a fool as Fia said, to only feel the light, ignoring the dark which gave the light its purpose?

She really did need Fia, the dark one and her siblings.

"Petr, it's only three weeks until the yule. Before it comes, there are quite a few things we must do."

C.J. Erick's story "When Darkness Falls on Edinburgh" was originally published in Metaphorosis on Friday, 15 December 2023

About the author

CJ Erick writes in multiple genres, publishes novels in a space fantasy series, and dabbles in poetry. He lives in Dallas area with his wife and their rescue superhero dog Saber-Girl, calls his sourdough bread starter "Ursula" (K. Le Guin), and cooks crazy-good Cajun food for a Midwest Yankee.

www.cjerickfiction.com, facebook.com/cj.erick.9, Instagram: cee_jay_erick

Koehl's Quality Impressions

Tim McDaniel

Early Wednesday morning, not much past 10:30, I wheezed my way through downtown in my old '31 Ford. Down to White Center, where the city sprawl collided with the suburban rents, resulting in rows of dingy cheap apartment buildings, absentee landlords and the retreats of the old or underemployed. I found the place easily. A building of wooden clapboard, still advertising 'covered parking' even though those parking spaces were filled with rusting Chevys, discarded washing machines, and mildewed mattresses.

I parked along the street and walked up to the front door, then leaned on the button next to the peeling paper with 'Linaman, Manager' penciled on it.

After a long while there was a muffled voice.

"Yeah?"

"Mr. Linaman?"

"Naw, he left months ago."

"You the manager now?"

"Yeah. You a cop or what? No one here been making any calls."

"Nothing like that. I have a small business proposal that you might be interested in."

"A business proposition, huh? So there's money involved?"

"There's money involved." I'd met plenty of guys like him in prison.

"Well come on up, then, I guess. 203."

The door opened, and I climbed the stairs. The thin carpet, perhaps originally a beige sort of color, was held together by stains, and the narrow staircase exuded the tang of cat piss.

Mr. Manager was, as I would have guessed, dressed in an old t-shirt and a pair of sweatpants, and smelled a lot like the staircase. I explained my needs, he articulated his, and we reached an agreement.

I checked out the deceased woman's room next. It was tiny, and the windows didn't open. There were a few sticks of shabby furniture, and one yellowing photograph on a wall, of a young man in a uniform standing in a desert somewhere. The room at least smelled a little better; a lavender-kind of scent lingered there. I closed the door behind me when I left to go back downstairs.

I left the building and took a deep breath. At least the apartment was still vacant. I wouldn't have to make any more deals on behalf of my client. Vampires, we called them, but not the blood-sucking kind. I made a commission on each deal, but they still made me feel like I needed to shower.

●

"Koehl's Quality Impressions" was stenciled in black gothic letters on the glass of my office door. A little crooked. All it needed was a cheesy little "While U Wait" card taped under it. Well, in this building, this neighborhood, I couldn't expect the clients I used to get at First Impressions; over there, Pichrenn's name still brought in the classy set, even this long after his death.

Was "Quality" accurate? Well, it's not bragging to say that I can raise ghosts with the best of them. I can make latent ghosts visible, clear as day, short-term or long. At least I can when I can afford to lay my hands on quality equipment. The gear I use now is so shoddy I'm lucky if Fred and Mary can even recognize dear jowly Aunt Greta.

So, yeah, clients were not lined up outside my door. I came in every day, though, in at nine or maybe ten or eleven and out at five or maybe four, when I wasn't out on a job. I couldn't afford to miss any walk-ins. I got the occasional referral of a double-booked or cheap client from my old friend Nol at First Imp, and some job orders from a few regulars, vampires, some of whom I knew from my prison days. But walk-ins, impulse buyers, were my main source of income. Sometimes people do act on whims. I stayed in the office daily, watching TV or reading or surfing for obits or drinking until I could justify the return to my apartment.

The glass on the door was at least frosted. A classy touch. Most of my clients didn't particularly want to be seen from the street, no more than I wanted passersby to see my empty reception room.

Empty it was, when I got back from arranging the vampire feeding. I hung my jacket on the rack near the door.

Ah. There was a new message for me on my computer. I went to the desk and jabbed the button.

"Hello, Koehl." I was sitting in the chair, and I didn't remember sitting down. Lindsay. "I have a job I'd like to discuss with you. I can come by tomorrow about eleven, if that's good for you."

I hadn't seen her since... when? Oh, yeah. Not since the trial.

God, how I wanted to see her again. And I also really wished that, tomorrow at eleven or so, I could be somewhere else, far away.

●

"I need you to come see me." Pichrenn's voice on the phone had been thin and uneven, air forced through rusty valves. I was in the middle of a job, taking the impression of a young couple's son, four years old at the time of death, but this was Pichrenn, so I called Nolan to take over for me.

This kind of thing wasn't unusual. The job I was doing was routine, though never tell a family that, and Pichrenn often called me away from those to attend him on more interesting cases. Or more high-profile. I figured, and hoped, he was grooming me to take over once he passed on.

I apologized to the couple, saying I had a family emergency, and took a cab over to the address Pichrenn had given me. I found him in one of those huge, lavish condos on 12th, squatting in the corner of a bedroom. The equipment was still boxed, lying in its contoured foam.

The room was dominated by an immense bed, brass. A window took up most of one wall, affording an impressive view of the city and the mountain, and ostentatious abstract paintings garnished the other walls.

There was another bit of apparent abstract art on the peach carpet, a dark red Rorshach image, all that physically remained of the room's former occupant: a bloodstain like an obscene starfish that had been crushed into the floor. There were additional random splashes and splatters on the mussed bed, and even on one of the walls.

Well, this family wasn't shy about displaying their money, if they could afford to keep the condo, untenanted (so to speak), for four and a half months after the murder of the husband. No wonder they could afford Pichrenn himself.

He stood up and looked down at the carpet stain, back straight, perfectly still, but his hands, jammed deep into his jacket pockets, were twisting and pinching the material. He did that a lot, as if his hands were the only vents for whatever emotions roiled within.

Lindsay was next to him, sitting on a clean part of the bed, composed and quiet. Her eyes were on Pichnrenn, but she was breathing a little too heavily.

"The Dudanna murder," Pichrenn said. I raised my eyebrows. The story had been a big one.

"The wife was the one who did it," Pichrenn said. "Made it look like a robbery, or tried to."

"Yeah," I said. "I saw it on TV. Hi, Lindsay."

She nodded at me, her eyes flashing secrets over Pichrenn's lowered bald head.

I said, "Our client, then, must be the dear departed's murderer's sister, is that right?"

Pichrenn smiled. "Right. The sister of the killer. That's what makes it interesting, isn't it?"

I squatted on the floor next to him and surveyed the scene. He was waiting, I knew, for me to see it. Our job, if we did it well enough, would be both a reflection on the murder, and a comment on the client. And of course we had to please our client while doing so, which sometimes meant hiding or disguising our own comments. We were portrait artists. Well, that's how we thought of ourselves. We wanted to do more than get a snapshot of a corpse. Our equipment amplified the energies embedded in the walls, the floor, the air, to reveal not a carcass, but the shade of a living man.

"Not a happy family, I take it," I said. "I mean between the sisters."

"I'd guess not."

"The wife got away with a slap on the wrist, as I recall. The best justice money could buy."

Pichrenn said nothing.

"Sis is, of course, married herself. An older gent, if I recall."

"Very happily married. There've been no reports of trouble."

"Right. And so there would be no jealousy of the sister who snagged the young movie-star-handsome millionaire, no sexual tension at family get-togethers, no younger-sister resentments or buried bitternesses."

"These people were the top predators of the social jungle, Scott. We're not talking about trailer trash."

"Course not."

"Would it make a difference if they were trailer trash? People all do the same things to each other, no matter their positions," Lindsay said. "Cheat on each other, sneak around."

I decided to ask Lindsay what she had meant the next time I was alone with her. But I knew I wouldn't. Betrayal was not something I wanted to discuss. And anyway, Lindsay had a way of making me forget scruples, even as they clearly gnawed at her.

But I had to say something. Something safe. "Sure it would," I said. "They couldn't afford us. They'd have to make peace with their dead and move on."

We were all silent for a time, then I stood up and squatted down again next to the box of highlighters. I took the first one out and stood up, looking the room over again. Then I crossed the room to the bedroom door and extended the tripod. After setting it in place, I put another highlighter just behind and to the left of where Pichrenn still stood. He observed my choices.

I pulled a third highlighter out of the box and placed it just in front of the window. I punched in some settings. Then I looked down at Pichrenn. He cocked his head.

"There was a lot of emotion flying around here, before and during," I said. "The whole area is bound to be saturated."

"Then we wouldn't need three highlighters," Pichrenn said. "I can almost see the remnants without the use of even one."

"You're sensitive, so you don't count. I've set up these two —" I pointed at the one near the door and the one near Pichrenn — "with complementary frequencies. They'll nearly cancel each other out, with just enough bleed-through to give us something to work with. As you say, it's so thick in here that even that amount should be plenty."

"Ummm."

"And the third one, near the window, I've set much lower."

"To pick up the background."

"Right," I said. "With only one, and with all the other energies flying around, all it'll probably pick up will be ghostly half-images, like something seen out of the corner of your eye."

"You did that at the Joshi place," Pichrenn said.

"Are you accusing me of repeating myself? But these will probably be a little weaker, more ghostly. I've been thinking about getting the chance to try this since the Caceres job. There, the energies were so weak there that half-images were the best I could get, but I did think the effect was an interesting one."

Pichrenn nodded. "And why here?" he asked. "A neat effect is just so much dazzle without a purpose to it."

"The energies released during the act," I said, "will be powerful, and I'm sure they'll be compelling as all hell. But they're all of violence, and terror, or its aftermath. We're sure to get some striking images. But what interests me just as much is the underlying tension. I doubt the victim was entirely shocked by his wife's deed."

I chanced a glance at Pichrenn, but his gaze remained focused on the floor, his brow creased. I would have given a pinkie to know his thoughts just then, to know why he wanted me there. Just for the job? Or was he sending me another message? "He knew, he must have known," I said, "that she was on the edge. He probably enjoyed baiting her, flirting with the sister, making her feel unwanted, bullying her, whatever. I don't know. But I'm sure there was something there. If we can display some of that, even as — or especially as — ghostly after-images behind the main action, I think it'll be something worth looking at."

"Hmmm," he said. Lindsay was nodding along.

"And I was thinking. They specified suppression of sounds, knocks, smells, temperature variations, I suppose?"

Pichrenn nodded.

"I don't know if it's totally ethical, but if we allowed a little of the subsonics to leak through..."

"Yes," said Lindsay. She looked over at me.

"Unsettling." Pichrenn got up, bones creaking, and shook a leg that had apparently gone numb. "Very interesting, Scott," he said. "You have a good grasp of things. I believe I'll leave this one in your hands."

I kept my face blank. There was no way he could have found out about what Lindsay and I had been up to. He had called to say he'd be late for a meeting up at his cabin, and things had just happened. And then they happened again, in other places at other times.

"The client paid for your personal attention," I said. "She's bound to be upset."

"I'll smooth things over with her," he said. "If she wants to pay for my judgment, she'll have to accept my judgment that you're the best one for this job."

Maybe that was all there was to it — that he thought I was best for the job.

It kind of makes me sorry that I killed the old guy.

●

Lindsay settled into the chair and leveled her eyes at me. Lindsay Ingham, Charles Pichrenn's former lover, or at least the final one. And mine. She used to breeze through the outer offices on her way to his inner sanctum, slim, elegant, and moneyed, with glossy black hair that bounced off the small of her back.

After Pichrenn's death, she'd pretty much disappeared. At the funeral it seemed to me, at least, that an understanding look had passed between us, an acknowledgement that I was still part of her world. But I had been out on a job when she came by the studio to pick up her mementos. She called me twice. I put off answering. But when she heard that I had taken Pichrenn's impression, she vanished. Felt like I'd betrayed him even unto death. Or maybe it was just guilt that she felt, however unwarranted. Our affair hadn't killed him.

Then the law finally caught up with me, and I saw her in the witness box at the trial, and there was prison. She didn't visit.

And now here she was, in my own little studio, in one of those new skirts that's tight in some places and loose in others, and a black blouse with ruffles around her neck. The air was low in oxygen just then, and my gaze stole back to her face, tracing the line of the chin, her cheeks and eyes and hair, whenever she looked down.

"So. Welcome to Koehl's Quality Impressions," I said. "It's uh, good to see you again, Lindsay."

Lindsay looked around her at the decor — the faded carpet, the Degas print on the wall. "Nice," she said. She didn't say it was nice to see *me* again.

"Yeah," I said. "High class all the way."

"Do you keep your equipment here?" she asked.

"I got a closet. This place came with every convenience. So, what have you been up to?"

"I remember you used to only use the best. You know, Charles really admired your ability to keep all of it in such top shape."

So she didn't want to get personal. No old friends and lovers catching up crap. "That's the trouble with the best stuff," I said. "It's temperamental." Like people. I waited for her to talk.

"Charles used to say you were the best in the studio," she finally said, not looking at me. "No knocks, no temperature swings or stopped clocks when you did a job."

The second mention of Pichrenn. "I miss him too, you know," I said, opening and closing a desk drawer for no reason. "I was there with him from the beginning."

"I know. Until the end. Well, if you miss him so much, stop by his place. You can see him anytime there, right?" Her voice had shifted out of neutral, but not in a direction I liked. "Sorry," she said. "I know you didn't mean… I mean, that you never wanted…"

"Don't worry about it. I'm past that. So what's up, Lindsay?" I leaned back in my chair. It creaked a little. I thought Lindsay had perhaps changed her perfume, but I couldn't be sure.

"I need a job done, Scott."

"And you came here? As far as I know they're still taking commissions at First Impressions. They're the best. And I know you always did like the best." I couldn't look too long into her eyes.

"If you're fishing for a compliment, I've given you too many already. Do you want to take the job?"

"I need to hear a little about it first," I said. A lie, but I didn't want her to know how far I'd sunk and how desperate I'd become. Oh, when I first got out on probation, I was the talk of the town, the indispensable impressionist and party guest. Offers both personal and professional came in the daily email. I had turned them all down; they had all been just a different kind of vampire, getting their jollies with a touch of death. But my fifteen minutes had ended.

Back to business. I clasped my hands on my desk. Clients liked it when you seemed to give them your full attention, and going to an impressionist is a little intimidating to some, like going to confession, or revealing your dirty little secrets to a psychiatrist. People take death seriously, even if it's not their own.

"It's my mother."

"I don't remember you talking much about her."

"No. We didn't have a lot of contact the last few years."

"So you had a fight. Teen angst, I suppose?" She didn't say anything. "But now you decide that you want to raise her. Planning to enact a little posthumous make up session, a sort of after- death mother-daughter heart to heart? You know it doesn't work that way." I don't know why I was being such a bastard.

"Look, I just owe it to her. There's nothing else I can do for her."

"'For her'? How's that? It's just a damn ghost, Lindsay. It's got as much self-awareness as a black and white photograph. Your mom, she's gone."

"Call it a gesture, then. It's too late for anything else." She looked down at the floor, as if the topic were too personal for her to go on. I didn't believe that for a second, but I let it ride. I didn't need to talk myself out of a job.

"OK. You're the customer." I slid a brochure over to her. Nice how desktop printing can make your hole-in-the-wall look like a real-live business. "Here are the rates."

She took it, but she didn't look down at the brochure. At least she didn't crease it; I could use it again next time if she didn't stick it in her purse. "I came to you because you're good. I don't want the effect spoiled by second-rate equipment."

"I don't really have the resources I once did."

"With the advance I'm prepared to pay, you can afford to get some of those resources again." I liked the sound of that; I missed the feel of properly tuned and maintained equipment, its quiet, even hum and ozone smell. The garbage I used now tended to sputter, and the focus kept going out unless you constantly kept on top of it.

Also, an advance that big could pay some of my less important bills, too. Rent and food came to mind.

Lindsay began tapping her code into my paypad.

I forced myself not to look. I pulled up an empty file on the computer, and started filling it out. "I'll need your current address." She took one of her cards out of her purse and passed it to me. I saw that nowadays she was employed at EarthTenders, Inc., a non-profit environmental umbrella. Part-time, no doubt. It was just the kind of feel-good job an over-indulged rich girl would have. It shouldn't have made me so bitter. If she spent her time suckling endangered wildebeest puppies, what was it to me?

"Any other legally interested parties?"

"Mom's latest ex has signed off on it. That satisfies your legal requirements, I believe."

"Sure does." I kept typing. "Visual, audio, olfactory?" Most people want only the visual, even though it's more work to suppress the taps and moans and temperature swings.

"Just the visual."

"Short-term, long-term, or permanent?"

"Short-term."

"OK." I stopped typing and looked at her, but she was doing her stare-at-the-floor act again. I saw a few wrinkles on her face that hadn't been there all those years before.

"I really just have to say goodbye," she said. "I don't need an endlessly repeating exhibition, for people to gawk at." Another little dig at me for raising Pichrenn. So I guess the guilt still gripped her. But I'd show her that nowadays I was immune to that kind of subtle reprimand. I was a businessman now, not some overpaid artiste.

"Short-term it shall be. Cause of death?"

"Her heart."

"OK, good. Place and time of death?"

"June 19th, this year. It was a Saturday. At 9:10 p.m. At 7th and Bell."

I typed. Then, "If the death occurred on the street itself, or in any public area, we'll need all kind of permits."

"That's not a problem. She actually died in a restaurant there, Grasso's. They've already given their permission." She fished some papers out of her purse and passed them across the desk. Standard release forms. The restaurant probably figured a ghost would be good for business, and maybe they were even right, at least for the short term. But I doubted it. "When can you do it?"

I pulled my appointment book out of a desk drawer and made a show of flipping through its blank pages. "How about this Thursday? Say one o'clock."

"That would be fine."

I didn't suppose the restaurant would object to that hour of the day. The raising of a ghost would be good entertainment for their lunch crowd.

After Lindsay left I sat in my chair, blinking. What the hell had I done? She'd reached out — clumsily, indirectly, but she had made contact. And all my defenses had shot up. I'd needed her, on many levels, after Pichrenn died. My friend, my mentor. According to the law, my victim. And I'd had no one to lean on, because she was dealing with her own issues.

I could still smell her. I didn't know if it was a perfume or just her, but now I knew it hadn't changed from back when. The office was suddenly small, dingy, dark and close. I had to get out.

I had to visit Pichrenn again.

The apartment building was now owned by a foundation that had agreed to allow suite 612 to remain vacant. They rented out the other rooms, and probably not one in ten of the current inhabitants knew that the former occupant up there on the sixth floor had not really left.

The doorman knew.

"Mr. Koehl. Good to see you again." Jacob removed his hat and put it under an arm. I noticed that his hair was graying, the tight curls looking like ash.

"Good to see you, Jacob."

Jacob turned to open the door for me. "Time for the renewal, Mr. Koehl?"

"No. Just a visit."

"Ah." Jacob led the way across the plush lobby to the bank of elevators. "Well, that's important. Remembering." He gently pressed the elevator call button, and the doors opened immediately.

"Yeah, I guess so," I said. We entered the elevator. "Many tourists come by lately, Jacob?"

"Not so many. There was an old lady eight, ten days ago, and some art student early this week."

The elevator car stopped. We paced the cream carpet down to 612. Jacob turned the key in the lock, then stepped back. "Have yourself a good visit, now, Mr. Koehl."

He never came in.

"Thank you, Jacob." I opened the door.

Usually he was in the big easy chair, head up, one hand touching his chin. He must have done that a lot, for it to have imprinted so strongly; he couldn't have planned a better portrait.

And, I must admit, I had done well with the material. Nothing flashy here, nothing avant-garde, not for him. A quiet study of a thoughtful, gentle man. I'd let a sound of even breathing come though. The legs were almost invisible, mere suggestions of lines and the drape of his trousers. But his body became more substantial as you moved up, and the chair back was nearly completely obscured by his torso. The head was preternaturally distinct, the dark eyes burning.

God, I missed him.

The foundation kept some equipment in a closet. I set it up the way I always did, going through the motions, and renewed the imprint. It wasn't time yet, I just needed to do something with my hands. Then I sat in a chair for a while. It doesn't do any good to talk to a ghost. I never know what to say, anyway.

●

I shouldn't have set the appointment for Thursday. It gave me three days to wait. Sure, I had wanted her to think I was busy, but I could've claimed a sudden cancellation. She'd have seen right through me, but then, she almost certainly already had anyway.

There was one thing I could do. I fed her check to my computer. Now I had the money, I could stop using the shoddy broadcasters that spit all over the spectrum, and the tuneless highlighters and the touchy suppressors. Now it would be topline stuff, paid for in full with Lindsay's advance.

At the shop they greeted me like an old friend who'd killed someone — fair enough. But once we got to going over the equipment — oh, the way those new suppressors squelch noise! — all awkwardnesses and discomforts were forgotten, and I walked out of there with the best stuff I'd ever worked with, and slaps on the back.

Then, of course, I had to go to the scene of death, to scout out the territory. I hoped my car still had some juice in the bat.

It was in a good part of town. A very good part, in fact, where I stuck out like a zombie at a wedding. Grasso's was the kind of place a Mafioso would kill to be murdered in — all indirect lighting, widely-spaced tables, dark reflective wood, candles, and hovering waiters. And expensive.

Conscious of my old jacket, my shoe with the loose sole, I didn't want to go in.

I knocked on the glass door anyway.

A guy in a billowy white shirt, his tie undone, peered out at me. I flashed him my business card, which should mean nothing, but flash any sort of ID when you aren't being asked to and people just start thinking police or Homeland Security. He opened the door.

"I'm afraid we're closed," he began.

"Yeah, I figured. Lindsay Ingham asked me to stop by."

"One moment, please." He disappeared into the bowels of the restaurant and soon came back with a Mr. Sarkouhi. Apparently there was no Grasso.

"Ms Ingham mentioned you would come to see the site, Mr. Koehl. Thank you for visiting before we open for dinner." Mr. Sarkouhi, comb-over plastered to his wine-colored skull, a thin moustache drooping against jowly cheeks, nodded me inside. "When you have prepared everything, of course, then we will go public, as they say. The table where it occurred is just through here."

Nothing special about the table. It was against one wall, a painting above it. But I saw some interesting possibilities, and the setting was appealing — death and money, death and elegance; these were and remain powerful combinations. They pushed buttons, and I found myself getting excited by the work ahead. Such a change from that which I had been getting lately.

I made some mental notes. Places I could shoot from, surrounding material resonances. I forgot that Mr. Sarkouhi was hovering behind me until he delicately cleared his throat.

"I'm almost finished, Mr. Sarkouhi. Just figuring the angles."

"Of course, Mr. Koehl. The passing of Ms Mehrer in our establishment was, I'm sure you understand, quite a shock."

"I'm sure it was."

"What I mean is, Ms Mehrer was more than a customer here. She was here so often, and she enjoyed a close relationship to those here, the staff and the other diners."

I could see what he was working up to. "Do you suppose they'll enjoy seeing her here again?"

"It might be disquieting to some."

"And yet Lindsay told me you agreed to the raising. She showed me the paperwork."

"Yes, that's true. It's just that, well…"

"I know. I guess you don't say no to Lindsay." I never could, for different reasons. Or maybe they weren't so different. "Mr. Sarkouhi, she's asked for just a temporary raising. I'll make sure it's as tasteful as I can. I don't know what else I can tell you."

"Thank you, Mr. Koehl. And my thanks, again, for coming when we are closed between lunch and dinner. I appreciate that you are trying to minimize the disruption."

"No problem." Actually, I hadn't even thought about the restaurant being open or not.

As Mr. Sarkouhi turned away, a thought struck me. "Mr. Sarkouhi. On the night in question, was Ms Mehrer dining alone?"

Mr. Sarkouhi's face flushed a deeper red. "Ah, no, Mr. Koehl. She was dining with her husband."

Her husband? Lindsay hadn't shown me any paperwork from him. And I would need it. As she well knew.

●

Back in the office, I called up the news stories about the death of Ms Mehrer on the computer.

Alicia Mehrer had indeed died of a heart attack on June 19th, at 9:10 p.m., at Grasso's. According to witnesses she murmured something, stood up, took a few steps and then collapsed, dying a few moments later.

I wondered at the last name. I looked up Lindsay's bio. Skimpy. She must have paid someone monstrous sums to keep her bio so short. But it did show that her dad, Joseph Ingham, had left the family when she was just seven. The mom remarried two years later. The second husband had died. Cancer. Then mom had married Joseph again, and divorced him again two years after that. Well. Sounded like an interesting family. Money and death, and Lindsay's family had a lot of both. But with a divorce on record, at least I wouldn't have to meet the old man to get a signature.

My computer search turned up plenty of gossip concerning the late Alicia and her ex Joseph. Curiosity got the better of me and I expanded the search a bit and came up with some charming hospital records. All of the sources agreed that Mr. Ingham had been one real bastard. The kind of guy a jury would wink at you for killing.

And yet, even after the abandonment and after the divorce, Alicia had kept coming back for more pain. Again and again.

Sex and death is another powerful combination; the oldest and the strongest of them all.

And why had Lindsay neglected to mention that her dad was with her mom at the time?

Closet skeletons can make a raising a lot more interesting.

●

Thursday. The restaurant door opened, and Lindsay entered with the grace of a predatory eel, dressed all in satiny black. She stood and watched me work for a while. Of course, a small crowd had already gathered; the equipment summons them as reliably as it summons ghosts. Mr. Sarkouhi stood prominently in the center, his arms folded in pride, surveying the crowd.

Lindsay came closer. "How's it going?" If she was so cool and commanding, why did her fingers clench her bag?

"Just finishing up the underlays now." I tightened a tripod leg, then checked the broadcast shadow.

"I've decided to go long-term, Scott."

I looked up. "What?"

"I said I've decided to go long-term. With an option for permanency."

I looked at Mr. Sarkouhi. "It's all right," Lindsay said. "Mr. Sarkouhi has given us permission."

"I'll need to see that for myself."

"Of course." She opened her purse without looking at it and took some papers out. She held them out to me.

"Why the change in plan?" I left her holding the papers and picked up another broadcaster.

Lindsay was silent for a short time. "Does it matter?" She allowed her hand to drop to her side, the papers slapping against her tailored slacks.

"No, I guess not." I extended the tripod legs on the broadcaster and set it up at a 45-degree angle to the first. I'd put a highlighter just between the two. "You just wanted to say goodbye — wasn't that the purpose of this raising?"

"Maybe I just thought I would need more time with her." I didn't even pretend to look convinced, and she continued, "She *was* my mother, Scott."

I flipped the test switch on the 'caster and checked the levels as it hummed. "Not a very private place for getting in your quality time with mom." I adjusted the levels and checked the output. I looked up at her.

Lindsay looked at me, her eyes just slightly narrowed. I knew why she had chosen me for the job. Not because I was the best, but because she knew that I would do it, that I would gratefully touch things more reputable studios sneered at.

Or there was another reason, but I veered away from that thought.

"Well, if you change your mind, remember I do collapsings, too," I said. "In fact, I lay more ghosts than women." It was a standard joke, and she gave it the response it deserved.

"Are you ready?"

"Another ten, fifteen minutes."

"Fine." Lindsay passed the papers to Mr. Sarkouhi and greeted some oldsters sitting at a nearby table. Mr. Sarkouhi stood there, one hand on his moustache, not looking at anything.

"I guess you'll be getting a permanent tourist attraction, right here at table eight, Mr. Sarkouhi," I said.

"Permanent, maybe." Sarkouhi looked less than thrilled.

"None of my business, but it seems to me that what might attract a crowd for a short while might grate on the nerves of your diners, if it's constantly in view. Of course, you'd be a better judge than me of what might pique a person's appetite."

Sarkouhi narrowed his eyes. "If you talk me into withdrawing my permission, Mr. Koehl, you'll lose the job."

"Last thing on my mind, Mr. Sarkouhi."

"I could revoke permission, though, at a later date. Couldn't I? I read the contract."

"Yeah, maybe. But Lindsay might try to sue if you try it. The lawyers would have to decide what your contract actually says. Better to just curtain off the table."

Sarkouhi met my eyes briefly, then nodded thoughtfully.

Memories intrude like unwanted ghosts.

The day Pichrenn died, I'd gone to see him at home. That memory was a persistent visitor. He'd been sick for some time, and he'd had his bedroom outfitted with all kinds of medical equipment and monitors. The place smelled of disinfectants and futility, and Pichrenn lay in his huge bed, looking over at me with eyes too bright in a head become too large.

His voice was as weak as his body, but he could still speak, was still coherent.

"Art," he told me. "That's been my life, Scott, these last thirty years."

"And you've done well," I said. "You know how impressions were looked at before you got into the field. Dodgy at best. You made a whole new artform. I guess not many can claim that distinction."

Pichrenn smiled sickly, not falling for the flattery, sincere though it was. "And now this." With an arm little more than papery skin stretched over knobby bones, he gestured at the IV feeds, the machine that beeped his heart along. "They tell me I could live ten more years like this."

What could I say to that?

"They're making advances all the time."

"So maybe I'll only lie here for eight years, or six. That's no way to be, Scott. But the law says I can't take the easy way out, with ten 'good' years ahead of me. Damn Republicans."

I looked away.

"Help me, Scott." He whispered it.

And then, "Make me a work of art."

"Huh?" But I knew.

There is no kind of death that can compare with a properly-conducted suicide. Despair, desperation, pain, a reckless courage, and even a strange sort of hope: that someone will stop you, that you'll be delivered into heaven, whatever. It makes for one hell of an impression.

And it's almost as hard to kevork as it is to do it yourself. Sure, lots of laws make it all right to kill someone, if they really want you to, and if the doctors have signed off on the sign-off. But that's not what Pichrenn was asking for, a sterile room and a certifiably painless fade out. My way would be less clinical.

But afterwards, I made the impression, and it's still drawing the occasional connoisseur. Maybe Pichrenn, or part of him, thought he was doing me a favor, giving me so much pain to work with.

●

Lindsay came over, ushered by a hostess. "Everything's ready?"

"Yep."

"Fine. Let's do this."

Sarkouhi raised his eyebrows at me. I nodded.

"I think your host would like to get everyone here for the unveiling," I said. "That's his payoff, right? That he can show this off to his customers."

"Who knows why anyone does anything. He gave his permission. That's all I needed."

"Still, we can give him a minute to get his people assembled." I made some final, unnecessary adjustments. "I have to say that I don't feel this will be representative of my best work, Lindsay. The image is fairly clear and sharp, but the background hum is, at best, just..."

"I don't need art. I just want to see Mother."

"Well, then everything's fine."

Sarkouhi, all smiles and broad gestures, led a small group of his well-fed and overdressed patrons into a semicircle around the table. I showed them where they could stand for the best view, then stood before them. I waited for their gossiping to slow to a trickle, their eyes to wander to me.

"Before I unveil this, I'd like to clear up a few common misconceptions about my craft, for those who may not be as deeply involved in the netherworld as I am," I said. I saw that Lindsay was annoyed with my delay, but hell, this was too good a chance to pass up. I just might pick up some high-class clients.

"First, what this is not." I started passing out business cards. "Ghosts are not self-aware, they're not beings. They can't see you or hear you. They're simply impressions, imprinted on the local area by the trauma of death. Or by other trauma, or other emotion. That's why you sometimes see ghosts of the living." I'd passed out all my cards. Time to wrap it up.

"The impressions are often of the moment of death, but not always." I went back to my equipment. "Dominant feelings, commitments left unfulfilled, unsaid messages, all these things can and do show up, and it's up to the artist to see that they do. And that's all I have to say. Let's see what we can see."

I checked my viewer. Yeah, I was satisfied with what I had called forth. I flipped the final switch.

At first there was nothing, except for the low hum of the 'caster. The smell of ozone grew in the air. Slowly an image started to form, in mid-air next to the table. It started as a grainy mist, like fine television snow, a vague human shape. It slowly intensified and clarified as the highlighters brought more of the energy out into visible forms, kicking it to the focusers. All this was needed to get the image formed in the first place — although of course natural ghosts do form, usually of an inferior quality, and with odd, annoying, aural and temperature effects — but once it was there, it would stay until properly laid, as long as it got boosted now and then.

The image continued to clear, and soon we were looking at a woman. It was a loop. Not uncommon. She moved, in jerky, uncertain movements, from the table to a spot a few feet away. Then suddenly we would see her lying on the floor, face down. Then she would be up again, moving around, as if confused. Her death had obviously come as a shock to her.

Her body, her clothes, were not too distinct — vague suggestions of a matronly form, decked out in some kind of conservative dark dress. Maybe the neckline was a bit lower, the dress a bit tighter, than society would choose to dictate. Was that a string of pearls around the fleshy neck? It was hard to tell.

But none of that mattered. Because the face — the face was clear, very clear. Real.

It was an aged face, but not heavily lined; Lindsay's mother would have been happy to hear that her face-lifts had survived her death. The forehead, fringed by curled white hair, was nearly smooth, the cheeks still full, the chin small and weak but still single.

You could see all that eventually. But it took time to take in, because what caught the attention were the ghost's eyes. They were startlingly blue in that papery face, and as the woman paced they sought something, something to be wary of. You could almost see a hunched form, a shadow, a dark aura, hovering at her back. And the expression in Mrs. Mehrer's eyes —

They were imploring. That's the word. But why? Was Ms Alicia Mehrer asking for mercy, for freedom? Or for understanding, compassion? There was shame in those eyes, too.

Even in death, she remained in thrall to her husband, bound to him by pain and need.

I couldn't have manufactured such a thing. But an impressionist can choose what to highlight — lives are complicated things — and I'd made sure that sick dependency came through. Call it art, showing a truth in place of the prettified picture that was asked for. Call it a stab at Lindsay. I don't know.

Maybe it was just what Lindsay had wanted to see. I had to look over at her. Her expression was at first smug, then horrified, lips parted and wide-eyed, but soon a mask slid down over her face. Her eyes narrowed and the right edge of her mouth curved up slightly. She coolly surveyed the onlookers; before her eyes met mine, I quickly looked down.

Then I looked at the crowd. I'd seen the same reactions a hundred times before. Some looked on in horror, lips curled, and clutched at the arms of those next to them. Some tried to avert their eyes, as if embarrassed, but their gazes were continually drawn back to the apparition before them. And some few leaned forward, drinking in the death.

●

Sarkouhi was watching the crowd, too. He seemed less than pleased. He saw me looking at him and walked over to me.

"Is this normal?" he asked in a low voice. "I mean, will it do anything else?"

"Some few do seem to react to things near them. Some look like they are trying to talk to you — the impressions can react to the impressed energies of those still living. Some act out the worries on their minds at the moment of death. Sometimes they even communicate what that was. Or try to. But, to answer your question, no. This is it. It's a fairly short action loop this time. She wasn't here long enough to lay down much more narrative."

Sarkouhi looked back at the impression, his face sour. I began packing up my stuff. Sarkouhi looked back at me.

"You're leaving?"

"Yep. Job's done."

"And this will just go on, repeating here in my place?"

"That's right." I folded a tripod and laid it gently in its foam-lined case. "I've pumped a lot of energy into the floor and walls, enough to keep it going for at least five or six weeks. And after that, I'll come back and pump it up some more. Can I use your phone? I have to call to have this stuff picked up." I couldn't just toss equipment of this caliber into my trunk, but it was humiliating to have to ask.

"Of course." He handed it over and I turned to the wall to give the man a moment, and sure enough, Sarkouhi went to talk to Lindsay.

Their conversation apparently didn't last too long, because when I clicked off and resumed packing, Sarkouhi was over by the other restaurant patrons. I guess he was trying to put a good face on the show, but the diners weren't buying. Several had already left, and a few in the back were realizing that they would have to pass uncomfortably close to the ghost to get to the door.

"Mrs. Sorensen!" Lindsay called, and one of the biddies looked up. A much younger man, his hair still dark, put a protective arm on her shoulder.

Lindsay made no attempt to get closer to her. "Enjoying the show, Mrs. Sorensen?"

"It's, ah..."

"Not sure? Perhaps your latest young man has an opinion — what's this one's name?"

The man scowled, whispered something to Mrs. Sorensen, and they turned away. Then she pulled away from him and looked back.

"I didn't know, Lindsay. I swear, I didn't know what he was doing to her." She turned and walked away.

Lindsay looked after them, her mouth fixed in its smile, her eyes full of hate.

Then she blinked and looked back at her mother for a moment. She strolled over to me. "Good work, as always."

"Thanks. And the rest of the money will be in my account when, exactly?"

"Oh, how you've come down in the world, Scott." She fished around in her purse and then started writing out a check.

"Yep. All the way down to the bottom line." I swiped her check through my reader. "Pleasure doing business. Please remember me whenever a loved one dies on you." I went back to the packing.

"This is my mother, Scott. You make me sound like one of your ghouls."

I folded a tripod and lay it gently in its foam. "The term is 'vampire.' But you're right. I know that you had me do this out of the love and respect you hold for your dear mom."

Lindsay moved in front of me, and spat her words. "You, of all people, have no right to judge me. I paid you for the job, and you did it. You didn't complain."

"I'm no judge, Lindsay." I closed and locked the lid on the case. I stood up. "They are, though." I nodded over to the last of the restaurant patrons. "You've given them a good show." I couldn't resist. "Was it the one you wanted?" I really was curious about that.

"You're done here, I think," she said, and walked out of the restaurant, almost striding through her mother's image.

Lindsay, Lindsay, Lindsay. Our shared betrayal of Pichrenn had eaten away at us both. Maybe my time in prison had given me a chance to let it go just a little more than she had, had convinced me that she was now out of reach, a subject of wistfulness and what-if. And how did she feel, now? No way would she think of me as out of her league; she could scrape me off the sidewalk any time she felt like it. But having me in her life would just remind her of what we had done to Pichrenn, how our relationship had been tainted from the start by that duplicity.

Sarkouhi headed over to me. I was getting downright popular. "This," he said, "is a bad business."

"Disappointed with the show? You're not alone."

"Oh, Mr. Koehl, I'm sure you have done an excellent job. But this is... It's not dignified."

"Death usually isn't."

He looked at me. "This isn't just death. How can I serve food, with this obscene thing here?"

Dear, dead Ms Mehrer continued her routine.

He hadn't thought of that before? Just what kind of idiot was he? Or, more to the point, what had Lindsay done or said to him? "You'd be surprised," I said. "This kind of show does bring a certain subset of the population. Not like your current crowd, though." I waved a hand at the people. "Like I said, you can always withdraw permission, Mr. Sarkouhi. These things are a lot easier to collapse than they are to bring out. And I work for reasonable rates."

"Ah. Mr. Koehl. As you reminded me, Lindsay Ingham has very many friends."

"She can make trouble for you, is that it? Not just legally."

"That is it."

"Looks like she's making trouble for you, anyway, Mr. Sarkouhi."

"That she is, Mr. Koehl."

As I climbed into my car I saw Lindsay watching the ghost through the window of the doorway, smoking an actual cigarette, the smoke making her features a little unclear. You can't do that in a restaurant. It's slow suicide. That wouldn't bother anyone, but even worse, it's public suicide.

●

The next day I was sitting in my office, staring out the window. I felt like shit. With the money and new stuff, paid bills, I should have felt like a pop star. Instead I kept seeing Ms Mehrer's face, and I felt like a whore.

The phone buzzed. I picked it up, and there was my vampire, Justin Hoben — excuse me, "John Robertson". The idiot called himself that, and then paid me through his personal account.

"John."

"You said to call today. You said that you would scout out the, that job we talked about."

"Yeah, John."

There was a pause. "Well?"

I didn't know why I was giving him a hard time. Lindsay's money would only last so long, and the bills would come due again eventually. So I roused myself. "Yeah, John. I checked it out. The manager is willing to go along, except he wants a cut. The usual amount, three hundred, and there's my fifty negotiating fee, on top of the baseline costs."

"Yeah, that's fine. When?"

I made a show of looking at my watch, although he wouldn't see it. "I guess I could squeeze it in late this afternoon, say four o'clock, if that works for you."

"Yeah, that would be good for me. Four o'clock."

I hung up. Sure, Mr. Hoben, that time works for you. I figured it would. Your wife thinks you're still at work, your office thinks you've left for the day. That works for you just fine.

It was sacrilege to use the new equipment for a job like this. Wiping grandma's priceless china with a rag made of old underwear. I could just as easily dig out my old stuff. My Mr. Robertson deserved no better.

But the lure of using that fine new gear was just too strong. My breath actually quickened as I thought about it. I felt like a pervert at a schoolyard. But I got it out anyway, and by three I was on my way.

Once there, it didn't take long for me to set up. Everything snapped into place just as it ought to, just as it used to. No sputtering, no loss of definition or control or focus, no stray signals. I played with the fine tuning, bringing out effects and details I hadn't been able to play with in years.

The old woman had died in the chair, just slumping further down, further down. No drama, just death. Her image flickered at the edges a bit; I toned it down, then brought it back up just to the edge of sight. She kept her eyes half closed, and she seemed to be mindlessly staring at something, probably a television set that the landlord sold off when the body was found. She wore a gray blouse, and a necklace of fat glass beads, red and brown. She also wore some fading blue jeans. She was barefoot.

Some current celebrities say in their wills that their houses or places of death should be destroyed, to forestall this kind of thing from ever happening to them. The rest of us can't afford that kind of protection, though there are restraint policies that are supposed to prevent the kind of thing I was doing. The very poor, though, are wide open to the predations of vampires after death.

My vampire knocked at the door. I opened it. "John."

"Mr. Koehl." Justin Hoben's eyes barely brushed me before they focused on the dying woman. His breath caught in his throat.

"I'll be outside." I went down the stairs and I heard Justin close the door and lock it.

I sat in the open door of my car. It's a shame I never took up smoking; it would pass the time. I watched the traffic go by, the single occupants of single vehicles. An hour or so later Justin came back out. His shirt was no longer tucked into his pants, and there was drying sweat on his flushed face. He walked up to me, and didn't look at me as he slipped me his check.

But after he turned away, he spoke.

"You're a genius," he said, his voice thick with emotion. "That was the best — the best I've ever had. Amazing." Still without looking at me, he said, "Thank you," then hurried away.

So the new equipment had an endorsement.

I went back upstairs, and put down the ghost.

●

Afterwards I drove slowly past Grasso's, though it wasn't on the way home. Grasso's didn't look to have many customers. I laughed, and went home, wishing I had eaten something so I could vomit it back up.

●

The next morning Lindsay was already in my office corridor when I arrived.

"Where the hell have you been?" she greeted me. She stubbed out her cigarette in her pocket ashtray. "It's almost noon."

"Hello, Miss. Did an appointment slip my mind?"

I unlocked the door and Lindsay followed me inside. She sat down, a firm line to her mouth and a hard look in her eye.

"Have a seat," I said. I seated myself behind my desk and rested my chin on my hands. "Something I can do for you?"

"More like something you did *to* me."

I leaned back. That gaze was a little too intense. "I don't understand, Lindsay. I did what you asked. The ghost hasn't collapsed, has it?"

"To hell with you, Koehl."

"Yep, anyone with one good eye can see the sick relationship she had with your dad. It's all there for everyone to see. And that's exactly what you wanted."

"It's disrespectful, mocking her like that. I wanted a tasteful —"

"In a restaurant. Yeah. Please, Lindsay."

"Go to hell." She folded her arms, looked away, and began to sniff.

"Cut the act, Lindsay. We both know what you wanted. You wanted to leave a bitter taste in the mouths of all her society friends. You hated them for not stepping in, or you hated them for leading perfect lives within calling distance. You hated her for what she allowed your dad to do to her, and you couldn't resist a little public humiliation. And I gave it to you. Just like you knew I would. Because I've got the eye to see it, and the technique to show it, and the desperation to accept the job in spite of all that."

She ended her pretense of crying, and just sat there. I wondered what she wanted, why she was here. To justify herself in my eyes — Oh, I never expected to see *that* — or to gloat with me over her triumph over her mother?

Gloat with *me*? Did Lindsay have no friends?

Did I care? "You always were a little self-centered. Justifiably so. But hardly blind — did you think the relationship obvious to her old friends would slip past me? I do know my work, Lindsay."

"Your work! Raising ghosts for perverts!"

"Don't worry. I don't discuss my clients with anyone."

I should have seen the slap coming. Maybe I did. Then Lindsay stood up and turned her back to me.

The inside of my cheek had been cut by a tooth, and I tasted blood.

"He hated you, you know. Towards the end. That was his parting shot — saddle you with a murder charge."

"Manslaughter." I kept the disinterested tone in my voice, but her words rang in my head. Pichrenn had hated me? I had practically been his son.

And yet — it rang true, also. It didn't come as big a surprise as it should have.

"He taught me well. I owed it all to him. He had no reason to resent me."

Lindsay turned back to me. "Idiot! It wasn't your skill he resented!"

"I never —"

"You didn't need to."

She glared at me, expecting me to — what? Kiss her? Slap her, like Bogart in some old movie? Explain away the thing we'd had behind the old man's back, when I'd been the favored son and it was clear that Lindsay would be free after the old guy had passed on?

I knew that there are ghosts all around us, hovering just at the edges of sight, on the fringes of our minds, as we go about our lives. I made my living revealing them. Now Lindsay was showing me others.

"Why do you keep renewing him, Scott? Why don't you let him fade out?" Her voice was flat.

I had no answer.

"He's gone, Scott. And you blamed me. You never returned my messages."

Had she left messages? I'd told myself for so long that she had cut me loose. But yes, she had left messages I had brushed off. After killing Pichrenn, how could I just go on, take up openly with his lover?

I couldn't think of anything to say, and Lindsay stalked out. Was I supposed to call her back?

Had all this been her way to get through to me?

●

I've always had trouble with moving on. Maybe everybody does. But I thought a lot about what Lindsay had said, there at the end. I sat in my apartment in the dark, the TV on with the sound turned low, and decided that maybe it was time to act, and maybe even time for Lindsay to take another peek at the sunlit world.

Me too. I not only have trouble moving on, I have trouble going back. Lindsay had reached out to me, coming to see me about a ghost; she had made contact, however awkwardly, and maybe that's the only way she could do it. Still, she had done it. She had tried to show me herself at her most vulnerable, most unappealing, most venal, and most real. I could, too.

●

I had no idea if she would show up or not. The message I'd left hadn't given her any details, any reason to see me, just the time and place. I watched Pichrenn in his chair, and tried not to think about it. About where she was now, what she was doing, that she was still in the world even though she wasn't in mine.

The door opened. "Scott."

Lindsay stood there.

"Lindsay."

She entered hesitantly. "I'm not sure what I'm doing here."

"Yeah. Neither am I. But I'm here."

She nodded as if that made sense. She crossed the room to the window. She hadn't looked at Pichrenn. She wasn't wearing black this time — light blues and yellows.

I joined her. "I need to tell you something, Lindsay."

She nodded, but didn't say anything.

It was easier talking when she wasn't looking at me. "It's like this. Yes, I killed Pichrenn. He asked me to do it, and maybe he had more than one motive. I don't know. But I know that I've never forgiven myself, for that and for — you know. Us. And afterwards I pushed you away, like it was your fault or something. But I'm tired of pushing."

She turned to me. Her eyes flickered to the impression, then back to me. "You don't have to —"

"Yeah, I do. I really do. Since I got out of prison, since even before that, I've been moping and cynical, and it's got me nowhere. Maybe I've been a little too much in love with death. Maybe that's a job hazard. But I'm tired of it. Finally, I'm just *tired* of it."

I went to the closet and pulled out a single piece of equipment. I didn't even need a tripod. I could just hold it and point it at the apparition.

"Scott — you're..?"

"Time to say goodbye."

I pointed, and pressed the button, and Pichrenn vanished.

Lindsay looked at the chair where the impression had been. I couldn't tell what she was thinking.

I held out the defocuser to Lindsay. She looked at it as if she didn't recognize it, but didn't take it. I put it on the chair.

"If you ever want it, here it is," I said. "It's easy to use. Runs on batteries. Just point, and push the nice red button." I walked to the door. Lindsay still hadn't moved.

At the door I turned. "I usually have dinner weeknights at a little place on Fifth, near Pike," I said. "Rommie's. It's easy to find. I'm usually there from seven-thirty to eight-thirty or so."

I walked out.

Maybe Lindsay was tired of death, too. Tired of looking back.

I'd have to wait and see.

Tim McDaniel's story "Koehl's Quality Impressions" was originally published in Metaphorosis on Friday, 27 April 2018

About the author

Tim McDaniel teaches English as a Second Language at Green River College, not far from Seattle. His short stories, mostly comedic, have appeared in a number of SF/F magazines, including F&SF, Analog, and Asimov's. He lives with his wife, newborn daughter (in spite of the fact that Tim is, by any sane measure, quite old), and dog, and his collection of plastic dinosaurs is the envy of all who encounter it. His author page at Amazon.com is www.amazon.com/author/tim-mcdaniel and many of his stories are available at Simily.co.

Spells for Going Forth by Day

V.G. Campen

I find Anubis about a mile past the Amtrak rails, where the sawgrass of the New Jersey salt marsh turns to swaying reeds of papyrus. He stands on a muddy creek bank holding a fishing pole and, though eight years have passed since I last saw him, he looks the same — a slender youth with the head of a jet-black jackal.

Anubis catches sight of me and morphs into fully human form, the most difficult shape for him to maintain. He turns away and begins pulling in his fishing line.

"Anubis," I call out. "It's me, Grace." At that he looks up and gives a short bark of surprise.

"Grace, a thousand pardons," he says, striding toward me, jackal-headed once again. "I did not recognize my little princess, all grown up." We embrace, and I inhale the scents of sandalwood and sun-warmed fur.

"Where is Matthew?" he asks, gazing over my shoulder, searching for my brother.

My throat tightens. "Hospital," I whisper. "Car accident."

Anubis holds me at arm's length and stares into my eyes, then nuzzles my face with his slender muzzle, casting about for the scent of death.

"He's not dead," I say.

"No," Anubis agrees. "Not dead." He releases me. "Come, I need help with these fish." He kneels and pulls a string of perch and mullet from the creek, then we push through the reeds to a clearing atop a slight rise where

Anubis has created a camp out of detritus dredged from the tidal creeks. Plastic chairs sit near a rusty metal drum that serves as a fire pit. I set to work gutting the fish, splitting their cool slick bodies from anus to operculum and drawing forth the entrails.

As children, Matthew and I spent long summer days with Anubis in the marsh, away from the chaos of our daily lives. He taught us how to set a bird's broken wing and mend a terrapin's cracked shell, gave anatomy lessons using the bodies of egrets and voles. Little wonder I'm now in med school and Matthew is — was — a science teacher. But one thing Anubis never taught us, despite our pleas, was mummification. "It is not a trick," he'd said. "It is a sacred ritual, an honor for the living and the dead."

Anubis stirs the ashes in the fire pit, uncovering smoldering wood and coaxing forth small flames. I sit listening to crickets and songbirds as he grills the fish. Feral cats gather around us, half-hidden in the vegetation, their eyes flashing green-gold in the shadows. Anubis breaks our silence. "It is good to see you, little one. That day you chased Matthew into the marsh is a treasure in my memory."

As usual, Matthew had forged a path and I'd followed. Three years older than I, restless and curious, he'd snuck out of our tiny apartment one Saturday morning while our mother slept, exhausted after another 60-hour workweek laboring at two menial jobs. I'd watched through the kitchen window as Matthew trotted across the parking lot, ignoring the group of men who gathered to smoke and drink no matter the hour. He'd clambered down the sloping concrete side of the storm water ditch that marked the boundary between asphalt and tidal marsh and disappeared from view. I hesitated, trying not to care, then grabbed a sweatshirt and ran after him.

I caught sight of my brother at the end of the ditch, where a trickle of dirty water spilled into the marsh. Matthew, hearing my sneakers slapping along the concrete behind him, sprinted into the grass and I followed, not knowing to stay on high ground. I floundered along the twisting creek beds and soon became mired knee-deep in mud exposed by the receding tide. Disoriented and panicked, I screamed for Matthew. When he found me, I was on the creek bank with my arms wrapped around a lean black dog who smelled of sandalwood and dust.

●

Anubis lifts the fish off the grill and begins singing in a low voice, summoning a dozen cats in from the sedge for their dinner. Grey, tabby, ginger, black — each one is sleek and elegant, wearing a collar made of bone and glass beads. While they eat, Anubis and I trade stories about Matthew. Even as an adult he found the time to visit the marsh, while I stayed away, succumbing to the demands of med school and the seduction of living in Manhattan.

"And what of Matthew now?" Anubis asks.

"He's on life support." *Irreversible coma*, to use a medical term. A *gomer*, in the slang of residents and interns. I start crying.

Anubis leans forward and licks at the tears on my cheek, though his amber eyes remain dry. Jackals do not weep. "Matthew was not afraid of anything in this life," he says. "You need not fear for him now. When his heart is weighed in the afterlife, it will be lighter than Maat's feather, filled with good deeds."

"But they want *me* to make the decision, to stop the ventilator. To let him go." I swipe my nose on my sleeve like a child. "And I still need him."

"It is no kindness to keep him in a world he cannot fully inhabit," Anubis says, "alone and apart from all he knows." A smoke-gray cat with green eyes leaps into his lap. Anubis strokes her head and adjusts her collar.

"Anubis, I'm a fraud," I blurt out. "How can I become a physician, how can I presume, if I can't handle this?"

Anubis stares across the marsh at a bank of thunderclouds massing on the horizon. "Perhaps, on this day, you should think of Matthew first."

My sorrow turns to anger, quick as the silvered turn of a minnow. "Do I disappoint you?" I stand abruptly, causing cats to scatter and dart back into the reeds. "Forget it. Forget me. I don't know why I thought the noble Lord of the

Necropolis would have sympathy for one mortal's struggle. All *you* care about are dusty old museum pieces."

"Those are the remains of people who worshipped me. You would do well to show respect."

"*Dust*," I shout. "Why are you even here? Hiding in a makeshift camp, keeping company with feral cats and stray children?"

Anubis goes still. His fur darkens beyond black, draining the light around him and creating an inky nimbus. My rage dissipates and I fear I've gone too far. As children we never questioned Anubis's presence in the marsh, accepting his stories of following sacred treasures plundered from Egyptian tombs and dispersed to collections across the world — including, of course, New York's Metropolitan Museum of Antiquities.

"You are correct," he says. "What remains is dust. I escorted their spirits to Osiris and set them on the path to the afterlife. My work in this world is done." Anubis exhales slowly, still gazing at the horizon. "My child, do you know what happens to gods when they are no longer revered?"

I shake my head and stay silent.

"Old gods are replaced by new gods," Anubis says. "Roman, Greek, Byzantine, each in turn with different ways of life and death. And now I am trapped."

I hear a subtle shift in his tone, a longing that pierces his customary reserve. "Trapped? Why are you trapped?"

"Because I have forgotten. I no longer remember how to pass between worlds and step upon the pathway. I do not have a tomb illustrated with maps, filled with inscriptions and incantations for my soul. No one builds a tomb for a god."

●

Three days later I return to the marsh carrying a daypack and a canvas shopping bag. Anubis sits cross-legged on the ground, plaiting a basket from slender blades of sea grass. When I up-end my bag and dump out tins of supermarket cat food, he raises an eyebrow and, though the sun is still high overhead, begins singing home the cats.

"I apologize for my words and behavior at our last meeting," I say. "I showed disrespect when you were trying to guide me." Anubis nods and returns to his basket-making while I dole out whitefish and tuna to the milling cats. When each has been served, I settle on the ground and pull from the backpack a heavy book, its cover embossed with the insignia of the Museum of Antiquities.

"What is this?" Anubis asks. His ears prick with curiosity. Matthew and I had often brought books to the marsh, both textbooks and novels, but I'd never thought to ask what Anubis wished to see.

"We call it the *Egyptian Book of the Dead*." I hand it to him and he rubs a finger over the raised lettering.

"A strange gift." He flips quickly through the introductory pages, baring his teeth at the photographs of mummies and sarcophagi, slowing when he reaches glossy reproductions of fragmented papyri and peeling murals. "It is the *Spells for Going Forth by Day*," he says, "and fragments of the *Book of Caverns* and the *Book of Dark Waters*."

"Can it set you on the path to your afterlife?"

He places the book in his lap and resumes plaiting the seagrass. "I think not. These are fragments from versions written centuries apart. Fragments out of context cannot, unfortunately, compensate for centuries of forgetting."

"There's more. Look at this." I extend a brochure advertising the Museum's newest exhibit: a full-sized recreation of a Fifth Dynasty royal burial chamber, one that had remained sealed and untouched until the last decade. "It's not the real thing, but with laser scanning and digitizing and I don't even understand it all, they recreated every surface down to the smallest detail — all the murals, every prayer and incantation."

Anubis reviews the brochure, then places it carefully inside the book and returns to weaving, his face impassive. The cats finish eating and begin cleaning their whiskers as the first evening star appears. Soon it will be too dark to hike safely out of the marsh, yet I remain sitting until Anubis puts the finished basket aside and I can no longer hold my tongue. "If I get you to the museum, to this tomb, is it enough?"

"I believe it might be," he says. "However, your duty is to Matthew, not to me."

"Let me help you. Please. Then I will be ready to help Matthew, I promise."

It is well past nightfall when Anubis finally responds. He hands me the basket, so tightly and perfectly woven it will hold water. "A gift for my princess," he says, and in the giving and accepting of this gift our agreement is made.

I spend the night in a chair by the fire pit, slapping at mosquitoes and dozing fitfully. Anubis, in the form of a jackal, curls on a bed of rushes with the *Book of the Dead* by his side. At first daylight I kneel and massage the muscles in his neck and shoulders, a familiarity he tolerates only when in jackal form. He yawns and blinks. "Every dawn is a victory," he says. "Remember that, Grace. Every day of life a triumph over the chaos of night."

●

Anubis huddles in the back seat of my rented car, his jackal head hidden under a blanket. He has spent the past weeks poring over the *Book of the Dead* and has become solemn and aloof. He no longer speaks, communicating instead by nods and glances. I maneuver through Manhattan traffic and pay an absurd amount to park in a garage adjacent to the museum. When Anubis shrugs off the blanket, he is fully human, though his face remains oddly canine, with deep amber eyes and pointed ears. Appearing in public is risky; in moments of emotion or stress his jackal head can unexpectedly re-assert itself. He wears a sweatshirt, lose khaki pants, and tennis shoes. No belt. Nothing metal that might set off a detector and incur a pat-down. I doubt he could maintain his form if touched disrespectfully. I hand him sunglasses and a hipster fedora to complete the costume.

We arrive in the museum's ornate 19th century entry hall a mere ten minutes before the final visitors are admitted, an hour before the museum closes. A guard rises from her chair behind the security table and points to my backpack. Instead of handing it over, I upend the bag and spill out a confusion of books, cosmetics, and keys, chattering inanely all the while. At the same time Anubis holds up his hands, palms outward, to show he carries nothing. The guard nods and Anubis saunters through the metal detector while I recover my belongings. Our plan is simple, based on clichéd movie tropes: wait until closing time and hope we are the last visitors in the Hall of Ancient Egypt, so that Anubis can enter the replicated tomb alone. If needed, I will create a diversion to distract any lingering visitors or nearby museum staff.

I rejoin Anubis on the far side of the rotunda, behind the massive skeletons of a *T. rex* and a triceratops locked in eternal battle, and we head toward an exhibit on fossils from the Gobi Desert. We'll wait to enter the Egyptian display, to avoid upsetting Anubis and drawing unwanted attention. In front of us, a toddler carried by his mother stares at Anubis over her shoulder. "Doggy," he says, and Anubis smiles a pointy-toothed grin and morphs for an instant to jackal-head, causing the child to shriek with laughter and allowing me, for a single breath, to see once again the old Anubis, my patient teacher and friend.

But the momentary shift in his head sends the fedora and sunglasses tumbling to the floor. I crouch to fetch them and, when I rise, Anubis is disappearing into the Hall of Ancient Egypt through a wide doorway flanked by granite obelisks. I mutter a curse and follow. Thankfully, the exhibit is nearly empty. One couple remains, busy posing next to burial masks and golden amulets, intent on documenting their visit with selfies. Beyond them, the recreated tomb occupies an elevated platform, dramatically lit by hidden spotlights. Velvet ropes delineate a pathway to the tomb's entrance steps.

Anubis has stopped in the middle of the room, in front of a large glass enclosure containing a Middle Kingdom mummy case, the lid removed to reveal the time-ravaged body. Canopic jars holding the dead man's lungs, liver, stomach, and intestines rest on wooden pedestals nearby. Anubis presses one hand against the glass, his head flickering rapidly between man and jackal. The light in the room dims. Shadows creep from under display cases and stretch over the marble floor toward the tomb.

The couple, startled, turn to see the Lord of the Necropolis striding toward them — jackal-headed, clad in loincloth and golden headpiece, trailing folds of darkness like a ceremonial robe. They run for the exit and Anubis follows, toppling the granite obelisks behind them to block the doorway. Alarms blare.

Anubis moves toward the tomb, barely visible now in the deepening shadows. I think he pauses and looks back at me before stepping across the threshold, but I cannot be certain. The darkness withdraws like a receding tide and the light returns, hazy with dust created by security guards clambering over granite rubble. They find me sobbing on the floor and, assuming my grief is fear, kneel to comfort me.

The tabloid headlines are campy and awful: *Nightmare at the Museum* and *Mummy's Revenge!* The stories describe the toppled obelisks and provide unofficial photos of the wreckage, as well as a single blurry photo of the masked figure who chased visitors from the exhibit. The museum, no surprise, declines comment and refuses to release any security camera footage.

I read each article to Matthew as I sit by his hospital bed holding his limp hand. When the stories are done, when there is nothing more to tell Matthew about Anubis, I summon the attending physician and watch as she disconnects his respirator. There are no canopic jars waiting for his organs; they will be dispatched with equal reverence to patients in need of transplants.

I leave the hospital and drive to the marsh, where I walk for miles beyond the Amtrak rails. The reeds remain reeds. There is no papyrus. The feral cats I glimpse are skinny and skittish, and none wears a collar of glass beads. Anubis is gone from this world. What is lost can never be replaced, yet the sun still warms my face and the creeks still pulse with the tides. I am at peace in this narrow space between earth and sky, once again willing to endure the chaos of the night for the promise of another dawn.

V.G. Campen's story "Spells for Going Forth by Day" was originally published in Metaphorosis on Friday, 5 March 2021

About the author

After decades of reading, V.G. Campen began to write. She has now published stories in multiple genres, including fantasy, horror, and science fiction. She lives in a kudzu-infested corner of North Carolina with one spouse, several pets, and too many books — and is, of course, working on a novel.

Dragons I Have Slain

B. Morris Allen

I collect dragon tears. It isn't difficult; they're insidious and subtle, and they seep through my armor and into my skin like ink, leaving me stained, soiled, sorrowful — a human map of misery. The Dragon Atlas, I call it — marked with the precise locations of honor and shame.

Dragons cry for the same reasons we do — pain, heartache, joy. We think of them as wise and cold, but wisdom is no antidote to empathy. Dragons are kings of empathy. That's what makes killing them so hard.

There was Vyurfang, short for something unpronounceable in dragon-tongue. I stood on his chest, his broken limbs splayed out across the rocks, the point of my longsword slipped between two diamond scales. I kept my back to him, and he turned his sky-dark eyes on my mirrored shield, and said "I am sorry, Solna," even as he tried to use my name against me. He cried as I slipped the blade home once, and again, and again, and again, through every chamber of his heart. He cried as his long body writhed in agony, as I came down to hold his head against my bosom and snap his tired neck. The tears soaked through the metal plate and the cotton gambeson and steeped my chest in sagacity and shrewdness, experience and acumen. I wash and wash, but I cannot get it out.

In the town, they hailed me as a savior, offered me fine wines, rich foods, soft beds. Handsome men, pretty women — I refused them all, and in the parlor of the inn they whispered to each other about dedication and purity as I shed my futile armor.

"Send up hot water," I told the landlord, "and keep it coming." I've done this before, and though no water can cleanse me, it's better to try than to despair. A dragon taught me that.

●

When we were girls, I was the dragon.

"Breathe fire, Solna," Elyndra commanded, and I would roar and cough on all fours, and she would hack off my head.

"Why must you play with that girl?" my mother asked, as if she could not see Elyndra's in-born grace, her golden beauty.

"Because her mother is scullery maid at the castle," my father replied. "And if she did not help us to sell our crop, who would buy it?"

●

After Vyurfang there was Cold-Heart, whose only weakness was in her mouth, into which I fired an iron quarrel when she spoke of duty and of passion. Her tears are etched into my forearms where I tore the quarrel out so that she would not lie with her mouth open and speechless as her body turned to stone.

And after Cold-Heart, there were Klarsharp, and Windclaw, and Sharpstone, and Zmeyra, and more others than I care to count. Each one marked me with their tears, wrote their passing on my skin. I feel the burden of it like a cloak of chain, slowing my steps, clouding my thoughts. Even when I sleep, it drags me down into nightmare, and when I wake, I force myself to stand only so that I can be doing, not thinking, even if that doing is only a slow march to one more death.

Dragons are a violent breed, with an instinct for survival so deep that even after death, they strive for life. Even while they hope to die, they try to fight. It is an instinct in them, I think, that they cannot suppress. I kill them this way and that way, and every time I think them dead, they twitch and claw and tear. And weep.

●

"I can't look you in the eye," Elyndra told me when we were older, almost blooded women. "A dragon can enthrall a man with a single glance."

"As you've enthralled Osal," I agreed, making a joke of heartbreak. "Though what you'll do with a thrall so small and weak, I can't say."

"I have you to protect me," she smiled, and kissed me on the cheek. "And Osal is clever, and his father is the glass-smith." But she wouldn't look me in the eye, and her kisses grew fewer as our bodies grew curves.

●

My armor, once of mirror-shined plate and tight-knit mail is rent now to tatters, discarded across fields and hillsides, caves and plains. Only my weapons remain: a sharp sword, a strong bow, and a promise, burdens now so heavy I can barely walk.

Today, it will end. Today, I will kill my last dragon, or she will kill me. There is always that hope. Today, I go without even my mirror shield to save me from enthralling dragon eyes. I will kill her with my eyes closed, or she will enslave me, or I will die. Today is the end.

They watch me as I go from the village. I have saved a pretty dress for today, a soft cotton gown they gave to me in Hatherton. The canvas baldric pulls against it, pricks the fine weave with coarse fiber until I give up and carry the sword in one hand, arbalest in the other, and the promise on my conscience. I hear the children snicker at a savior in a sun dress, hear parents chide them in quiet, tolerant voices.

I have kept my boots, for the way is muddy, and there are streams I must cross. At the first, I slip the sword under one arm, and pull the dress up to my thighs. It is easier than plate, and more comfortable. The children laugh and point, and make jokes about dragons' legs, but they come no further. We are too close now for childish dares.

It was daring that brought me to this day, and desperation. Desperation to catch the eye of Elyndra, a spare, fine willow to my tall and sturdy walnut. Daring to think she might value strength and commitment over craft or intellect.

●

When we were women grown, Elyndra went in to the castle, as a lady's under-maid, and I followed her. No lace and fripperies for me, no delicate embroideries on satin underthings, but canvas straps and heavy pikes.

"I'm sorry," Elyndra said when we met in the evenings. "But we must use what we have. I'm pretty. You're strong. Best not to argue with fate." Fate decreed that her mistress invite Olas to show the Countess and court his tricks of glass and wire, and that I enlist as guard trainee.

"You're no nearer Elyndra in the guard than here at home," said my mother when I packed to leave home. "And with your father gone, I need your help."

"I will send my wages," I mumbled.

"Elyndra is a tramp, and a shameless one," said my mother, and she gazed past father's empty chair to the widow Remble's shack. "She'll no more be with you than you'll be a hero, with all your belts and spears and bruises."

The dragon came not long after, a long dark shape like a storm cloud spread thin by wind. It settled on the mountain behind the castle, on the steep slopes that fell off in cliffs to the river below.

"They've written to the Queen," Elyndra said, eyes wide. "They say she'll send a hero! Osal told me so. He said it will be a hero, with landboats so full of armor it'll take ten men to row each one. The Countess herself has ordered him to make a special far-sight device so that she can see the dragon from her tower. And with the pay from it," she looked away, a slight flush across her perfect skin. "Well, you know."

I found a sword easily enough, a rusty piece of steel from the practice racks. Armor I did without, going forth as near-naked then as I do now, though more sensibly dressed in cotton trousers and tunic. I crossed the shallow valley below the castle, went quiet into the dark of the mountains, and climbed through the mist, glad it muffled my scrabbling steps from the dragon whose shadow filled the tap-rooms.

I found him just above the treeline, in a cave less tunnel than scrape, a shallow overhang of rock exposed to cold winds that fell down from the ice above to the cliff below. I had no mirror, for I was brave, not shrewd, and when he opened his eyes to me, I was lost.

I spent untold centuries in delirious contentment, washed in cerulean tides that hinted love and warmth and certainty until he closed his eyes again and I was free. I wept for loss and fell to my knees to beg him to take me back, my sword discarded dull and evil at my side.

"Have they never told you, girl, to beware a dragon's eyes? Do they not tell tales at night of the cunning of the serpent?" His voice was the slow rumble of an avalanche awakening, and my bones trembled with its might, so that I could not answer. He opened his eyes again, but held back his captivating powers. "Are we so disregarded now, that they send out naked children to do us in? Are you the best there is?"

I told him then, in stumbling, stuttered words of my plan, my hopes, my dreams. Reflected in dragon eyes, Elyndra seemed distant, a slender and a frail reed on which to rest my faith, and I saw clearly now how mad my thoughts had been, how palpable her disinterest in me, how evident her hopes of wealth and position.

"I'm the least there is," I replied as my future fell around me, and I saw in his eyes that even my self-pity was an appeal for deliverance.

"Yet you are the tool I have," he said, "and we must both make do." He snaked his head down from his cave to hang beside me in the chill air. "I cannot give you love," he said. "Though I see you need it, that is the one magic dragons do not have." A lucent tear escaped one lapis eye, and, unthinking, I stretched a hand to touch it. Under my finger, the tear smeared against hard scale, and I felt it enter me, sliding past barriers of skin and flesh to touch my spirit.

"A dragon's tears are potent," he said. "Fools hope to sell them. The wisest know them for a burden, and a shackle." I touched my tear-stained finger to my chest, felt it write destiny on my heart.

"I have no love to give you," he repeated, though I could see in his eyes a love of land and peoples and of me. "I have pain and duty and despondency, and if you want them, they are yours." In that moment, I forsook Elyndra and happiness and hope, and gave myself to fate.

"Our era is done," he said. "The time of dragons and of flight. We have long seen its end arriving. You humans have brought it, with your carts and roads and machines. You have spelled an end to magic with your studies, your scrutiny, your relentless logic."

I thought of the Osal, with his contraptions of wire and melted sand that made my head hurt, and the carter rowing his silly land-boat down dusty roads. I opened my mouth to protest their futility, but the dragon shook his head.

"We have had our time. We have had our peaks and our valleys, our empires and our isolation, our enchantments and our everyday. It is your turn now."

"Our turn for what?" I blurted, mind still full of flight and fantasy.

"For yourselves."

"But why? Stay with us. Guide us." I touched my tear-marked finger to his cold face above the fangs.

"We cannot. Most of us are already gone. Only a few are left — those unaware, or unlucky, and myself, and my queen." He turned his long body and stretched out wings the color of rain-flecked slate that spread out and above me to block the sun. With a snap, he flung them out and down. They crashed against the rock, sending dust and gravel into the icy wind.

When the dust had settled, he spoke again. "These are no more than ornament now. I cannot fly. None of us can, for flight is more magic than mundane. And a dragon that cannot fly is no dragon. Without flight..." I could see the clouds in his eyes, the conflict of desire and memory. "Without flight," he said quietly, "a dragon cannot live. Does not wish to live."

I wept to see him as he saw himself, a master of sky and land reduced to a creeping lizard, wings no more than a hindrance. I wept again as a dragon's true sight showed this to be not self-pity but truth, not despair but acceptance.

"Our instincts are strong," he continued. "Too strong. Those of us who could set them aside have done so. They cast themselves from the heavens while they could still fly, drowned themselves in bitter seas, starved themselves in hidden caverns. They were the lucky ones. The others try, but they fail. They cast themselves from cliffs too low to kill, topple boulders they can dislodge at need, challenge champions they cannot help but battle against. They are broken in body and in spirit, but dragon bodies heal even when the spirit cannot. And yet they try, failing over and over again, and achieving only pain."

I looked about me. Fine dust had settled on the dragon's useless wings, torn and crumpled at the tips where they had struck the rock, and leaking drops of emerald blood onto soil from which sprang moss and fern. Beside me, my discarded sword mocked my brash ignorance. I pulled my courage about me as best I could. "Let me help," I said, as if a foolish girl with a rusty sword were of some value.

Wisdom is not kindness, and truth is not comfort. I saw, through his eyes and my own, how unequal I was to the offer I made, how much he would have preferred a more accomplished servant, how little choice he had. I saw his dismay at my inadequacy, his determination to exceed it.

"You are not the tool I hoped for," he admitted. "Yet my queen set me to wait here among the humans, and you are the one who has come. We must make the best of it. In the face of failure, we cannot succeed if we do not try."

We agreed then, how I would search out his fellows, and kill them despite themselves. He gave me a small sack of gems from the small hoard he had carried, taught me how to use a mirror, how to find a dragon's weak points, how best to use them, and how to be sure of death.

"These are the secrets of the ancients," he rumbled, laughing. "For centuries, we have kept them from you humans, and now I show you freely the chinks in my armor. It is," he bared his fangs, "a bitter irony."

When we had done, and I had memorized and practiced and repeated to his satisfaction, night was well upon us.

"Come and sleep under my wing," he said, "and tomorrow we will finish."

Had any human ever slept with a dragon? I wondered, as I snuggled close against the fine scales with their scent of oats and pepper.

"You are the first," he answered. "The last. The only."

In the morning, I watched as he he flung himself from the cliff, and fell, and soared for one last moment, like leaves of autumn gold defiant in the sun. And then I climbed down to his broken, bloody body to wipe away his last tears and cut off his head.

I took them with into town — the tears invisibly traced across my palms, the head across broad shoulders, with flowers springing up in my path where emerald blood had trickled down my back and legs into the soil. I felt my body stronger and harder than I had ever known it, and my heart more desolate.

I delivered the head to the Countess, and she gave me honor, gold, and armor. All went as the dragon had predicted. 'The dragon,' I called him, for only now did I realize that I had never learned his name, and because the humans did not care. They looked at me, with my dragon-marked skin, and looked away.

I set off to the next town afoot, spurning the carter and his land-boat. Only as I left did I think to look for Elyndra. I found her, in her cotton dress that shone like satin, saw her wide-eyed fear as she stood next to Osal for protection against the horror and hero I had become.

●

I am still the horror. I kill noble, beautiful creatures when they are weak and defenseless. The map of tears across my body has grown so heavy now that only my sword keeps me upright. I dull its sharp point, stabbing it into the stone of the mountain as I climb. At the last narrow scramble, the arbalest grew too heavy, and I left it beside the path for some foolish child to find. It is hard to care about the humans now that I have seen so many in so much foolishness. They celebrate the death of dragons as if it were an accomplishment. If that is their future, they deserve it.

I can sense the last one near me now, smell her pepper scent around a ridge of jagged rock This the queen, of course. The last dragon. The last of my burdens, of my impossible task. I put down my sword to tug my gown straight, brush the burrs from its hem. It is tight at the waist and shoulders, and it leaves my arms naked to the wind, but it is the best I have, the only good thing I have.

I leave my sword where it lies. In a queen, the instinct for survival may be stronger. She may kill me on sight — sear me and my pretty dress with a breath of fire, or rend me with her fangs. I can hope.

I step out around the ridge. She is vast, this queen, the size of houses. Her scales are violet and indigo and blue and black in the autumn sun, and her wings form caverns across the slanted meadow. Her eyes are the green of forests and rain. I lean my spirit toward them... and do not fall.

"You are proof against us now, child," she says, but I have enough dragon in me now to know it for a joke, to know that she holds back her power.

"I cannot kill you," I say, letting my shoulders slump. Let there be an end to death at last. My arms are cold, and the dress does little to warm the rest of me.

"There is no need," she replies, and rests her head beside me on the ground.

"I cannot kill you," I insist. "I will not kill you. I have done enough." I look up to her forest eyes, and beg them for release. "Let me rest. Let me finish." We both know what I mean.

"We have used you hard," she admits. "We have been unfair, even cruel." I see the truth of it in her gaze.

We are silent for a time. "He used his power," I realize at last, and know it true. "It was not my choice. All this killing. All this death."

I think back on all the bodies, the blood. I feel the tracery of tears burn across my hands, my chest, my back. Not bravely, freely chosen. Not voluntary service to a dying race, but an unwitting tool — a fool of death.

I sit, and wait for my own tears to flow, to fill the hollow of my disillusion.

"He could not help it," she says at last. "It is the way of dragons, to control, to master, to deceive."

"To enslave," I spit, though I cannot muster anger.

"Yes. Yet our time is ended. Your technology drains the world of magic, but it is your will that prevails — that indomitable will that fights tyranny, resists oppression."

She smiles her dragon smile, all fangs and sharp eyes. "Even you, little one. Not the strongest of your race, nor the best. But even you have come this morning to refuse me. Thus we reach our end, when an unarmed young human denies a dragon queen."

"I will not kill you," I say again, bitter now with the knowledge that I have been used, that I am as poor a vessel as I once feared — that I was chosen for my very weakness. Relief grows in me as well; I am done forever with that task, done with blood, done with dragons and their deaths.

"No other could have done it. Strong, determined, implacable. Enthralled." She shows me the truth of it, shows me her gratitude. Perhaps I have done well. Perhaps not. Perhaps I am only tired. Whatever the truth, I want no more of it.

"I will not kill you," I say a fourth time.

"Even a timeworn dragon queen is a queen." She shakes her wings, and a breeze blows through my hair. "I have one more flight left in me, and I will take it until it ends. But we owe you thanks, we dragons. What boon can I give you, who have given us so much?"

"Death and blood," I say, for that is what I have given. What I was forced to give.

"Dignity," she replies. "And for a dragon, that is a great deal."

I am dull now, with disillusion. I want no more revelations, no boons. I want... I do not know, and I sit in silence, my pretty, foolish dress a dusty folly, poor shield against the mountain cold. I want no more killing, no more effort, no more decisions, no more plans. No more weapons. No more tears. Above all, no more tears.

"Take me with you." On that final flight, the last voyage of the last dragon.

She looks at me, forest eyes impenetrable as oak.

"Very well," she agrees, and her eyes glint with moisture.

She gathers me into one huge paw, and I see the razor claws pressing into her scales as she stretches them to keep me safe. It hurts her, but I do not care. Why should I be the only one to hurt? And if she slips, and the claws close in, what matter? The dragon tears on my skin reproach me, show me the child that I am acting. I tell them silently to let me die as a I choose, and they do not argue with my wisdom, little as it is.

We rise with a clap of thunder and a rush of wind, and then we are high above the land, and in the village below, the humans run like raindrops, away, away, away.

We fly over the land I have known all my life, over the sites of my bloody executioner's work, and of my birth and childhood. It is small, inconsequential, the sites of my great and awful deeds a tiny patch of green and brown upon the great sprawl of land and sea beneath us. There is too much of it! The mountain I climbed this morning, no more than a foothill for a range of granite peaks, with beyond them the glint of water. We follow rivers to the west, and I silently urge the queen on, further, faster, to see more before the end.

She slithers her head down to me like a goose, so that she is flying one way, facing the other, then turns her head back toward the front, her long neck forming a loop that ends above my head. "There are lands below even the bards have not heard of, lands where dragons and their deaths are a matter of legend," she says through the wind of her passage. "There are lands that speak different tongues, even between humans. Lands of carters and craft, lands of farmers and hard work, lands of battle and lands of peace, lands of beauty and of plainness."

"This is what we give you," she says, and I feel her wingbeats falter. "These were our lands, that now are yours." We slip in the air as the magic fades and I sense her muscles straining.

We sink lower and lower, and my heart aches for all the lands I have not seen, the magic of horizon and discovery. Soon, the flight must end, and the queen and I will reach the end of our voyage, and the beginning of peace.

We are hilltop-high now, above a green land of forests and rain and ocean. "This was my favorite," she says, and there is regret in the soughing of her voice. "Here I was my happiest." She swoops low over the waves on a warm, sandy beach, and I feel her tears bathing my body as her claws shift and the end nears. I close my eyes, and feel her joy and sorrow as she remembers happiness and her race dies. "I hope there is room for me in your Atlas," she says. Then the claws open, and I am falling, falling, into the waves.

I strike hard, and the breath whooshes out of me and the cold green is all around me, and I am sorry. I kick out for the surface, and the air, and as my head breaks through, I see a dark arrowhead against the sky, climbing, climbing out to sea. And then it falls.

It's better to try than to despair. A dragon taught me that. I hold the lesson close as a current carries me to an uncharted shore of hope and life, and the salt water washes me clean.

B. Morris Allen's story "Dragons I Have Slain" was originally published in Metaphorosis on Friday, 2 December 2016

About the author

B. Morris Allen grew up in a house full of books that traveled the world. Nowadays, they're e-books, and lighter to carry, but they're still multiplying. He's been a biochemist, an activist, and a lawyer, and now works as a foreign aid consultant. When he's not roaming foreign countries fighting corruption, he's on the Oregon coast, chatting with seals. In the occasional free moment, he edits Metaphorosis magazine, and works on his own speculative stories of love and disaster.

www.BMorrisAllen.com

Copyright

Title information

Sages of Metaphorosis

ISBN: 978-1-64076-301-2 (e-book)
ISBN: 978-1-64076-302-9 (paperback)
ISBN: 978-1-64076-303-6 (hardcover)

Copyright

Metaphorosis Publishing

Metaphorosis offers beautifully written science fiction and fantasy. Our imprints include:

Metaphorosis Magazine

Plant Based Press

Verdage

Vestige

Joyful Heave

You can also find us:
@metaphorosis.bsky.social (Bluesky)
@Metaphorosis@writing.exchange (Mastodon)
www.facebook.com/metaphorosis

Help keep Metaphorosis running at
Patreon.com/metaphorosis

See more about some of our books on the following pages.

Metaphorosis
a magazine of speculative fiction

Metaphorosis is an online speculative fiction magazine dedicated to quality writing. We publish an original story every week (2016-2023) or month (2024), along with author bios, interviews, and notes on story origins.

We also publish monthly print and e-book issues, as well as yearly Best of and Complete anthologies.

Come and see us online at magazine.Metaphorosis.com.

The Metaphorosis Library Collection

Plant Based Press

Vegan-friendly science fiction and fantasy, including anthologies of the year's best SFF stories, from 2016-2020.

Chambers of the Heart
speculative stories
by
B. Morris Allen

A heart that's a building, a dog that's a program, a woman sinking irretrievably — stories about love, loss, and movement.

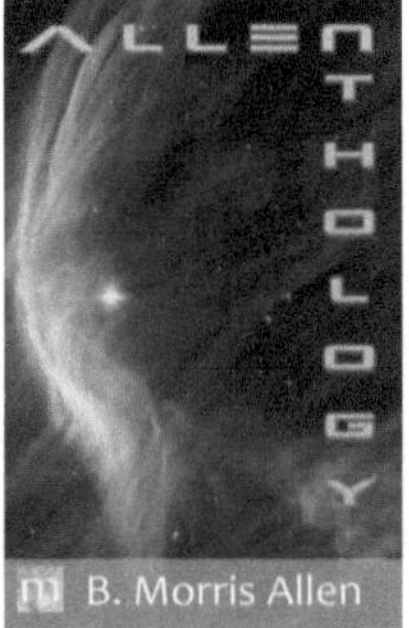

Susurrus

A darkly romantic story of magic, love, and suffering.

Allenthology: Volume I

Including three full collections of SFF stories.

Verdage

Science fiction and fantasy books for writers — full of great stories, often with an additional focus on the craft of speculative fiction writing.

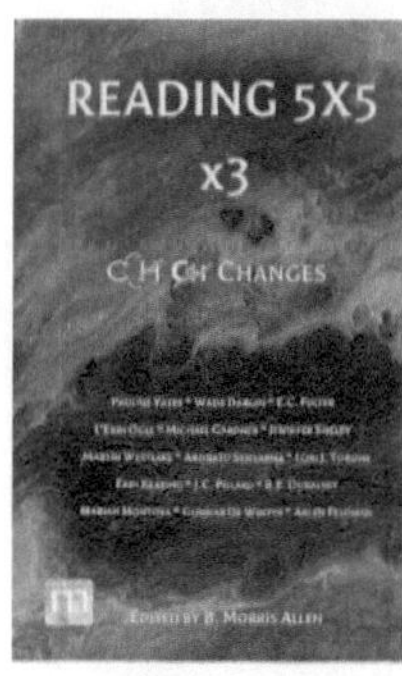

Reading 5X5 x3

Changes

How do stories move from 'maybe' to published?

Here are 15 case studies of stories published in *Metaphorosis* magazine.

Reading 5X5 x2

Duets

How do authors' voices change when they collaborate?

A round-robin of five talented science fiction and fantasy authors collaborating with each other and writing solo.

Including stories by Evan Marcroft, David Gallay, J. Tynan Burke, L'Erin Ogle, and Douglas Anstruther.

Score

an SFF symphony

An anthology with an emotional score from the heights of joy to the depths of despair — but always with a little hope shining through.

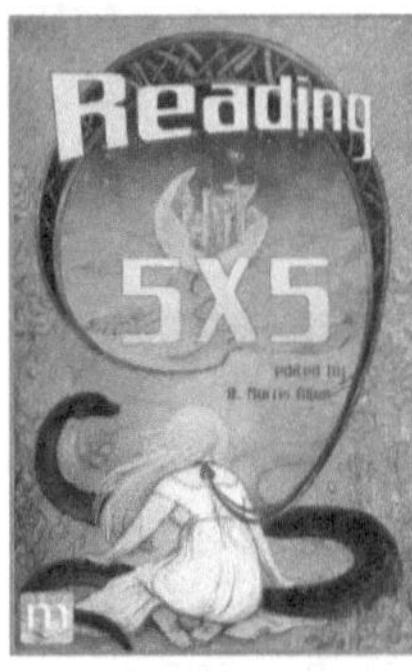

Reading 5X5

Five stories, five times

See how different writers take on the same material.

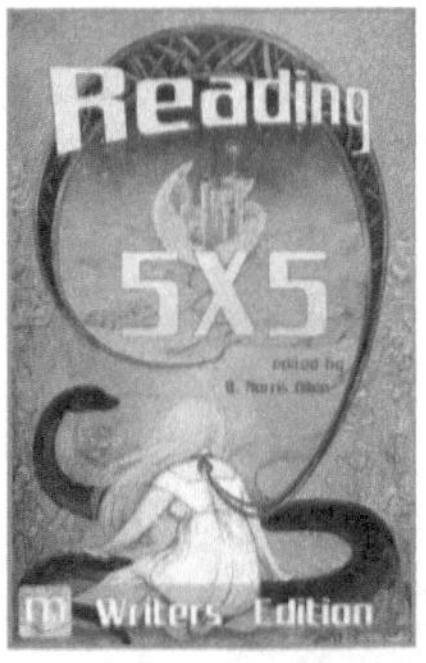

Reading 5X5

Writers' Edition

Two extra stories, the story seed, and authors' notes on writing.

Vestige

Novelettes, novellas, and novels by Metaphorosis authors.

The Nocturnals
Mariah Montoya

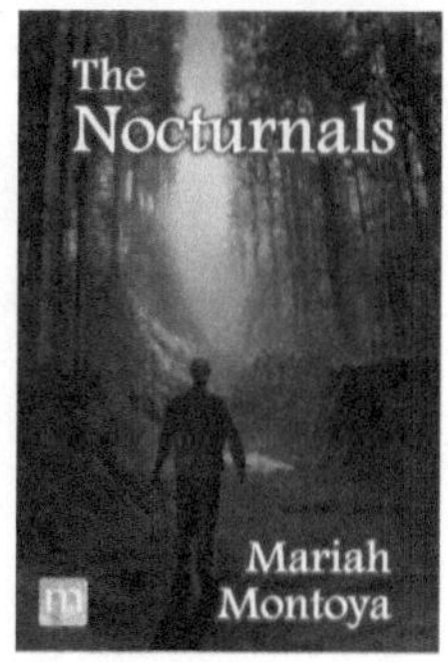

Night is Dangerous. Day is deadly.
Where day and night last thirty years, humans move constantly stay ahead of the night and cruel Nocturnals that call it home. But a boy is lost out there.

Science fiction and fantasy anthologies with innovative and unusual themes.

Museum Piece
an unusual collection

A gallery of the strange and outrageous

Step right up and enter a world of wonder and oddities! These museums are not your typical tourist traps. From the Museum of Lost Dreams to the Museum of Fine Regrets, each exhibit will take you on a journey you won't soon forget.